'This book stole my heart . . . inventive, heartbreaking and empathetic, it's a book about whether it's better to have loved and lost, or never to have loved at all. Women's fiction at its finest'
**Gillian McAllister**

'Big ugly cry incoming! You'd have to be made of stone not to fall for this love story'
***Red***

'A wonderful high-concept love story. I adored it'
**Richard Roper**

'Heartbreaking and compulsive in equal measure'
**Kate Riordan**

'A brilliant read'
***Bella***

'You might need a tissue at the ready, but this is an epic romance that will absorb and transport'
***Platinum Magazine***

'Amazing concept, a beautiful love story'
**Eva Woods**

'I. Am. Broken. It's exquisite, beautiful and tender and has left me utterly bereft!'
**Emma Cooper**

'Heartfelt and beautifully written'
**Kate Eberlen**

'Heartbreaker'
***Cosmopolitan***

'This beautifully rendered work is both heartbreaking and life-affirming. Readers should be prepared to cry'
**Publishers Weekly**

'An epic, beautifully written novel'
**Roxie Cooper**

'Enthralling, immersive and deliriously romantic. An exquisitely written emotional thriller with characters I will never forget'
**Katie Marsh**

'Heartbreaking, hopeful and completely original – *The Sight of You* is a love story that stays with you long after the final page'
**Dani Atkins**

'Just wonderful - the perfect 'will they, won't they' romance with a unique premise. It's stayed with me long after I finished with an ending I cried buckets over'
**Lorna Cook**

'One of those rare books that stays in your heart long after the final page . . . I'm utterly bereft now it's finished. Beautiful, lyrical and yet packs an emotional punch that will leave you reeling'
**Penny Parkes**

'What an astonishing book. I just loved it. One of those rare books that is beautifully written and utterly life affirming'
**Kate Thompson**

'A beautiful read about following your heart. This is a total triumph'
**Fabulous Magazine**

Holly Miller grew up in Bedfordshire. Since university she has worked as a marketer, editor and copywriter. Holly currently lives in Norfolk with her partner and their dog.

HOLLY MILLER

# the
# sight
# of
# you

HODDER

First published in Great Britain in 2020 by Hodder & Stoughton
An Hachette UK company

This paperback edition published in 2021

1

A CIP catalogue record for this title is available from the British Library

Paperback ISBN 978 1 529 32438 9
eBook ISBN 978 1 529 32436 5

Typeset in Garamond MT Std by Palimpsest Book Production Limited, Falkirk, Stirlingshire

Printed and bound in Great Britain by Clays Ltd, Elcograf S.p.A.

Hodder & Stoughton policy is to use papers that are natural, renewable and recyclable
products and made from wood grown in sustainable forests. The logging and
manufacturing processes are expected to conform to the environmental
regulations of the country of origin.

Hodder & Stoughton Ltd
Carmelite House
50 Victoria Embankment
London EC4Y 0DZ

www.hodder.co.uk

# PROLOGUE

# 1

## Callie

*Joel, I'm so sorry. To see you again like that . . . Why did I get on the train? I should have waited for the next one. It wouldn't have mattered. I missed my stop anyway, and we were late for the wedding.*

*Because the whole way to London, I could only think of you, about what you might have written in the note you gave me. Then when I finally opened it, I stared at it for so long that, by the time I next looked up, Blackfriars had come and gone.*

*There was an ocean of things I wanted – needed – to say to you, too. But my mind just misfired when I saw you. Maybe I was scared of saying too much.*

*What if today was it, though, Joel? What if today was the last time I'll see your face, hear your voice?*

*Time's rushing by, and I know what's coming.*

*I wish I'd stayed. Just a few minutes more. I'm sorry.*

# PART ONE

# 2

## Joel

It's one in the morning and I'm standing bare-chested at my living-room window. The sky is still and blistered with stars, the moon a marble.

Any minute now, my neighbour Steve will leave the flat above mine. He'll head down to his car, the baby squirming furiously in her carrier. He takes Poppy for drives in the middle of the night, tries to soothe her to sleep with the rumble of tyres and his playlist of farmyard-animal sounds.

Here it comes. The sleep-slackened tread of his feet on the stairs, Poppy grizzling. His trademark mishandling of our fractious front door. I watch as he approaches the car, flicks the lock, hesitates. He's confused, knows something's not right. But his brain's still catching up.

Eventually it clicks. He swears, puts a hand to his head. Makes two disbelieving laps of the vehicle.

*Sorry, Steve – it's all four tyres. Someone's definitely let them down. You're not going anywhere tonight.*

For a moment he's a statue, lit up by the laboratory glow of the streetlight. Then something makes him stare straight into the window I'm looking out of.

I hold my nerve. As long as I stay still, it must be nearly impossible for him to see me. My blinds are shut, the flat silent and dark as a reptile resting. He can't know I have my eye pressed against a single slat. That I'm watching everything.

For a moment our gazes are soldered together before he looks away, shaking his head as Poppy treats the street to a timely scream.

A light springs on in the house opposite. Brightness strikes the darkened street, exasperation drifting down from the window. 'Come on, mate!'

Steve lifts a hand, then turns to come back inside. I hear the two of them trail upstairs, Poppy wailing determinedly as they go. Steve's used to keeping strange hours, but Hayley will be trying to sleep. She's recently returned to her job at a prestigious London law firm, which means it matters if she nods off in meetings.

Still. My tasks for tonight are complete. I cross them off in my notebook then sit down on the sofa, parting the blinds so I can look at the stars.

I reward myself with a shot of whisky, because that's what I do on special occasions. Then I make it a double and down it, fast.

Twenty minutes later, I'm ready to crash. I'm after a very specific kind of sleep, and everything I've done tonight should help me achieve it.

'He's ever so hot,' says my eighty-something near-neighbour Iris, when I pitch up at her house a few hours later to walk her yellow Labrador, Rufus.

It's not yet eight in the morning, which might account for why I haven't got a clue who she's talking about. Her neighbour, Bill, who pops round most mornings with a nugget of gossip or weird little leaflet? The postman, who's just waved jauntily at us through the living-room window?

Postmen. They're always either inanely cheerful or miserable as sin. Never a middle ground.

'He's been sleeping on the kitchen tiles to stay cool.'

Of course. She's talking about the dog. This happens more often than I'd like: being too exhausted to make simple conversation with someone at least twice my age. 'Good idea.' I smile. 'Might try it myself.'

She shoots me a look. 'That will hardly endear you to the ladies now, will it?'

Ah, The Ladies. Who are they, again? Iris seems convinced there's a queue of them somewhere, keen to put their lives on hold to hang out with a guy like me.

'Do you think he can cope?' she asks, gesturing at Rufus. 'Out there, in this heat?'

I used to be a vet. I'm not any more. But I think Iris takes comfort from my one-time credentials.

'It's cooler today,' I assure her. She's right that it has been warm lately, since we're only just in September. 'We'll go down to the boating lake, have a paddle.'

She smiles. 'You too?'

I shake my head. 'Prefer to commit my public-order offences after hours. More exciting that way.'

She lights up like my lame jokes are the highlight of her day. 'We're so fortunate to have you, aren't we, Rufus?'

To be fair, Iris is pretty awesome herself. She wears earrings shaped like fruit and has a Premium subscription to Spotify.

I bend down to clip on Rufus's lead as he eases to his feet. 'He is still a touch on the heavy side, Iris. That won't be helping his heat tolerance. How's his diet going?'

She shrugs. 'He can smell cheese from fifty paces, Joel. What can I say?'

I sigh. I've been lecturing Iris about Rufus's food for nearly eight years now. 'What was our deal? I'd walk him, you'd take care of the rest.'

'I know, I know.' She starts to shoo us from the living room with her walking stick. 'But I just can't resist the look on his face.'

I've got three dogs in tow by the time I make it to the park. (I walk two others along with Rufus, for ex-clients who aren't too mobile. There's a fourth as well, a Great Dane called Bruno. But he's socially unhinged and formidably strong, so I take him out after dark.)

Though the air's freshened up overnight, I keep my promise to Iris about the boating lake. Unclipping the dogs' leads, I feel myself brighten as they canter like horses into the water.

I take a breath. Attempt to persuade myself again that what I did last night was right.

It had to be. Because here's the thing: almost my whole life, I've been having prophetic dreams. The kind of lucid, lifelike visions that startle me from sleep. They show me what's going to happen, days, weeks, years down the line. And the subjects, always, are the people I love.

The dreams come every week or so, the ratio of good to bad to neutral fairly even. But it's the dark premonitions I fear most: the accidents and illnesses, pain and misfortune. They're why I'm constantly edgy, always on high alert. Wondering when I might next have to re-route the course of fate, race to intervene in someone's best-laid plans.

Or, worse, save a life.

I track my canine charges from the bank of the lake, giving a group of fellow dog-walkers a smile and a necessarily wide berth. They gather most mornings by the bridge, beckoning me over if I make the mistake of eye contact. I've kept my distance ever since the time they started swapping tips on sleeping well, their talk turning to home remedies and therapies, pills and routines. (I made my excuses and vanished. Haven't hung out with them since.)

The whole thing just cut a little deep. Because, in pursuit of a dreamless night, I've tried the lot. Diets, meditation, affirmations. Lavender and white noise. Milky drinks. Sleeping tablets with added side effects, essential oils. Exercise so punishing I'd have to stop to spew. Sporadic periods of hard boozing in my twenties, under the misguided notion I could alter my sleep cycles. But years of experimenting proved my cycles to be untouchable. And nothing I do has ever been able to change that.

Still, simple mathematics dictates that less sleep must equal fewer dreams. So, these days, I stay up till the small hours, aided by screen time and a pretty hardcore caffeine habit. Then I allow myself a short, sharp spell of rest. I've trained my mind to expect it: snapping out of slumber after just a few hours.

Which is why, now, I'm in urgent need of coffee. Whistling the dogs from the water, I head back towards the path along the river. On the road to my right, real life is grinding into gear. Rush-hour traffic, cyclists, commuters on foot, delivery vans. A discordant orchestra, tuning up for a standard weekday morning.

It makes me oddly nostalgic for normality. I've not got too much headspace at the moment for gainful employment, friendships or health. The worry and lack of sleep leave me constantly knackered, distracted, jittery.

If only to prevent the whole thing from burying me, I live by some loose-ish rules: exercise daily, not too much booze, steer clear of love.

I've confessed the truth to just two people in my life. And the second time, I swore it would be the last. Which is why I can't tell Steve that last night, I was acting on a fevered premonition about Poppy. My goddaughter, whom I love like I do my own nieces. I saw the whole thing: Steve exhausted, forgetting to brake at the crossroads with Poppy in the back. I watched his car barrel into a lamppost at thirty miles an hour. In the aftermath of the accident, she had to be cut from the car.

So I took the necessary action. Which was worthy of that double whisky, if I do say so myself.

I put the dogs back on their leads and make for home. I'll need to avoid Steve, for a while at least. The longer I can keep my head down, the less likely he'll be to connect me to what happened last night.

Once I've dropped the dogs off, I'll seek out a café to hole up in, I think. A place where I can drink coffee quietly in a corner, anonymous and unobserved.

# 3

## Callie

'You can't tell me it's never happened to you before.' Dot and I are wiping tables in the coffee shop after closing, exchanging theories on the customer who walked out without paying earlier. This is always my favourite time of day – winding down and trading stories, restoring the shine to the room. Beyond the window, the early-September air is warm and delicate as peach skin.

'Maybe it was an honest mistake,' I say.

Dot pushes a hand through her crop of bleach-blonde hair. 'Seriously. How long have you worked here?'

'Eighteen months.' It sounds more incredible every time I say it.

'Eighteen months, and you've not yet had a walk-out.' Dot shakes her head. 'You must have the right kind of face.'

'I'm sure he just forgot. I think Murphy distracted him.'

Murphy's my dog, a black-and-tan crossbreed. Well, he's sort of mine. Anyway, he's living the dream being pet-in-residence at the coffee shop, because there's no end of people here willing to fuss him and sneak him illicit titbits.

Dot snorts. 'The only thing that guy forgot was his wallet.'

I'd never seen him before. Then again, I'd never seen a lot of today's customers before. The rival café at the top of the hill usually absorbs the commuter footfall of Eversford, the market town where I've lived my whole life. But it closed this morning without warning, and its regulars began drifting mutely in as soon as we opened, all pinstripes and aftershave and well-polished shoes.

But this customer was different. In fact, I'd be slightly embarrassed to admit just how much he stood out to me. He couldn't have been en route to any office – his dark hair was solely bed-worthy, and he seemed saddled by exhaustion, like he'd had a rough night. At first he appeared distracted as I came to take his order, but when he finally turned his eyes to me, they gripped tight and didn't let go.

We exchanged no more than a couple of words, but I do recall that before he walked out without paying – and between bouts of scribbling in a notebook – he formed something of a silent bond with Murphy.

'I think he might have been a writer. He had a notebook with him.'

Dot disagrees through her nose. 'Of course – starving writer. Trust you to put a romantic spin on theft.'

'Yes, but if it was up to you we'd have one of those signs, like you get in petrol stations. *If you do not have the means to pay . . .*'

'Now *that* is an excellent idea.'

'It wasn't a suggestion.'

'Maybe next time I'll floor him with my best roundhouse.'

I don't doubt it would be good – Dot's recently taken up kickboxing, committing to it with an energy I envy. She's always doing the next thing, running wild through life like a creature uncaged.

By contrast, she thinks I've shrunk back from the world – that I've slunk into its corners, started blinking into bright light. She's probably right.

'No martial-arts moves on the customers,' I tell her. 'Café policy.'

'Anyway, there won't be a next time. I've memorised his face. If I see him in town, I'm demanding that tenner back.'

'He only had a coffee.'

Dot shrugs. 'Call it our tax on eat-and-run.'

I smile and move past her into the back office to print the order for tomorrow's delivery. I've been gone only a minute when I hear her calling out, 'We're closed! Come back tomorrow!'

As I stick my head around the office doorway, I recognise the figure at the door. And so, it seems, does Murphy – he's sniffing the hinges expectantly, tail wagging.

'It's him,' I say, feeling my stomach skitter slightly. Tall and lean, grey T-shirt, dark jeans. Skin that hints at a summer spent outside. 'The guy who forgot to pay.'

'Oh.'

'Nice detective skills, Sherlock.'

With a huff Dot unlocks the deadbolt and turns the key, cranking the door just a notch. I don't hear what he says but assume he's come to settle up as she's unhooking the chain now, opening the door to let him in. Murphy scoots backwards as he enters, tail wagging, paws dancing.

'I walked out without paying earlier,' he says gruffly, with disarming remorse. 'Completely unintentional. Here.' He passes Dot a twenty, rubs a hand through his hair, glances at me. His eyes are wide, dark as damp earth.

'I'll get your change,' I say.

'No, keep it. Thanks. Sorry about that.'

'Take something with you. Another coffee, some cake? As a thank-you for being so honest.' Aside from anything else, something in his demeanour seems to plead for kindness.

There's some *drømmekage* left, an airy Danish sponge topped with caramelised coconut that roughly translates as *dream cake*. I box up a slice and offer it to him.

He pauses for a moment, rubs the crescent of stubble along his jaw uncertainly. Then he takes the box, his fingertips nudging mine. 'Thanks.' He dips his head and leaves, a warm breath of velvet air drifting into the shop as he goes.

'Well,' says Dot. '*He* was a man of few words.'

'I think I threw him with the cake.'

'Yeah, what was all that about? *Another coffee?* she parrots. '*Some drømmekage?*'

I only just resist the urge to blush. 'At least he came back to settle up. Which proves you to be an outrageous cynic.'

'Hardly. With that slab of *drømmekage* you're still barely in profit.'

'That's not the point.'

Dot raises a micro-bladed brow. 'Our boss might disagree. Or at least his accountant would.'

'No, Ben would tell you to have more faith in human nature. You know – give people a chance.'

'So, what are you doing tonight?' Dot has a smile in her eye as she moves past me into the office for her jacket. 'Sleeping rough for charity? Launching a pop-up soup kitchen?'

'Very funny. I might just hang out at Ben's for a bit, see how he's doing.'

Dot doesn't reply. I know she thinks I'm weighed down by worrying about Ben, that I spend too much time mired in my memories.

'How about you?'

She reappears, sunglasses propped on top of her head. 'Water-skiing.'

I smile. *Of course – what else?*

'You should come.'

'No, I'm inherently clumsy.'

'So? Water's soft.'

'No, I'd better . . .'

She levels a look at me. 'You know what I think, Cal.'

'I do.'

'Joined Tinder yet?'

'No.' *Please don't nag me.*

'Or I can set you up with someone . . .'

'I know.' Dot can do anything. 'Have fun tonight.'

'I'd say the same to you, but . . .' She winks affectionately. 'See you tomorrow.' And, in a parting cloud of Gucci Bloom, she's gone.

After she leaves, I knock the lights off one by one before taking my customary final pew near the window, to breathe in the fading scent of bread and coffee beans. Like a reflex, I slip my phone from my pocket, tap through to Grace's number and dial.

*No. You can't go on like this. Stop.*

I cut off the call and snap the screen back to lock. Calling her is a habit I've been trying hard to break lately, but the sight of her name on my phone always gives me a lift, like a bright blast of sunlight on a rubble-grey day.

Allowing my gaze to unspool through the window, I unexpectedly find myself staring into the watchful, peat-dark eyes of the notebook man from earlier. With a jolt I start to smile, but I'm too late – he looks down at the pavement and makes himself a shadow, striding swiftly away into the evening's mellow light.

He's not carrying the cake box any more. Either he's already eaten it, or he tossed it into the first bin he saw.

# 4

## Joel

I lurch awake at two a.m. Easing out of bed, I grab my notebook, trying not to disturb her.

Last week's warm weather has dissipated, and the flat's a bit chilly. I pull on a hoodie and jogging bottoms, make for the kitchen.

Sitting up at the breakfast bar, I scribble everything down.

My younger brother Doug will be chuffed, anyway. I dreamt about his daughter, Bella, gaining a sports scholarship to the local private school, the year she turns ten. An outstanding county swimmer, apparently, winning fistfuls of medals every weekend. Strange how things work out. Doug was banned from swimming at our local pool as a kid, after one too many dive bombs and flipping off the life-guards.

Bella's not even three yet. But Doug's view is that it's never too early to schedule in potential. He's already got four-year-old Buddy playing tennis, watches *Britain's Got Talent* for tips on pushy parenting.

Then again, my dream has confirmed it's going to pay off. I make and triple-underline a note about mentioning local swimming clubs to him, ASAP.

'Joel?'

Melissa's watching me from the doorway, still as a spy.

'Bad dream?'

I shake my head, tell her the dream was good.

Melissa's wearing my T-shirt, and she'll probably wear it home, too.

She thinks it's cute, doing that. But I'd rather not have to keep an inventory of my own wardrobe.

She approaches me now, hops onto a stool. Crosses her bare legs, runs a hand through her mane of sandy hair. 'Was I in it?' She throws me a wink that's both coy and outrageous.

*That would actually be impossible*, I want to say, but won't. She knows nothing about the nature of my dreaming, and that's the way it's going to stay.

For almost three years now Melissa and I have been seeing each other every month or so, usually with little contact in-between. Steve's stopped her for a chat more often than I'd like, as though he thinks it might be worth getting to know her. Even Melissa finds this idea amusing, has started talking to him in the hallway just to provoke me.

I glance up at the kitchen clock. Stifle a yawn. 'It's the middle of the night. You should go back to bed.'

'Nah.' She sighs languidly, picks at a fingernail. 'I'm awake now. May as well stay up with you.'

'What time do you start work?' Melissa manages media relations at the London branch of an African mining company. Her morning shifts frequently kick off at six a.m.

'Too early,' she says, eyes pinwheeling displeasure. 'I'll call in sick.'

I'd been planning a dog-walk with my friend Kieran first thing, was hoping to have breakfast at the café. I've been back several times now, following last week's non-payment debacle.

Initially, I admit, I felt some kind of moral duty to return. But now it's more about the dog-in-residence and great coffee. And the warm welcome I get, despite being a less-than-exemplary customer the first time I set foot in the place.

'Actually . . . I've sort of made plans.' My stomach flexes with guilt, even as I say it.

She tilts her head. 'Charming. You know, I still can't figure out why you're single.'

'You're single,' I point out, like I do every time she comes over.

'Yeah. But I want to be.'

It's one of Melissa's theories. That I'm desperate for a relationship, dying to be someone's boyfriend. I'd been single for five years before meeting her, a fact she delights in like a cat with a mouse. Sometimes she even tells me off for being too clingy, when I message her after a month of radio silence to see if she fancies a takeaway.

She's wrong, though. I was straight with her from the off, asked if she was okay with keeping things casual. She laughed and said yes. Told me I was full of myself.

'You know, one day, I'm going to open that notebook while you're asleep and see exactly what it is you write in there.'

I half laugh and look down, not quite trusting myself to reply to that one.

'Is it something I could sell to the papers?'

Maybe she could: everything's in there. A dream every week for twenty-eight years, and I've been keeping notes for the past twenty-two.

I write it all down in case I need to act. But from time to time I do have to watch a bad dream play out. I let them slide if they're less than serious, or when I can't see a way to intervene. Neither option's ideal, for a man with my mindset.

Still. Like diamonds in the dirt, happier dreams glimmer between the bad. Promotions, pregnancies, little twists of good luck. And then there are the dull ones, about life's mundanities, routines. Haircuts and food shops, housework and homework. I might see what Doug's eating for dinner (*offal, seriously?*). Or I'll find out whether Dad will top the local badminton league, or if my niece will forget her PE kit.

The relevant times and dates are bright in my mind whenever I wake.

They lodge there like knowing my own birthday, or on which day in December Christmas falls.

I pay attention to everything, even the tame stuff. Keep track of it all in my notebook. In case there's a pattern, a clue in there somewhere. Something I can't afford to miss.

I glance now at my notebook on the worktop. Brace myself in case Melissa tries to snatch it. She clocks me straight away and smiles creamily, tells me to relax.

'Do you want a coffee?' I say, to try to dim the glint in her eye. Still, I feel a twinge of remorse. Despite her swagger, I'm sure she wouldn't mind coming over here just once and getting her full eight hours like a normal person.

'You know, with all your money you could afford to buy a proper coffee machine. Nobody drinks instant any more.'

From out of nowhere, a vision of the café drifts into my mind. Of Callie setting down my drink, and the cobbled-street view from my window seat. It alarms me slightly and I push it away, spoon coffee between two mugs. 'All my what money?'

'I love how you make out like you're poor. You used to be a vet, and now you don't work.'

That's only partly true. Yes, I've got savings. But only because I realised in time that my job was hanging in the balance. And they won't last for ever.

'Sugar?' I ask, to steer her off-topic.

'I'm sweet enough.'

'That's debatable.'

She ignores me. 'So – will you?'

'Will I what?'

'Buy a proper coffee machine.'

I fold my arms, turn to face her. 'For once a month when you come round?'

She winks at me. 'You know, if you actually started treating me properly, you might be in with a chance of this going somewhere.'

I return the wink, clink spoon against mug. 'Instant it is.'

I had my first prophetic dream at just seven years old, when I was as tight with my cousin Luke as it was possible to be. Born only three days apart, we spent every spare moment together. Computer games, bike rides, roaming wild with the dogs.

One night, I dreamt that as Luke took his usual shortcut across the playing field to school, a black dog charged at him from out of nowhere. I woke at three a.m., just as the dog was clamping its jaws around Luke's face. Thumping through my mind like a migraine was the date when this was all going to go down.

I had just hours to stop it.

Over an untouched breakfast, I told Mum everything, begged her to call Dad's sister, Luke's mother. She quietly refused, projected calm, assured me it was just a bad dream. Promised I'd find Luke waiting for me at school, totally fine.

But Luke wasn't at school, totally fine. So I ran to his house, hard enough to taste blood at the back of my throat. A man I didn't recognise answered the door. *He's in hospital,* he told me gruffly. *Got attacked by a dog this morning over the playing field.*

Mum rang my aunt that evening and all the details came out. A black dog had attacked Luke on his way to school. He needed plastic surgery on his face, left arm and throat. He was lucky to be alive.

After putting down the phone, Mum took me into the living room, where we sat quite still on the sofa together. Dad hadn't come home yet. I can still remember the scent of the chicken noodle soup she'd made me. The weirdly comforting sound of my siblings bickering upstairs.

'It's just coincidence, Joel,' Mum kept saying. (I wonder, now, if she was trying to convince herself.) 'You know what that is, don't you? That's when something happens by chance.'

Mum worked in Dad's accountancy firm back then. She earned her living like he did, from dealing in logic, looking at facts. And the fact was, people were not psychic.

'I *knew* it would happen,' I sobbed, inconsolable. 'I could have stopped it.'

'I know it seems that way, Joel,' she whispered, 'but it was just coincidence. You need to remember that.'

We never told anyone. Dad would have dismissed me as delusional, and my siblings were still too young to understand or possibly care. *Let's just keep it between us*, Mum said. So we did.

Even today, the rest of my family still don't know the truth. They think I'm anxious and paranoid. That my garbled warnings and manic interventions are down to unresolved grief over Mum. Doug thinks I should take a pill for it, because Doug thinks there's a pill for everything. (Spoiler: there isn't.)

Does Tamsin, my sister, suspect there's more to it? Possibly. But I deliberately keep the details vague, and she doesn't ask.

I can't say I've never been tempted to tell them everything. But if the urge ever comes, I only have to think back to the one time I was naive enough to consult a professional. The derision in his eyes and the sneer on his lips were enough to make me vow I would never confide in anyone again.

# 5

## Callie

A Friday night in mid-September brings with it a typically dispiriting call from my letting agent.

'Bad news, I'm afraid, Miss Cooper.'

I frown, remind Ian he can call me Callie – we've had enough dealings, over the years.

He repeats my first name slowly, like he's writing it down for the first time ever. 'All right, then. Now, Mr Wright has just informed us he's selling his property.'

'Which property? What?'

'Your flat. Ninety-two B. No, wait – C.'

'It's okay, I know my address. You're really evicting me?'

'We prefer to say you're being given notice. You get a month.'

'But why? Why's he selling?'

'No longer commercially viable.'

'I'm a person. I'm viable. I pay my rent.'

'Now, don't get upset.'

'Do you think . . . he might sell it to another landlord? I could be a sitting tenant.' I like how it sounds, at least – enhanced rights, making demands on my landlord for once and not the other way around.

'Oh, no. He definitely wants you out. He needs to spruce the place up.'

'That's good to know. Except I don't have anywhere else to go.'

'Not on benefits, are you?'

'No, but—'

'Plenty of properties on at the moment. I'll email you.'

Nothing quite matches being evicted, I realise, for making you feel like a complete and colossal failure. 'Way to start my weekend, Ian.' I wonder if he makes all of his eviction calls on Friday nights.

'Yeah? No worries.'

'No, I was being . . . Look,' I say desperately, 'could you find me somewhere with a proper garden?' My flat's on the top floor, so I don't have access to the one here – but even if I did, it would be like hanging out in a scrap-metal yard. It's covered almost completely with tarmac, and filled with various items of junk – rusty sun-loungers, a broken rotary laundry line, a decaying collection of kitchen chairs and three out-of-service wheelbarrows. I don't mind scruffy, a touch of mess – so much better than a sterile show-home garden – but this one's an ongoing tetanus risk.

Ian chortles. 'Budget still the same?'

'Less, if anything.'

'Funny. Oh, and Callie – I take it you got those bees sorted?'

'Bees?' I say innocently.

Ian hesitates. I hear him tapping furiously. 'Yeah, here it is. They were going in and out of the soffits, next to your living-room window.'

They were indeed – the couple next door reported it, I think. I palmed Ian off when he called, told him I had a friend who could help. It comes as no surprise at all that he's only thinking to follow up now, months later.

I was so desperate to protect it, the happy little home the bees were building. They were doing no harm – unlike their detractors, who had brick-woven their front garden and replaced all their grass with the fake stuff only days after moving in.

'Oh, yes,' I say cheerfully. 'All sorted.'

'Nice one. Don't want them hibernating over winter.'

I smile. The nest will be empty now, the bees long gone. 'Actually, bees don't—'

'What's that?'

'Never mind.'

Ending the call, I sling my head back against the sofa. Turfed out at the age of thirty-four. Well, there's an excuse for a full pint of ice cream if ever I heard one.

There was a hawthorn tree in the next-door garden, before the couple ripped it up to accommodate their makeshift car park. It was in full blossom at the time. The cloud of petals as they launched it into the skip they'd hired brought to my mind windy spring days from my childhood, and the sweet joy of a dash through nature's confetti, cheered on by my dad.

It reminded me, too, of the hawthorn tree I could see from my desk at the paint-tin company where I used to work. I loved it, that solitary spur of life on the concrete boundary of the industrial estate. Perhaps it was planted by a bird, or someone as desperate as I felt back then. For years I watched it through the seasons, admired the buds of its blossom in spring, its rich commotion of greenery in summer, and autumn's rusty splendour. I even loved it in winter, the geometry of its leafless branches as pleasing to me as a gallery sculpture.

I'd walk over to it each lunchtime, sometimes just to touch the bark or look up at its leaves. On warmer days I'd eat my sandwich beneath it, perched on the edge of the verge. By my third summer someone had clearly taken pity on me, dumping an ageing wooden bench out there.

But at the start of my sixth summer, the tree was cut down to make room for a smoking shelter. It tugged at my gut in a way I couldn't explain, to see a huddle of grey faces where leaves and branches had once stood, staring blankly into space from beneath that lifeless dome of Perspex.

I look out of my window now, down at where the neighbours' hawthorn used to be. I should probably get online, start searching for somewhere else to live. Funny how easy it is for one person to uproot another's life, just when they least expect it.

# 6

## Joel

I'm down by the river, thinking about what happened earlier. Or didn't happen. It's hard to say, exactly.

It was strange, when Callie set down my double espresso at the café first thing. Our eyes met, and I felt heat chase a shiver across my skin as I struggled to loosen my gaze.

Irises stippled hazel, like sunlight on sand. Long, carefree hair the colour of conkers. A complexion of the palest vanilla. And a double-take smile that couldn't have been for me.

But, apparently, it was.

Callie nodded at Murphy, who was up against my knee enjoying a head scratch. 'I hope he's not pestering you.'

During my now near-daily visits to the café over the past week or so, I've formed a pretty strong bond with her dog. 'This guy? Oh, no. We have an understanding.'

'You do?'

'Sure. He keeps me company, and I throw him cake crumbs when you're not looking.'

'Would you like some?' An affable smile. 'We have a fresh batch of dream cake just in.'

'Sorry?'

'The *drømmekage*. It's Danish – it means "dream cake".'

I hated the name. But, let's face it, that cake was the culinary equivalent of crack. 'I would, actually. Thanks.'

She returned almost instantly, setting down an oversized slice on a plate in front of me. 'Enjoy.'

Our eyes met again. Once more, I found I couldn't look away. 'Cheers.'

She lingered. Fiddled with her necklace. It was rose-gold and delicate, the shape of a swallow in flight. 'So, busy day? Are you off to work?'

For the first time in a long while, I felt frustrated that I couldn't say yes. That I had not one interesting thing to tell her about myself. I'm not even sure why I wanted to, exactly. There was just something about her. The way she moved, the shine of her smile. The chime of her laugh, full and sweet like the scent of spring.

*Pull yourself together, Joel.*

'I have this theory about you,' she said then.

I thought fleetingly of Melissa, who's arrived at enough theories about me to pen her own massive, meaningless thesis.

'I think you're a writer.' Callie indicated my notebook and pen.

Again I had the urge to impress her. Captivate her somehow, say something winning. Unsurprisingly, I fell short. 'Just incoherent ramblings, I'm afraid.'

She didn't seem too disappointed. 'So what do you—'

But all at once, from behind us, a customer was trying to get her attention. I turned to see Dot dashing between tables, grimacing apologetically.

Callie smiled. Tipped her head towards the counter. 'Well, I'd better . . .'

It was odd, the urge I had to stretch out my hand as she walked away. To draw her gently back towards me, feel warmed by her presence again.

I trained myself a long time ago not to dwell on passing attractions. But this was solar-plexus level, a feeling I haven't had for years. Like she'd brought back to life a part of me I thought I'd buried for good.

I left pretty soon after that. Resisted the reflex to glance at her on my way out.

'Joel! Hey, Joel!'

I'm still trying to dislodge this morning from my thoughts when I realise I'm being heckled. This isn't usually the best way to get my attention, but I recognise the voice. It's Steve's, and he's chasing me.

I've been avoiding him since letting down his tyres last week. Now, though, I guess, my misdemeanours are quite literally about to catch up with me.

I'm half minded to sprint for the boating lake, attempt a pedalo-based getaway with my small herd of dogs in tow. But then I remember Steve could definitely outrun me, wrestle me to the ground and get me to submit, all in the space of about ten seconds.

Steve's a personal trainer, holds loathsome outdoor boot-camp classes for people with masochistic tendencies. He must have just finished one, because he's sweating as he swigs from an oversized muscle milkshake. He's in jógging bottoms and trainers, a T-shirt that looks like it's been sprayed to his body.

'All right, hounds,' he says, to my motley crew of three, falling into step at my shoulder.

He seems relaxed. Still, that could just be the endorphins. I keep striding purposefully, guard firmly up. If he asks me about his tyres, I'll deny all knowledge.

'What's going on, mate?'

Or I could just say nothing at all.

Steve gets straight to the point, because he's efficient like that. 'Joel, I know it was you who let down my tyres last week.' His voice is low but firm, like I'm a kid he's caught nicking cigarettes from the corner shop. 'I've been asking around, got Rodney to check his footage. It's all on CCTV.'

Ah, Rodney. The eyes of our street. A walking, talking citizen's arrest. I might have known he'd be my downfall. The clues have been there for months, ever since he got broadband installed last summer just so he could tweet the police.

Self-reproach snakes through me. I want to say something, but don't know what. So I just stuff my hands deeper into my pockets, keep walking.

'You know,' Steve's saying, 'after you'd done it, you rested your head against the wheel arch. You felt bad, didn't you?'

Of course I did, all rationale aside. Because, for so many years, Steve felt more like family to me than a friend.

'I *know* you didn't want to be doing what you did, mate. So just tell me why.'

Even the thought of that conversation feels like standing on the edge of a cliff. Racing heart, prickling skin, speech shrivelling to sawdust in my mouth.

'I had to tell Hayley,' Steve says, when I fail to enlighten him.

This comes as no surprise: they function properly, the two of them. Sharing everything, withholding nothing.

'She's not happy. Actually, she's fuming. She can't understand what the hell you were thinking. I mean, I had *Poppy* with me—'

'The tyres were right down. You couldn't have driven away, even if you'd wanted to.'

Steve grabs my arm now, pulls me to a halt. The strength of his grip renders me pretty helpless: I'm forced to meet his eye.

'Poppy's your goddaughter, Joel. The least you could do is tell me why.'

'It wasn't . . . I promise I had good reason.'

He waits to hear it.

'I can't explain. I'm sorry. But it wasn't malicious.'

Steve sighs, releases my arm. 'Look, Joel, all of this . . . It's kind of confirmed what me and Hayley have been thinking for a while. We need more space anyway, now we've got Poppy, so I should tell you . . . we're going to do it. We're moving out.'

A breath of regret. 'Sorry.' I need him to know this. 'Really, I am.'

'We probably won't sell. Not at first, anyway – we'll get a tenant in. The mortgage is nearly paid off, so . . .' He pauses, looks at me as though he's let slip something really offensive. 'Just heard that back in my head. What a middle-class arsehole.'

Steve and Hayley were sensible, bought their flat off our landlord when prices were still reasonable. 'Not at all. You work hard. Hang on to the place.'

He nods slowly. 'I wish you could tell me what's going on, mate. I'm . . . worried about you.'

'Everything's under control.'

'Joel. I think I might be able to help. Did I ever tell you—'

'Sorry,' I say quickly, before he can finish. 'Need to get going. These dogs won't walk themselves.'

They absolutely would, of course. But right now they're the only excuse I've got.


I've lived in Eversford my entire life, have been Steve and Hayley's oddball downstairs neighbour for nearly a decade.

I tried to avoid them when they first moved in. But Steve's a pretty hard man to dodge. He's his own boss, which meant he had time to do stuff like put my bins out and take in packages and intimidate the landlord over the cavernous crack in our side wall. So that was how we went from neighbours to friends.

Vicky, my girlfriend back then, was keen to nurture the new relationship. She kept making arrangements with Hayley for the four of us: sundowners in the back garden, bank-holiday barbecues, birthday celebrations in town. She suggested Bonfire Nights at the local park,

Halloweens ducking trick-or-treaters with the aid of rum, darkened windows and horror films.

Vicky left me on her birthday, after three years together. Presented me with a list she'd made, a slim column of pros against a litany of damning cons. My emotional detachment topped the list, but no less significant were my general dysfunction and constant edginess. My reluctance to let myself go of an evening, and apparent inability to sleep. The notebook I never let her look at was on there too, as was my permanent air of distraction.

None of it was new to me, nor was any of it unfair. Vicky deserved far more from a boyfriend than the lukewarmth I was offering her.

It didn't help, I'm sure, that I kept the dreaming from her. But Vicky had always reminded me a bit of Doug, in that she wasn't famed for her empathy. Though there was a lot about her I admired (ambition, sense of humour, inner drive), she was also the sort of person who'd shrug if she ran over a rabbit.

When she left, I succumbed to heavy drinking for a few months. I'd tried it before, in my last two years at uni, after reading about its disruptive effects on sleep. I knew it wasn't the answer, not really. That it wouldn't actually work. But I suppose I convinced myself things might be different this time.

They weren't, so I shelved it. Just in time, probably, as I'd been starting to succumb to the dangerous warmth of dependency. And the thought of tackling that on top of everything else felt about as attractive as signing up to swim the Channel, or picking a fight at my local kung fu club.

In the years that followed Vicky leaving, Steve and Hayley always felt more like family to me than friends. It was almost as if they were putting their arms around my pain. And when Poppy was born this year, I think they thought that being her godfather might actually be good for me.

At the christening, I held Poppy proudly for a photograph. She was like a writhing puppy against me, warm and adorable. I looked down at her face, felt her weighty preciousness, was overwhelmed with love.

Furious with myself, I passed her back. Got drunk, smashed two wine glasses. Had to be hailed an early taxi home.

That did it. Things have been strained ever since.

## 7

# Callie

Towards the end of the month, Ben suggests a night at the pub, where a friend-of-a-friend's having a birthday do. I'm almost too tired after finishing work, but I've been reluctant to let Ben down of late – his progress is still so tentative, like he's emerging from hibernation after the bitterest winter.

Joel was one of the last customers to leave tonight and, for a rash half-second as he closed the door behind him, I thought I might dart into the street and invite him along. He's by far the best thing about working at the café right now – he can sink me with just a smile, fluster me with the briefest of glances. I've found myself waiting each day to see him, wondering what I could say to make him laugh.

But at the last moment, I changed my mind, because I'm fairly certain asking him to the pub would be crossing a line. The poor man should be able to enjoy a coffee in peace without being harassed for a date by loitering baristas. Anyway, someone this lovely is bound to be taken – even though, as Dot points out, he's always alone.

Really, I remind myself, we hardly know each other – just well enough for smiles and passed remarks, like stars from companion galaxies exchanging winks across swathes of limitless sky.

The birthday party's in the beer garden where, luckily, it's still warm enough to sit out. I spot my friend Esther and her husband Gavin, and a bunch of people we all knew slightly better when Grace was alive. If she was here now she'd be working the patio, the earthy roll of her laugh like a snatch of familiar, well-loved music.

For a moment, I pause to listen out for it. Because, you know – just in case.

I slide onto the bench next to Esther, Murphy settling down at my feet. A waterfall of honeysuckle plunges from the pergola above our heads, vivid-green and frothing with creamy blooms. 'Where's Ben?'

'Held up at work. I think he's feeling a bit low.'

'Blue-low, or black-low?'

'Well, he's on his way. So blue-low, I suppose.' Esther, arms bare in a butter-yellow top, pushes a pint of cider towards me.

I met Esther and Grace on our first day of primary school. I was comfortable sliding into their shadow from the off, admiring but never matching their daring. They shared an outspokenness that frequently got them turfed out of lessons, and manifested itself years later in evenings spent shouting at *Question Time*, in arguments across the top of my head about government policy and climate change and feminist theory. They buzzed off each other, fierce and feverish. And then Grace was taken suddenly and violently away, leaving Esther to fight solo for all their principles, their most ardent passions.

Grace was killed eighteen months ago, by a taxi driver who was over the limit. He swerved off the road, and Grace died on the pavement where she'd been walking.

It was instant, they told us. She wouldn't have suffered.

While we're waiting for Ben, the conversation turns to work. 'Tried my hand at your dream job today, Cal,' Gavin says to me, sipping his lager.

I smile, slightly puzzled. 'How do you mean?'

Gavin's an architect, and each year his team volunteer their time for a local good cause. He tells me he's spent eight hours today undertaking habitat management at Waterfen – our local nature reserve, my private haven.

'You can imagine how that went.' Esther winks. She works long hours for low pay as a policy manager for a social-welfare charity. 'Eight hours of outdoor graft for desk junkies.'

Inhaling the honeysuckle, I picture a day spent spellbound by meandering hedgerows and wild woodlands, tawny reed beds threaded together by a cool ribbon of river. I do occasional volunteer work down at Waterfen, submit quarterly reports. It's piecemeal and unpaid – breeding-bird surveys, habitat monitoring – but that's okay. It satisfies my cravings for horizons unhemmed by buildings, earth unmuddied by people, air unsullied by artifice.

I smile at Gavin. 'Sounds interesting.'

He grimaces with the sort of self-loathing only unplanned exertion has the power to induce. 'That's one way of putting it. I thought I was *fit*. And let's just say that restacking log piles five times my height, lugging fence posts around and breaking my back pulling up whatever-it-was is not my idea of fun.'

I register the scratches along his forearms. There's a faint dusting of nature, too, still visible in his hair. 'Ragwort?'

'What?'

'Was that what you were pulling up?'

'Yeah, whatever,' he mutters darkly, swigging his lager. 'It was hell.'

'Sounds like heaven to me.'

'Well, the warden said they're advertising for an assistant's role soon. Be better use of your ecology degree than serving coffee. Why don't you—'

Even as Esther cuts him short with a cough, I feel something stir inside me, the waking flex of a sleeping creature.

'Why don't you what?' Ben plonks his rugby-player's physique next to me, pint in hand, surveying our faces expectantly. He embodies exactly the end of a working day – shirt sleeves rolled up, hair askew, eyes off-duty.

'Nothing,' I say quickly. In the drained glass to my right, I notice a ladybird out of its depth in the dregs. I slide my fingers against the tidemark, perform a rescue. It flits away.

'There's a job coming up at Waterfen,' Gavin says. 'You know – the nature place, where you can go and be tortured for charity? Apparently it's Callie's dream career, so—' He breaks off and shoots Esther a look, which is his usual way of objecting to being kicked in the shin.

Ben straightens up from ruffling Murphy's ears. 'I thought you loved the café.'

His bafflement scours me like sandpaper. 'I do,' I assure him quickly, ignoring Gavin's raised eyebrow. 'Don't worry. I'm not going anywhere.'

Ben's expression becomes relief, and I know what it means – that for the café to be in safe hands would mean the world to Grace. Leaving my job to become manager after she died seemed so obvious it was almost logic. Ben was committed to a marketing role he loved, while I was stagnating at the paint-tin company. I'd been there for eleven years – eleven years of organising my boss's diary, making her coffee, answering her phone. It was only ever supposed to be a stop-gap after uni, a quick way to make rent – but three months in, it became permanent, and a decade after that, worthy of a long-service award that amused Grace no end. 'Ten years loyal to one woman,' she'd teased, when I turned up at hers with the bottle of champagne I'd received. 'It's like a weird little marriage.'

That was just a year before she died.

I adopted Murphy from Ben not long afterwards. He'd been Grace's dog, really, but there was a no-canines policy at Ben's office, and plenty of love going spare at the coffee shop.

Owning a café was the first steady anything Grace had done in the six years since we'd left uni – but even that started out as a whim. She used an inheritance to impulse-buy the lease on an old children's clothing shop, taking us all by surprise. She'd been travelling the world in the interim, working as she went – waitressing, telesales, handing out flyers in costume. Occasionally she'd call me from some faraway country, regale me with her latest adventures and disasters, and I'd come off the phone piqued and envious. I'd fantasise briefly about catching a flight myself, feeling the dopamine thrill of having finally fled my own tiny patch of globe.

I wondered, often, what it would be like to take off like that. I was drawn to places of vast wilderness, endless skylines, dizzying panoramas. We'd learnt one term in school about South America, and ever since, I'd lusted over a particular national park in the far north of Chile. Our geography teacher had visited, just two summers earlier, and by the end of the lesson we all felt we'd journeyed there with her. I related her adventures to my dad that night, asked if we could holiday in Chile next summer. He laughed and said we'd ask Mum, which I knew immediately to be his way of saying no. He was probably correct in thinking that no one in their right mind would acquiesce to such a request from a ten-year-old.

So I travelled to the *altiplano* in my mind instead, pored over pictures of snow-capped volcanoes and sweeping vistas, dreamt at night of alpacas and llamas, falcons and flamingos. It became my escape, whenever I needed one – to drift off to that corner of Chile, made fable by my imagination.

I always promised myself I'd go. But after leaving university I had precious few savings, and I wasn't too sure I suited Grace's legendary work-as-you-go approach. I had none of her boldness, and far too much of my own self-doubt. The timing never seemed quite right – I was job-hunting, trying to save, working hard, dating. And so the years slipped by, and Chile remained a far-flung dream.

I know it's always seemed to Ben that managing the café was a welcome route out of a job I was bored stiff in. But all it's really done is remind me that serving coffee isn't my passion. I'm still living in the town where I was born, and meanwhile there's a world out there – pulsating with possibility as it turns, turns, turns.

# 8

## Joel

I'm accidentally-on-purpose walking past the vet's practice where I used to work. I do this at least once a week. Don't ask me why.

Maybe I'm pretending I still work there, that I'm about to pass through the swing doors like nothing ever changed. Say hi to Alison on the front desk, pause to chat with Kieran on the way to my consulting room.

I spot him in the car park. He's outside the rear door with his back to the brick wall, taking five.

I cross the road and head over. Raise a hand as he sees me.

'Hey.' He straightens up. 'How you doing?'

'Good, thanks.' I nod like it's true, though we both know it's not. 'You?'

'Needed some fresh air.'

Joining Kieran against the wall, I steal a glance at his navy-blue uniform. It's identical to the one back at my flat. The same uniform I was proud to wear, once.

We tip our faces towards late-September sunshine. 'Bad day?' I ask him.

'Not great. Remember Jet Mansfield?'

'Sure.' The deaf Border collie, with an adorable ancient owner, Annie. She adopted Jet shortly after her husband died. The pair of them were devoted to each other.

'I amputated his front leg six months ago. Sarcoma.'

I look at him, take a guess. 'And now it's back?'

'Just had to break the news to Annie.'

'How'd it go?'

'About as well as you'd think.'

'What's she going to do?'

'Fortunately she agreed with me.'

*Max pain relief*, I think, *and a comfy bed.*

'I doubt he's got longer than a month.'

I picture Annie taking Jet home. She'll be doing her best to pretend everything's normal. Shaking food into his bowl as she tries not to cry. 'You okay?'

'I guess.' Kieran smiles faintly, looks at me. 'Sort of nice having you out here again. Feels like the old days.'

I've kept Kieran in the dark about my dreams: I always feared him assuming mental instability, pitying me. Thinking privately, even, that it was a good job I left.

Since he's my friend and ex-boss, Kieran's respect means everything to me. It's part of the reason I quit, jumped before I was pushed.

I force a smile. 'Yeah.'

'Fancy a job?'

I keep the smile but shake my head. 'Too much on right now.'

'Yeah,' Kieran says, 'you do strike me as a guy with a really packed schedule. Just wandering past, were you?'

'Yep,' I say, straightening up, clearing my throat. 'Speaking of which, I should get going.'

'Hit me up any time,' Kieran calls out, as I head off across the car park.

I raise a hand, keep walking.


My route home takes me past the café. As I approach, I see Callie outside locking up, Murphy at her heels.

I've dropped in most days since my first visit nearly three weeks ago now. Sometimes it's Dot who serves me, sometimes it's Callie. But I always find myself hoping for Callie. Once or twice, I've even made an adolescent play for time until I can see she's become free. Pretended to mislay my wallet, dithered over a sandwich or croissant.

I'm most unlike myself, I've found, whenever I'm around her.

This morning I was seated near a customer who unwisely decided to disagree with Dot on the definition of brioche (Dot's view: it's not a cake). Mid-debate, Callie caught my eye from another table she was serving. We both struggled not to laugh, until eventually she was forced to seek refuge behind the counter. Meanwhile, I had to put my head in my hands for fear of completely losing it.

When eventually she came to take my order, I pretended to deliberate before loudly requesting brioche. At which point she started laughing all over again.

It's been a long time since I've laughed like that with anyone.

Which is why, now, I'm hesitating. Watching her turn the key, check the handle, take a final scan of the shop front. It's a moment perfect for approaching her, inviting her out for an after-work drink. But, just in time, I check myself.

An image of Vicky's pros-and-cons list fires like a flash-bulb in my mind. I think of Kate too, before her, in bed with someone else.

My life to date: intermittent stabs at normality (school, uni, girlfriends, work) between pockets of instability (wild-eyed experiments, heavy drinking, solitude).

Honestly, dating? With someone as lovely as Callie, I wouldn't know where to start.

*Forget it. What's the point? Ridiculous.*

Besides, I've no actual evidence that she'd even be interested. To her I'm probably just another customer, and a slightly peculiar one at that.

So instead I just watch, like I'm peering through a keyhole into another life. Callie's wearing a pale denim jacket now, has pulled her dark hair into a topknot. Murmuring something in a low voice to Murphy, she slips on a pair of sunglasses. And then together they start to walk away.

I experience a rare rush of wishing it was me by her side. One arm around her shoulders, high on her laughter as it mingles with mine.

## 9

# Callie

In early October, a fortnight or so since my evening at the pub with Ben and the others, I take the morning off work to go flat-hunting.

True to form, Ian's first offering is a damp basement bedsit where I spot mousetraps in a kitchen cupboard. 'I don't want to live with mice, but I don't want to break their necks either,' I confess.

Ian looks at me as if he's never met anyone so entitled in all his life. 'You'll be homeless at this rate,' he chides – though he's smiling like it's funny, which it's not.

In the living room of my next appointment – a first-floor flat in a Victorian terrace, where the landlord, Steve, wants to meet prospective tenants himself – I notice a framed picture. It's of a dog almost identical to Murphy, made up of hundreds of tiny paw prints.

'That's Hayley's,' Steve says, following my eye. A personal trainer, he's head-to-toe in gym wear. 'My wife. She's a real dog person. Actually, that reminds me – I did ask Ian to check, but you've not got any pets, have you?'

I cross my fingers and tell him no. It was pointless asking Ian to show me pet-friendly flats, mainly because they don't exist.

Still, so far, I'm impressed. The street is pleasant and tree-lined – which bodes well for a dawn chorus – and only a couple over from where I live now. The rent's fifty quid more expensive a month, but then so was the bedsit and this is easily fifty quid nicer. It's a bit stuffy up here beneath the rafters, but the communal hallway doesn't smell of sick or urine, which, on a budget like mine, is depressingly rare.

'There's outside space,' Steve says, when I ask if there's a garden, 'if that counts.'

We both know it doesn't – that *outside space* is really only code for somewhere to keep the bins – but I force my face to look interested. 'Oh?'

He takes me over to the kitchen window, where I stare miserably down onto another concrete nightmare, this one crazy-paved, straight out of the seventies.

I long, so much, for a lawn. Just something green to look at.

'That all belongs to the guy downstairs,' Steve says. 'Well, not actually *belongs* – he rents, like you. Sorry it's so scruffy. I'm sure he wouldn't mind tidying up if I asked.'

'No,' I say quickly, because those dead leaves and old bricks, rotting wood and dodgy fence panels are truly the only things going in that oversized patio's favour. 'Don't. It's good for the nature, all that stuff.'

Steve frowns. 'The . . . ?'

'You know – the beetles and insects. Moths, spiders. They prefer . . . a bit of mess. For shelter, and . . .' I trail off, then switch on a smile because I really don't want to lose this flat on account of appearing deranged. 'So, what's he like? The downstairs neighbour.'

Steve pauses for a long time, which forces me to wonder why a simple description like *nice guy* or *decent bloke* wouldn't cover it.

'Well, he keeps himself to himself,' he says eventually, which I'm fairly sure is a neutral way of saying anti-social. 'You'd barely see him, probably.'

I try briefly to picture this person, elusive as a polecat, slinking between shadows, nocturnal and nervous. Maybe a little domestic mystery is what Dot has in mind when she says I need more excitement in my life.

\* \* \*

Dot wrinkles her nose when I relate all this to her later that afternoon. A party girl at heart, she doesn't really see the point of neighbours unless you can spend half your time hanging out in their flat sharing weed and flipping through their record collection. 'You misspelt cappuccino,' she points out. 'Two *c*s.'

It's been a slow afternoon, maybe because storm clouds are filling the sky. I'm balanced on a stepladder, rewriting every one of our smudged menu items in bright white chalk pen and my best calligraphy.

I lift a cloth to the board, wipe out half of the offending word and try again.

'Mind you,' Dot says, 'I suppose he might be hot.'

'Don't start.'

She shrugs, then starts anyway. 'I still think you should let me introduce you to my kickboxing teacher.'

'No, thanks. He sounds terrifying. And please don't bring him in here.' Dot's got form on this, inviting guys she thinks I might like in for coffee and cake. I've told her to stop, that it's weird while I'm at work – not much different from going on a date in your office, running them through your hobbies, top holidays and favourite films between bouts of photocopying.

Naturally, Dot persists. 'What about that guy I met speed-dating?'

'Dot, I'm not going out with your speed-dating rejects. How desperate do you think I am?'

Dot looks at me as though she wishes the question wasn't rhetorical. But before she can open her mouth to say as much, we're interrupted by someone clearing their throat.

Turning to see Joel behind the counter, I palpitate with embarrassment as I try not to imagine how long he's been standing there. I never even noticed him walk in.

'Sorry to interrupt.' His eyes are wondrous, near-black.

He's been coming to the café almost every day for at least a month now, usually first thing, sometimes late afternoon. He always sits in the same seat by the window, asks me and Dot how we are, fusses Murphy, tips generously, and brings his crockery to the counter on his way out. I've often spotted him brushing the crumbs from his table into a paper napkin, or wiping it down because he's spilt a splash of coffee.

Dot leaves me to it, shoulders shaking with mirth as she heads into the back office.

'Sorry,' I fluster, clattering down the stepladder. 'We were . . . Never mind. Idle gossip.'

'No worries. Just wanted to—'

'Of course. Sorry. What can I get you?'

He orders an egg-and-tomato sandwich – he's vegetarian, I discovered, like me – and a double espresso. He's dressed for the cooler weather today in a charcoal crew-necked jumper, brown boots and black jeans.

'Speed-dating,' I find myself saying, rolling my eyes as I scribble down his order. 'My idea of hell.'

Joel smiles. 'Yeah.'

'I mean, it's bad enough being judged by one person on a blind date, but twenty people lining up to do it, with scorecards?' I affect a shudder. 'Can't think of anything worse. Isn't it better to just meet naturally, and then . . . ?' Catching his eye, I trail off, the silence that follows more than overdue.

He clears his throat and shifts his weight, like all he wants to do is make a break for the table by the window. 'Couldn't agree more.'

*Brilliant, Callie. Now he thinks you're trying to hit on him. Really running with the desperate theme today.*

'Don't wait,' I say hastily. 'I'll bring everything over.'

'You've gone all clammy.' Dot laughs, re-emerging from the office once Joel's walked away, Murphy at his heels as if the pair of them arrived together.

I let out a hoot of laughter, then hand her his order, clambering up the steps to finish writing where I left off. 'What?'

'You're all pink and flustered.' She picks up some tongs, reaches into the cabinet for Joel's sandwich.

Outside, rain starts pelting the pavement with a shower of misty bullets. I lift the pen and start writing again. 'I have no idea what you're talking about.'

'Was he flirting with you?'

'Definitely not.'

'You know he comes in here virtually every day?'

With a shrug I turn to her, though it's Joel in my peripheral vision. 'I think he's just bonded with Murphy.'

'Yeah,' Dot says, pursing her lips. 'Murphy. That must be it. He really, *really* likes your dog.'

'You can't stay here all night, Cal.'

'I don't want to wake him.'

'I'll do it, then.'

'No! Don't. Give him five minutes. There's plenty I can be getting on with.'

Dot tilts her head and looks at him, like she's taking in a particularly nuanced piece of art. 'So what's his deal, do you reckon?'

'How do you mean?'

'Does he have a job? He always seems a bit . . .'

'What?'

'. . . vagrant.'

I like that about Joel, the raw appeal of imperfection. 'Does it matter?'

'Oh, you have *such* a soft spot for him.'

'I do not.'

'Whatever. I approve. You could do far worse.'

'Thanks, Dot. You can go now.'

'Fine. But can you please not stay here watching him sleep until midnight?'

'I promise I won't.'

She demonstrates her faith in me by banging the door hard on her way out, giving me a double thumbs-up through the window.

Joel stirs, so I head over to his table, Murphy at my side.

'We're about to close,' I tell him gently.

He blinks as he looks up and around. 'Sorry?'

'You dropped off there.'

For a moment or two he stares at me before jerking into a sitting position, swearing softly. 'Sorry. That's embarrassing.'

'Not at all. Happens all the time.'

'It does?'

I hesitate, then smile. 'No, but . . . it's fine. Really.'

'Oh, and you're trying to go home.' He scrambles to his feet, slides his notebook into his pocket, picks up his espresso cup and plate.

'I'll take it.'

'No, please, let me—'

In the next second, the cup and plate have shattered on the floor, like the shells of dropped eggs.

Joel shuts his eyes briefly, then looks at me and winces. 'It's customers like me who really make this job, isn't it?'

'It's fine.' I laugh, not wanting to admit that, in fact, it is. 'You go. I'll clear it up.'

He ignores me and bends down, starts collecting fragments. I tell Murphy to stay where he is, then join Joel on the floor to help.

We pick up the remaining shards, fingertips occasionally brushing. I find myself trying not to look at him while my heartbeat goes bananas.

Ceramic cleared, we get to our feet as a drumroll of thunder sounds from outside. The sky has ripened now, and the clouds are plum-purple.

'Can I pay you for the breakage?'

'Not at all. It was my fault.'

Joel does something to my stomach with his eyes. 'Listen, sorry you've had to throw me out.'

'Oh, that's okay. I had to do the same with a couple who were on a first date once.'

He seems surprised. 'Bored each other to sleep?'

I laugh. 'No. They were just so . . . absorbed in each other, they didn't notice everyone else had left.'

I can see him thinking this over. 'Absorbed in . . . scintillating conversation?'

'Not exactly. I sort of had to prise them apart.'

'Ah, the joy of youth.'

'Afraid not. They were mid-fifties, easily.'

Now he laughs too. 'Strangely, I don't feel as bad now.'

I grin. 'Good.'

By the door, Joel stops to fuss Murphy for a couple of moments more, then says goodbye and leaves. I watch him walk away and cross the road, swept along with the stormy air.

As he reaches the opposite pavement, he glances back over his shoulder. I look quickly down, scrub hard at a table that's already gleaming.

# 10

## Joel

We're gathered in the fug of Dad's steamed-up kitchen, preparing Sunday lunch. My niece Amber is thundering through the house in a dinosaur costume, which, due to its impressive tail, has reduced her spatial awareness to approximately zero.

'Well, it's getting ridiculous, if you ask me,' Dad's saying to Doug, like I'm nowhere to be seen.

'Nobody did ask you,' I point out.

Doug kicked off today's Morgan family spat by asking if I'd managed to find a job yet. When I didn't reply, he simply carried on talking to Dad about it, as if I'd got up and left the room.

'Unemployment's at the root of all your problems, I'm sure.' Dad peers at me over the rim of his glasses, carrot and peeler in hand. 'The sooner you go back, the better.'

Not another quicksand of a conversation about how I couldn't carry on. About how bad I felt at the surgery that final morning. (They don't know the extent of it: that I'd been drinking heavily again, was hungover and incompetent, sleep-deprived and sad.) The time to go had come.

It visits me like voltage sometimes, how much I miss it. Like when I'm walking my pack of dogs in the park. Or if I pass a cat, sprawled out and sun-drunk on a garden wall. If I smell disinfectant (synonymous, always, with long hours at the surgery). Or when I spend time with Kieran, laughing the way we used to.

'They're not holding my job open, Dad. I left.'

He tuts. 'What a waste of a degree.'

It's not his words that slice me open so much as his disdain. Fortunately, a six-year-old stegosaurus is approaching at speed. 'Uncle – Joel – you're – it!' Amber squeals, ramming the spikes of her spine against my shins.

I beam at her, delighted. 'It's as if you knew.'

'Bad luck,' jeers Doug, from over by the sink, slow-witted as a snail.

'Back in a minute. Just got to deal with a dinosaur.' I wipe my hands on a tea towel, hurtle into the fray with my best Mesozoic-era roar.

Later, Tamsin comes and leans against the fridge while I'm washing up.

Her husband Neil's on drying. He doesn't really do chit-chat, but he's amenable and thoughtful in a way that makes me happy he married my sister.

'Heard Dad giving you a hard time earlier,' she says, nibbling a fingernail.

'Nothing new there.'

'He doesn't mean it, you know.'

Three years my junior, my sister's almost a whole foot shorter than me. Like Doug, she's red-haired, though she has a vast glossy shock of it that strangers frequently approach her to rave about. (I'd wager this doesn't happen too often to Doug and his buzz-cut.)

She seems tired today, distracted. More like me than herself.

'Thanks for being nice,' I say, 'but he absolutely does.'

'He just worries.' (Subtext: *we all do*.)

'Points for the dinosaur costume, by the way.'

Tamsin rolls her eyes, but smiles. 'She wore it for a party last week and now it's her new favourite thing. Still, it livened up our trip to the Co-op yesterday. We like to be a bit eccentric in this family, don't we?'

*Well, yes, we do.* 'True.'

'Hey, I've been meaning to ask. What was with the To Let sign outside your place a few weeks back? You're not moving, are you?'

Steve and Hayley left last night, and I couldn't think of a good way to apologise for having been such a lousy friend and neighbour. So I lay low for the evening. Failed to answer the final knock on my door.

'No,' I tell her. 'Steve and Hayley.'

'Something you said?'

'Probably.' I concentrate on removing every last scrap of gravy from the jug.

I sense her taking me in. 'Okay. Well, we're heading off.'

'Already? Sure you don't want to stay? Any minute now Dad's bound to ask why I haven't got a girlfriend.'

Normally this is the kind of lame quip that would make Tamsin laugh. But when I look up, the light's worked loose from her eyes. 'I just . . . let's just say . . .'

'We're not pregnant,' Neil says quietly, dropping the tea towel. He reaches out for my sister's hand. 'We just found out.'

I feel their pain strike the back of my throat. 'Sorry.'

Tamsin nods. 'I told Dad and Doug I've got a headache.'

'Sure.'

'I'll get our stuff.' Neil leaves the room, patting me on the back as he goes.

'Don't forget our dinosaur,' Tamsin calls after him. Her voice is parchment-thin.

'I'm sorry, Tam,' I manage, once we're alone.

She nods, tips her head back against the fridge. 'God. I want this so badly, Joel.'

I remember the day Amber was born. I raced up to the hospital, spent the afternoon staring down at my brand-new niece in her little cot. I was puffed-up with pride, thinking, *My sister's made a baby. Look, everyone — an actual living human!*

'I mean, at what point . . . at what point do you . . . ?' She heaves out a breath. 'It's been five years. *Five.*'

'It'll happen for you,' I say quietly.

'You can't know that.'

*But I do.* I know because I dreamt it just two months ago. Tamsin in hospital, me at her side, holding her hand. And next to the bed, the best part of all. A baby boy, Harry, asleep in a cot.

She doesn't know it yet, but he's coming next Christmas.

I grab her hand, give it a squeeze. 'Yeah, I do. Hang in there, Tam, please. I promise it'll all work out.'

Washing-up done, I take a few steps down Dad's back-garden path. It's mid-October, and the air is thick with an autumn chill. A grubby chasm of cloud is squatting over the nearby houses, spitting drizzle.

Mum loved this garden, called it her sanctuary. I miss her every day.

She passed away from breast cancer when I was thirteen. I dreamt about it four years ahead of time, one awful ice-bound night in November.

The dream struck me with fear in a way I'd never known. I told no one what I'd seen: I was terrified of scaring Mum, enraging Dad. Breaking up our family. Would I be blamed? Was I causing these things to happen? I became almost mute: wouldn't speak, refused to smile. How could I be happy, knowing what I knew? The colour had been washed from my world. I feared falling asleep, grew almost allergic to shutting my eyes.

She finally told us at Christmas three years later. We were lined up on the sofa like a row of errant toddlers. I'll never forget the expression on her face. Because she wasn't looking at Dad, who was standing stiffly by, emotions already fenced-off. Or at Tamsin, who was weeping. Or at Doug, so quiet he was barely breathing. She was looking at me, because she knew I already knew. *Why?* her eyes implored me. *Why didn't you tell me?*

Not giving her every last damn chance to live remains the biggest regret of my life.


Behind me, the back door slams. Doug.

'Hello, little brother.' Calling me that is my younger brother's private joke that only he finds funny. He congratulates himself with a swig of beer.

I resist the urge to comment on his jumper. I'm sure he probably thinks of it as golfing apparel, despite never having swung a club in his life.

From out of nowhere, Doug produces a packet of fags. I stare at him sparking up. 'What are you—'

'I tell you what.' He drags then exhales. 'It's actually kind of exciting, trying not to get caught.' He glances over his shoulder towards the living-room window. His wife Lou's in there with their kids Bella and Buddy, trying to persuade them off the iPad and towards Dad's game of Boggle.

Doug takes a couple of furtive steps left, so he's shielded by the crab-apple tree.

I have to laugh. 'You are tragic.' My own breath looks like smoke in the frigid air.

'Yep. Lou and I don't have much fun, these days. My life is essentially work, gym, TV, sleep. Talk about dull.'

*An uneventful life*, I think, not without a pang of jealousy. *Don't knock it.* 'So, you're a smoker with a gym membership,' I remark conversationally. 'Kind of a bad investment, wouldn't you say?'

He ignores me. Takes another drag, eyes narrowing. 'Speaking of fun.'

I wait. Doug's definition of fun is almost never the same as mine.

'This "anxiety" of yours . . .' He gives the word air quotes, just to demonstrate his manliness. 'Lou's talking about going on holiday next year. Fuerteventura. The kids' first time abroad.'

I breathe through a couple of minor palpitations. 'Nice.'

'Yeah, one of those all-inclusive places.'

A thought cartwheels my way. 'What – with kids' clubs? Swimming pools and stuff?'

Doug shrugs. 'Probably.'

'You should get Bella involved. Lou said she's a proper little fish.'

Doug snorts. 'Okay, well, cheers for the parenting advice. Anyway, the whole thing depends on whether you're planning to turn up at the airport, waving your arms above your head and ordering us not to get on the plane.'

Well, I would if his plane was going down. Fortunately for Doug, it's unlikely. I happen to know his chances of dying in a commercial jet crash are about one in eleven million.

Still, I reckon I deserve a little more credit. It's doubtful I'd be that blatant, unless it was a hands-down emergency. Yes, I come out with weird warnings, strange bits of advice, but I've tried to be subtle, over the years. Like when I steered Doug gently clear of a pub brawl that would have fractured his jaw. Advised Lou against a trip to a dodgy dentist, her fated trigger for months of chronic neck pain. Intercepted them both before they got mugged in town. (I reported the guy in question, though the most I could actually lay claim to was 'witnessing suspicious behaviour', the irony of which did not escape me.)

'Maybe a holiday is what *you* need,' Doug says. 'When was the last time you went anywhere?'

I fail to reply. Who admits, in this Instagram age with the world at our fingertips, that they've never once left the UK?

'Oh, I know,' Doug says. 'Magaluf, 2003.'

(I'd lied, of course. Told my family I'd gone abroad with the lads I'd met in my first year of uni. In fact, I moved into my second-year house-share early, then eavesdropped on their stories when they eventually joined me. Repeated them to Doug like they were my own.)

Doug shakes his head. 'A lads' holiday at uni and nothing since. And you say *I'm* tragic.'

'I'm happy here.' By which I mean it's good to know I can get some-where fast if I dream something heart-stopping and need to intervene.

'Oh, yeah. You do seem really happy, Joel.' Doug's eyebrows draw together as he drags on his fag again. 'You know what you need? A good—'

'All right,' I cut in, before he can say it. I shove my hands in my pockets. Stamp my feet against the cold.

'It's not natural. Going for so long without a girlfriend.'

Unwittingly, he's reminded me of my conversation with Callie last week about speed-dating. I remember taking in the loop of her hand-writing as she scribbled down my order. How her hair slipped free from its knot, flew with her breath as she spoke. The earrings she was wearing, a pair of birds in sterling silver.

But most of all I remember the lodestone pull of her eyes. It was so powerful, I almost leant forward to suggest we try a date of our own sometime. But at the last moment I righted myself. Turned quickly, walked away. For fear of her reading my mind. For fear of what it meant.

Because I've guarded against feelings like this for almost an entire decade. And now they're jumping me without warning, robbing me of my vigilance.

'You're talking about sex, not a girlfriend,' I say to Doug.

Doug snorts, as if there's next to no chance of either. 'There are tablets you can take, you know. Just buy them online if you're embarrassed.'

I know he's referring to my supposed anxiety. But I can't resist the urge to goad him. 'Bit young for the little blue diamonds, aren't you?'

He goes very still for a moment. Puffs out his chest. 'I mean it, Joel, about the holiday. This will be our first time abroad, with the kids. You do anything to mess that up, we're done. I have to put my family first.'

I swallow and nod, serious now. *I just want to keep you all safe.*

'Mum's been gone twenty-two years, mate. It's time to grow up.' He claps me on the shoulder. Passes me his lit cigarette. Goes back inside.

I stare at the spot of grass where the rabbit hutches used to be. For so many years, this house was alive with animals. Dogs and rabbits, guinea pigs and ducks. But Dad let them all go naturally after Mum died. And now the place only really feels animated when there are dinosaurs doing laps of it.

The pain of losing Mum was worse than anything I've known. If my own life depended on it, I'm not sure I could go through that again.

I stay where I am for a couple of moments, my stomach a clenched fist of regrets.

# 11

## Callie

Several weeks on from my eviction and, with the help of Mum and Dad, I've finally moved into my new flat. I feel slightly guilty – I've got too many belongings really, enough boxes filled with knick-knacks to warrant three pairs of hands. But they seem happy to overlook all my clutter. I think they're privately pleased I asked for their help.

They leave at about half six so Mum can make it home for her book club. Then Dad returns a couple of hours later with Murphy in the back of the car.

I meet him out on the darkened street, beneath a sky salted with stars. We thought it best to carry out a clandestine handover, under cover of nightfall.

'Thanks for everything, Dad.'

'No worries, darling.' He passes me Murphy's lead. 'You know we're more than happy to lend a hand.'

'I feel a bit old for all this, really,' I confess, the cold air making my breath opaque. 'It's like you're moving me into university digs all over again.'

Dad smiles. 'Come on. You're never too old to need your parents.'

I smile back at him. No matter how ineffectual I think I am, my dad's always got something reassuring to say.

He tucks me under his arm, pulls me close to the warm wall of his chest. I draw in the familiar coal-tar scent of him, take a second to love him all over again.

'Now, you're sure you don't want us to keep the dog for a few days?' he says. 'Give you a chance to run it by your neighbour?'

That would be the sensible option, but I can't relinquish Murphy, even for one night. It's still hard to look at him, sometimes, without wondering if he's thinking about where Grace has gone.

Dad reads my expression as he draws away, gently squeezes my shoulder. 'All right. But don't you think you should at least tell your letting agent?'

I look down at Murphy, who blinks back at me like he'd quite fancy getting some shut-eye. 'Ian's not really the sort of person you should be honest with, Dad.'

Dad, man of principle that he is, appears to consider challenging me on this before changing his mind.

'Thanks for the plants,' I tell him again, as he kisses me goodbye.

It was his house-warming gift to me – a winter window-box he'd potted up himself with primulas and ferns, a twist of variegated ivy, some heather and cyclamen. 'Thought it might improve your view,' he said, as he gave it to me earlier. My eyes beaded with tears as I thanked him, picturing the time he must have spent finding the box, choosing the plants, positioning them just so.

As Dad heads off, I glance at my new neighbour's front window, but since the blinds are down and everything's dark, I assume he's out. I know I won't be able to keep Murphy a secret for long, so I'm hoping I'll be able to win him over somehow.

Putting my key to the front-door lock, I realise that, strangely, it doesn't fit. I stare down at it for a couple of moments before it comes to me. The door to my flat and the communal front door both have Yale locks, and I've only brought my flat key outside.

I take a step back and look up at my window. I haven't left it open – not that I fancy my chances of successfully scaling a plastic drainpipe. Then I wonder if perhaps the neighbour's been forward-thinking enough to break the terms of his tenancy agreement by leaving a key under a flowerpot. But there aren't any flowerpots out here, or anything you could really hide a key under.

I'm starting to resign myself to calling my parents and staying the night at their place when the front door swings open.

We both stop still, temporarily wordless.

'Hello.' I feel a whoosh of unexpected pleasure. 'What . . . what are you doing here?'

'I live here. What are *you* doing here?' He squats down to greet Murphy, who's writhing with excitement on the end of his lead. 'Hello, you.'

'You . . . live *here*?'

Eyes alight, Joel straightens up. He always looks so classic, and tonight is no exception – navy-blue collared jacket, skinny jeans, brown boots. 'Nearly ten years now.'

For a moment I am speechless with happiness, before I realise he's waiting for me to explain my presence on his doorstep. 'I just moved in.'

It takes him a second. 'To Steve's place?'

'Yes.'

His smile comes easily. 'That's great.'

'I can't believe it.'

'So we'll be neighbours.' He rubs his chin. 'Well, how've you been? You know – in the twelve hours since I last saw you.'

We chatted briefly in the café this morning, remarking on the two women sitting closest to the counter who'd come in laden with bags of Christmas wrapping paper. Such crassness should be banned until at least December, we agreed, before we realised simultaneously that in fact we do quite enjoy the early onslaught of Easter eggs in February.

Time to confess. 'Actually, I've locked myself out. I forgot to put the outside key on my key-ring.'

'Did the same when I moved in,' he says, in that lovely low voice of his. Still holding the door open, he steps aside to let me past. He smells delicious, of sandalwood and spice. I try not to feel too self-conscious of my moving-day outfit – tracksuit bottoms, and an ancient grey jumper with holes in both elbows. At least it's dark, I suppose.

'Thank you.' On the doormat, I pause. 'Listen, I'm not supposed to have Murphy here, but—'

'Won't breathe a word.'

'Thank you,' I say, my shoulders dropping with relief. *Thank God it's you.*

'I know it's tough to find landlords who accept them.'

I wonder if he's speaking from experience. Being particularly enchanted by his rapport with Murphy, I asked him once if he had a dog, but he told me no. Perhaps he has done, in the past.

He's checking his watch. 'Listen, sorry to be . . . I was just on my way out.'

'Not at all. Don't let me hold you up.'

'The back garden's all paved, I'm afraid,' he says, 'but if you need to take him out last thing, there's a green at the end of the cul-de-sac there.'

'Oh, I didn't know. Thanks.'

His mouth remains steady, a fault line in the intriguing geography of his face. 'Well, goodnight,' he says softly, eventually, before striding off down the front path into the night.

# 12

## Joel

When I get back from walking Bruno, less than an hour after meeting my new neighbour, I stop in the hallway. Glance up the staircase that leads to Steve's flat.

Not Steve's. Callie's. She's in the flat above me, right now. I picture her moving through it as she makes the space her own. Long hair kissing her shoulder blades, unpacking boxes with that steady self-containment I've come to know so well. Maybe she's lit a candle, put on some music. Something urban but chilled. I noticed her bottle-green nail polish this morning as she set down my coffee. Caught the nectar of her perfume. Felt the strangest urge to cover her hand with mine, look up and say, *Shall we go somewhere?*

I shut my eyes. *Stop thinking about her. Just . . . stop.*

Still, I find myself lingering. She might have heard the outside door clunk closed as I came in. Perhaps she'll pop her head out, suggest a nightcap, ask to borrow some sugar. She'll make me laugh, maybe, like she does every day in the coffee shop. The queen of dry anecdotes, self-deprecating jokes.

But then I take a breath. Make an effort to come to my senses. *This will pass*, I tell myself. Like a squall, or tidal surge. *It feels bigger than it is. Give it time, it will pass.*

The next night Callie and Murphy walk through the front door as I'm just getting in. I've been at Kieran's: a catch-up over curry with him, his wife Zoë and their two kids.

'Anything interesting?' Callie lets Murphy off the lead so he can pelt towards me. His tail swipes the air as though it's been weeks since he's seen me, not hours.

I'm sifting through post. 'Sorry. Unless you fancy my gas bill. Or taking out a personal loan in Steve's name.'

Callie's snug in a green parka with furry hood, a grey knitted scarf looped around her neck. 'The best I can usually hope for is a bank statement. Or a circular from that frozen-food hellhole down the road.'

I smile. 'How's the flat?'

'Love it. It's loads better than my last place. More space, less damp.' She sighs happily, then raises an eyebrow. 'Jury's still out on the downstairs neighbour, though.'

I laugh. 'Yeah, I don't blame you. I'd give him a wide berth, if I were you. Looks dodgy.'

She laughs too, pitching her door keys from palm to palm.

'Are you just getting in from work?' I say. 'It's late.'

'Oh, no, I . . . went somewhere afterwards.'

It's like the engine's cut out in my brain. 'Sorry. I was aiming for neighbourly concern there, not trying to sound like your dad.'

'Oh, that's okay. I'm essentially my mum in disguise. I told a customer he'd catch his death today.'

'Ha. What did he say?'

'Nothing at first. Then he frowned and asked what I meant. He was early twenties, tops. Probably still a student.'

I'm relieved she doesn't seem to be holding my lack of social skills against me. Still, give it time. 'Right.' I lift the wad of envelopes. 'Better get on with this personal loan. These forms won't falsify themselves.'

She laughs politely, smoothes a wayward wave of hair back behind her ears.

I hesitate then tilt forward slightly (because there's nothing quite like someone leaning in to explain their own joke). 'Just kidding. I'd be the world's worst fraudster. Can barely buy booze without breaking into a sweat.'

Obviously, I can't get into my flat quickly enough after that.

Why – *why* – was I talking to her about booze and sweat and financial crime?

I haven't felt clumsy like this in a while. Fat-tongued and foolish, struggling to make sense. Like an amateur actor bungling lines. No wonder she laughed so politely, hesitated before we parted like she was waiting for some sort of excruciating closing gag.

How have I even got to this point? What happened to turning away from girls I get a feeling about, from smiles that tug at my gut, looks that land in my spine?

I'd fallen for Kate, hard. After coupling up at the end of our second term at uni, we'd been dating for nearly a year. Had she not been on my course, I doubt our paths would have crossed. But we saw each other most days, and she was funny, gentle, warm.

Kate always put my flaws down to the stress of studying, I think. Patchy sleep and restlessness, bouts of distraction, the occasional disappearing act? Well, that was all fairly consistent with being a student.

But then I dreamt about her sleeping with someone else six years into our supposed future. She was in a flat I'd never seen before, naked on a mattress I assumed to be half mine. The guy she was with looked older than either of us (a colleague-to-be?). Anyway, he seemed pretty confident, life-choice-wise.

It was the photo of us both on the nightstand that told me she was cheating. I debated hanging in there, wondered if I could stop it. But spending the next six years on the edge of my seat? That wasn't how relationships were supposed to be. Anyway, the damage was already done. Some things in life you just can't un-see.

So I ended it. Came up with something painfully ironic about being unable to envisage a future. It was an odd feeling, apologising for breaking her heart when it was fated to be the other way around.

Getting over Kate wasn't easy. It took me a while to stop dreaming about her. For the flames of what I felt for her to burn fully out. But five years on I met Vicky. She was the lead in a play I went to see, and we got chatting in the bar afterwards. Quite how we ended up back at my place that night, I still don't know. The competition was stiff, and much more cultured than me.

At the start I tried to hide who I was. Live up to the man Vicky must have mistaken me for. And for a while I succeeded, until the day we moved in together. The proximity was like a grand reveal of the person she'd really met, and Vicky quickly grew impatient. Of my edginess and sleeping habits, the early-morning note-taking. Of my emotional restraint and tendency towards distraction. We started to bicker. Passive-aggression kicked in as we began detoxing from the drug of newly knowing each other. The torch beam was dimming, the air sneaking free from the neck of the balloon.

The whole time we were together, I didn't dream about Vicky once. After just six months I knew what that meant, and a part of me was relieved. A relationship without love was pointless, yes, but wasn't it better that way? No love meant no added complications. No agonising dreams, no lose-lose scenarios to sweat over. No premonitions of infidelity. I didn't love Vicky, and it almost felt more reassuring than if I had.

Who knows? Perhaps on some level, the whole thing was a master-class in self-sabotage.

Anyway. After she left, I made a decision, beautiful in its simplicity. I would never fall in love again.

# 13

## Callie

I'm sitting alone at Waterfen, thinking about Grace.

We first came here as children, scampering like rabbits across the wooden bridge linking public park to nature reserve. Clattering along its boardwalks and meandering sandy footpaths, we would sink our feet into marshy pools, scoop up damselflies with glistening wet hands. Grace would talk while I wandered in her wake, floating through clouds of frothing white meadowsweet, drunk as a bee on nature's sumptuous song. We'd roam our private jungle of sedge and reed, the green bejewelled with magenta blazes of rosebay willowherb, staying out till dusk while the landscape cooled around us. And our chatter would always blossom with jokes and school and dreams.

Back then Grace loved Waterfen for what it represented – illusory freedom, putting off her homework. But I loved Waterfen for what it was – something raw and unhewn, the way the world was meant to be. An immersive theatre of wilderness, paradise on a stage.

It was at Waterfen that we discovered our tree. A majestic old willow by the reserve's furthest boundary, its boughs bent over the water's edge like the heads of watchful herons. We scaled its furrowed trunk, became mermaids behind its leafy waterfall, smiled to each other as beneath the soles of our dangling feet, walkers wandered unknowingly on. We carved our initials into the rugged rivets of its bark.

I climb the tree now, just as we always used to, even though it's wet,

even though it's cold. The initials are still here, mossy and rain-smoothed.
I run my finger through the dint of them, trying not to picture the
engraving on Grace's headstone.

Ben and I came up with it together.

*Grace Garvey. Adored wife, daughter, niece and granddaughter. Lover of life.*
*Uncompromisingly unique.*

I never told anyone about our tree. It was just for Grace and me,
always.

After uni, when I moved back to Eversford, I was directionless at
first. Grace was still travelling and Esther was in London temporarily,
having just met Gavin. And my parents couldn't fill the gap my friends
had left. It was coming to Waterfen that kept me going – surrounding
myself with greenery and things with wings.

I think again about the reserve job Gavin mentioned all those weeks
back. I've been checking the Waterfen website daily – but nothing. Still,
I know how slowly things can move forward in charities, that it can take
an age for the simplest of outlays to get approved.

But even if a job did come up, I'm not completely sure I could give
Ben my notice. Could I really hand Grace's dream to someone else,
discard it like an heirloom I no longer wanted?

And yet . . . I have dreams of my own. Like working here at Waterfen,
smelling the earthy sweetness of rain on a reed bed as corvids call and
starlings swarm the sky. Getting wet and hot and muddy, breathless with
hard work and happiness. Giving back just a little of what this place
gives me.

*I'm sorry*, I whisper to Grace's ghost. *I know the café was your dream.*
*But I'm just not sure it will ever be mine.*

As I'm walking home, I feel all at once emboldened – maybe from
thinking about Grace, or about moving on from the coffee shop
somehow. I want to seize the moment, and ask Joel up to my flat for

a drink. After all, we've been neighbours for a whole week now. He can always say no.

'This is homely,' Joel says, as I show him into the living room.

Unwinding my scarf, I'm about to discard it as I always do on the arm of the sofa before changing my mind, rolling it up neatly on the console table by the door instead. Because, realistically, *homely* could be code for *pigsty*. I still haven't finished emptying boxes, and I should have tidied, of course, before asking him up.

He appeared to deliberate, earlier, before saying yes. Instantly I panicked, afraid I'd made him feel awkward, obliged him to be polite. So I opened my mouth to attempt an excruciating backtrack – but before I could crucify myself, he said yes.

I hope he wasn't expecting my flat to look stylish or sophisticated. I have no furniture that didn't come flat-packed, no artwork I didn't pluck from a rack, no shiny ornaments or co-ordinated accessories. Just a muddle of mismatched items I've collected over the years, like the futon with the patchwork throw hiding coffee and red wine stains, a scattering of ring-marked cork coasters, and a variety of nature-themed mugs, courtesy of my friends and family. There are two bookcases in clashing shades of veneer stuffed with books on wildlife and nature, some *very* uncool trinkets – birds and woodland creatures, my loved ones running with a theme again – and a ramshackle jungle of plants on the inside windowsill. Nothing that says I'm an adult, successful, or remotely winning at life. And that's before Joel's tripped over any of the untouched boxes I have yet to deal with, half blocking the kitchen doorway.

I make a sixty-second diversion to the bedroom to change, hyper-ventilate, smooth down my hair and apply a swift rub of nude lipstick. Then I head back to the living room, offer Joel a drink. 'I have coffee, tea or . . . mid-range wine.'

He hesitates for a moment, then asks for a small glass of wine.

As Joel moves over to my bookcase, Murphy at his heels, I fetch the bottle from the fridge and pour two glasses. I watch his fingers as he draws them slowly across the spines of my books, the sleeves of his sweater slightly too long for his wrists. I try to filter out his slow, lingering movements, the slender physique, the measured and thoughtful demeanour I would love to get to know better.

'*Plant glossary. Guide to trees. Lichens. Moths.*'

'I'm not very cool, I'm afraid,' I confess.

I fear this to be something of an understatement – growing up, I was always the one with my eyes mortifyingly trained on a nature book or, worse, an episode of *Countryfile* with my dad. I'd be barefoot outside as soon as winter became spring, collecting sticks and leaves and eggshells, getting mud on my face and twigs in my hair.

Sometimes in summer, when the skies were hot and still, Dad would set up a bulb in the garden to shine overnight. A wooden box fitted beneath it, and early next morning we'd marvel at the moths we'd attracted that had danced through the dark as we dreamt. Elephant hawk-moths in bubblegum-pink, garden tigers exquisite as any butterfly, and my favourite, white ermine, with their regal fur coats. We'd add them to our list then stow them safely in the undergrowth away from prying beaks, so they could shelter from the daylight before darkness fell again.

My ex Piers used to rib me for being a nature nerd. He was the kind of guy who killed spiders with slippers, crushed wasps beneath pint glasses, squashed moths as they slept. And every time he did, a little bit more of my love for him died too.

'Nothing uncool about having a passion,' Joel says.

'I'm just a hobbyist, really.'

'No potential for a career?'

I pass him a wine glass, decide the story's too long. 'Maybe.'

We clink gently. I take a chilled sip, feel a rush to my bloodstream that I suspect isn't fully down to the alcohol.

He's leaning over to inspect my row of pots on the windowsill. 'What are you growing?'

'Those ones at the end are herbs. These are just house plants.' I offer up a smile. 'I like the greenery.'

Moving on to my other bookcase, he examines my tiny library of travel books – a guide to Chile, *Birds of South America*, a collection of maps. Books on the Baltic states – hand-me-downs from a one-time friend of Mum's, who'd travelled there in her youth. I guess my parents thought they might go some day, but evidently they never got round to it. The furthest we ever went in my childhood were Spain and Portugal, the odd camping trip to France.

I've spent hours lost between the pages of those books, armchair-travelling to unspoilt outposts and lunar landscapes, where civilisation vanishes from view and earth submits to sky.

'You're a globe-trotter,' Joel surmises.

I think of Grace, how she'd laugh at this. 'In my dreams, maybe.'

He seems to swallow, before gesturing to the books. 'You've not . . .'

'Not yet. I hope I will, some day.' I sip my wine. 'There's this . . . national park in Chile, way up in the north. It's always been kind of my ambition to go there.'

He looks over at me. 'Yeah?'

I nod. 'We learnt about it at school. I remember our teacher calling it . . . a UNESCO Biosphere Reserve.' I laugh, pronouncing the words precisely for effect. 'It just sounded so exotic, so exciting. Like some-where in outer space.'

He laughs too. 'You're right, it does.'

A girl on my course at uni had been, claimed to have spotted a bird there so rare it's almost myth. It made me want to go even more, that idea of being outsmarted by nature.

'I'm kind of drawn to remote places,' I confess. 'You know – where the earth feels bigger than you.'

He smiles. 'Yeah, humbling, isn't it? Like when you look up at the stars and remember how tiny we all are.'

Together we move to the sofa. Joel drops his free hand to Murphy's head, lets his fingers fondle his ears.

I sip my wine. 'So where's the most interesting place you've been?'

'Actually . . . I've never been abroad.' He exhales and looks embarrassed, as if he's just confessed to hating football, or disliking the Beatles. 'How dull is that?'

Though surprised, I'm also a little relieved that he doesn't carry with him travel stories from every continent, as Grace did, tales to make my life seem even more mundane than it already is. 'Not at all. I'm hardly adventurous. Is there any reason you . . . ?'

'It's complicated.' I wonder what the story is, but before I can ask, he's changing the subject, asking how long I've been at the café.

'Actually, it belonged to my friend, Grace. She . . .' The words buckle on my tongue. 'Sorry. She passed away quite recently.'

He doesn't say anything for a few moments. Then, very quietly, 'I'm really sorry. What happened?'

'It was a hit-and-run, a taxi driver. He was drunk.'

The soft stretch of a pause. I feel his gaze sweep gently across me, comforting as a lamp in fog.

'Did they—'

I nod quickly. 'He got six years.'

I go on to tell him everything, then – about Grace and adopting Murphy, quitting my job to take on the café. 'I was a PA before, at a factory. They manufacture metal packaging. You know – for drinks cans, aerosols, paints . . . Actually, never mind. I'm boring myself just thinking about it.' I put a hand to my face and laugh. 'So what is it you do?'

He seems uneasy suddenly. 'Did. Actually, I was a vet.'

Incredible – for a moment, I'm not sure what to say. My instinct, irrationally, is to wonder why he never mentioned it, before I realise there's no reason at all why he should have. 'But you're not any more?'

'Taking some time out.'

'Burnout?'

'You could say that.'

'I imagine being a vet can be stressful. Like being a doctor.'

'Yeah, it can be.'

'Do you ever miss it?'

He seems to cast around for a response, then tells me he walks dogs as a favour for some of the older folk in the area, that it helps to stave off any pangs of regret.

I smile, happy to be reminded there are genuinely good people left in the world.

Joel sips his wine, his hand seeming large around the stem of the glass. He does have vet's hands, I think. Capable, trustworthy.

'So where's Steve moved to?' I ask.

'The new development by the marina.'

'Oh, I spent most of my childhood down there. At the nature reserve.'

'Waterfen?'

'Yes,' I say, pleased. 'Do you know it?'

He nods, and I look again into his spilt-ink eyes. 'It's an excellent place to empty your head. If you know what I mean.'

'I do,' I say.

We chat for a few minutes more until we've finished our wine. But before I can offer him a refill he's thanked me, given Murphy a parting pat and made his way to the door, where he hesitates for just a moment before leaning forward to peck me on the cheek.

The graze of his skin against mine brings a heat to my face I'm still thinking about hours later.

# 14

## Joel

At Halloween, Melissa decides to drive all the way from Watford to drag me to the corner shop (something about week-old tangerines not really cutting it on the trick-or-treating scene).

Over a week has passed since my drink with Callie in her flat. I've thought a lot about reciprocating, have rolled the conversation around my mind in the hope of making it smooth and seamless.

But then I remember all the reasons I have to resist whatever it is I'm feeling for her. To honour my commitment to non-commitment. Not that doing so is easy, when you live on different floors of the same house. Callie's unguarded and charming whenever I bump into her, and a far more considerate neighbour than I am. She sorts our mail, reminds me when I forget about bin day. Leaves the occasional cake boxed up on my doormat after her shift.

But my favourite thing about living in the flat below Callie is the power ballads that pelt forth from her shower most mornings. She's a shocking singer, but I've discovered I don't care. As it turns out, I love waking to the sound of her unique and strident discord.

I could stop going to the café, I suppose. But that seems extreme action to take on account of a crush. I'm a man in my mid-thirties, not a boy of fifteen.

'We should really terrify the kids tonight,' Melissa suggests, as we walk to the shop, 'and send you to answer the door.'

'I'm very nice to children, actually.'

'Come on. You're the least kid-friendly person I've ever met.'

'Inaccurate. I love kids. My nieces and nephew will vouch for that.'

'You don't like *Toy Story*.'

'So what?'

She shrugs. 'It's weird. Everyone likes *Toy Story*.'

'You know what I think's weird? Grown-ups watching cartoons.'

Melissa brushes a strand of platinum wig hair from her face. The party she'd been going to in Watford has fallen through but, unsurprisingly, she's sticking with her costume (Julia Roberts's character in *Pretty Woman*. Obviously. Earlier she produced a can of silver hairspray, asked if I wanted to be Richard Gere. I said I did not).

'Look, can you just walk behind me? I don't want anyone to know I'm with you.'

'Ha.' She loops her arm through mine. 'I love embarrassing you, Joel. You're so uptight and twitchy.'

Well, I can't really argue with that.


I lose Melissa by the confectionery, grab a few essentials while I'm here. Baked beans, white bread, tomato soup, pizza. Maybe one day I'll work out how to cook and do a Big Shop, like most people my age. But for now, cans and things in packets suit me fine.

'Happy Halloween, again,' says a voice, gentle as a breeze.

I turn, and it's her. She made me a pumpkin spice latte this morning, brought it to my table with a little meringue ghost and a smile that still hasn't left my head.

'You know,' she says, 'we forgot to talk about who's going to be on trick-or-treater duty tonight.'

I feign giving this some thought. 'Well, actually I don't believe in trick-or-treaters.'

'Interesting.'

'My theory is, if you pretend they don't exist, they go away.'

Callie nods slowly. 'My theory is, you're closest to the outside door. Are you honestly going to make me run down a full flight of stairs every time?'

I tease her with a raised eyebrow. 'I might.'

'All right. I'll make it fair.' She holds up a couple of packets of Halloween-themed Haribo. 'I'll buy the treats. But we have to split the leftovers later.'

We share a look. It travels to my stomach, in long, lucid loops.

But now I'm tasting Melissa's perfume, feeling her arms lasso my waist. My heart sags a little, which isn't really fair on Melissa. Still, in my defence, she is dressed as a prostitute.

'I've got the Haribo, babe. Let's go.'

I clear my throat. 'Melissa, this is Callie.'

In Callie's green-gold eyes, something dwindles. 'Hello.'

'Hello,' Melissa says, mimicking her tone exactly. 'What are you dressed as?'

Callie looks surprised, then at me.

Mortified, I shake my head at Melissa. 'You're the only one in costume.'

'I'd better get going,' Callie says politely. 'Nice to see you.'

Melissa takes me by the hand and leads me towards the till, boots click-clacking against the lino. 'Who was that bitch?'

'Hey.' I stop, drop her hand. 'That's a bit strong.'

Her face lifts. 'Joel! I'm just messing with you. See what I mean about you being all tense and edgy?'

'You're not exactly helping.'

'So who is she?'

'My new upstairs neighbour. She moved in when Steve left.'

'You know what you need?'

'To pay for this and go home? Preferably alone?'

'Ha. You love me really.'

*No,* I think. *I really, really don't.*

I'm sitting on the living-room floor, back to the wall, pizza box next to my knees. Like always, I've ordered a large pepperoni to share at Melissa's request. But she never eats more than two pieces, and I have to pick all the pepperoni off.

She crouches next to me, extracts a slice from the box. 'Hey, you know we've been doing this nearly three years now?'

'That long?'

A sceptical smile. 'As if you don't remember the exact date you first laid eyes on me.'

I don't, actually. But I do remember the occasion. A late-night exercise class, when I'd been going through a phase of thinking high-intensity spinning might be the answer to all my problems. (It almost was, in that I nearly dropped down dead halfway through the first session.)

Melissa meandered over to me afterwards, all Lycra and swinging ponytail and make-up firmly in place. I was bent double at the time, doing my best not to throw up.

'New Year resolution?'

It was January, as it happened. But I didn't really go in for things like that. 'Just want to get fit,' I gasped.

'How's it going?'

'Making progress.'

'Wow. How bad were you before?'

After a shower and a protein shake we went back to my place. I was surprised when she called a couple of weeks later, but so it went on.

Above our heads now, the creak of Callie's floorboards. I picture her moving through the flat, wine glass in hand. Taking time at the window to drink in the stars.

I can't help wondering what she thinks of me, after our encounter at the shop earlier. Has she concluded Melissa's my girlfriend? That I'm as shallow as I am untrustworthy?

Maybe, I think, it would be for the best if she did.

'Dominic hates pizza,' Melissa says, settling down by my side.

I don't recognise the name. But I do recognise the way she lays it down, like a parcel to be unwrapped. It's not the first time, and we've never claimed to be exclusive. What we are suits us both. That's why we've worked so well for so long.

I sling three oily salami saucers into the box, play along. 'Who's Dominic?'

'Someone I've been seeing.'

'Older man?'

'What makes you say that?'

I shrug. 'You're a Richard Gere short of a party.'

She smiles thinly. 'No, actually.'

'Was it his do you were supposed to be at tonight?'

She sets her mouth in a way that implies it was. 'We argued. He wants me to move into his place.'

'How long have you been . . . ?'

'Three weeks.'

I masticate my carbs. 'Sounds a bit full-on.'

She slackens her jaw slightly. 'Don't tell me you're jealous.'

'Look, in all honesty, if you've met someone you like, then . . .'

'Then what?'

'. . . then I don't think we should be doing this. I want you to be happy. I've told you that.'

We sit quite still for a while. I can feel a pulse, but we're so close together it's hard to know if it's hers or mine. 'We can just hang out tonight,' I say. 'Nothing has to happen.'

She snakes around to kiss me on the mouth. 'Thanks. But I want it to, pizza-breath.'

Ah, Melissa. I can always count on her to say the perfect thing.

That night, I dream of something so disturbing it has me by the throat.

Saturday night about a year from now, and I'm standing in Dad's kitchen. He's kicking off about something, jabbing an index finger in my direction. The words are hot with fury as they leave his mouth.

But they are words I can't begin to comprehend.

'You're not even my son! I'm not even your father!'

He says them twice during his minute-long monologue. I just stand in front of him, a little afraid, a lot stunned.

And then he strides from the room, orders me to leave him alone. On the other side of the kitchen, an open-mouthed Tamsin drops a bowl of strawberry jelly. It splatters across the floor and my feet. Stains them like blood.

And now I'm at the foot of the stairs. Staring upwards, shouting after him.

'Dad? What the hell are you talking about? *Dad!*'

# 15

## Callie

A few nights after Halloween, Joel catches me in the hallway.

'Listen, I wanted to apologise.'

Without warning my face blooms as I wonder if he's saying sorry for the sounds I heard drifting up through my floorboards, late into Thursday night.

I was in bed, watching a documentary about plastic in the ocean. At first I heard only a few thumps – enough to make me mute the laptop in puzzlement – but then, as the thumping became more rhythmical, overlaid with grunts and gasps, I switched the whole thing off and simply listened, motionless. I couldn't help but picture Joel, wondering what he looked like, imagining how it might feel to be Melissa. I felt my skin creep with heat as my pulse began to thud, then – just as I was shutting my eyes to let the picture fully unfold – there came a final, decisive exclamation before everything fell quiet. Guiltily, I fired up the laptop again and attempted to focus very hard on the grim footage of plastic being washed up on an Indonesian beach. But for the rest of the night and the next couple of days, the scene refused to loosen from my mind.

Between an unexpectedly busy weekend in the café and my barely being at home, we've only passed pleasantries since – and facing him now, I'm struggling to meet his eye. I hope he can't tell that I didn't find it shocking or offensive – quite the opposite, in fact. He looks a bit embarrassed too, and I can't think what else he'd be saying sorry for, so I run with it. 'You really don't need to apologise.'

'We'd had a drink.'

'Absolutely.'

'She's not like that all the time.'

'Right.'

'She gets a bit more forthright after—'

I hold up one hand. 'Got it. Honestly.'

'And that costume was just—'

'There's really no need—'

'Well. I just wanted to say she was only joking. But she shouldn't have spoken to you like that.'

'Are you . . . talking about what Melissa said to me in the shop?'

'Yes . . . What are *you* talking about?'

I swallow. 'Never mind. Crossed wires, I think.'

There's no chance now, of course, to mention the shouting I heard much later the same night. It rang out like gunshots, shocked me awake. There was no female voice, so they can't have been rowing – Joel must have been dreaming. But bringing it up now would feel odd and intrusive, like I'm some sort of voyeur, a.k.a. every neighbour's worst nightmare.

Joel looks bemused but smiles like he doesn't mind. 'How's Murphy with fireworks?' It's Guy Fawkes this evening and already the sky is a disco, a nightclub of bass and neon.

'Ben offered to have him. His mum and dad live out in the sticks. No near neighbours for miles.'

'Good thinking.'

I rustle up a smile. 'So, do you have any Guy Fawkes plans?'

'Absolutely not,' he says, deadpan. 'Can't stand the bloke.'

I laugh. 'Dot and her water-skiing lot are having a party at the country park.'

Possibility balloons between us. I want to invite him, I do, but surely he has a girlfriend?

I take a breath, search my stomach for daring. 'So if you're not doing anything . . . ?'

The slowest of smiles, the most agonising of waits. 'Okay,' he says eventually, his voice going gravelly. 'Yeah, I'd like that.'

# 16

## Joel

I did have plans actually: shivering in Doug's back garden with the rest of my family, watching two-thirds of his fireworks fail to achieve lift-off. But I'd been thinking of cancelling anyway. I'm fairly exhausted after a few sleep-scant nights. Plus my dream about Dad has pretty much floored me. I've not been able to forget it, have been scouring every photo I have of us together. Rereading messages on my phone with tears in my eyes, like you do when someone's died.

I think back to it now. *You're not even my son! I'm not even your father!*

It's just not the kind of thing you say off the cuff to hurt someone. I've got plenty of other shortcomings he could choose from to do that.

Which can only mean there must be something in it.

I need to find out more about what I foresaw that night. But asking Dad outright? The sheer gravity of that conversation just doesn't feel viable. Not yet, anyway. I need to go to his house while he's out, I think. Uncover the truth for myself.

I meet Callie out the front ten minutes later. The early-November air is frost-filled and muddled with stars, the moon halogen-bright. It lends a strange midsummer quality to a sky already ablaze.

There's nothing to suggest that spending this evening with Callie is a date, I remind myself. We're just neighbours, off to enjoy the fireworks. Exactly as I used to with Steve and Hayley. A tradition, platonic, no strings.

We set off towards the river. Callie's face is parcelled between the grey woollen hat pulled down low over her head, and the soft red scarf she's coiled up to her chin. Our hands are stuffed into our pockets, shoulders occasionally bumping.

'So how long have you been seeing Melissa?' She sounds genuinely curious. Which I suppose you would be if you'd met Melissa.

I laugh uncomfortably. 'That's . . . not quite as it seems.'

I feel her look at me. 'No?'

'I'm not sure I can explain. Or I'm not sure I want to.'

'Why not?'

'You might think worse of me.'

We walk a few more paces.

'Friends with benefits?' she guesses.

'Yep.'

'That's not so bad.'

'It's not good.'

'But life's not perfect.'

'No,' I agree, thinking, *Ain't that the truth.*

Above our heads, a boom, then a waterfall of light that turns us temporarily technicolour.


A subtle hum of music leads us to Dot and the water-skiers by the boathouse in the country park. There's an impeccably organised drinks table, and a health-and-safety-compliant bonfire in an incinerator identical to the one my dad has for his garden-leaf mulch. It's been a while since I've attended a party with people other than my family. But there's something charming about the wholesomeness of this. The man toasting marshmallows, the parade of people carrying baked potatoes back and forth. The children swooping sparklers through the air.

Dot flings her arms around me when we arrive. She's rocking an early-sixties vibe, all lacquered lashes and backcombed hair. Her coat looks slightly military, her jewellery vintage.

Planting a kiss on my left cheek, she presses a cup of something into my hands. 'Hello, Customer. I knew it.'

'You knew what?' I say, amused.

'What are we drinking?' Callie asks quickly, her cheeks pink from the cold and the walk.

'Bonfire Night punch. My contribution.'

'What's in it?'

Dot shrugs, which I suppose is how most people make punch. 'Bit of everything. Mostly rum.'

I take a sip. It's good, super-sweet and strong. Like tropical fruit juice under the influence. I'd been planning to hunt down some coffee, but I guess I can get my fix later.

'I have my eye on a man,' Dot confides, looping an arm through mine.

I meet Callie's eye, smile.

'He's over there. The blond one with his back to us, faffing about with the marshmallows. What do you think?'

I struggle to judge a man I don't know from the back of his head. 'Well, he seems helpful. Capable.'

Dot mainlines her punch in silence. 'Oh, you're right,' she says eventually, coming up for air. 'He's *so* not my type. He's the club treasurer, for God's sake! Just look at how carefully he's turning those marshmallows.'

'I didn't mean—'

'No, it's true. What was I thinking? There's not even a hint of pyro-maniac in that man.'

'Sorry,' I say mildly, wondering how I've managed to divert Cupid's arrow so dramatically in the space of less than thirty seconds.

'Right. More booze.' Dot heads off towards the boathouse.

'Something I said?'

Callie laughs. 'To be fair, you didn't have very much to go on.'

'Although pyromaniacs are top of her list, apparently.'

'I wouldn't worry. Dot's benchmark for the perfect guy is literally inexplicable.'

We walk a few feet to the dark edge of the lake. It's actually an infilled gravel quarry, fringed by trees and sandy footpaths. The water's an inkwell, flecked with moonlight.

'I like Dot's nickname for me.'

'Customer? Unique, isn't it?'

'Stops me getting ideas above my station, I suppose.'

She laughs again. 'She does know your name. I think it must have had something to do with the punch.'

'What did she mean when she said *I knew it?*'

Callie lets out a staccato breath. 'You know, I have no idea.'

At a regulation distance from the boathouse, Dot's marshmallow man switches roles. A crowd draws together, dark like gathered penguins, as a stream of fireworks roars obligingly to life.

The air becomes abstract art, pigment-filled. A Jackson Pollock with the sound up high.

'I feel a bit like a teenager,' Callie says, as the first run of rockets scatters to a close. 'Hanging around the country park after dark, drinking homemade punch.'

I feign a light bulb. 'Knew I recognised you from somewhere.'

Laughing, Callie turns to me. Then hesitates. 'Oh, you have . . . Dot's lipstick on your face.'

'Ah.'

'Do you want me to . . . ?'

Before I can answer she's removed her glove, raised her hand to my cold cheek. Slowly, she rubs the mark away with a warm press of thumb. 'There you go.'

Inside me, something swings. I fight the urge to grasp her hand as she lowers it, tell her how beautiful she is. 'Thank you,' I manage.

From the group, a voice shouts Callie's name. We start making our way back up the grass slope towards the boathouse.

'Joining us?' Dot asks, striding purposefully forward.

'For what?'

She indicates the water. 'Firing up the Jet Skis.'

Callie coughs on her punch. 'You're joking. It's freezing.'

'That's what wetsuits are for.'

'Dot, you've been drinking. Are you sure that's safe?'

'Of course,' Dot says. 'Nathan's a fully trained instructor.'

Callie wrinkles her nose. She's probably thinking, like me, that Nathan must in fact only be part-qualified, given he clearly skipped the module on not being an irresponsible jackass.

Dot waves a hand. 'Oh, don't worry, he's been on the lemonade all night.' She turns to me. 'Fancy joining us, Customer?'

'Ah, no, thanks. You don't want to see me in a wetsuit. Believe me.'

Dot chortles. 'We're all friends here.'

'I think we'll sit this one out,' Callie says.

Dot throws one arm around Callie's shoulders, kisses her hair. It makes me strangely envious. 'What am I always telling you?'

Callie shrugs. Dot jogs off back towards the boathouse, presumably to recruit more people to the cause of her open-water death wish.

I take another sip of punch. 'What is she always telling you?'

Callie hesitates. 'Fancy a walk?'


'Sorry about Dot. She thinks I'm old and boring.'

We wind along the footpath leading into Waterfen, the nature reserve. The moon seems brighter somehow, a giant hole punched into the dark card of sky.

Though she's by my side, Callie's leading the way. She's as familiar with the route as a bird on migration, the constellations her compass.

'How old is Dot?' I've been curious about this.

'Twenties,' Callie says, like most people would say *Monday*, or *in-laws*.

'So "old" would make you . . .'

'Thirty-four.' She glances at me. 'You?'

'Even older. Thirty-five. All hope is lost.'

We cross the wooden footbridge marking the entrance to the reserve. Our footsteps are high-pitched, hollow against the boardwalk. Shadows lengthen the spines of the trees, their darkened arms reaching out to greet us in the gloom.

'Dot's always telling me to . . . Oh, what's the phrase?'

'Grab life by the—'

'Exactly. She wants me to kickbox and water-ski.'

'Is that what you want?'

Callie smiles. The hair not covered by her hat is beginning to glisten, damp with tiny droplets of night air. 'Put it this way, I've held out so far.'

'Maybe you're just different.'

She's quiet for a moment, like she's giving this some thought. 'Maybe.'

We head further into the reserve, the boardwalk a winding artery through its sensory system. The fireworks become distant aftershocks. We are steeped in the sounds of nature at night: the lone hoot of a tawny owl, the rustle of lumbering mammals. From deep in the woods drifts the occasional churr of a creature stirring.

'Just so you know,' I say, 'I have no idea where we are right now.' The dark's disorienting, screwing with my sense of direction.

Her laugh ripples. 'Don't worry. I've come here at night often enough.'

'Light sleeper?'

'Sometimes,' she admits.

\*    \*    \*

We swap the boardwalk for a churned-up channel of footpath running along a narrow dyke. Eventually, where the treeline parts like a curtain, Callie stops. She moves her head closer to mine. I catch the scent of her shampoo, a sharp twist of citrus, feel it climb inside me.

'This is one of my favourite views,' she whispers.

The footpath looks over a wide sweep of marsh. It's plump with rush, adorned with the jewellery of silvery wading pools. Roosting wildfowl scatter the earth's wet surface. Following Callie's outstretched finger, I make out a group of grazing deer. Their dainty forms are slender and sculptural, washed over by moonlight.

We squat down on the footpath to watch. The wet-wool scent of the undergrowth rises to meet us.

'Beautiful, aren't they?' she whispers, transfixed.

I nod, because who wouldn't find this beautiful?

There's a gently rolling undercurrent of sound – waves of crepuscular whistling, sweet swells of companionable gargling. I ask Callie where it's coming from.

'That's the widgeon and teal, noisy lot.'

My eyes rest again on the deer. 'They're like a work of art.'

'I love seeing them like this. They're nervy, and they've got a real talent for hiding. Apparently they can smell people up to a hundred metres away.'

We watch a while longer, curious as camouflaged mammals in our little nest of undergrowth. Then Callie smiles at me, a silent signal for us to move on.

# 17

## Callie

We keep talking, hardly pausing for breath, walking side by side as the path broadens out then sweeps round to hug the river.

I tell Joel about my parents and their work – Mum's dressmaking business, and Dad's job as an oncologist. He asks how long I've been into nature, and I say basically my whole life. It was Dad who first brought me to Waterfen, who created a little space in his vegetable patch just for me. He'd smile when I freaked Mum out by adopting invertebrates from the garden, would talk me down from the inevitable tears when I was parted from them. He taught me how to tell apart frogs and toads, pointed out the difference between buzzards and sparrow hawks, high in the sky. Early on summer mornings we would sit in the garden together, where he'd narrate the dawn chorus for me, from first bird to last. We made bug hotels and houses for hedgehogs, pressed flowers and pond-dipped, mixed up compost for the worms and woodlice.

I describe the degree I never used, tell Joel about the assistant warden's role here I still haven't applied for. The vacancy went live on the website a couple of weeks ago, and the closing date's this Friday.

He asks what's holding me back.

I think about it for a couple of moments. 'The idea of change, maybe. I feel like we're all just about getting onto an even keel again, after Grace. And the job's only a fixed-term contract, so there are no guarantees long-term.'

'Be worth it, though?'

I frown. 'I'm risk-averse, I guess. My parents were always quite . . . sensible, you know? It's the reason I never really travelled, probably. Staying the same has just always seemed safer, somehow. Like . . . if you don't pursue your dreams, you can't feel bad if you never achieve them.'

'Taking on the café must have felt like a risk,' he observes softly. 'Quitting your old job, after so many years.'

He's right, it did, but all my thoughts back then were distorted by grief. I barely considered the fear because the sadness was so much worse – like insanity, some days. And agreeing to work at the café seemed like a way of honouring Grace – a leap of faith, doing something on a whim. Because that was how she had always lived her life.

We continue along our path. Joel looks lovely tonight, insulated from the elements by a dark woollen coat and scarf. He suits winter, I think, with all its layers and understated appeal, its subtle complications.

As we walk I ask if he's named after anyone, like for example Billy Joel, and he says, no, of course not, that would be madness, before asking the same question of me – except he comes up understandably short on anyone famous named Callie.

'Actually,' I say, 'my dad suggested calling me Carrie one night over dinner, when Mum was pregnant with me. They were throwing baby names back and forth – but typical Dad, he had his mouth full at the time.' I smile. 'Chocolate torte, apparently.'

'She thought he said Callie?'

I nod. 'And Mum loved it so much, he didn't have the heart to break it to her. So Callie it was. He only told her when I turned eighteen – he made a little speech about it at the restaurant on my birthday. And I had chocolate torte instead of cake, of course.'

'That is quite possibly the best baby-naming story ever.'

'Thanks. I think so too.'

I ask Joel about his family, my mind reeling in sympathy as he reveals his mother died when he was only thirteen. He doesn't say much when I ask – just that she had cancer, and that they were very close.

We walk a little further until, out of habit, I pause on the path beneath the old willow. 'Grace and I used to spend hours in this tree when we were kids. You know once you're up there—'

'—you can spy on the world unseen.'

'You did that too?'

As he nods I feel the warmth of a new connection, the thump of ignition in my belly.

'Well,' Joel says, after a moment, 'they do say fireworks are best appreciated from height.'

So together we climb, embarrassingly ungainly, into the crook of the willow's broad shoulders, where I show him the initials Grace and I carved into the bark. Beyond our private landscape, the peculiar arson of Bonfire Night still dances across the horizon, gunpowder thumping like the footsteps of giants.

We stare out at it for maybe twenty minutes more until silence finally descends and the sky falls back to sleep.

We're about to climb down when a barn owl emerges from the shadows, its pale trajectory enchanting as snowfall. We watch it glide by before it banks steeply up, then vanishes like vapour behind the trees.

The following night, I get back to my flat after dinner at Esther's to find a white cardboard box on the doormat. Inside there is a slice of chocolate torte from the Sicilian pastry shop in town I love but can't afford. And there's a scribbled note.

*Your story made me smile.*

*J*

*P.S. Wasn't sure if it was my place to say this last night, but please have your own best interests at heart. Apply for that job.*

# 18

## Joel

The chocolate torte was a mistake. I know that now. Going to the pastry shop, choosing the best-looking slice, watching them box it up. My heart was hopping so hard the whole time, I never even stopped to think.

I just want to do nice things for her. Bring a smile to her face, a small lift to her day. I'm not even sure why. But I've felt that way since we first met.

So I was disappointed when she didn't answer her door. Felt a little bit crushed that I had to write a note.

I only acknowledged the truth minutes later, back in my flat. Reminded myself that if I had a single shred of decency I would throw whatever it is that's unfolding between us up to the wind. Because nothing has changed since my mum died or Vicky left, or I broke up with Kate. And nothing ever will.

But the fact is, we're separated solely by floorboards. And the following morning, just as I'm thinking I should try harder to keep my distance, there's a knock on my door.

I stand in the middle of my living room, ready to answer. But then I remember all the reasons I shouldn't and shut my eyes. Wait for her to leave.

Walking the dogs through the park mid-afternoon, I contact Dad to say I can't make lunch this Sunday.

I feel a sting in my throat as I send him the message. One more relationship crumbling, because I know too much. Yet another moment I can never rewind.

I play it all back now in my mind. Picture his face as he said the words.

*You're not even my son! I'm not even your father!*

Is that why I never quite saw eye-to-eye with him? Why I constantly felt I was a disappointment, somehow? It always seemed like Doug was the son he'd been waiting for, which for a while I put down to their shared passions. Everything from model trains and red meat to rugby and numbers (Doug took over the accountancy firm from Dad when he retired).

But maybe, for the first time, there's an indication it ran deeper than that.

Would it not make a strange sort of sense if it was true? Even though that would bring with it another life-altering question: who, and where, is my real father?

# 19

## Callie

The morning after finding the chocolate torte, I make the mistake of mentioning it to Dot. She becomes animated with strategy, giddy with tactics, the self-appointed line commander of my love life.

But I don't want to apply tactics to Joel. Tactics were what I needed to handle Piers, when even at the beginning time spent together always came with a flipside – like burning your tongue on something lovely, or trying on a gorgeous outfit only to feel slightly fat.

By contrast, being around Joel is always so straightforward, so enjoyable. He warms me through, rather than leaves me cold. Added to which, ever since that night I heard him with Melissa through the floorboards, I've been in no doubt as to just how hot I think he is.

I stopped at his flat on my way to work this morning, but when I knocked there was no response, or audible movement inside. So I slipped a note under the door.

It simply read:

*That chocolate torte made me smile (a lot). Thank you.*
*C*
*P.S. I've applied for the job.*

# 20

## Joel

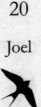

Steve's invited me to join him for some sort of healthy juice. He's asked me three times now. Frankly, it's the kind of invitation I'd usually decline, but I still feel guilty about how things turned out between us. So, a few days after Bonfire Night, I meet him in the café at the gym where he works. I expect this to be a form of atonement in itself.

I was right. A speaker above our heads discharges a migrainous throb of house music I've fled nightclubs in the past to escape. And that's before Steve's slid a juice across the table to me that looks worryingly like tomato soup.

'What's in it?' I'm pretty tired today, and I'm hoping that, against all odds, it might contain some caffeine.

'Carrot and beetroot. Kale. Orange juice. It's cleansing,' he says. Like that justifies the part where they liquidised raw vegetables and flogged him the output for nearly a fiver.

Still, atonement.

We catch up for ten minutes or so. He shows me photos of the new house on his phone. Reminds me Poppy turns one in the new year, tells me Hayley's doing well back at work. It's hard, as he talks, not to be distracted by his biceps. I see them twitching beneath his skin, like there's only so long they can be parted from the dumbbell station.

I feel more than a bit out of place here, in my jeans, long sleeves and boots.

Eventually he puts his phone away. 'How's Callie?'

I keep it neutral. 'Great. Really nice neighbour. Seems like a good tenant.' I think about her note to me, propped up in my kitchen now. About how hard it's been recently to think of her in purely platonic terms.

'All right,' Steve says, smiling wryly. 'You can thank me later.'

I say nothing. Unfortunately this gives me no choice but to take another sip of pulverised vegetable.

'So how's everything? You know – life, work, health.'

'No change, really.'

'Still no job?' he muses, like we're talking about someone else. 'You must be burning through your savings.'

I mumble acknowledgement. It's a sore point, predominantly because I am. I lived like a monk to build them up in the first place, cashed in an ISA inherited from a great-aunt. I'm careful with it (trips to the coffee shop my sole indulgence). And I'm lucky to have a financially illiterate landlord, who's put my rent up once in ten years. But the money won't last for ever.

Steve's never shied away from asking personal questions, which I mostly attribute to the confidence that must come with having a gladiator-grade physique. But he has a warmth about him, too. Affability honed like an extra muscle from years of talking to clients, listening to their problems while they force out sit-ups and try not to spew.

Steve sets down his smoothie. Rubs at something that isn't there on our table. And then, just like that, a hand grenade of a question. 'Did I ever mention I have a master's in neuropsychology?'

I manage to tell him, no, he did not mention that.

'What I'm saying is . . . if you ever wanted to talk . . .' He opens the damn door and leaves it swinging by its hinges. But the landscape beyond looks cold and uncertain.

'Why? I mean, if you're a neuropsychologist, why do you work here?'

'Does there have to be a reason?'

I look at Steve busting out of his vest in front of me. Then I try and fail to picture him wearing a white coat. 'Yes,' I say, blinking. 'There does, as it happens.'

A shrug. 'I joined a gym to help me deal with the stress of studying, then realised my heart was more in this than that. So I started training people part-time during my PhD, and felt like I was born to do it.'

Jesus. A PhD. 'You're a doctor?' Why did his mail never reflect this, alert me to this code-red situation?

'Nah. Dropped out after three years. Though sometimes Hayley does like to call me Doctor—'

I raise a hand to cut him off, then lower it. 'Why are you telling me this?'

'I thought you might like to know.'

'Know, as in avail myself of your services?'

From out of nowhere, my university GP sneers into my mind. I can still picture his face like he's sitting right in front of me. The side-eye, the derision. The inexplicable irritation.

Steve's shaking his head. 'Not like that. I'm no counsellor. But I suppose I just wanted to say that if you ever fancy a chat, I might understand more than you think. I don't just lift weights.'

Can't say I ever judged him before. But I wouldn't necessarily have gone with brain specialist if I was asked to take a punt on his former career path. 'You ever regret it?'

'Regret what?'

'Not pursuing it.'

'Never. I wouldn't have met Hayley, and we wouldn't have Poppy.' He looks around the café. 'And this is loads better than a career in some anonymous lab. I still get to make a positive difference to people's minds. Just in a more direct way.'

'How come you never invited me to train with you?' (I'm curious more than anything.)

'I guess you never really struck me as the working-out type.'

'I go walking,' I protest.

'No offence, Joel, but so does my nan.'

'Well, isn't motivation part of the gig?' I've seen Steve in the park before, yelling at groaning boot-camp participants that pain is just weakness leaving the body.

'You've still got to want it.'

I look down at my half-drunk tomato soup. If Steve already senses me to be a lost cause, then this sorry orange mess can stay firmly in the glass where it belongs.

'Look, mate. I only wanted to say, if you ever need anything—'

'Actually, there is something you could do for me.' I've got a favour to ask him, to do with Callie.

I leave a short while later, disoriented and a little exposed. As if I've lost layers of myself to the wintry wind. Like a scarf whipped away I won't ever get back.

All the way home, I think about what Steve's told me. About heading down a certain path, before taking a chance on the one thing that made him happy.

And for me, that thing is knowing Callie. She makes me happy when I see her at home or at the café. I don't want to stop spending time with her. She touches parts of me I'd forgotten were there.

Better to know her as a friend than not to know her at all. Even though, in another life, it might have been something more.

University. A time when intensive studying, a claustrophobic social scene and periods of zero sleep were screwing with my already messy mind. I kept skipping lectures, or turning up to them exhausted. My degree seemed at risk when it had barely begun, and something had to change.

So, once I hit my second term, I decided to make a doctor's appointment.

It took me a couple of months to work up to it. Luke's accident and Mum's death still loomed large, as if I feared I might be held retro-actively responsible. Or maybe I'd be declared mentally ill, sectioned against my will. (I could only imagine the reaction of my dad, king of the stiff upper lip, if that was ever to happen.)

I'd not met my university GP before. He was old, which might have been reassuring if he hadn't looked so impatient before I'd even sat down.

The consulting room was gloomy, enclosed by vertical blinds. It smelt clinical. Of disinfectant and disinterest.

'Insomnia,' was his barked summation of the story I spent a breathless two minutes imparting to him. At that point I was giddy with hope, purely because I'd made it through the door. Surely, now, I'd get the help I was so desperate for. Perhaps he'd even know of a cure.

'Yes,' I replied. 'Because of the dreams. My premonitions.'

He stopped typing then, narrowed his eyes. I guess he didn't fancy logging that bit. A smile feathered his lips, which were flaky in a way I was sure there was a cream for. 'Friends, Mr Morgan?'

'Sorry?'

'Have you lots of friends here, or have you struggled? To fit in.'

The truth was I had always struggled. I withdrew from my peers at school, after what happened to Luke. Became something of a loner. My dreams took up the headspace I needed for socialising, so I could count the friends I'd made here on one hand. But that was the damn symptom, not the cause. Surely a doctor of all people should have been able to figure that out.

'Drugs?' he continued, when I didn't respond.

'If there's something that could work, I'll try anything.'

A condescending smile. 'No. I'm referring to recreational drugs. Do you take them?'

'Oh. No. Never.'

He disbelieved me by way of full eye contact. 'And you're not on medication.'

'No.' I tried again. 'Look, I dreamt my mum was going to die. And then she did. She died of cancer.' I could have choked on those words.

'Fresh air,' he clipped, as if I hadn't even spoken. 'Get some exercise, stop drinking, take these.' He scribbled out a prescription and handed it to me.

'I do exercise, and I don't drink much—'

'They're for the insomnia. Make sure you read the leaflet.'

'But the insomnia . . .' I said shakily '. . . isn't really the problem. It's more of a side effect.'

He shifted in his chair, cleared the clag from his throat. 'Did you manage to get a seat in the waiting room just now, Mr Morgan?'

'Yes, I—'

'Lucky you. Sometimes, it's standing-room only. Students are a sickly bunch.' He leant forward, stabbed his jotter with a biro like he was angry. Like I'd deliberately flouted a rule that was clear to everyone except me. 'I can only deal with *one problem per appointment*.' The expression on his face was total disdain. It ate into my gut like acid.

I don't know what it was (bad day, personal problems) but something about my presence that afternoon had really irritated him. Out of nowhere, I was reminded of my dad.

A silence settled then, drawn out by the ticking of the clock on his desk. Cheap white plastic, a pharmaceutical-company logo emblazoned across it in purple.

But I had to try. One last time. It had taken so much for me to book the appointment, work up the courage to walk through the surgery door. Repeat the words I'd been practising for days in my bathroom mirror.

'Is there anything neurological . . . Could there be something wrong with my brain? With the premonitions—'

I was cut off by his laugh. An actual laugh. One that, against all the odds, lit up his humourless face. 'Well, you cannot predict the future, obviously. I don't know if this is some sort of joke, or a dare you've been put up to, but you're wasting my time. Get out of my surgery.'

# 21

## Callie

A week or so after Bonfire Night, when I see Joel first thing at the coffee shop, I know what I'm going to do. I've been practising how to pitch it to him – but now my mouth's gone dry and I'm wobbling slightly, which probably isn't going to help.

I set down his double espresso, the cup twitching from my hand. 'Morning.'

'Hey.' He looks up. Though his eyes are tired, his smile is warm.

My heart's like a fist trying to break down my ribcage. 'I . . . got an email last night. They've invited me for an interview at Waterfen.'

His whole face lifts. 'Wow, congratulations. That's brilliant news.'

I abseil into my next question. *Don't think about it, just do it.* 'So, that new Italian place by the river's been getting rave reviews. Excellent *spaghetti al pomodoro*, apparently. Fancy trying it tonight, helping me prep?'

He looks slightly taken aback – though to be fair that's maybe because it's nine in the morning, there's a queue at the counter for coffee-to-go, and I'm lingering by his table, waffling on about spaghetti.

Then, from out of nowhere, the woman at the next table leans over and chimes in. 'I tried it last night. Top-notch. Definitely recommend.' She makes a chef's kiss with her fingers.

I want to give her an actual kiss. But instead I simply smile, look back at Joel and wait, stomach writhing in silent agony.

Finally, he swallows, gives me the answer I've been praying for. 'Yeah, okay. Why not?'

As we wait to be shown to our table at the restaurant, Joel's describing his afternoon dog walk.

'. . . so Tinkerbell – that's the Maltese – makes a break for it by the bins. And I'm running after her, shouting her name, over and over . . .'

He does a quick impression. Already I'm laughing so hard there are tears in my eyes.

'She's essentially a thug disguised as a mop. Very outward-ranging.'

'Outward-ranging?'

'Ah, that's the technical term for *Screw you, I'm off.*'

'Well, you can hardly blame her.' I dab at my eyes with the corner of my scarf. 'I mean, to Tinkerbell you're probably just a booster vaccination on legs.'

He laughs too. 'Fair point. Hadn't thought of that.'

'I still can't believe you walk people's dogs for free. Are the owners really attractive, or something?'

'Well, let's see. There's Iris – she's eighty-five. And Mary's getting on for ninety. And I tell you, if I was fifty years older—'

Still laughing, I put up a hand. 'I know I started it, but now I wish I hadn't.'

A waiter approaches to show us to our table.

'Sorry.' Joel smiles. 'I'll dial down the borderline humour now.'

'No, don't,' I plead. 'Borderline humour's my favourite.'

*I'm feeling it,* I think, as we're seated at a cosy corner table. Joel makes me warm with pleasure as ever . . . but then again, he can be hard to read. I'm not sure if it's mixed signals exactly, but I just don't know if he sees me as anything more than a friend. Occasionally when I meet his eye, and feel that magnet-clamp deep in my chest, I think perhaps he does – but then it's as if something shifts in his brain, and he folds up all his feelings and shoves them away, out of reach.

Besides, I'm still unclear on quite what the deal is with him and

Melissa. He's said they're friends with benefits, but that could mean any one of a thousand things. I want to ask, but I'm not sure if I will. Sometimes I sense a certain guardedness about him, and the last thing I want to do is cause offence.

'I love drinking wine from these,' I say, as our waiter sets down a carafe of red wine and two tumblers. 'They make me feel like I'm at a pavement café somewhere in the Med.'

Joel smiles as he pours, hands me a glass.

'By the way, I wanted to thank you,' I say. 'For talking to Steve.'

Joel met him at the weekend, explained the Murphy situation, squared the whole thing up so I didn't have to worry about being caught out.

'You already thanked me.'

Yes, I did, when he told me – but only in stammered sentences as my tear ducts geared up. 'Well, this is my official thank-you.'

He raises his glass to mine, eyes twinkling. 'No, this is your official congratulations.'

'It feels a bit premature,' I confess. 'I still have to get the job, and it doesn't help that I'm terrible at interviews.'

'I don't believe that for a minute.'

'Oh, it's true. I shake, sweat – everything. All they'll need to say is, *Why do you want to work in nature conservation, Miss Cooper?* and I'll probably start weeping.'

I feel his gaze resting on me. 'Well, if you do,' he says, 'it'll only go to show them how passionate you are.'

Though it's icy outside, it's cosy in the restaurant, and Joel's removed his jumper. He looks lovely bare-armed across the table from me, warm and calm. After some deliberation, I decided to go smart-casual tonight – my nicest jeans, and the silk blouse strewn with stars that Grace convinced me I should buy, only weeks before she died.

I take a sip of wine. 'What did you say in your interview – when they asked why you wanted to be a vet?'

'They didn't, really. Not for my job, anyway.' His face is part-obscured by his glass. 'That was more about specialities and equipment and certificates.'

'But they must have done for your course at uni.' I nudge his knee with mine. 'Please tell me. I need all the help I can get.'

'Okay. But remember, I'm not even a vet any more. What do I know, really?'

'Humour me.'

'Well, I grew up around animals. Dad wasn't a fan, but he did anything to make Mum happy. And she loved them. We had rabbits, guinea pigs, ducks, chickens. I'd volunteer at the local animal rescue too, cleaning out cages. That's where we got our dog, Scamp. He was my best friend. We did everything together – explored the woods, spent hours down by the river. He was always with me. We were inseparable.

'And Scamp loved to run. I never tried to stop him because he could never be parted from me for long. Anyway, one evening, we were out on a forest track and he bolted after a rabbit. Which was pretty normal for him – except this time, he didn't come back. So I started calling him and calling him, but . . . nothing.' The pitch of Joel's voice dips a little. 'I stayed out until dark looking for him, then went home to get Mum.' He pauses. 'Eventually we found him. He'd tried to run through a barbed-wire fence, but impaled himself halfway. The blood loss was . . . Well, he didn't stand a chance. But it was as though he'd been waiting for us to find him. He was struggling for breath, and he looked up at me like he wanted to say sorry for running off. A few seconds later, he died in my arms.'

I feel my eyes dampen with tears.

'Anyway, I told him I loved him. And then I just held him until the warmth had left his body. That was the day I knew I wanted to care for animals. At my interview, I wasn't supposed to be soppy and say I loved animals. I was supposed to talk about my work experience and future plans, what skills I would bring to the job. But for me, there was no other word to convey how I felt. Anything else would have fallen way short. It was love.' He exhales, then looks up at me.

I'm smiling softly, though my heart is peeling apart. 'Sounds like you're still a vet to me.'

Over piles of pasta and ciabatta, Joel casts a glance around the restaurant. 'You know, I imagine Italy to be . . . not at all like these charming *faux*-frescos.'

I laugh. They've made a good stab at it, but the stencilled temples and pretend piazzas won't be giving Michelangelo a run for his money any time soon.

'You should add Rome to your list,' he says, breaking off a hunk of bread, dipping it in oil. 'One of Europe's greenest cities, apparently.'

'Actually, I've been once. And it is – it's beautiful.'

'Family holiday?' he asks lightly. I sense he's offering up the wrong answer in the hope of exchanging it for the right one.

'No, I went with my ex. Piers.'

Joel sips his wine, doesn't comment.

I try to work out what to say, how best to describe a holiday that was wonderful and torturous all at once. 'I just . . . spent a lot of time exploring by myself, in the parks and the ruins, walking along the river. I found this incredible rose garden . . .' I relive that blue-sky day, how the air swelled with scent. 'Anyway, Piers barely left the hotel. He spent most of the time by the pool. We were the opposite of each other, really. He was a bit of a playboy, super-flash. Rome was actually our third date. His idea, not mine.'

Joel smiles. 'Flash indeed.'

'He attracted drama – you know? Got into fights, debt. He'd disappear from time to time. Was always falling out with people, lurching from crisis to crisis. I thought at the beginning maybe I should go for someone who was totally not my type . . .' I trail off. 'That was a mistake. Turns out we have types for a reason.'

Joel winds spaghetti around his fork, face clouded with thought. 'Better to play it safe, you mean?'

For a moment I'm not quite sure how to answer. 'Or avoid drama at least, I suppose. Yeah.'

Something passes over his face then that I can't quite identify, but it's gone as quickly as it appeared.

# 22
## Joel

When we got back from the restaurant last night, I toyed with the idea of inviting Callie in for a coffee. For a few seconds, I had the words ready to go.

But at the last moment, I stopped myself.

Callie told me she's not interested in drama: another red-flag reminder of why this can't go any further. All my life, my days and moods have tracked my dreams, played out in ups and downs. As Vicky once pointed out, I'm the exact opposite of stable, the antithesis to steady.

So I let the words dissolve, sweet but only fleeting, like sherbet on my tongue.

I made an excruciating mess of saying goodnight, obviously. I deliberated awkwardly, then went in for a double air-kiss neither she nor I was prepared for. Topped it off by mumbling something inexplicable about the Continent as our noses collided.

I've been keeping my head down ever since.

I've dropped in at my dad's in the hope of uncovering the truth about my dream. Luckily, he spends each Friday across town, immersed in his woodworking hobby. Comes home covered with sawdust and shavings, the scent of split timber.

I dreamt he sawed off a fingertip once, bemused him with a gift shortly afterwards of some cut-resistant gloves. It worked out all right in the end, because Dad's reached that age where he rotates between gloves. Leather for driving, latex for the petrol station. Rubber for washing-up, and a pair with longer cuffs for scrubbing down the loo.

He keeps boxes of Mum's stuff in Tamsin's old room. I've rarely looked at them since they came into being, and now I remember why.

He divided who she was into categories. Perhaps he had to. People talk about grieving as a process, and he processed the hell out of this. *CLOTHES. BOOKS. SHOES. MISC. PAPERWORK.*

I set down my coffee cup, pull out the *MISC* box. I need to work quickly: like me, Dad's fairly reliable in his habits and routines but, ever the would-be copper, he does a good sideline in catching people out.

The box is full of photographs bundled up with rubber bands, old articles she'd ripped from newspapers and magazines. Ticket stubs and trinkets, like the hand-blown glass ring dish Dad gave her for Christmas one year. Boxes of jewellery, even a couple of bottles of perfume. (I don't dare touch them, let alone lift them up. I'm too afraid to be reunited with her scent, to feel the warmth of her arms around me again. During chemo her skin became too sensitive for perfume, and she kept saying she didn't feel herself without it. For a long time after she died, the house didn't feel like itself either. Not when the kiss of her fragrance had been permanently extinguished.)

I flick through the photographs. They're mostly family ones that didn't make it into the albums downstairs. None offer any clues. So I turn to the box marked *PAPERWORK*. I guess I'm imagining a birth certificate or a stash of letters. Some other paper-based link to my past, maybe. But there's nothing. Just reams of financial and insurance correspondence, a fat wodge of hospital letters. It's strange to see the first one, the letter to Mum's GP from her consultant, confirming the results of the biopsy.

A few words on a page, and all our lives were changed for ever.

I look down at my notebook again, at what Dad said to me in my dream. The sadness curls and boils inside me, made even more potent by the memories I've just been sifting through.

Then, downstairs, a door bangs.

'Joel?'

My sister. I relax. 'Hey,' I call out.

'Saw your car.'

'Hold on.' I cram the stuff back into the boxes, leave them where they are on the carpet. Jog downstairs to greet her. I feel a shoring-up inside as we hug, remembering the news she'll be sharing next spring. It helps, a bit, thinking of new life when I'm once again knee-deep in loss. 'Aren't you supposed to be at work?'

'On my lunch break.' She lifts a carrier bag. The sleeves of her fuchsia shirt are rolled up to the elbows. 'Just putting some bits and pieces in the fridge.'

'Like what?'

'Stuff he can heat up.'

I stare at her. 'How long have you been doing that?'

'It's no big deal.' She turns away from me, heads into the kitchen. Opening the fridge, she starts stacking it with plastic boxes.

'Since you left home?'

A shrug. 'Oh, maybe. It started back then, I suppose, and I just . . . never wanted to stop. It seemed mean, somehow.'

I've seen those boxes in there so many times. I always just assumed Dad to be mildly neurotic about his personal nutrition. Had never even thought to ask.

It's something children do, take care of their parents as they get older. Did I never think to ask because on some level I sensed something wasn't quite right?

A flash-flood of sadness. I feel it physically now, whenever I look at Tamsin. We might only be half-siblings: is that why we're so different in appearance? Tamsin and Doug with their rust-red hair and eyes the colour of summer sky, versus me, dark like their shadow. I'd get the occasional comment from classmates when I was younger, but Mum reassured me she looked nothing like her sister, either. To me that was explanation enough. So I just accepted it, made it my stock response if anyone ribbed me. Thought nothing more about it.

I try to calm my mind with cheerier thoughts. Like Amber's stellar upcoming performance in the nativity play. And the bike she'll get for Christmas, unbeknown yet to even Tamsin and Neil.

As Tamsin finishes organising the contents of the fridge, I attempt to refocus. 'Hey, Tam. Do you know if anything weird ever went on between Dad and Mum?'

'Weird how?' She straightens up.

Her frown flags my thoughtlessness. I can't let her think I've uncovered evidence of an affair or something. Not before I have proof, anyway. 'Never mind. Forget it. Shouldn't have said anything.'

'You know,' she muses, her thoughts clearly drifting, 'I do sometimes wonder if we should get Dad dating.'

I force a smile. 'Can't imagine Dad letting his guard down enough.'

She smiles back. 'I know someone else like that.'

I shift the weight to my other leg.

'I *want* you to find someone.' She sidles up to me, squeezes my arm. 'You're so lovely.'

'And you're so biased. Anyway, I'm happily unattached.' The more I say it, the more I might start to believe it.

'I want you to find true love.' Tamsin seems more determined about this than ideally I'd like.

'I'm not interested in true love. Really.'

'Well, you must want to meet a girl at least. Doug says you're virtually celibate.'

*I have met a girl, Tam. And she's charming, and beguiling, beautiful as a butterfly. But there are too many reasons it can't work.*

'Doug says a lot of things.'

'So it's not true?'

I don't exactly fancy going into the finer details of me and Melissa with my little sister. 'Okay, just so you know? We're not having this conversation.'

'It's been a long time since Vicky.'

Even picturing Vicky's face reminds me how unfair it would be to drag Callie into my little vortex of dysfunction. 'Vicky's better off without me.'

Tamsin persists. 'Have I ever told you about Beth? I work with her and she's completely lovely. I could introduce you—'

As Tamsin continues to talk Beth up, my phone buzzes. A light-hearted message from Callie, something about a package she's taken in for me. There are emojis. I'm relieved to have confirmation that last night's double-kiss fiasco hasn't put her off knowing me for good.

I peck my sister on the cheek. 'Love you, Tam.' Exiting the kitchen, I start climbing the stairs.

'What exactly are you doing here again?' she calls.

'Research,' I mumble, safe in the knowledge she probably can't hear me.

# 23

## Callie

Over a week has passed since my meal out with Joel, since he moved me to tears with his story about Scamp. I held that moment in my mind during my interview at Waterfen yesterday, kept close what he said about passion.

I'm out shopping in town when I receive the call, and have a conversation that makes me altitudinous with joy.

I'd planned to nip back to my flat and at least run a brush through my hair, but when I get home the urge to hammer on Joel's door is just too strong.

He's dripping wet when he opens it, with only a towel around his waist. Water droplets are scattered like dew across his soap-smooth skin.

I flounder, trying to focus on what it was I came here to tell him.

'Sorry,' he says, before I can speak. 'Wanted to answer the door before you—'

'Joel, I got it.'

'You got what?'

'Fiona just called. I got the job at Waterfen – a one-year contract.'

'Callie, that's incredible. Congratulations.'

As our eyes meet – just for a moment, before he softly half laughs and turns his gaze to the floor – I realise how much I like him, enough not to care if this is the right thing to do.

He lifts his head as I step forward. We hesitate for a moment, faces so close our noses are almost touching. My blood is abuzz. I could measure my heartbeat in kilowatts. And now I'm reaching up on tiptoe to kiss him, and he's kissing me back – gently at first, like a question, but then fuller and stronger as our mouths lock together. I feel the heat of his hand in my hair, and now we're drawing even closer, his body warm and firm against me, wet from the shower. I feel him shiver with pleasure and for spoonfuls of seconds I can think of nothing but the taste of him, the wet press of his lips against mine, the sweet corkscrew of his shower-gel scent.

Eventually, I pull away and draw breath.

'Sorry,' he murmurs, glancing down at my T-shirt, damp now from his soaked skin.

Outside, it's started raining, a comforting percussive rhythm against car roofs and paving slabs, the bare bones of the trees.

I smile and bite my lip. 'That's okay.'

'Callie, I—' He opens the door a little wider to let me in. 'Can you give me, like, five minutes? Should probably throw some clothes on.'

Suddenly, I feel shy. My heart is racing, piston-fast. 'I need to let Murph out anyway. I'll just go and do that.'

He nods. 'I'll leave the door on the latch.'

# 24

## Joel

I'm staring myself down in the bathroom mirror, the porthole I smeared into the steam creeping closed already.

I've been struggling to gather my breath, as if someone's pulled a drawstring very tight around my lungs.

*I want to stop this, but I can't. I don't have it in me to fight it any more. I like her too much.*

I lean over the sink, lower my head. The idea of Callie and me . . . It feels natural and inescapable. Like the first clear sky of spring. A sapling stretching tall from a forest floor.

And that kiss . . . well, I've already relived it countless times in the space of mere minutes.

But still I feel set adrift. Untethered and unsafe. I think again about the vow I made years ago to protect my heart and sanity.

And what about her heart, her sanity?

I look up, stare at what's left of my reflection. And now here it comes. The reflex I've trained myself into, like compressing a brake in my brain. I think of how little she actually knows about me. Of what her face might do if I told her the full story.

And yet . . . all the logic in the world still has to counteract that kiss. Which is why, when the buzzer goes as I'm getting dressed, I scramble for it.

Because, despite everything, five minutes without Callie already feels like too long.

I press the intercom. 'Hi.'

'Hey, babe.'

My heart dives for cover. 'Melissa?'

She laughs. 'Joel.'

'What are you—'

'You didn't seriously forget?'

A shiver passes through me. I rest my forehead against the intercom. *Please, please let it not be her birthday.*

'Are you going to let me in? It's pouring out here.'

I shut my eyes. *Do I really want to be that guy?* 'Sorry. Hang on.' I buzz her in, so at least I can explain.

I haven't seen her since Halloween nearly a month ago. I vaguely remember mention of her birthday as we began to kiss that evening, slipped into our familiar routine. There's even a chance I might have murmured something about her coming over tonight. This is all my fault.

I open my front door.

'This is a wind-up, isn't it?' Standing in the hallway, she flips back her hood. Loosens her coat. Her skin is summer-holiday brown.

I shake my head. 'I'm sorry. I've actually . . . made other plans.'

Until ten minutes ago that wasn't strictly true. So I feel doubly dishonest for saying it.

'Other plans, like, a girl?'

My eyes tell her yes.

'But you let me come all the way over here anyway.'

'I forgot,' I finally admit. 'I'm sorry.'

She doesn't say anything. For a moment, I think she might start crying. I've never seen Melissa cry, have sometimes wondered if she even knows how.

She recovers temporarily. 'Well, can I come in for a pee at least? I'm bursting.'

'Of course. Sorry. Of course you can.'

And it's while I'm unthinkingly stepping aside to let her into my flat that I look up. Callie's at the top of the stairs, still as a startled fawn, Murphy by her feet.

But before I can open my mouth to say her name, she's disappeared.

# PART TWO

# 25

## Callie

*Tell me it gets easier. Missing you. I thought it would, but it only seems to be getting harder.*

*I want to hear your voice in real life, not just in my head. I want to laugh with you and kiss you. Tell you about all the things I've been doing. Have you hold me in your arms, feel your face close to mine.*

*But I know writing this is as close as I'm going to get to a conversation. So for now I'll pretend you're here by my side, that I'm talking to you. Maybe it'll help — stop me wanting to see you, just one more time.*

*I wish you were here, so much. I'm missing you, Joel, more than I can bear.*

## 26

## Joel

Melissa's in the bathroom with the door ajar, part-way through a speech. Meanwhile I'm lapping the living room, desperate to sprint up the stairs and tell Callie this isn't what it looks like. (I even find myself wondering if I might actually have time, before Melissa wraps up what's turning out to be the longest pee in history.)

'. . . I mean, you don't forget anything. You never have. You even know my *mum's* birthday, for God's sake.'

Finally the flush, then running water.

'So who is she?' She reappears, stops still in the doorway, folds her arms. My heart gives way a little when I take in the elegance of her dress, the curls she's heated into her hair.

'It's the girl from upstairs, isn't it? The one from the shop. I could tell you liked her when you got all bristly with me.'

I think about Dominic, the guy she'd been sort-of-seeing earlier this month. I don't want to call her out on it, exactly. But the arrangement between Melissa and me has always been just that. An arrangement.

'Why . . . why are you making me feel bad?'

'I'm not. Maybe you just . . . feel bad.'

'I am sorry, Melissa.'

'So now I've got to drive all the way back to Watford in that shitty storm?'

An explosion of rain hits the windowpane then, like sarcastic applause aimed squarely at me.

I stare back at Melissa, think of all the times she's driven up the M1 to see me. Of my never returning the favour because I hate being away from home. Of her accepting all my quirks, rarely questioning my behaviour.

Arrangement or no arrangement, Melissa's given me way more than I've ever given her.

I sigh. 'Of course not. Of course you can stay. I just need to—'

She smiles sardonically. 'Don't blow her off on my account.'

A moment passes.

'Listen, Melissa . . . nothing can happen tonight. Between you and me.'

Her smile expands, like I've just said something adorable. 'Oh, you're being all principled and everything.'

'Hardly.' I look down at my feet.

'I thought you were never going to have a relationship. I thought no-strings was all you ever wanted.'

'It was, but then . . .' Faltering, I catch her eye at just the wrong angle.

There's a long pause.

'Well, she must be really special,' is all she says. Then she sparks up a fag, heads into the kitchen to help herself to wine.

## 27

# Callie

Once I've shut the door on what I've seen, I wrap myself up in my most comforting wool cardigan and weave my hair into a plait. Then I tip a small shot of whisky into my seabirds-of-Scotland mug – the nearest clean receptacle – attempting to savour the burn as I sling it slightly tragically back.

Then, a knock on the door.

Cautiously, I open it.

'I'm so sorry, Callie.' Joel looks wretched. 'I had no idea she was coming.'

He's slipped on jeans and a T-shirt now, and his hair's roughed-up, like he's just rubbed a towel across it. I try not to picture the way he looked downstairs when I knocked – warm and bare-chested, breathing hard, wanting me.

Or so I thought.

'It's okay.' I permitted myself a few silent tears over the whisky, and now I'm worried Joel can tell. 'I did know about her, and I chose to ignore it.' All the signs were there, I guess, but to me he just didn't seem the type.

'No, Melissa and I . . . we're not together. Honestly. What we have is just . . . it's . . .'

As his words sputter into stillness, I realise I'd been hoping he would have something more mitigating to say.

He tries again, voice low. 'I said Melissa could stay. Just for tonight. She's had a long drive. But I promise you, nothing will happen.'

I blink back memories of hearing them together, the night of Halloween. 'You really don't need to—'

'No, Callie, I like you a lot—'

I cut him off with a nod but say nothing, because I'm not really sure what that means any more.

Above our heads, rain pummels the stairwell skylight, like it's trying to get in.

'Can I come by tomorrow?'

I frown. 'I don't know if that's—'

'Please, Callie.' He takes a couple of breaths, as if every word is broken glass inside his mind. 'This is just horrible timing. Nothing more.'

'I'm about to go out,' I say softly, even though I didn't know it until now. 'I'd better get ready.'

He looks so stricken, and suddenly I feel angry at the waste of it all. Aside from anything else, that kiss was hands-down the best of my life.

He whistles out a breath. 'Okay. Well, have a good time.'

'I'll try.'

But still he doesn't turn to leave, which gives me no choice but to say goodnight before ever-so-softly shutting the door in his face.

# 28

## Joel

Though I feel the strongest urge I've had in a long time to punch something, I just about manage to resist breaking my knuckles on the nearest wall. I want to knock on Callie's door again, make a better attempt at explaining myself. But she gave me a chance and I did nothing with it. So instead I go back downstairs, craving time to think.

When I get inside, Melissa's lost the dress. She's bare-legged now in one of my T-shirts, caramel hair shaken loose around her shoulders. She stops me by the front door, glass of red wine in hand. Running a finger along the dent of my cheekbone, she brings her freckled face close to mine. She smells of fag smoke and a perfume so familiar I've come to associate it purely with kissing her.

'I won't tell anyone, gorgeous.'

As gently as I can I move away, make for the kitchen. 'That wouldn't be a very good idea.'

She settles down on the sofa. Arranges herself cross-legged so if I looked, I'd see her underwear. 'Can I ask you something?'

'Are you hungry? Shall I order pizza?'

'What does she have that I don't?'

*It really isn't that simple*, I want to say. *How much I like Callie – it's not about pros and cons, comparisons or preferences.*

Even though it sounds crazy, the connection I have with Callie feels . . . more fundamental than that. Innate and elemental. Like a lightning strike or moving tide. A hurricane of feelings.

I picture how Callie looked at me just now, eyes scattered through with fragments of green and gold, like something beautiful that was broken.

'Pepperoni?' I say softly, so I don't have to answer the question.

# 29

## Callie

I leave the flat a short while later, summoning Esther to town for impromptu mojitos. I simply couldn't bear it if I heard Joel and Melissa going at it again – at least if I'm out I won't feel like I'm celebrating my new job by lying in bed wearing noise-cancelling headphones.

We sit up at the bar, and I drink too quickly, in the way people do when they're trying to blunt the edges of something, and for almost an hour I don't even mention Joel.

But eventually Esther asks, so I tell her about Melissa.

'Wait. Isn't she a prostitute?' Esther says, memory now muddied by mojitos.

'No, she just dressed as one, for Halloween.'

'How do you dress as a prostitute?'

'*Pretty Woman.*'

Esther winces disapproval, of both the film and Halloween. 'And she's *staying over*?'

'He said she'd had a long drive.'

Her expression becomes so pitying it's almost humiliating. 'Please tell me you don't believe that. This is Piers, all over again.'

'Joel's not Piers. He couldn't be more different.'

Esther torments an ice cube with her straw. 'Don't you remember when Piers cancelled dinner because his "cousin" was staying over – who turned out to be that girl he met at the golf course?'

I shrug and sip my drink in an effort to soothe the sting of recollection. It doesn't work as well as I'd hoped.

Esther attempts to squeeze sense into my hand. 'I'm just not sure he sounds like a great long-term prospect, Cal.'

'Why not?' I say, desperate for her to come up with a single argument I can convincingly disprove.

She lowers her face to mine in drunken solemnity. 'He's ditched you for a girl who turned up on his doorstep.'

To be honest, I'm quite drunk now too, which makes that doubly hard to argue with.


The next morning I'm out of coffee, but I can't risk running into Melissa, so I sit down next to my living-room window and wait for her to leave. The sky is goose-feather grey, the air rich with late-November rain. From a nearby tree that will blossom in spring comes the drill of a robin's alarm call. I watch the world begin to wake, lengthen its ligaments. Curtains nudge open and the street stirs with its familiar symphony of footsteps and closing doors, shuddering engines. Silhouettes solidify as the sky grows gradually whiter and lighter, shot through with the steam from flaring boilers.

Sooner than I expected she is there, sidestepping puddles, sugar-brown hair long and loose around her shoulders. She has one of those coats with the *faux*-fur collars, and a car that probably cost twenty times my monthly rent. Flicking the lock, she climbs straight in without looking back.

I set out as soon as her brake lights wink at me from the end of the road.


Unfortunately, she hasn't got very far, because I bump into her by the corner-shop chiller cabinet. She's one of those awful people who don't need make-up to turn heads, who seem to have the skin tone and the lashes and the bone structure built in.

To my surprise, she smiles, and it's a much friendlier smile than the last one she gave me. I'm hoping that's not because she's just had the night of her life, though I have to concede it's a definite possibility.

'Can't drive without it,' she says, lifting up her carton of iced coffee. I suppose that's what people do in awkward situations – make small-talk about whatever it is they're in the middle of doing. 'He was out of milk, and I hate it black.'

*He*, I think. *No need for a name. We're both only thinking about one guy.*

A beat or two passes, and I realise Melissa's waiting for me to say something. 'Listen, if I'd known you two were—'

'We never said we were serious. That's not really Joel's style, if I'm honest.'

I'm unable to tell if she cares. 'Right.'

'He hasn't told you, has he? About his . . . issues.'

I say no, because I guess I'd know if he had. As Melissa inclines her head and lowers her voice I feel a lick of guilt because, last night's events aside, Joel's been nothing but lovely to me. Yet here I am, helping her gossip about him *in absentia*. She's beckoning me forward, teasing me into crossing a line.

I don't ask, but she tells me anyway.

'He's a real loner, you know. A bit . . . disturbed. He's dead against having any kind of relationship. And have you ever seen that notebook he carries around with him?'

I want to leave, but she's throwing scraps of information at me now like bait.

'Do you know what's in it?'

Finally, she's got me. I bite. 'No.'

She hesitates, no doubt by design, and chews on her lip. 'Oh, maybe I should let him tell you.'

I'm gripped by the sudden urge to grab her arm and press her to continue, but right at the last moment, I resist. *If there's something Joel needs to tell me, that's up to him.*

'Okay,' I say, with a shrug, making to move past her.

'It's a bit mad. You probably wouldn't believe me if I told you.'

I meet her eye. 'I don't want to know. Please?'

A self-satisfied smile. 'You're right. If I were you, I'd want to stay blissfully ignorant too.'

'Excuse me,' I say softly. 'I'm running late. I'd better go.'

I glance at Joel's door on my way back into the flat, but I don't stop. I just keep moving.

# 30

## Joel

Steve rests rock-solid glutes on the edge of a table in his gym's tiny office. 'You're in luck. My next client's not till twelve.'

I stay by the door, hands in my back pockets, wishing I'd thrown on a couple of extra layers. Steve's gym is unheated, since it's one of those places where people take sweating seriously.

My heartbeat's racing in time to the house music on the other side of the door. And not because of the coffee I've just necked. *This is it. No going back. Please . . . you've got to believe me, Steve.*

'I need to know I can trust you.'

Steve folds his arms. Quite a feat when your biceps resemble bowling balls. 'Of course.'

'No, really. I've got to know that what I say won't go any further. Including Hayley.'

He sizes me up, like I've asked if he can turn me into Arnie. 'You mixed up in anything illegal?'

'No.'

'Okay. Then this goes no further.'

I'm standing on the cliff edge again. Only this time I'm actually going to jump. I feel it physically, the dizzying, hazardous height of the thing. It's the first time since uni, since I got laughed out of the doctor's surgery. 'When you were studying . . . did you ever come across people who were psychic?'

A silence, fully wired.

'That depends on what you mean by psychic,' Steve says eventually.

'What . . . what are the options?'

He shifts his weight against the table. 'Stage psychics. Clairvoyants, with premium-rate phone numbers—'

'No. I mean people who really can predict the future.'

A moment of contemplation. Longer this time. 'You?'

My stomach seesaws. I step off the cliff. 'Yes.'

'What are we talking here? World events? Lottery numbers?'

'Nothing like that. I have . . . dreams.'

'About what?'

'I see what's going to happen to the people I love.'

I had no idea that silence could be so unnerving until now. My heart hopscotches as I study his face for signs of disbelief.

Miraculously, none appear.

'Go on.'

I can't quite compute that he hasn't yet laughed, or suggested I head out for a very long walk. His composure is such that I almost forget what I need to say next.

'Go on, Joel. I'm listening.'

So I take a breath and start to talk about Poppy. His daughter, my goddaughter. I describe my dream – the chilling sight of Steve forgetting to brake at the crossroads, ploughing into a lamppost. And everything that followed. I tell him it's why I let down his tyres, back in September.

Swearing softly, he works his jaw. Looks over at the window like he quite fancies punching the thing from its frame. 'What else?'

I move on: to Luke, to my mum and the cancer. To my sister's soon-to-be-pregnancy. I tell him about Kate, and my dad.

I hand him my notebook so he can see. It's the first time in my life I've shared it. Steve may as well be looking straight into my brain – at my dreams, thoughts and plans, anxieties and ideas. Anything even loosely relevant goes straight down on the page.

Will he think I'm crazy? Laugh, as my GP did all those years ago? Signpost me towards some sort of mental-health assessment?

And what would I do then? Because this stuff is as real as it gets.

Steve flicks tentatively through the notebook. 'Any patterns?'

'Nope. I have one most weeks. Good, neutral, bad. I never know what's next.'

Unsurprisingly, I guess, I foresee more good or neutral things than bad. Because that reflects the balance of my loved ones' lives. But the bad stuff, when it comes, outweighs the rest a hundredfold.

I'm desperate for all of it to stop. Because I want to be with Callie.

Steve turns round, rips the front page off the motivational desk calendar behind him. The entry underneath it orders me to hustle for that muscle.

He picks up a pen, starts to write. 'Have you seen doctors?'

'Just one, at uni.'

'And he said?'

'To get out of his surgery and never come back.'

Still scribbling, Steve raises an eyebrow. 'He didn't suggest this could be linked to anxiety?'

'He didn't suggest anything. And, Steve, even if I am anxious . . . *I can predict the future.*'

'Ever dreamt anything that hasn't come true?'

'They don't come true if I step in. Every dream I have . . . it's prophetic.'

Steve carries on writing. But I'm starting to feel deflated, because he hasn't scrambled to his feet yet with the light bulb I'm so desperate for.

I think, deep down, I knew he wouldn't. That walking away from this conversation with an instant solution would have been nothing short of a miracle.

'Have you ever had a serious illness?'

'Does this count?'

'No.'

'Then no.'

'A head injury? Any knock to the head at all that you can remember?'

'No. Nothing. Why?'

'My knowledge is a little rusty, but I'm wondering if it might be something to do with your temporal and frontal lobes. Your right hemisphere, possibly.' He waves the pen around his forehead, like that will help me understand.

And I do, broadly, thanks to my veterinary neuroscience lectures at uni. But I've never been able to build a bridge between my medical knowledge and the dreams. It's what I'd been hoping Steve could do.

Steve lowers the pen. 'Look, Joel, I haven't studied this stuff for nearly twenty years. I could throw some titbits at you, but really I'd be guessing. I do still have a few contacts, though. I'm wondering if Diana Johansen might be able to help.'

'Who's she?'

'A leading neuroscientist, now. I studied with her. I'm sure I could get her to see you. She heads up a university research team, has contacts everywhere.'

'You think she could investigate?'

'Maybe. I don't know how it all works, these days. For anything official she'd have to apply for funding. There'd need to be ethical approvals, and you might have to undergo some detailed medical exams.'

'You mean,' I say heavily, 'there's no quick solution.'

'You didn't really think there'd be a pill for this, did you?' His voice softens, like he's comforting a teething baby.

It drops through my chest then: the hopelessness, heavy as a falling barbell. 'I guess not.'

'Look, I'll do what I can, I promise.' Steve meets my eye. 'And . . . thank you, Joel. For trusting me.'

I nod acknowledgement, and a few seconds pass.

Steve rubs his chin. 'I have to say, I'm kind of relieved.'

'Relieved?'

'Well, this explains a lot. Is this why you pushed Vicky away?'

'Probably.'

'What about Callie?'

I blink, rapid-fire. 'What?'

'She's the real reason you're here, isn't she?'

'Why would you say that?'

'I called her last week – just to check in, see if there was anything she wanted. I asked how you were getting on, and . . .' He grins. 'Let's just say I couldn't shut her up.'

I know hearing this should make me happy. But all that was before last night, of course. Before the sweetness of our kiss turned quickly sour.

We still haven't spoken. I left the flat about an hour after Melissa this morning, but there was no sign of Callie.

'Have you told her any of this?'

'No.'

'So who else knows?'

'Just you. And that doctor from years ago.'

'You've not told your family? Friends?'

'No. No one.'

Steve whistles out a breath. 'Look, Joel, I don't know much, but I know that talking's a good thing.'

'Only with the right audience. That's why I came to you.'

'But if you talked to Callie, she might understand. You won't know until you try.'

I say nothing.

'Okay.' He hangs one hand off the back of his neck. With the weight, I wonder, of everything I've told him? 'Let me talk to Diana, as a first step.'

'Thank you.'

'Hey, I should be thanking *you*. That night, you saved Poppy from . . .' But the rest of his sentence goes AWOL, and I know why. Because it's too damn hard even to picture some things, let alone put words to them.

We just stare at each other then, while workout music pumps through the office door. It's like we're drinkers turfed out of an anonymous backstreet bar, trying to remember which way is home.

'So you believe what I'm telling you?' Even now, I'm not sure I dare trust it's true.

'Yes,' he says gently. 'I believe you, Joel.'

Somewhere deep inside me, a years-old knot works free.

'I wish I could give you all the answers you want. But I'll call Diana this afternoon. I'm on your side, Joel. We'll crack this, I promise – even if it takes a team effort.'

It's that phrase, *team effort*, that sends my thoughts scattering. The idea of being subject matter, a laboratory experiment. Did Steve mention medical tests, ethical approvals? Maybe talking to Diana would invite publicity, attract attention. Turn her into one of those celebrity scientists who are always popping up in inappropriate places, like quiz shows and radio phone-ins about rising house prices.

'Let me think about it,' I say quickly. 'Don't call Diana yet. Got a few things I need to do first.'

True to my word, I think about it all the way home. Steve's right. I should trust Callie. Tell her everything.

But more than that: for the first time in my life, I think I might actually want to.

# 31

## Callie

At three o'clock, he shows up.

'Hi,' he says, across the counter. He looks sturdy and sincere in a woodsy sort of way, in a soot-grey coat and a black woollen hat. 'Have you got five minutes?'

'She has the whole afternoon,' I hear Dot say, before I can reply. I turn, and she motions to the clock. 'Seriously. Two hours left until closing and we're virtually dead. A bit like that dude.' She jerks her head at the old man in the flat cap by the window. 'Go. Make me happy, please. Promise I'll call if they start queuing out of the door.'

Dot doesn't know what happened last night. I haven't even told her we kissed.

When I look back at Joel, I feel sadness settle in my chest – it feels so wrong not to see him smiling.

'I have an interesting selection of dogs outside,' he ventures. 'Fancy bringing Murph for a wander?'

Outside, I introduce Murphy to Joel's dogs, who all seem very keen to make their introductions by sniffing one another's rear ends.

'The yellow Lab's Rufus. The Maltese is Tinkerbell, and the Dalmatian's Spot. There's another one – Bruno – but he's not cut out for socialising, so I walk him separately.'

We set off down the street, the dogs straining on their leads ahead of us. A suspension of wintry mist makes the world feel underwater, the sun a bright-white blowhole in the sky.

'So, Callie. Are you by any chance a fan of the cakewalk?'

'The dance?'

'No, this is a bit different. Some would say better.'

Despite everything, I smile. 'Go on.'

'Well, essentially it involves an idiot treating you to cake, followed by a walk at the country park while he apologises and attempts to explain himself.'

I think about Melissa, about how devastated I felt last night when I saw her and Joel together. But one look at Joel's face is all I need to decide that I have to hear him out.

We stop at the Sicilian pastry shop, then head on to the park, where we let the dogs off. They scatter like ferrets from a cage, kicking up mud as they go.

'Here. Last one's yours.' Joel extends the paper bag to me like a peace offering.

I take the final *sfinca* – Sicilian ricotta dough balls, gilded with sugar and narcotically sweet.

He brushes sugar from his fingers. 'So, I never got to congratulate you properly last night about the job. It's fantastic. Brilliant news.'

I glance at him, feeling shy suddenly. 'I wouldn't have applied if it wasn't for you. And what you told me, about passion counting – it really helped.'

As we walk, I catch the spice of Joel's scent on the air. It evokes straight away our kiss from last night and its base-of-spine thrill, heated and deep. A kiss I had hoped meant something magic to both of us.

'I'm so sorry about what happened, Callie.'

'The kiss?'

'No! That part was . . . amazing. I meant . . . Melissa. I forgot she was coming. We arranged it weeks ago.'

He's telling the truth. One look at the tension on his face is enough to convince me of that.

'I bumped into her this morning at the shop,' I confide. 'We didn't talk for very long. I sort of . . . ran off.'

Ahead of us, the dogs are bounding around one another in circles, their playful yapping offsetting the gravity in the air somehow.

'There's more to everything that's happened than Melissa. And I want to tell you about it, but . . . I know you want to avoid drama. After Piers.' Appearing to catch himself, Joel briefly shuts his eyes. 'Sorry. That came out wrong. It's not up to you to indulge me.'

'It's okay,' I assure him softly, wondering what he could be about to say. 'You can tell me anything.'

He releases the self-soothing breath of a man about to jump from a very high diving board. 'Sorry. This . . . this is harder than I thought.'

'I don't want to make you feel uncomfortable.'

'You don't. I feel more comfortable with you than I have with anyone in a long time.'

We're by the leisure pontoon, where lines of pedalos are shackled up for the winter. A low mist is shifting like breath across the surface of the lake, a kind of spectral camouflage for courting mallards and groups of braying greylags. On the opposite bank, the boathouse from Bonfire Night lies still and deserted.

'I have—' Joel breaks off and rubs the back of his neck. 'Sorry. This is really hard.'

I reach out and touch his arm to let him know it's okay. But inside I'm starting to feel almost as afraid as Joel looks.

'I have dreams, Callie.' His voice wavers, like weak reception on a radio. 'I dream about . . . what's going to happen to the people I love.'

Seconds swim by.

'Oh . . . I . . .'

Joel ventures a smile. 'Just to say, I know how that sounds.'

I try to think. 'When you say you see what's going to happen . . .'

'I can see into the future. Days, months, sometimes years in advance.'

'Are you—'

'Serious?' He looks at me. 'Unfortunately, yes.'

'No, I was going to say—'

'Sorry. I interrupted. Twice.'

'It's okay. I was just going to ask if you're sure that the dreams . . . aren't a coincidence.'

'If only they were.'

We stand at the edge of the lake. I have no idea what to do or say next. How can this be true? And yet Joel comes across as one of the most sincere people I've ever met.

'Just so you know, if you're thinking of making a run for it,' he says, tilting his head in the direction we've come from, 'I absolutely wouldn't blame you. I can just . . . become the weird guy downstairs again, if you like. No hard feelings. I promise.'

I rush to reassure him. 'You never were the weird guy downstairs to me.' But still. What he's told me is seismic, a vast loophole in logic, and I don't have a clue what to do with it. 'Listen, Joel, everything you've just said . . . it defies science. Reality.'

'It does. But I can try to explain.'

So we carry on walking as he describes his cousin Luke and the dog attack, his mum dying of cancer, his family and losses and near-misses and tortured nights spent wondering. He recounts the horrible experience he had with his university GP. He confesses he hates being away from home, for fear of dreaming something awful that he needs to intercept, and I realise that must be why he's never travelled.

When he mentions a dream he had at Halloween, in which his dad claimed not to be his real father, something slots into place in my mind.

'I heard you,' I say. 'I heard you call out that night, in your sleep.'

His dismay is almost palpable. 'Sorry. In my dream . . . I was shouting after him.'

'No, don't be. I just . . . I could hear how upset you were. Have you—'

'Talked to him? No.'

'Why . . . why not?'

As he laughs softly, I see his eyes are wet with emotion. It takes him a moment to reply. 'What the hell would I say?'

After that he carries on talking for almost ten minutes straight, and when eventually he's done, we share a look that gives me goosebumps.

'Callie, I know this stuff might not be easy to understand. Or even believe. I didn't believe it myself, not for a long time. It took me years to come to terms with it. So I'm hardly expecting you to buy the whole story right now, today.'

'I don't *not* believe you.'

'Oh.' His face flexes with relief. 'Well, that's more than I was expecting.'

From the lake, two mute swans take flight, the pounding of their wings like the rushing of sonogram heartbeats.

'So . . . who else knows?'

'Hardly anyone. Steve. He's got a friend who might be able to help, but . . . I'm not holding my breath.'

I remember what Melissa said to me earlier, in the shop. 'I think Melissa knows.'

'I never told her. She just thinks I have trouble sleeping.'

Repeating what she said, I feel unexpectedly guilty for maligning her. She's not been unpleasant to me exactly – territorial, yes, but that's forgivable. 'She asked if I knew what was in your notebook.'

'She's bluffing,' he says. 'I don't let it out of my sight.'

We talk some more. He tells me his sister Tamsin will be pregnant next year – I can barely fathom the idea that he knows this ahead of time – and then he sketches out the mechanics of sleep cycles against my palm with one finger, turning my insides to skittles. He shows me his notebook, tells me he's tried self-medicating – with lavender and warm milk, getting blackout-drunk, herbal teas, sleeping tablets, supplements and white noise. But none of it ever works.

For his own sanity he limits sleep, these days, and has cut down on booze, believes exercise helps his mood.

'Is there anything you can do?' I ask him then. 'To stop the dreams . . . coming true?'

'Things like accidents, if I can get there in time.' He swallows. 'Stuff like cancer's harder. Or impossible.'

I take his hand, feel the weight of his burden as if it was my own.

Much later, once we're back at the house, Joel says, out of nowhere, 'I'll look after Murph, if you like. When you start at Waterfen.'

My mind about-turns. I'd been reluctantly investigating doggy day care. 'You can't do that.'

'Why not?'

I look down at Murphy gazing up at me. 'Because that's too big an ask.'

'You're not asking. I'm offering. I'm around during the day. I'll watch him, take him out with the other dogs. He'll love it.'

I'm hugely touched. 'I don't know what to say.'

'Say yes.'

'I . . . that would be . . .'

'It's no problem, really.'

An image of Joel-the-vet alights in my mind. I already know he would have been steady-handed and temperate, reassuring and kind. 'I can just picture you as a vet,' I say.

He looks down at our hallway carpet, stuffs his hands into his pockets. 'I wouldn't,' he says gruffly. 'I wasn't very good at it.'

'How do you mean?'

'That day at the coffee shop, when I fell asleep – that's who I'd become at work. The only difference was, I left before they asked me to.'

'How long is it since you quit?'

'Three years.' He clears his throat. 'Ploughed every spare penny I had into savings before that. Dull as hell, but I guess I thought I might need them one day.'

'There's nothing dull about buying yourself freedom.'

He smiles as though that's just about the nicest thing anyone's ever said to him. And all at once, I'm leaning forward to kiss him. Everything inside me ignites as I lose myself in him, against him, his mouth moving to my neck, my collarbone, back to my neck. I push his T-shirt up, feel the firmness of his stomach, his bare skin hot beneath my fingers. Our kissing becomes fiercer, and we move back against the wall, bodies hotwired and mouths wild, every movement a tiny frenzy as we let each other know just how much we want this.

It takes a superhuman effort to part, minutes later.

Breathing in shivers, I push back my hair. 'I should . . .'

Joel's chest is heaving too. He reaches out to touch my wrist. 'See you tomorrow?'

The most thrilling of promises. 'Yes. See you tomorrow. Yes.'

# 32

## Joel

I take a minute or two to come round when I wake. No dreams.

Relieved, I roll onto my back and stare skywards. Towards where my bedroom ends and Callie's begins.

'I think the universe might want us to give this a go,' I whisper to the patch of scruffy ceiling where I imagine her bed to be.

I already know I can't wait to see her. Knock on her door, suggest coffee or brunch. Experience the effervescent rush of kissing her again.

All the reasons I shouldn't are still there: falling for her, fearing what I might see if I do, and everything that brings with it.

But all the reasons I should are slowly beginning to outweigh them.

She knows about my dreams. I bared my soul to the first person I've truly cared about since Kate. To Callie, who's breathed hope into my heart. Yet still she stopped me for that full-on kiss in the hallway last night. Something's drawing us together, powerful as gravity. And now, after all these weeks, perhaps I'm finally ready to let gravity win.

I've watched possibility drift by over the years, connections I've held myself back from pursuing. Like Kieran's cousin Ruby, who played footsie under the table with me five minutes after we met. The whip-smart veterinary nurse I got chatting to in a gin bar, that time Doug persuaded me out. The girl behind the counter in the post office, whose filthy joke about package sizes still causes me to smile and swerve the place in equal measure.

But Callie eclipses them all.

I turn my face into my pillow, permit myself a smile. And as I do, the reluctant clunk of Callie's water pipes stirs into life. The sound of her running shower is like a standing ovation against my ceiling. And now, here it comes: the first tuneless verse of this morning's song.

'I Want to Know What Love Is'.

Couldn't have put it better myself.

I resist knocking on her door for almost twenty-three minutes.

'Morning,' she says shyly, when eventually I give in. She's wearing jeans and a pair of slippers, an oversized knitted jumper the colour of morning mist.

*Oh, my word, she looks beautiful. What was I going to say, again?*

I smile at her. 'How's your appetite? Scale of one to ten.'

She bites her bottom lip, tucks a strand of damp hair behind her ear. 'A solid nine.'

'Can I tempt you to breakfast?'

'Always.'

'What do you fancy?'

She blushes a little. 'Um, I'm a sucker for pancakes.'

'Handy. I know just the spot.'

The pancake joint's tiny. It's fairly new to town, but already has a cult following with queues out of the door, even on Sundays in late November. But today we get lucky with the last two stools in the window. Callie's excited, says she's been wanting to try this place since it opened.

The waitress who seats us is curt as cold air, but I assure Callie the pancakes will be worth it.

'Poor woman. I might be crabby too, if I had this many covers first thing on a Sunday,' Callie confesses. I've noticed that about her, that she always gives people the benefit of the doubt. She inclines her head to mine. 'Have to say, I'm in a bit of a frenzy about these pancakes now.'

My stomach flips with hunger and something else.

She surveys the room. 'Look how packed it is. If I was any sort of business woman, I'd be jealous.'

'It's just an illusion. This place is microscopic.'

She nudges me with her elbow. 'I had a nice time, you know. Yesterday.'

Hope hoists a flag in my stomach as she holds my gaze. Still, I have to ask. 'Nice in comparison to . . . dental work? Doing your taxes?'

She laughs and winces at the same time. 'Sorry. *Nice* is a terrible word.'

'In the context of everything I told you, believe me, *nice* is the best word ever.'

Our pancakes arrive a few minutes later, huge stacks of syrup-soaked buttermilk pillows. Sticky and caramelly, they're daubed with whipped butter.

Callie studies them earnestly. 'Okay, *now* I get the queues.'

We start to eat. I try to gauge her frame of mind, read the light and shade of her body language like a sundial. Is she as happy and relaxed as she appears? Unfazed, even, by my revelations yesterday? I can hardly believe she could be.

Eventually, chest drum-tight, I ask if she's had a chance to think about what I told her.

She wipes her mouth. Turns to face me. 'Yes. And I don't want to let it stop what we're doing. This, us.'

Relief rushes through me, and yet . . . 'I know it might be hard to believe what I've told you, Callie.'

She takes my hand. 'No, I—'

'I've been trying to think . . . of a way I can prove it to you.'

'You don't have to do that.'

'But I want to.'

She sips her coffee, waits.

'Tomorrow night, there's going to be a burst water main on Market Street. Middle of rush-hour, gridlock. My sister's going to get caught up in it, miss her yoga class.'

I see Callie's mind turning this over. *Consequences aside*, she's thinking, *there's no way he could bring about a burst water main, even if he was that nuts.*

'Joel, you really don't need to do this—'

'I do,' I insist. 'Just so you know I'm not crazy.'

As we're finishing our coffee Callie asks about Vicky. All at once I'm grateful to be facing the window, rather than struggling to meet her eye across a table.

'We broke up eight years ago.'

'How long were you together?'

'Three years.'

'Were you happy?'

I stare out at the frosty street. 'At first.'

'Who ended it?'

'She did. I think she just wanted someone normal, by then.'

Callie wraps her hands around her mug. Waits for me to elaborate.

'I wasn't a very good boyfriend,' I admit. 'I was . . . pretty self-absorbed. A bit messed-up. Bad company, probably.'

'You're very honest.' She seems impressed.

'None of that bothers you?'

She turns to look at me, face open as a leaf to rain. 'You don't have to be flawless to be lovable.'

'No,' I agree. 'But ideally you should have more pros than cons.'

I don't tell her I kept the list Vicky gave me, at the end. I can still recite it, word for word.

'Did you ever dream about Vicky?'

'You mean, did I love her?'

Callie's features seem suddenly to contract with shyness. 'Yes.'

'No. I never dreamt about her.'

'So have you ever . . . been in love?'

Behind us, a group of students are called to their table. They rush past, an eddy of energy and optimism that evokes a strange kind of nostalgia in me. For what, I'm not exactly sure.

'Once. A long time ago.' I glance at her, clear my throat. Offer up the briefest details of my relationship with Kate. 'Feel free to flee at any time,' I say, when I'm done.

'You keep saying that.'

'Hardly selling myself here.' *Not that I ever thought I'd want to.*

She sneaks a palm over my hand. Though her skin is warm, it makes me shiver. 'Yes, you are.'

I meet her eye. And, somewhere inside me, an anchor lifts.

# 33

## Callie

I'm online, eyes wide, reading a news update on the website of Eversford's local paper.

> *A burst water main is causing major delays in the town centre this evening. Traffic is at a standstill on Market Street and adjoining roads, with drivers reporting delays of up to an hour . . .*

I exhale. It's not as if I didn't believe Joel before, but this has made it real and indisputable. It makes me want to draw him to me, hold him tight and never let go.

I'm not exactly sure why, but I wanted to see the thing for myself – it felt almost miraculous – so I knocked on Joel's door, asked if he fancied a fast-food hit. We've installed ourselves in the window of a burger joint on Market Street, with front-row seats overlooking the chaos.

'Am I a bad person?'

Joel swirls a chip in ketchup. 'Why? Because you wanted to run down here and rubber-neck?'

I grimace. 'Just to be clear, I wouldn't have if it was an accident, or—'

'Hey, it's fine,' he says, rocking into me gently with his elbow. 'I do it myself, sometimes.'

'Just to check you're not dreaming?'

He laughs, and after that we eat in silence for a little while.

'Well,' he says eventually, 'if nothing else, you can't say I don't know how to show a girl a good time. Fast food and gridlock at rush-hour – what more could you want?'

'You're off the hook – this was totally my suggestion.' I think again about why we're here. 'It's mad, though, isn't it? *You knew this was going to happen.*'

His smile fades a little. 'Believe me, the novelty wears off pretty quickly.'

Beyond the window, car doors open. An altercation between two pent-up drivers unfolds.

As they square up to each other with their chests and fists, Joel grabs his drink. 'Fancy making a move? Not sure I want to watch this bit.'

'It's not your fault, you know,' I tell him, as we exit the restaurant and walk swiftly away, drinks in hand. 'It's a burst pipe. You couldn't have stopped it.'

'I could have done something. Called the water company – they'd have checked it out.'

'No one's been hurt,' I remind him softly.

'No,' he agrees. 'And showing this to you tonight felt more important.'

# 34

## Joel

We head back to Callie's place. I'm relieved to have been able to prove myself to her, even though she didn't ask me to. But the whole episode has left me slightly unsettled. So when we get in I change the subject, ask about her day.

She tells me she gave Ben her notice at the café this lunchtime.

'How'd he take it?'

'Better than I thought. He's going to promote Dot, I think, then find someone to replace her.' A sigh. 'He was really nice about it, actually. So supportive. Which kind of made me feel worse – like I'm turning my back on him. Maybe even Grace too.'

We're sharing the sofa, though only our gazes are touching. Beyond the window, a scallop of moon is suspended in the darkness. The sky is wired with stars.

'He was supportive because it's a great move for you,' I assure her. 'The start of a whole new chapter.'

Callie's braided her hair, draped it over one shoulder. It exposes her slender neck, the drop earrings she's wearing set with real pressed flowers. 'I guess it's been a long time coming. I had this weird fear, just after Grace's funeral. I kept waking up in the middle of the night, wondering what people would say about me if I died. Fixating on it, almost. Esther thought I was trying to avoid dwelling on Grace. You know – blanking out the sadness by stressing about my own failings.'

I think back to my mum. How intently I started obsessing over my dreams after she died. That's when I began hardcore note-taking, recording every damn thing I saw.

'I was worried my eulogy would read like a CV,' Callie says. 'You know – *Extremely reliable. Recipient of a long-service award at Eversford Metal Packaging. Punctual, hard-working* . . . That was what gave me the final push, I guess. To quit my office job and take on the café. I went a bit mad, I think, for a couple of months.'

'Mad how?'

She shrugs. 'Doing loads of ill-advised stuff. Like, deciding what I needed was a really bizarre haircut with a fringe, which I absolutely hated, obviously. Then I thought I'd paint my entire flat dark grey, but it looked *awful* and I had a meltdown halfway through about my damage deposit, so I had to paint it all back again.' She lets out a self-reproachful breath. 'What else? Signed up to online dating – disastrous. Got drunk and . . .' She trails off.

'Oh, no.' I laugh. 'You can't stop there. Got drunk and . . . eloped? Got arrested? Racked up a five-figure bar bill?'

Her voice drops to a whisper. 'I got a *tattoo*.'

I grin. 'Excellent.'

A pause.

'So what is it?'

'What is what?'

'The tattoo.'

She bites her lip. 'Never mind.'

'How, what and where?'

'It's a *very* long story.'

I check an invisible watch. 'Oh, I have time.'

'Okay. Well, I got drunk, then . . . I got a tattoo.' She exhales, folds her hands demurely in her lap.

I'm not letting her off that easy. 'You already told me that. I'm going to need details, I'm afraid.'

She chews her lip again. Tucks a wayward strand of hair back into her plait. 'Well, I had it in my head that I wanted a bird . . . but I was drunk, and I couldn't quite get across what I meant. I wanted a swallow – it was supposed to be elegant, and beautiful. Delicate, you know? I tried to draw it for them, but I'm a *terrible* artist and . . .'

'Where is it?'

'On my hip.'

I raise an eyebrow. 'Can I see it?'

'Okay, but you can't laugh.'

'I promise.'

She lowers the waistband of her jeans just enough.

I look down at it. Then up at her. 'It's a . . . wow.'

'I know.'

It *is* a swallow. I think. But if it is, it's on steroids. Bright red and blue, and unexpectedly sizeable. Hearty and plump, with cartoon curves. There's a blank scroll in its beak, and an intensity to its expression I can only presume to be accidental.

Or maybe her tattooist was high at the time.

'It's quite . . . I mean, it's . . .'

Her eyes go wide. 'You don't need to be nice about it, honestly. I cried when I saw it sober. I started desperately googling laser tattoo removal, vowed never to do anything daring again.'

'What was supposed to . . .' I clear my throat '. . . go in the scroll?'

'Oh, they thought I wanted that, for someone's name. I'm surprised they didn't just make something up, stick it in there without asking.'

'Christ. The mind boggles.'

She doffs me with a cushion. 'You promised you wouldn't laugh.'

'I'm not. I think it's charming.'

'It's not charming. It's graffiti that won't wash off. I'm building up to going back, having it lasered.'

I reach out, take her hand. 'I think you should be proud of it. Sod lasering the thing. It's part of your story.'

She starts laughing, lips pink and full from the press of her teeth. 'Are you serious?'

'Too right. You did something crazy, brave. You should see that tattoo and feel nothing but happiness.' I glance down at her hip again. But it's when I look back up at her that I feel happiness: the full, synaptic rush of it. 'Keep doing crazy stuff,' I say, squeezing her hand.

'Really? Crazy like this tattoo?'

I grin. 'Why not? So long as it's a good kind of crazy. *Your* kind of crazy.'

'I have a feeling Waterfen's going to be pretty wild. For me, anyway,' she says, laughing. 'What's next – fancy coming with me to Chile?'

She's joking, I know that really. But being with Callie is the closest I've ever come to escaping life as I know it. Because even just getting to know her is like time spent in a foreign country. Somewhere I've often wondered about, but never had the courage to explore.

We lean forward at the same time. Fall into a kiss, fly into orbit.

# 35

## Callie

It's Esther's birthday, and she's invited me and Joel to a party at her house.

'I haven't been to a house party for years,' he confesses, as we're getting ready.

'How come?'

'They're not really my . . . natural habitat.' He says it's to do with the gradual sliding-away of friendships, his lifelong feeling of being an outsider.

I'm ironing my dress for tonight, the belted navy one that skims my hips just right and goes perfectly with peep-toe heels and a fearless lipstick. 'Don't worry. No one will know.'

He kisses me. 'You hope.'

'Well, I don't care if they do,' I murmur.

I have a feeling Joel and I turning up together is going to be the talk of the party, but he seems nervous, so I decide to keep that to myself.

Esther greets us at the door wearing a badge that says *FORTY AND FABULOUS.*

'Gav's attempt at irony,' she says, kissing us both. 'I'm thirty-six.'

'I'm Joel,' he says, extending a hand.

Esther beams like that's the funniest thing she's heard all year. 'You. Are. Hilarious. Come on. Everyone's going to love you.'

As we're walking down the hall I keep expecting Grace to emerge from a doorway, bright-cheeked and gin-glazed, a full glass in each hand and unlimited kisses for everyone.

The nice thing about Joel is that his outgoing warmth belies his hermit mindset. We've barely got drinks in our hands before Gavin pulls him into conversation about sustainability in architecture, which eventually turns into a debate with Esther on attempts by the middle classes to raffle off their homes, and after that I don't get to speak to him again for ages. Every time I glance over to check he's okay, he's locked in conversation with someone new, and eventually I nearly lose him among a crowd of people I don't recognise. But our eyes intermittently find each other, satellites across a solar system, and whenever they do, my stomach ripples with stars.

By the time I feel a hand around my waist I realise that one or maybe even two hours have passed.

It's Esther. 'Just wanted to say how proud I am of you.'

'Proud?'

'Yeah, for chasing your dreams. I should have encouraged you more, all these years.'

She did, I think. She always insisted I'd caved too quickly when my initial flurry of interviews and applications after uni came to nothing, refused to let me jettison my dreams. *You're the only person I know who can name a bird from its flight pattern*, she would tell me out of nowhere on a crisp winter's morning, when I'd pointed out the flock of pintails above our heads, a run of stitches against the sky's puckered fabric. *And who else can identify a tree just by looking at its bark? You should pursue your passions, Cal. Life is for living.*

But by then my confidence had already taken a beating from that first round of rejections. Ecology was so competitive – it felt safer and less heart-breaking to suspend my ambitions, assure Esther I'd pursue it again soon. So, after a while, she stopped bringing it up.

'You did,' I tell her now. 'I just don't think I was ready to listen at the time.'

'Love that necklace,' she says, nodding at my clavicle. 'I was with her when she bought it.'

It's a tiny pewter acorn, a Christmas gift from Grace not long after she'd met Ben. She was trying to make a point, I think, about acorns and oak trees and getting off my backside.

Esther hugs me again, then lopes off to locate Gavin.

Later, I find Joel chatting to Gavin and Esther in the basement kitchen. It's a relief to see they don't appear to be holding against him the way we started, with all the confusion over Melissa. Or that, at the very least, they've agreed to wait until tomorrow before ribbing me about it over WhatsApp.

'Hey.' I loop my arms around Joel. He's shed his jumper somewhere, is warm and soft-skinned in just a T-shirt. His fragrance is familiar already, like the scent of returning blossom. 'I lost you.'

'Hey. I lost you, I think.'

'You hang up. No, *you* hang up,' Esther says. She's on the red wine now, her lips vermilion.

I smile. 'What are you guys talking about?'

'Ben,' Esther says. 'He's on about quitting his job and selling the house, moving away maybe.'

'Really?' I've not spoken to Ben much tonight, but he did seem quite tipsy when I saw him in the queue for the downstairs loo.

'We're trying to decide if we should talk him out of it,' Gavin says.

'No, why?'

Esther bites a fingernail. 'Well, in case he's being rash.'

I curl my arm more tightly around the warm column of Joel's torso. 'But Grace has been gone nearly two years now,' I say quietly.

We all take a moment.

'I mean, it's great, isn't it,' I continue, 'if Ben's finally feeling hopeful? He's not said anything optimistic like that since she died.'

'So long as he's moving on, as opposed to running away,' Esther says sagely, as, somewhere nearby, a glass smashes.

Gavin sticks his head out of the kitchen doorway to have a look. 'That's Ben. Oh, Christ, he's retching.'

'Honestly, house guests,' Esther says, winking as she swigs back the last of her wine. Then she and Gavin exit the room, leaving Joel and me alone.

Outside, the patio forms a black axis across the basement windowpane. The night air is cloudy, milky with mist.

'Think he'll be okay?' Joel asks me.

'Oh, definitely. Esther's excellent in a crisis.' I frown. 'I just hope . . .' He waits.

'. . . that Ben's not worrying about the café. I don't mean me leaving so much as . . . things changing. Moving on.'

Joel looks thoughtful. 'But maybe in the long run, it'll turn out okay if they do. If he's already talking about making a fresh start . . .'

I try to smile. 'Yeah. I'll talk to him, I guess. Once he's recovered from tonight.'

Joel lets his eyes travel the room. 'This is a really great place.'

'I know.' I draw my fingers along the notches and grooves in the old oak worktops. 'It's so cosy and traditional.'

He nods. 'Like a proper family home.'

'They were trying for a baby,' I say suddenly, without really knowing why. 'Esther and Gavin.'

'Oh, sorry, I didn't mean—'

'No, I know, I just . . .'

'So they were . . .'

'Trying. Before Grace died. But then they stopped.'

'Death does that, I guess. Makes you take stock. Press pause.'

My smile feels weak as water. 'As long as you remember to press play again at some point.'

We both stand still for a second, listening to the anguish of American blues mewl down through the floorboards, before Joel leans across and kisses me. It feels sublime being down here together, tucked away in the warm belly of the house, like marsupials safe from the outside world.

'I smudged you,' he says, when we part momentarily.

His lips are smeared red from mine. 'Ditto.' And then I lean forward and kiss him again. Insistent and impassioned, our bodies are soon tight, our mouths wet and hot. We become each other's pulse right there in the open palm of the kitchen, warmed by the breath of the Aga and sheltered by the creaking, gently steepling walls of the room.

# 36

## Joel

Callie's dozed off next to me in bed, all rumpled clothing and ruffled hair. We took our kiss from Esther's kitchen earlier straight back home. To the front step while I grappled with the key, then into the hallway. Then through the door to my flat and half onto my sofa, before finally we made it to the bedroom. Together we fell against the mattress, mapping each other out with fevered hands. Heartbeats hammering, skin dampening. At one point I knocked the lamp from my nightstand with my foot (how were we *that* way up?), plunging us deliciously into darkness. I felt her pelvis twitch as she laughed, making me frenzied with desire.

It's been a week since we first kissed and I'm falling for her, hard. But I want to do this properly. Go slow. Take our time. She means so much to me already that not rushing things just seems to make sense.

Which is how she's ended up curled against my hip like a cat while I watch a TED Talk about human stampedes, headphones firmly on.

Maybe I feel like this because of Melissa. Because my brain's trying to draw a line between her and Callie, somehow. Or perhaps I need to believe I won't mess this up before we do much more than kiss.

Anyway. We'd cut a strange picture, I think, if you were looking down on us from above. Me in my own little world. Callie asleep by my side, fully clothed.

# 37

## Callie

The sun is an oily flare, high in the sky of a tart early-December morning. It's my first day at Waterfen and I'm in the middle of marshland, jolting along in the cab of a tractor that, strangely, I appear to be driving. My new boss, Fiona, is on the fold-out seat next to me, a trailer full of fence posts rolling along behind us as a small battalion of other staff members and volunteers track the deep rents of our tyre marks on foot.

I clench and unclench the steering wheel a few times, just to check this is really happening and I haven't wandered off-piste from my sleep into one of Joel's dreams.

It's hard not to be distracted by my surroundings as we drive. The landscape glints with winter, sunlight sparking off crystallised ground. Twice we catch the tawny dart of a deer fleeing through undergrowth, as a hen harrier loop-the-loops against the sky's flawless easel.

'It's not possible to get tractors stuck, is it?' We're approaching a patch of bright wet ground that bears an unnerving resemblance to bog.

'Oh, yes – it is,' Fiona says cheerfully. Dark-haired and ruddy-cheeked, she has the no-nonsense disposition of a midwife.

'So what do you do if you get stuck?'

'Oh, you don't.'

'Don't what?'

'Get stuck,' she says, with a smile. 'Do that and you really are screwed.'

I keep my eyes on the quagmire ahead. 'Right. Got it.'

She laughs. 'Relax. It's just like driving a car. You'll feel if you start to lose traction.' I sense her glancing at me. 'You do drive a car, don't you? Forgot to check your licence back there.'

I grin and confirm that, yes, I am in fact qualified to drive. After nearly two years of working in the café, where the smallest spill of coffee felt like a TripAdvisor slating waiting to happen, Fiona's relaxed approach is like permission to breathe. I can already feel my brain switching lanes, a changing-down of gears in my mind. Perhaps I'd even be getting emotional about it, if I wasn't in charge of agricultural machinery and trying to avoid a headfirst plunge into the nearest ditch.

I'll come to love this tractor in time, Fiona assures me. She describes hypnotic sun-swamped summers of topping and weed-wiping, long, meditative afternoons spent circling meadows in the fen, the air mottled with sunlight and sprinkled with butterflies. She tells me I've arrived at the worst possible time of year. 'Which is actually a good thing,' she adds, 'because the way I look at it, the weather can only get better from here on in.'

'I sort of like winter, though,' I tell her.

Her smile is all sympathy. 'We've not started clearing out the dyke system yet.'

The morning is spent erecting a fence line with posts and stock-proof fencing wire, which is terrifying in a high-tensile kind of way. I'm petrified of getting it wrong and ricocheting one or more of my workmates into the back of an ambulance. But the trepidation invigorates me – it's an unexpected stimulant, having to focus so hard on not decapitating someone, or driving the tractor into a bog, or losing my footing and falling into a dyke. It's like the adrenalin shot I've been craving since the day I started working at the paint-tin company.

We take lunch on top of reed stacks, deep in the middle of the fen. Hot and heaving from the morning's work, we shed fleeces and jackets, even though it's not far above freezing. We watch the pivot and plunge of a hunting kestrel, the cold air washing like water over our sweating skin. From a nearby belt of bare-branched trees, the chipping of jack-daws falls like rain.

As we inhale our soup and sandwiches, the conversation turns to wanderlust. Dave, a volunteer and recent ecology graduate, is leaving next week to work on a conservation project in Brazil, monitoring and researching wildlife at a state park reserve. I've been completely in awe since the moment he told me.

Fiona asks us all for our bucket-list destinations.

'Latvia,' says Liam. Blunt and broad-shouldered, with hair the colour of honey, he's Fiona's permanent assistant, coming on board five years ago after realising exactly how bad he was at financial auditing. 'Beauty, peace and quiet, no one around to annoy you.'

'You've already been to Latvia,' Fiona points out. 'That doesn't count.'

I smile, think of my guidebooks back at the flat, wonder if Liam and I might turn out to have a lot in common.

Liam shrugs. 'Don't want to go anywhere else.'

'Not somewhere more exotic?' Dave says, though the smile in his eyes tells me they've had this conversation before. 'Africa maybe?'

'Nah. You know I'm cold-blooded. Anyway, I've seen as much of the world as I want to see.'

Fiona turns to me. 'How about you, Callie? Dream destination?'

'Lauca National Park,' I say. 'You know, in—'

'Chile,' everyone choruses.

I lean forward slightly. 'There's this bird there—'

Dave starts laughing. 'Ah, the famed diademed sandpiper-plover.'

Liam snorts, upturns his crisps packet towards his mouth. 'You've got a better chance of seeing a snow leopard.'

'Or a unicorn.' Dave chortles.

'I know someone who's seen one,' Fiona says.

I nod eagerly, remembering the girl on my course at uni. 'So do I.'

Dave smiles. 'Well, if you ever get a picture, make sure you send it to me.'

Fiona meets my eye. 'Take no notice. My friend says the place is stunning, real once-in-a-lifetime stuff. And that bird would be an epic find.'

'Right,' Liam says, crushing his empty packet and checking his watch. 'This is all very nice and everything, but that fence line needs finishing off.'

'You'll have to get used to him, I'm afraid,' Fiona says to me, with a wink. 'He's a bit like a husky. Always itching to keep moving.'

I like Liam already – he seems like my sort of guy. So I'm first to jump eagerly down from the reed stack and follow him back to the fence line.

I knock on Joel's door when I get home, smiling as he winches me into a hug. 'Sorry – I'm all sweaty and horrible.'

'Sweaty and lovely,' he insists. 'Tell me everything.'

I describe my day, show him the blisters peppering my palms. 'I didn't realise how unfit I am. But on the plus side, I did learn how to drive a tractor.'

'On day one? That's throwing you in at the deep end.'

'Yep. Mind you, at least I didn't have time to panic first.'

'Nice people?'

'Yes, really nice. Really great.' I smile down at Murphy. 'How was he?'

'Well, he did pine for you at first. But I won him round with my killer combination of walks, ball, treats and tummy rubs.' He drops his voice to a whisper. 'Between you and me, I think he's developed a soft spot for Tinkerbell.'

I laugh. 'Tinkerbell's far too old for him. She's nearly ten.'

'Hey, don't knock it. The distraction worked wonders.'

Inside, I feel a slackening of tension, like the sag of a sail as a storm subsides. 'Thank you so much.'

'You're more than welcome. Drink?' He heads over to the fridge, withdrawing a bottle and searching out a corkscrew.

Joel's flat puts mine to shame – it's always so clean and orderly, a capsule of calm. In the living room, there's just a two-seater sofa with a teal-coloured throw spread demurely across its shoulders, a decent-sized TV, Bluetooth speaker and not a lot else – aside from a succulent on the hearth and a coffee table, normally bearing his notebook and pen.

I flop onto the sofa. 'You bought proper wine.'

'Sorry?'

'If it's got a cork that means it's posh. Or did I make that up?'

'Well,' he says, pouring a glassful, 'it's a good thing, apparently. For the cork forests. I've been reading up, now that you work in nature conservation and everything.' He crosses the room and passes me a glass that feels cold as frost. 'Here, get stuck into this and I'll run you a bath.'

*Oh, my heart. My heart is singing.*

'Thank you,' I manage, but he's already disappeared into the bathroom to turn on the hot tap. I watch him as he goes – the spread of his shoulders, his dark jostle of hair – and feel an intimate sense of longing.

After several intense weeks together, Joel and I still haven't had sex. I know he's reluctant to rush things, that his feelings around relationships are complicated, that he doubts his own competence in matters of the heart. So I'm happy to take things slowly. What we're doing feels right for us.

When the bath's run and I go in there, Joel's lit a candle, set a freshly laundered towel to warm on the rail. It's like a slow-dance of tender gestures, all the things I used to do for Piers that he'd never do back, presumably because he didn't think I was worth the trouble.

Until recently, Joel probably didn't even own a candle, let alone the lavender bubble bath he's poured into the water. It's like he's been waiting for years to have someone he can do this for.

# 38

## Joel

It's halfway through Callie's first week at Waterfen, and we're walking home from dinner at the home of my ex-boss Kieran and his wife Zoë. After the warmth of their underfloor-heated den (they live in a blond-brick, double-fronted villa on one of Eversford's most expensive avenues), the outside world feels scaldingly cold.

'Is Kieran your only real friend?' Callie asks me gently as we walk, our breath aerosol-white in the December air.

'Steve's a good friend.' Better than most, given all he's put up with from me.

'Why?'

'Why what?'

'Why are Kieran and Steve your only real friends?' Her arm hooked into mine, she asks the question like it's no big deal. Except I know it is. I guess she's wondering if a guy without a serious personality defect can really make it to halfway through his thirties without a crew to show for it. An ever-present stag-night-in-waiting. Doug, who has his own faithful cohort (old school pals, rugby mates, work colleagues, friends-in-law) has never thought so. He's forever ribbing me about the lack of barbecues on my birthday, summers devoid of wedding invitations. World Cups come and gone without a squad to raise a glass with.

'I guess after the dreaming started,' I admit, 'I wasn't very focused on making friends. It felt like a full-time job at times. Trying to keep track of everything, hold my mind together. Still does, if I'm honest.'

Last night being a case in point. I dreamt about a near relative's debit card being cloned, his bank account emptied. I've got a few months, but what to do? Tell him to pay cash-only until June, beef up his internet security? I deliberated all morning, eventually opted to send him an email. Fabricated something about a friend being hot on this stuff. What he does with it, I guess, is up to him.

When I next looked up it was nearly midday. I could barely remember Callie leaving my flat to go to work. I never took the time to kiss her as she woke, make her a coffee, ask if she fancied doing something this weekend. Tiny chances to connect, fluttering from my fingers.

'It's a shame,' Callie says now.

I clear my throat. 'You don't miss what you never had. And friendships aren't too easy to invest in when you have to keep to yourself all the stuff that defines you.'

'Maybe it doesn't have to define you.'

*But it does*, I think. *I don't have a choice about that.*

We walk on, past wrought-iron railings laced with frills of winter jasmine.

'Well, my friends love you,' Callie says. 'I couldn't keep up with my messages the day after Esther's party.'

I smile. 'That's good.' Because if you can't be normal then pulling off a decent impression of it is the next best thing, I guess.

'You know, what you think of yourself isn't always how other people see you.'

I taste the sweetness of her words, compress her hand with the crease of my elbow. 'Speaking of which . . . have you always thought of yourself as a secret *Mastermind* contender?'

She laughs. 'What?'

'How does one person amass so much general knowledge? You know *everything*.' (We played a trivia game after dinner. And to cut a long story short, Callie wiped the floor with all of us.)

Unsurprisingly, she's pure modesty. 'As if. I was only good on science and nature.'

'And geography. I mean, where did you pick up so many random facts about Peru? And I don't know anyone else who could name the capital of Tanzania off the top of their head.'

Callie sinks her chin into her scarf. 'Ha. Piers used to hate that about me.'

'Hate what?' It's hard to imagine Callie with any loathsome qualities at all.

'That I knew lots of random facts. He thought I was trying to show him up.'

'Like a kid,' I suggest, not particularly inclined to go all out and batter him. The guy messed up his chance with the best girl in the world. He's already a hundred–nil down.

'Let's just say, if he'd lost like you did tonight, he'd have sulked for a week.'

I feign indignation with my eyebrows. 'Hold on – like *I* did? I wasn't as bad as Zoë. She didn't even know who invented the telephone.'

Callie starts laughing. Grips my arm a little harder. 'Don't you just know she was dying to say *Mr Telephone*?'

'Yep, and she only reined it in because Kieran kept kicking her.'

Fizzing with mirth, our eyes meet. We start contorting with laughter. A solitary late-night dog-walker gives us a wide berth, glancing over his shoulder as he strides away up the otherwise silent street.

I don't tell Callie about Kieran cornering me in the kitchen earlier, while I was helping to clear plates. (I learnt years ago from Tamsin that when you've got kids, it's the little things you appreciate.)

'Where did you find this girl?'

His question was rhetorical. Callie had already told them the story over parsnip soup, one hand gripping mine, the sole of her foot in the crook of my ankle. So I just smiled.

'I'm happy for you, mate.'

'Thanks.'

'Seems like things are finally beginning to turn around for you.'

I started stacking plates in the dishwasher. From the dining room I could hear Zoë shrieking with laughter at something Callie had said. The splash of more wine being decanted between glasses.

I turned to face him. 'I'm sorry I let you down.'

'Joel.' Speaking gently, he reached out to me, resting the heel of one hand against my collarbone. 'We've done this.'

Over the years we worked together, Kieran turned out to be the kind of stabilising influence I hadn't fully realised I needed. Composed and tiller-steady, he was forever the firm eye over my most difficult clients and clinical decisions. When the hard work was done, we'd go out for a pint, games of pool. And I'd wait for the laughter lines that always shot to his eyes in the moments before he lost it. Because whenever they did, that was it: I'd be gone too.

There were lines on his face that came later as well. But they were furrows of frustration as he watched me move further and further away from the life I'd built. He never lost his cool with me, though. He just waited patiently, like he was watching for the current carrying me away to about-turn. For me to begin the long and painstaking swim back to shore.

I pulled out the top tray of the dishwasher, started upturning soup bowls into it. Kieran's hand dropped away.

'It was one time, Joel.' Like he needed to say it.

*One time too many.*

'What happened wasn't your fault.'

Some things you can be told a million times and never quite believe. Like when a bird flies from Alaska to New Zealand without once pausing for breath. Or a loved one slips away in their sleep, while the whole time you've been sitting next to them, holding their hand.

For a few moments the room was silent as outer space.

'Hey, can you do me a favour?' Kieran said then. 'It's to do with Callie.'

A wry glance. 'Don't cock it up?'

Kieran shrugged. 'Yeah. I like the way she looks at you. As if you're the only person in the room. That's a rare thing.'

I gripped the edge of the work surface then. Hoped Kieran wouldn't notice. 'Tell me how I can have that and not break it somehow.'

He noticed. 'It's actually pretty simple.'

'Enlighten me. Please.' Although he can't, of course he can't. Because he has no idea what drives my deepest fears.

'You just have to commit. Jump. Feet first, no holding back.'

We rejoined Zoë and Callie in the dining room after that. But for the rest of the night, all I could think was, *How the hell do you commit to a relationship when you're too scared to fall in love?*

# 39

## Callie

By the end of my first fortnight at Waterfen, I feel a rekindling inside me.

I've never been so connected to my body. I marvel at the twitch and flex of long-dormant ligaments as my bloodstream fires, my lungs expand and my muscles slowly wake. I am lifting logs and forking reed and wading through water, tasting all the while the coarse appeal of breathlessness. I laugh at the absurdity of sub-zero sweating, delight in the satisfaction of a scythe smoothly swung. And I begin to crave the opioid flood of exhaustion that comes at night, the swamp of analgesia as I sink into Joel's sofa and he rubs out the knots in my back with his thumbs.

I think back to how Piers used to tease me when I struggled to open jam jars or twist the cork from a bottle of fizz. *Just look at me now*, I tell him in my mind, as I load up the trailer with twenty-kilo logs, feeling the burn in my back as I pull weeds from the dykes, tossing them aside to form lofty piles, new high-rise homes for the mice.

Every day the world is turning between my fingers, above my head, beneath my feet. I feel a terrestrial sense of homecoming.


On Friday afternoon Fiona asks if I'm married. It's hard to tell out here, I suppose, where nobody wears their wedding rings for fear of them entering the ecosystem.

We're reed-cutting in the fen. I'm on forking duty with Fiona, following Liam and a couple of volunteers on the brush-cutters. The wind today has teeth, and it's angling the drizzle sideways, but the work's so hot and heavy I'm already down to just a T-shirt.

How alive and on-fire I've been feeling of late is because of Joel too, of course. I'm wildly attracted to him in a way that's utterly new to me. To feel his hands explore my body and his mouth against mine is like a daily dose of dynamite, deep inside.

But he still wants to wait, before we take it any further. He whispers as much to me sometimes when we're together, always breaking off before we reach the point of no return. *I don't want to rush this. Is that okay? You mean too much to me.*

So different from Piers or anyone else I've dated. And though, of course, I'm aching to have sex with Joel, at the same time the self-restraint and the holding back makes everything feel even more highly charged.

'No,' I say to Fiona. 'I'm not married.'

'Living with someone?'

Smiling, I push the hair from my eyes. 'Sort of. I'm dating the guy who lives in the downstairs flat.'

Fiona forks reed like she's slaying it for dinner. I envy her technique, perfected over many years – she can pick up double what I can, and I know I'm slowing her down. 'Yeah? What's he like?'

I begin to describe him – I love talking about Joel, tasting his name on my tongue. But as the words leave my mouth I start to feel almost childish, as though I'm telling her about an imaginary friend. Fiona probably thinks a month barely counts as a fling, let alone a relationship, though it's difficult to know for sure. There's much less opportunity for the nuances of body language when you're halfway through a workout in the middle of a reed bed.

'What does he do?'

'He used to be a vet.'

She doesn't respond for a few moments. Then, 'Wait. Joel. Not Joel Morgan?'

'Yes! Do you know him?'

She nods, still forking. 'He saved my German shepherd's life. She ate a baited fishing hook on the beach and swallowed it with the line.'

'Ouch. Poor thing.'

'I know. And she's not a fan of male vets, either. But Joel was excellent. Very calm. Lovely guy – I'll never forget how he was with her.'

I'm more than happy to accept a compliment on his behalf. 'That sounds like Joel.'

'I popped back a week later to say thanks properly, but they said he'd left.'

We carry on forking for a few moments. My breath is pneumatic and my palms are burning with blisters, even through my heavy-duty gloves.

'So what's he doing now, then?'

'Just taking a bit of time out,' I say, as smoothly as I can manage, like it's no big deal. 'He does dog-walking as a favour for some neighbours, the ones who can't get out much.'

'Oh. Well, tell him to hurry back. He was an amazing vet. One of a kind.'

'Thank you. I will.'

'And if he's as nice to people as he is to animals, I'd say you've got a good one there.'

A few hours later, I meet Joel in town for a post-work Chinese. I'm ravenous, having essentially just clocked off from a heavy weights workout, eight hours long.

'Dropped into the café earlier. Dot says hello,' he tells me. He's been going there less often now, since I moved on. He looks tired tonight

– he's not slept much this week – but still his eyes are warm and full, searching my face for the story of my day.

'You mean they've not filed for bankruptcy yet?'

'Hey, you've only been gone a few weeks. Corporate collapses take time.'

Smiling, I sip my water. 'Is it weird without me there?'

'A bit. Especially when Dot pulls up a chair at my table and refuses to leave.'

'Did you meet Sophie? Dot said she started this week.' Sophie is Ben's enthusiastic new hire who, according to Dot, has already suggested introducing a uniform, scrapping table service and – in Dot's words – 'recklessly violating the menu with avocado'.

Grace was allergic to avocado. It gave her cramps so severe she had to curl up in a ball.

Rubbing my leg with his foot, Joel fixes me with pitchy eyes. 'Yep. Though she's not a patch on you, of course. She's a bit . . . brisk.'

I frown, breaking open a spring roll with my fingers. Grace so wanted the café to be friendly, a place without code for the size of your coffee cup, where you could wander in solo without feeling self-conscious.

Sometimes you could hear her laughter from the street, spilling into the air like confetti. She'd be outside often too, chatting to passers-by as she wiped down the pavement tables. Grace gave her whole self to the world around her – like a lit window at night, you couldn't walk past somewhere she was and not feel warmed through.

When Joel asks about my day, I tell him Fiona's dog story. 'She says you saved her German shepherd's life, the week before you left.'

He refills our water glasses from the jug – mine first, then his own. 'Fish hook?'

'That's the one.' I find it highly impressive, to be honest, that someone could bring a fish-hooked dog in here right now and Joel would know exactly what to do.

'Nice dog, as I recall.'

'She doesn't normally like male vets, apparently.'

'Fiona or the dog?'

I smile. 'The dog.'

'Oh, she was all right. Dogs like that are usually just afraid.'

'Perhaps she knew.'

'Knew what?'

'That you were one of the good guys.'

He shifts in his seat, uneasy as ever with being paid a compliment.

'Fiona told me to tell you not to take too long out. She said you were excellent – her words, not mine. Although I do happen to think you're pretty excellent too.'

'Help yourself to chow mein,' he mumbles bashfully, gesturing with a chopstick. 'Don't let it get cold.'

# 40

## Joel

Callie and I have just emerged from our local garden-centre-cum-department-store, after spending an hour under optical and acoustic assault from a winter wonderland more illuminated than Blackpool. The place was Christmas on hallucinogens, a psychosis of over-stimulation. Tambourines disguised as sleigh bells, the latent fug of gingerbread lattes. An infantry of hard-selling elves.

I usually borrow my Christmas cheer from my sister. But when Callie discovered we could rent a tree from the garden centre, who'd then return it to the growers for reuse next year, she asked if I fancied entering into the spirit of things.

I said I did. But that was before I agreed to help manoeuvre a fir tree through a packed car park three days before Christmas.

'So this is why people buy fakes,' I gasp.

'But the plastic ones are so joyless.'

I jerk my head back towards the garden centre. 'I have never in my life been anywhere more joyless than that wonderland. On which I think they're overselling themselves, by the way.'

'I think you're just upset you didn't get to meet Santa.'

'I'm definitely not. He was wearing sunglasses.'

'Too many lights?'

I shake my head. 'Too many last night. He was hanging, one hundred per cent.'

Callie laughs. 'Poor guy. Imagine his torment.'

'I'm trying not to. Screaming kids. Christmas music on loop. The overwhelming urge to hurl . . . Now you come to mention it, sounds a bit like Christmas with my family.'

Finally we reach the car and lean the tree against the bumper. I put my hands at the small of my back, reel in fresh air. Steve would be horrified if he could see the full extent of my poor upper-body strength. I'm not sure I'd last five minutes doing Callie's job (unlike me, she's barely broken a sweat).

'Anyway.' She hooks a foot over the rear tyre, ready for our first attempt at launching the thing onto the car roof. 'The best thing about a real tree is that it will make your flat smell gorgeous.'

'Hang on, when did we say it was going in my flat?'

She smiles. 'Um, how do I put this?'

'You're thinking I'll never make it up the stairs, aren't you?'

She was right, actually. So we stand the tree in my living room's bay window. Adorn the branches with tinsel and trinkets, fairy lights, tiny chocolates. It makes me feel slightly wistful for times past.

My dad pretty much abandoned the idea of Christmas after Mum died. There were never any decorations, no special food in the fridge. The extent of the effort he went to was buying us all gift cards for the shopping centre in town.

I think everyone was quietly relieved when Amber was born and Tamsin offered to host. She'd inherited Mum's appetite for fun, after all. I knew things were looking up when she confessed, tipsy one night at mine, that she planned on 'tearing Christmas a new one this year'. The sentiment, at least, was bang-on.

We're finally out of shiny stuff. I step up behind Callie, cocoon her with my arms. She leans back on my chest, and I rest my face against the fragrant flourish of her hair. We stay like that for a couple of moments, trading heartbeats. *You must feel mine going crazy*, I want to say. *I'm falling for you, Callie.*

'You know,' she whispers, 'I'm starting to think . . . that this year, Christmas might actually be enjoyable.'

The sentiment's achingly familiar. 'Guess your last one was pretty rough.'

She turns to face me. Her eyes are nightlight-soft. 'It must be a hard time of year for you, too.'

'Easier since the kids came along. We just make it about them, now.'

She smiles. 'I bet they love it.'

'It's all down to my brother and sister, really. I just show up with the gifts. Let the children clamber all over me. Try not to drink too much.'

'Ah. The mantra of doting uncles everywhere.'

'Oh, and I referee as well. My lot almost came to blows last year. Charades.'

'What else?'

'The clue was "Good Vibrations" by the Beach Boys. My brother was drunk. Thought he'd try and make it dirty.'

She starts laughing. 'Oh, no.'

'Yeah, it was pretty funny. Me and Tamsin had our hands across the kids' eyes. Dad was stone-cold sober and appalled. They took it out to the garden in the end. I had to intervene.'

Callie smiles, like I've just told her a really heart-warming story. 'I'd love to meet your family.'

'It's a bit hard . . . spending time with them right now.' I try to swallow the sadness away, caught out by a tripwire of nostalgia that might soon mean something else to me entirely. Though I've not yet uncovered any evidence about my father, I still can't shake the potency of my dream. 'Knowing what I know about my dad – or think I know – I'm not sure how I feel.'

She gives my hand a supportive squeeze.

'But it's Christmas,' I concede. 'So I'll definitely see them at some point, and you should come.'

'I'd like that.'

We sit down on the sofa together. Across the room, the log fire roars molten lava. 'How about you? You going to your parents'?'

'We usually go to my aunt's on Christmas Day. It's a sort of family tradition. But my cousins are a bit obnoxious. I'm just not sure I'll feel fully . . . festive if I spend it with them.'

My heart back-flips as an idea lands. 'Well, hey, since we're both avoiding our families, why don't we spend it together?'

She kisses me. 'I'd love that. Just got to . . . let Mum and Dad know.'

'I don't want to cause any—'

'No, it's fine,' she says quickly. 'It won't be a problem, I promise.'

A few moments pass. Then she gets up and moves towards the window. Lowers the blinds, asks me to switch off the lights. I oblige.

She squats down and plugs in the fairy lights we've draped across the tree. A mini supernova erupts, washing the walls with a multi-coloured glow. 'Maybe this is the year we start seeing Christmas differently,' Callie whispers.

I push away all thoughts of the future, and the past. Because in this moment, tonight, I'm happier than I've felt in a long time. 'I think you could be right.'

# 41

## Callie

In the end, the only way I could square spending Christmas Day with Joel was by agreeing to go to Mum and Dad's for dinner on Christmas Eve so they could meet this mystery man of mine. I think a small part of Mum didn't believe he even existed.

Joel delighted them, of course. He asked all the best questions, laughed at Dad's jokes, spoke warmly to Mum.

Before we left, as Joel was using the bathroom, Mum whispered to me, 'Well, I think he's lovely, darling. Very down-to-earth.'

Meanwhile Dad, with his arm around Mum's shoulders, said, 'Nice lad.' And their shared smile in that moment was all the approval I needed.

I wake on Christmas morning to the sound of clattering in the kitchen. Heading in there, I find Joel barefooted in jeans and a checked shirt, staring blankly at a saucepan. Murphy's sitting hopefully at his feet.

Joel glances over his shoulder and smiles. 'I was going to ask how you like your eggs, but there's a flaw in the plan.'

I hop onto a stool. 'What's that?'

'I have no idea what to do with eggs.' He breaks into a grin, passes me a Buck's Fizz. 'Will this make up for it? Happy Christmas.'

Lunch goes more smoothly than breakfast, mainly because Joel's had the foresight to purchase the entire contents of a supermarket freezer aisle, so it's simply a case of dividing it between oven and microwave.

I get a twist of guilty pleasure as I think of what my mum – home-cooking's sternest advocate – would say if she knew we were cooking pre-roasted potatoes, gravy from granules and bread sauce from a packet that pings when it's done. Something about it feels deliciously rebellious.

When I tell him this on the sofa after lunch, Joel grins. 'If using a microwave is what you think of as rebellious, your parents got *very* lucky.'

'Oh, they still haven't seen my tattoo.'

'Don't think they'd approve?'

'You do remember my tattoo, don't you?'

For a few moments he holds my gaze, then says softly, 'Not sure. Maybe I need a quick reminder.'

My stomach is all flames as I smile and oblige, lowering my jeans to reveal the inked patch of skin. Joel leans forward and then his mouth is on mine, the most heartfelt of kisses, before he draws away, starts to trace the bird's outline with a single finger. At least a minute passes before slowly, gently, he works his hand down inside my jeans, inching lower and lower without once breaking eye contact. He lets his fingers brush the edges of my underwear again and again, a tease so prolonged it's almost unbearable. And then, finally, he moves his hand between my legs, whereupon I roll back my head and close my eyes, soar off high into the sky.

'I got you something,' he murmurs later, breath sweet and warm against my hair, one finger still tracing the ink on my hip.

He fetches a gift from beneath the tree. Sitting up, I feel his eyes on me as I unwrap it and break into a smile. It's a carafe and two tumblers, identical to the ones we drank from that night at the Italian restaurant, before my interview at Waterfen.

'So you can always be at a pavement café,' he says, 'somewhere in the Med.'

I'm touched almost to tears as I lean across and kiss him, whisper my thank-you.

'Oh, and . . . there's this.'

Unwrapping his second parcel, my fingertips make contact with the soft white cotton of a T-shirt bearing a black tractor motif and the slogan, *MY OTHER CAR'S A TRACTOR.* I laugh. 'Excellent choice.'

'Saw it, and thought of you.'

'You just happened across this?'

'Well, no. I had it specially made at the screen-printing place.'

Of course he did. 'Thank you. I love it.'

He takes my hand. 'All right. Come on. I reckon it's dark enough now.'

'Should I . . . be nervous?'

He laughs. 'I'd say, with me, that's never a bad policy.'

So with Joel's hand across my eyes, I walk as erratically as a minutes-old foal into the garden. I enjoy the sensation of it – the warmth of his palm against my face, guiding me safely through the blackness.

Eventually, I feel a cold clamp of outside air, and Joel removes his hand. I inhale sharply. The back fence is aglow with hundreds of fairy lights, our own tiny galaxy of fireflies.

'Now that . . . is an achievement,' I murmur, after a couple of moments. 'To make a criminally ugly garden look so beautiful.'

'Yeah,' he says softly. 'Doesn't scrub up too bad, does it?'

But before I can reply, he's taking my hand, leading me round to the shed. Hitherto redundant, its door is welded shut by an impenetrable crust of ivy. Now, though, there's a brand-new wooden nest box peeping out from beneath its eaves. 'Thought we might get some chicks to watch next year. Robins, maybe.'

*Oh, I've been waiting to meet you my whole life*, I think, as I pull him towards me for a kiss.

\* \* \*

Later, Joel goes out to walk Murphy. He takes him round the block sometimes, late at night – another way, I suppose, to help him ward off the wind-down towards sleep.

While he's out, I call Grace. I know it's crazy, but we never failed to speak on Christmas Day, so I need to dial her number, at least. That's been one of the toughest things about losing her – to train myself out of those everyday reflexes.

I imagine, as I always do, that tonight will be the night she'll answer. That I'll ask her where she's been all this time, and she'll tell me she got held up chatting to so-and-so, one of the infinite number of people who loved her.

But I'm greeted only by the flatline beep of her voicemail.

'Happy Christmas, Gracie. It's going really well here. I wish you could meet Joel. I think . . . I think you'd really like him. Anyway, just to say . . . I love you.'

And then for a little while I let myself cry, because I miss her, because it's Christmas.

# 42

## Joel

Deep into Christmas night and I'm still awake. Callie's nestled against me, twitching in her sleep like an animal dreaming.

I was overcome with anger, earlier. Not towards Callie, but myself. For not being able to take pleasure in the present she'd given me. The pamphlet and voucher, printed on paper so thick and creamy it seemed more like wedding stationery.

A wellness retreat for a week, food and expenses included. Just for me, not her. I guess she couldn't afford the package for two.

They major on sleep therapy, she told me, so enthusiastic she kept tripping over her words. (I didn't have the heart to remind her I've no interest in sleeping deeply, now or in the future.) They'll teach me how to meditate, practise yoga. She asked me again about Diana, mentioned perhaps getting in touch with Steve to get the ball rolling. She said next year could be the year everything turns around.

I'd forgotten what it was like to be hopeful, optimistic about change. The idea of it seems so strange now. Like viewing somewhere I once lived from high up in space. I think again about the time and money I've devoted to experimenting, over the years. To the lavender and white noise. The sleeping tablets and hard booze, and God-knows-what-else I've ordered online. And I've come up short every time. *This problem has no solution, Callie.*

For a while now the drug of spending time with her has been numbing my fear of consequence. But (well-intentioned as it was) her gift has only really reminded me that my dreams are going nowhere.

After she fell asleep, I googled the retreat on the iPad. My heart seared silently in two: the whole thing cost her almost as much as three months' rent.

I turn to my nightstand and pick up my Christmas card from her. Two polar bears rubbing noses, signed inside with love.

I stare at the word until it burns a hole in my brain.

# 43

## Callie

We lie in on Boxing Day morning but chink the blinds, suffusing the room with glacial light. I'm running an unhurried fingertip across Joel's bare chest, mapping the contours of his muscles, the lovely landscape of his bones. His notebook's lying closed on his lap, a pen tucked into the elastic that holds it shut, so I guess he must have had a dream last night.

'How are you feeling about today?' I ask him. I've tried and failed to picture being in Joel's position, unexpectedly having cause to question my paternity.

'Good. I'm looking forward to them meeting you.'

Eight whole members of a brand-new family – as nerve-racking as a panel interview for a job you really, really want. I think of Joel impressing my parents on Christmas Eve, and hope I can do the same.

Still. 'No, I meant . . . about your dad.'

He turns to look at me. 'Well, aside from anything else, ten hours in his company could be challenging.'

I have a feeling he's skirting the subject. It's too painful, perhaps. 'Surely he won't give you a hard time at Christmas.'

'I'm sort of hoping you being there will help.' He grimaces. 'Although I should probably warn you, my brother and his wife are going to fall out after lunch.'

'Oh, do they—'

'I dreamt it,' he clarifies quietly. 'Something about rationing the kids' chocolate intake. But if we do the washing-up, we can duck it.'

'Good idea.' But though I'm smiling, inside I'm blown away – his foresight still astounds me every time.

Unsurprisingly, Joel's not dwelling on it. Instead he's exhaling, glancing at the clock on his nightstand. 'We should probably get ready.'

'Soon,' I whisper, letting one fingertip linger against his bare chest before winding it slowly down towards his stomach.

'Yeah, you're right,' he murmurs, as his eyes flutter closed. 'I mean, it's Christmas. No need to rush.'

The contrast between Joel and his siblings, when I meet them, is hard to ignore. Not only in mannerisms, but appearance too – darkness against copper, like a bloom out of season, a rare bird on home soil.

I notice a subtle shift in his demeanour when we arrive. As I watch him crouch to kiss his nieces and nephew, shake hands with Neil and clap his brother on the back, there's no trace of unease. It reminds me just how practised he is in keeping his feelings to himself.

Tamsin's brought lunch – a mountainous feast of leftovers from yesterday, crammed with flavour in the way food is when infusion's had a night to work its magic. As soon as we sit down, Joel's foot finds mine beneath the table while, above it, our gazes tango. *Thank you*, he seems to be saying, *for doing this*.

As we eat there is some gentle jibing, mainly from Doug. 'Don't plants have feelings too?' is how he reacts to the news I'm vegetarian like his brother. And then, when I'm talking about using chainsaws, 'Bet you run away when the tree falls over, ha.' Later, though, there's a settled breath of silence around the table when Lou asks about my parents, and I reveal my dad used to be an oncologist.

After lunch, as Doug starts handing round chocolate selection boxes, Joel and I escape to do the washing-up. Once in the kitchen, I can't help listening out for evidence of an argument – and, sure enough, it comes. Raised voices, slammed doors and, at one point, the sound of someone running upstairs.

Eventually there's talk of going for a walk, I guess in the hope that the fresh air will calm everyone down. So I offer to show Joel's family a nearby field where I happen to know you can watch red kites flying in to roost at dusk. The kids seem disproportionately excited by the idea, until Tamsin explains to them with a smile that, no, we're not going out to fly kites. I feel awful, as if I've just proposed a trip to the cinema, then downgraded it to the supermarket. Still, I'm sure the birds will win them round.

A twilight tide laps the corduroy furrows of the field, chasing down the sinking sun. At its far edge, against the sky's fiery shoulder, the birds are circling above a copse, gliding on the breeze. They spread like smoke, growing in number from two to eight then twenty. Twenty-five. Thirty. With Joel by my side, I crouch next to Buddy as he strokes Murphy's head, share the tricks and twists of the kites' winged wizardry. Spellbound, Buddy watches them carried on the hands of the wind, like specks of soot in the gloaming, until slowly, one by one, they begin to spill from the sky.

And that's how I spend Boxing Day night – introducing Joel and his family to nature's subtle majesty. I couldn't have asked for more.

## 44

## Joel

It was scarily straightforward in the end, to open the door on an entirely different life. I could easily have missed it: that quick glint in the darkness of Dad's loft, where I'd been sent to fetch two extra chairs before our Boxing Day lunch.

It was the dust bag for Mum's one concession to indulgence, a large leather shopper the colour of marzipan. That holdall accompanied her everywhere. Quick trips to the shop, bus journeys into town. Long drives to see our grandparents in Lincolnshire. And, eventually, her final trip to hospital.

I noticed the dust bag's crest. It was identical to the gold-embossed one I knew so well from the shopper. Lifting the thing up, it felt heavier than it should have. So I opened the dust bag, and then the holdall inside.

A heart-puncturing onrush of scent. Decades-old leather, memories mildewed-over. In the bag were the things she'd taken with her for her last-ever stay in hospital. He'd never unpacked them.

Her cotton-soft nightdress with the candy-pink floral print. I held it up to the loft's strobing strip-light, remembered how my chin had rested against its neckline the very last time I hugged her. A toothbrush with the bristles splayed (very Mum, so fastidious about hygiene she'd make her gums bleed). And her glasses. I turned them over in my hands. They used to nestle in the contours of her face so perfectly, seemed to magnify her kindness somehow.

And the book she was reading too. It was a thriller by an author whose name I'd never registered, though I do remember she'd been trying and failing to get through it for months. One of the pages was turned down, about two-thirds of the way in. It must have been the place she'd reached when she died.

I flicked fruitlessly through it, then landed on the inside front cover. And there it was.

Later, I drive us home. Callie's feet are on the dashboard, Santa socks on full display (cheers, Dad).

The traffic's heavy tonight, but I don't mind. I'd like to stay in this car with Callie for ever, going nowhere fast. A slow burn of good feelings, always.

It's been a decent day. The chaos of Christmas and hyperactive kids meant I could at least take a break from worrying about the situation with Dad. Plus I'm buoyed by the thought that, after dreaming last night, I'll likely be dream-free for the next few days. The feeling's as close as I ever come to relaxation.

'Want to know a secret about Doug?'

'Always,' Callie says.

'He's got a phobia of trees.'

She laughs, which is what most people do when this comes to light.

'He's afraid of branches falling on his head. Works from home in high winds. An official dendrophobe, apparently.' I look across at her. 'So all that ribbing about you running the other way while you're chain-sawing was just machismo. Bluster.'

She smiles sleepily, rests her cheek against the rain-mottled window. 'I thought as much. He's quite alpha male, your brother, isn't he?'

I nod, then frown. 'It doesn't work like that anyway, does it – you cut and run? Is that where the expression comes from?'

'No, isn't that to do with boats? Anyway, if you've made your cut right, you should know exactly where a tree is going to fall.'

'Good,' I say, a bit too emphatically.

Up ahead, the road becomes a river of red neon.

Callie puts a hand on my leg as I brake for the traffic. 'Joel, do you ever think . . .' Her voice is languid now in the warmth of the car. 'I mean, have you ever thought of your dreams as being . . . you know . . . a gift?'

'A gift?'

'Yeah, I mean . . . being able to see the future is pretty powerful.' Her fingers play against my thigh. 'That night with the water main, in town, really made me think.'

'What did you think?'

I feel her look across at me. 'That in some ways your dreams put you in a position of privilege. Knowing things that no one else does.'

'No.' My voice is stiff. 'I've never really thought of them like that.'

'Sorry,' she says, after a couple of moments. 'I didn't mean to diminish what they do to you.'

The traffic moves. 'No, it's . . . I know what you're saying.' As always my mind's muddled with conflicting feelings. 'Anyway . . . thank you for today. Meeting someone's family for the first time is kind of intense.'

'I made you meet mine. And I had a great day – your family is lovely.'

'You were a total hit with the kids. Sorry about Buddy.' He refused to be parted from Callie (not me) as we were leaving. We could still hear him screaming as we got into the car.

'Don't be. He's adorable. So are Amber and Bella. I've always loved kids. It was a real toss-up between going into childcare or nature conservation when I left school.' She laughs. 'Funny how I ended up doing neither in the end.'

'Doesn't matter. You're doing it now.'

'True.' She sighs happily. 'So what was it you said you found earlier, in the loft?'

I feel the heat of stolen treasure in the pocket of my coat. 'A book, in my mum's hospital bag. With a phone number and an initial inside.'

'What's the initial?'

'W.'

'Anyone you know?'

'Don't think so. I looked up the area code – it's Newquay. I've never been. None of us have, I don't think.'

'Maybe she got it from a charity shop. Or borrowed it from a friend.'

'Yeah, maybe.'

I turn past the surgery. Glance at it quickly, as if to check it's still standing. We're almost home.

'Do you think my dad's curmudgeonly?' I say.

'That's a good word. Curmudgeonly.'

I smile.

'No. I think he's very straight-talking. But he looks at you with love in his eyes.'

Is that really what Callie sees? My own perspective is so distorted now. 'That's probably the dull glaze of disappointment,' I say. 'How many times did he mention I'm no longer a vet?'

'It's not disappointment. He just doesn't understand.'

'Maybe. Pretty sure he wishes he had two of Doug, though.'

'How long have you felt like this?' She sounds crushed on my behalf.

'My entire life. It makes me think . . .'

'Go on,' she urges, after a beat. 'What does it make you think?'

'That maybe it's true. That I'm not really his son.'

# 45

## Callie

A couple of weeks into the new year, I go to Cambridge for a hen do. Alana's an old colleague of mine from the paint-tin company, though she was one of those transient types with ambition, which explains how she's now several corporate ladders away from where we started out.

A financial-services head hunter, she must have forgotten I no longer work at the factory, because twice she presses her business card into my palm and insists she can hook me up. The first time she did it I thought she meant drugs, and was almost too nervous to unfold my hand.

The hen's one of those events where I can't work out if everyone secretly despises each other. There are six bridesmaids, but they're phone-checking more than they're mingling, and the maid-of-honour booked cocktail punting – which would have been fine if it wasn't mid-January and Alana wasn't terrified of water. So we call it off and find a bar instead, where the maid-of-honour heads straight to the loos to flip out, forcing the rest of the bridal party into protracted negotiations to appease her.

I organised Grace's hen do, off-road buggy driving near Brighton, an attempt to recreate – at least in part – her fabled Dubai dune-buggy experience. Afterwards there was curry, then pints in a proper pub, the two things Grace said she always missed most when she was travelling. And, to top off the day, it rained – and it was the right sort of rain, British rain. Cold, unforgiving, *Four Weddings* rain was Grace's preferred precipitation type.

She leant over to me halfway through a pint of John Smith's. Her mascara was running by then because we'd been laughing so hard. I remember making a mental note to buy her some of the waterproof stuff so she didn't end up looking like a Halloween bride at her own wedding. 'I want you to get married, Cal.'

'What?'

'I *so* want you to get married.'

'Why?'

She looked around the pub. 'So I can do all this for you.'

Putting a fingertip to the apple of her cheek, I wiped away some of the black. 'When I meet the man I want to marry, you'll be the first to know.'

I hadn't even met Piers back then, not that marriage would ever be on the cards between us. And before that I'd really had only flings, a few dates that had progressed before going invariably nowhere.

It still makes me sad to think of it now, that Grace never will get to meet the man I want to marry.

The hen do goes from bad to worse when everyone starts to bicker about whose idea the punting was, so I sneak outside to call Joel.

'How's it going?'

'Horribly, actually. It's the most passive-aggressive hen do I've ever been on.'

'That doesn't bode well for the big day.'

'Tell me about it. I'm thinking of giving them the slip. Fancy being my co-conspirator?'

I hear him smile into the phone. 'Always. Think they'll mind?'

'Alana's limbering up for a brawl with her maid-of-honour as we speak, so I doubt it.' I hesitate. 'How does a night in a low-end hotel sound to you?'

I'm booked in at a budget place on the outskirts of the city. The maid-of-honour chose it, for the discount on the group booking, but

Alana turned purple when she saw it. It's the kind of hotel that could only really pass for decent if both your eyes were closed and you liked all your surfaces to come with a slightly sticky sheen.

'Low-end, you say?'

'It's very poorly rated on TripAdvisor.'

'Say no more. I'm there.'

An hour or so later, he knocks on my hotel-room door.

'Wow,' he says, when I open it. 'You look incredible.'

Excited for an opportunity to escape my wellies and fleece, tonight I made an effort by way of a black dress and fairly extreme heel, curling my hair, giving my eyeliner a sizeable flick. The effect's diminished now – my shoes are off and my hair's lost its bounce – so it's extra-nice that Joel still thinks I look lovely.

'I'm trying to work out if it's good or bad that the guy on the front desk didn't bat an eyelid when I bowled straight past him,' Joel says, putting his arms around me.

I smile and kiss him hello. 'I'd say good. Definitely. Thank you for saving my night.'

'Oh, I'm really just here for the free biscuits.'

I wince. 'Sorry. There was only one shortbread, and I got a bit peckish.'

'Ah. How was it?'

I laugh. 'Stale.'

Together we sink onto the mattress. Or, at least, we try to, before it becomes apparent that the bed frame represents something of a death-wish to the coccyx.

Joel grimaces bravely. 'Oh, they really don't want you to lie in here, do they?'

'I'm sorry. This place is worse than I thought. Barely worth half a star.'

He tries and fails to indent the mattress with his palm. 'No, you're being too harsh. This, for example, is a very handy feature. Saves setting an alarm for the morning, see?'

The bed's really two singles – the hen party was an odd number, and when the maid-of-honour asked, I said I didn't mind not sharing. So I've pushed them together, which has only made the set-up feel even more shambolic than it did before.

I survey the room again. 'Urgh, easily the most soulless place I've ever stayed. Are those curtains . . . *plastic*?'

'Now, soulless is a tad unfair.' He leans over to kiss me. 'Wait here a moment. Don't drink all the UHT milk. Be back in two secs.'

Fifteen minutes later he returns, sticks his head around the door.

'Shut your eyes. That UHT had better be where I left it.'

I laugh and comply, moving my hands to my face so I'm not tempted to peek. My senses sharpen as I feel his footsteps, hear the bite of a lighter and a tap released. Then follows the sound of something tearing, a tinny trickle of music. Finally a click, and behind my eyelids, nightfall.

'Okay. Open your eyes.'

There are tea-lights on the desk now, a wonky bunch of flowers in a mug. Music's playing low on his phone, and in his hand a champagne bottle is ready to pop. He shrugs sweetly. 'Turns out the soul's self-service.'

'How did you . . . ?'

'Well, I stole the tea-lights from the dining room. But I bought the champagne, then asked a friendly maintenance man if he'd care to donate his lighter to the good cause of romance. Oh, and I swiped the flowers from the lobby.' He winks. 'Because who doesn't love a nylon carnation? Sorry – they're a bit dusty.'

I'm not sure if anyone's ever made me laugh and cry at the same time, but that's what I'm doing as I climb off the bed and go over to him, roping his waist with my arms. 'You've just turned the worst night ever into the best night ever.'

Our faces are close now. We're almost-but-not-quite kissing.

'Want to make it even better?' he whispers.

'Yes.' The word is molten on my tongue. 'I really, really do.'

He bends to kiss me, and it's a kiss that's full of fireworks, of weeks-long anticipation. Now, exhilaratingly, both our bodies are on fast-forward – in an instant our hands are everywhere, grasping at limbs and pulling off clothing and tugging at hair. Fully charged, we undress in what seems like seconds before collapsing in a tangle on our cobbled-together bed. And now he's peeling back the silk of my underwear before that final dizzying moment – after so many weeks of waiting – that I know we've both been anticipating for so long.

'Callie,' he gasps, his face against mine, 'you're everything to me.'

'You are to me too,' I breathe back, spun over with ecstasy. I want to tell him I love him – because I do, I've known it for weeks – but instead I shut my eyes, feel him start to move inside me, and right here, right now, this is everything I ever wanted.

## 46

## Joel

'Oh, no. Rufus hates Valentine's too.' Callie laughs as Iris's dog cocks his leg against a bus shelter. The poster on it is advertising a rom-com film, release date 14 February.

'Why? Who else hates Valentine's?' I ask.

'Only everyone I know, fanatically.'

'Fanatical hate. Sounds reasonable. Why, again?'

'Oh, you know, because it's a cynical corporate ploy and commercial schmaltz. A symbol of rank consumerism. Did I tell you Esther holds an anti-Valentine's party every year?'

I try not to laugh. 'But I thought Esther had her very own library of Hugh Grant DVDs.'

'She's not anti-love, just its commercialisation.'

'Because those high-budget films are resolutely not-for-profit.'

'She would say she chose to buy them—'

'All thirty of them.'

'—whereas Valentine's is thrust upon her. Us. The world.'

'So what do you do at these parties, then – burn roses? Flush chocolates down the loo?'

Callie stops to untangle Murphy's lead from around his front leg. 'Not exactly. But they are intense. They're very . . . immersive.'

'What – you sit in a circle and chant about how much you hate Valentine's?'

She straightens up, face zipped closed. It's impossible to know where she falls on this one. 'Well, you have to hold a view, at least. And there's always a theme. Last year was zombies.'

'She having one this year?'

'Yep. The theme is heavy metal through the ages.'

'Wow.' I rub my chin, attempt nonchalance. 'So who would you go as? If you went to the party, I mean.'

Her mouth wriggles, like she's wrestling a smile. 'Not sure. I haven't said if I'll go yet.'

She doesn't, in the end. Instead she calls dibs on the evening two weeks in advance. Asks me to meet her at the café, eight o'clock on Valentine's night.

It's a first for me. Fully buying into Valentine's. If you'd asked me in the past, I'd have sided firmly with Esther on swerving the thing altogether. The idea of celebrating love has never been straightforward for me.

But then I met Callie.

I arrive fifteen minutes early, with a bottle of wine and a bunch of flowers. (I say 'bunch'. It turns out no one wants to look too try-hard on Valentine's Day: all the normal flowers had sold out by the time I made it to the shop. So I've ended up with a bouquet the size of a small planet, containing fifteen different types of flower and sprouting exotic greenery like it has its own microclimate. But I could hardly turn up empty-handed, so there you go.)

All the blinds are down at the café. But light is flickering inside, inviting as a woodland cottage.

She laughs when she opens the door. 'I can't see your face.'

'Yeah. Just so you know, I fully realise flowers this ridiculous should be a deal-breaker.'

She peers around the bouquet. 'That depends on who's carrying them.'

'A disorganised idiot. Sorry. I left it too late. Sling them in the bin if you want. It's quite an experience, walking down the street with them on Valentine's. There was heckling.'

'You might be the only person I've ever known who'd apologise for bringing me flowers.'

'Hey, they warrant it.'

'No, I love them.'

'Well, there are enough here to start your own botanic garden, I suppose.' I set the bouquet on the counter. 'You look beautiful, by the way.'

Her hair is a dark twist on top of her head. She's shimmering in a sleeveless metallic top, the fabric fluid as smelted gold.

'Thanks. I had my themed outfit all ready for Esther's party. So I thought, why not?' She makes a ta-da with her arms.

Gold top, gold earrings shaped like flamingos. A dusting of gold on her eyelids. It takes me a moment. 'Heavy metal through the ages . . . you're gold.'

'I decided to subvert the theme.'

'Glad to hear it.' I glance down at my own outfit. Plain blue shirt and black jeans. Safe as you like. 'But I feel a bit underdressed now. You should have told me.'

'Why – what would you have come as?'

I crouch down to say a quick hello to Murphy. 'Well, I do have a gold lamé jumpsuit. But I keep that for special occasions.'

'More special than this?'

'All I can say is, Let's Boogie Night at the Archway does take some beating.'

'Now that I would pay to see.'

'This feels like stepping back in time.' I straighten up, take off my coat. 'Turning up at the café, looking forward to seeing you.'

The shyest of smiles. 'I always looked forward to seeing you too.'

On my table by the window, where I sit whenever I'm here, Callie's arranged candles, cutlery, glasses. There's an ice bucket chilling a bottle of wine, and Ella Fitzgerald in the air.

'I asked Ben if we could come here for the evening. I thought it might be nice, since it's where we met. Sorry if it's cheesy.'

I kiss her. 'Not a bit. It's lovely.'

'You think? I promise I won't serve you espressos and eggs on toast.'

'You cooked?'

'Well, no – not with a panini press and a microwave. I talked nicely to the bistro down the road.'


We dig into goat's cheese tarts, fat and brown from the bistro's oven. Our glasses are full, the candles glowing romantically between us.

'You know,' I tell Callie, 'at Christmas, when I was poking around in my dad's loft, I found a receipt from my mum and dad's honeymoon, thirty-four years ago.'

Her face gives way briefly, as if by 'receipt' I mean 'abandoned puppy'. 'What was it for?'

Through the café's speakers, Ella defers gracefully to Etta James.

'A posh meal out in Christchurch. Guess what the total came to? Three courses, and drinks.'

A smile. 'Twenty quid?'

'Eight pounds thirty-nine.'

'That's amazing. Like . . . holding someone's history in your hand.'

'Mum was sentimental. She kept stuff like that. She showed us the bus ticket once that Dad bought her at the end of their first date.'

'She was an old romantic.'

'She tried, I guess. Dad was much less soppy than she was.' I smile, shake my head. 'You know, Valentine's was always a bit of a nightmare for us at the surgery.'

'No, really? How come?'

My mind becomes a memory. 'Dogs breaking into chocolates, cats chewing flowers. Wrapping paper and sticky tape in stomachs. Candles knocked over. The list was endless.'

Callie sips her wine, lowers the glass. I could look into her eyes all day and not once want to blink. 'Ouch. That's enough to make anyone a Valentine's cynic.'

'Almost,' I say, 'but not quite.'

After dessert, I take her hand. 'This was an amazing night.'

'It was.'

'It scares me, how great this feels.'

Our fingers become a knot. Tight, inextricable. 'Why?'

'Because I never . . .' She knows some of what I feel about love. But not my decision to avoid it, the romantic kind, for ever. And the timing's hardly right to fill her in on all that tonight.

'I love being with you, Joel,' she whispers.

'I love . . . being with you too.'

'Actually,' she says, more boldly, 'I love *you*. I'm not afraid to say it. I love you, Joel.'

Maybe reflexively, I look down at the table. She's sketched a heart into the chocolate sauce on the dessert plate we shared, bookended it with our initials.

The *C* goes first.

'I love you,' she whispers again, like she needs to make sure I know it absolutely.

'You're scared to say it, aren't you?'

I thought Callie was asleep. I'm trying to stay awake, half listening to a TED Talk while the other half of me looks at the book I discovered at Dad's. I've been wondering what to do with it for weeks. Should I act on what I found, or leave the past where it lies?

I could track down the address for the landline, find out who lives there. But then what? Now I've got the chance to take things further, I feel suddenly afraid. Because of what I may find out. Because of what it may mean.

At first I don't catch what she says. I slide my headphones down around my neck.

'You're scared to say, *I love you.*'

She's wearing my ancient Nike T-shirt, hair bunched up around her face. She looks so sweetly vulnerable that, for a moment, I wonder if she's talking in her sleep.

'I'm not scared to be with you.' Not strictly true. But I am at least curious about the future now. I'm beyond complete paralysis.

Still, love . . . love is the thing I don't yet dare succumb to.

'You're afraid to love me. You think it'll be bad luck if you say it.'

'You know how I feel about you.' But even as the words leave my mouth, I'm cringing inside. Contender for the lamest half-sentiment in the English language?

I know Callie wants me to explore this. She's asked me once or twice about following up on that appointment with Diana. About booking my place at the retreat she gave me for Christmas (futile though I'm sure it would be). And of course I don't blame her.

Maybe I shouldn't even be sleeping with her, if I can't so much as tell her I love her.

I reach for her hand beneath the covers. The room is cold this Valentine's night, but her skin feels duvet-warm.

'I know you love me.' Her voice winds down to a murmur. 'You don't have to be scared.'

*I'm not scared*, I think. *I'm terrified.*

## 47

# Callie

With the sliding of the weeks, spring is trickling in, and the world is getting brighter, lighter. After so long spent flattened by winter, the earth seems to be developing dimensions. Its lungs are slowly filling with the fledgling dawn chorus, and foliage is fattening its limbs. Butterflies become stray sparks among explosions of ochre daffodils, and at Waterfen, the breeding season is blooming. I love hearing the chiffchaffs whistle me in to work, as redshanks reel and lapwings hassle harriers in an ever-expanding sky above my head.

Though there's lots that I love about winter, after weeks spent clearing dykes and waddling about in waders it's a relief to feel the earth hardening beneath my feet as the light lengthens and the sun slowly warms, like an egg about to hatch. The air has shrugged off the scent of soil and stagnant water, swapping it for the sweetness of April blossom and nectar. And as nature repairs itself, so do we – we set down the chainsaws and brush-cutters, and begin mending fences and servicing machinery, enjoying the gentler jobs of tugging thistles from the ground, mowing meadows. I become consumed by breeding-bird surveys and spend hours inclining my eyes to the sky, or tuning my ears towards elongated undergrowth as I wait to catch a flash of flight, the telltale turn of a feather, a mellow segment of song.

In our nest box on the garden shed, a pair of robins has set up home. Joel and I see the female occasionally, a delicious dart of orange, her beak to capacity with dead leaves and moss, bedding for her eggs.

It's a privilege to watch her, like she's trusting our company and the little wooden home Joel chose. I hope we can catch the chicks fledging in a few weeks, clumsy bundles of brown wobbling their way into the world.

And down by the river, the willow tree is growing full and fleshy with greenery. I climb it sometimes after work, just for five minutes, to feel the warmth of its bark and its comforting bulk, to be close to Grace again, examine how our initials have weathered yet another winter. With every changing season, I worry she's going to fade away, like an autumn leaf absorbed by the earth, patterns tarnished and colours dulled, until its character and complexity are simply dust in the dirt.

I always tell her I love her, up there in that tree. It feels a bit like saying it to Joel, in that I'm waiting for a reply that will probably never come.

We're off to a book launch, a friend of Zoë's, when I decide to broach the subject. I've been thinking about it for a while – since Christmas, really – and although it's a risk and I know it could backfire, I'm going to do it.

I'd been planning to ask him tomorrow at breakfast, a long, lazy window over coffee for him to consider the question, no pressure. But as I'm curling my hair cross-legged in front of Joel's bedroom mirror, and he's standing behind me buttoning his shirt, it seems so opportune. Because here is a snapshot, right now, of how we could be – at home and comfortable, together.

'Don't freak out,' is how I begin.

*Oh, good one, Callie.*

In the mirror, Joel smiles. 'Wouldn't dream of it.'

'I've been thinking . . .'

He nods, like, *Keep going.*

'. . . about whether or not . . . I mean, would it make sense . . . ?'

And then I clam up completely. I can't find the words, now that his reflection is looking at mine, those carbon-dark eyes pulling my gaze to his.

He waits. 'Still not freaking out . . .'

I take a breath and jump. 'I was thinking perhaps we should move in together.'

In the mirror, he stays still. The seconds stretch. 'Is that . . . what you want?'

I catch his eye. *Oh, you're freaking out now.* But I decide to be brave anyway, give him the nod that I feel in my heart. 'Yes. You?'

'I hadn't really . . .'

'It's too soon,' I surmise.

'No, not like that—'

'Don't worry,' I say gently. 'You don't have to say anything just now.'

The tiniest part of me is hoping he'll protest and offer me a yes or a no, but he doesn't. He simply says, 'All right. Thanks.'

We're crammed into the under-ventilated bookshop where the launch is, so when Joel takes my hand as the speeches are coming to a close, whispering that he needs a breather, I'm secretly relieved.

'Do we have to buy a copy?' he says, once we're out on the pavement, both pleased to be in the open air. It's been warm today, and the early-evening breeze across our faces is still streaked with sunshine.

Softly, I shove his arm. 'Yes! It's a book launch. Why else are we here?'

'I just don't quite *get* it. Is it sci-fi or erotica?'

I smile. 'Just think of it as erotic sci-fi.'

He laughs. 'Aha. Knew there was a catchy term for it.'

'Well, of course. Robots need love too.'

Post-work shoppers move past us on the street. There's a couple eating ice creams, a guy sauntering along in a T-shirt and Ray-Bans. The sight of them feels headily optimistic in a way that seems unique to spring, like birds building nests or buds becoming blossom.

'I'm sorry, Cal,' Joel says suddenly. 'About earlier. I honestly . . . God. I handled that really badly.'

Oh, the moving-in. It was a mistake, I see that now. 'No, I sprang it on you. Don't—'

'I've been thinking. About what you said.' He clears his throat. 'How would you feel about . . . moving into mine?'

My heart sprouts wings. 'Into yours?'

'Yeah. I mean, don't get me wrong, I love your flat, but would mine make more sense, with the garden and Murph, and . . . ?'

I can't hold back my grin. 'Are you sure? You don't have to—'

'I know. But this feels right.'

'It does.'

'As long as you're cool with . . . you know. Everything.'

'I wouldn't have asked you, otherwise.' Yes, I lose him first thing in the morning occasionally, to fairly intense note-taking and sequences of monosyllables. If we spend the night together, we rarely fall asleep in tandem – often he's out with Murphy, long after I've gone to bed, or he simply stays up to avoid sleep. And sometimes our rest is disturbed, if a dream wakes him. But so what? No imperfection can touch how much I love him.

He dips his head now, sets his mouth close to mine. 'This is all assuming you don't secretly hate my flat, of course.'

'I secretly love it more than mine.'

'So we're doing this?'

'We're doing this.'

For a split-second before Joel kisses me, it seems as if he wants to say something else. But as I hold my breath to hear it, his mouth meets mine and the moment moves on.

# 48

## Joel

Callie's face is flecked with dirt, sprigs of hair poking free from her ponytail. She's leaning against me on the sofa, warmly content at the end of a sun-filled day at Waterfen. I'm happy for her, after so many weeks spent weighed down by winter. Fingers frozen, clothes clotted with mud. Not that she ever complained.

Beyond the window, the Friday-night light is vacating the sky.

Murphy has rested his chin on my sister's knee, trained his eyes patiently on her face. Like he knows exactly what she's here to say.

'I'm pregnant.'

I'm on my feet straight away, wrapping Tamsin in my arms. I hope she can't tell that, though my joy is real, my surprise is manufactured. Because I've already met Harry in my dreams. Kissed his flawless forehead, wondered at his pinky newness. Felt steam-rollered by love.

'You're the best mum I know,' I murmur into her hair. 'Congratulations.'

I open an arm for Callie to join the hug. The three of us stand knitted together, laughing and wiping away tears.

While Callie's getting more drinks, I ask Tamsin how far along she is. (I already know she's around eight weeks, of course. It never stops feeling awkward – being intimate with someone else's private information before they are.)

I smile as she confirms it. 'Neil must be chuffed.'

'Oh, you know Neil. If we won the lottery he'd just say, *Cool.*' She carries on stroking Murphy. 'But, yes. I think this is one of the only times I've ever seen a tear come to his eye.'

'So, a Christmas baby.' Callie hands Tamsin another herbal tea. (I got it in especially, as soon as I dreamt about Harry.) 'That's exciting.'

Tamsin hoots. 'Remind me of that on their birthday next year, and all the years after that. Shocking planning.'

'Will you find out what you're having?'

'No. Want it to be a surprise.'

I shoot Callie a smile, look quickly away. It seems all wrong that we know the best part (*You're having a boy, and you're going to call him Harry*) seven whole months before Tamsin will. Though already I can feel a familiar undertow of fear: *I only ever want to dream good things about him.*

Tamsin sips her tea. She's wearing a cream-and-navy-checked cotton dress, a pair of those sandals with woven soles. The sunglasses on top of her head hold back her copper waterfall of hair. 'Mum was about eight weeks with Doug, I think, when she married Dad.'

There's a slightly awkward picture of it somewhere. Me, not yet two, sandwiched between my parents standing stiffly on the register-office steps.

In my mind, the awkwardness mutates. Did they look uncomfortable because the child on Mum's hip was another man's? Did Dad know anything for sure? Or did he sense it subconsciously?

*What happened, Mum? Why did we never talk about it?*

'This one was conceived out of wedlock,' Tamsin says to Callie. She winks at me. 'We think that's why he's a bit . . . you know. Errant.'

My blood ripples. *Conceived out of wedlock – or someone else's son?*

Resting a hand against her still-flat stomach, Tamsin looks at Callie. 'I can hardly believe it, you know. Neil and I have been trying on and off since Amber was a year old. I honestly didn't think this would happen for us again.'

'We're so happy for you,' Callie says.

'I just hope . . .' Tamsin falters.

My gut twists. 'Don't,' I whisper.

'But it's been such a long time coming. What if something—'

'It won't.'

'You don't know that.'

'I do. I do know.' More slowly, my eyes repeat it for her. *I do. I do know.*

'How?'

Callie grips my hand. I force my expression into neutral. Today isn't about me, it's about Tamsin. 'Just trust me, okay?' I say. 'Everything will be fine. I promise.'

It seems to be enough. She nods, just once. Uses the tissue Callie's passed her to dab away stray tears. 'I guess this is what happens when you want something too much.'

'No such thing as too much.'

She manages a smile. 'So what about you?'

'What about me?'

'Not *you*. You *two*. Fancy making me an auntie?'

I keep hold of Callie's hand but deadpan the question. 'Tam, it's been six months.' Callie's not even moved in yet officially. But she has told Steve. And molehills of her stuff have started springing up across the flat. I glance at her herbs and house plants, lined up now on the windowsill. She brought them down yesterday, along with her window-box, and the sudden burst of greenery felt like a flurry of fresh air. This week she's got plans to fill the patio with flowerpots, plant them with summer blooms for the bees and the butterflies.

'Stranger things have happened,' Tamsin says.

*They have. And they do. All the time.* And then, unexpectedly, a thunderbolt of a thought. One that involves Callie being pregnant, and me rapturous with happiness.

Despite everything that frightens me about love, I can't help thinking it would be a strange kind of wonderful. To look down at Callie's belly, and know our baby son or daughter was snugly cocooned inside it.

But 'Sisters,' is all I say. I cast the idea aside. Bury my face in my mug.

After Callie falls asleep that night, I take Murphy for a turn around the block. While I'm out, a message springs to life on my phone. It's from Melissa. She asks what I'm up to, says it's been too long. Tells me not to be a stranger.

It's not the first time. She got in touch at Christmas, then again in February. On both occasions I drafted replies, then failed to press send. Illogically, messaging her to finish things felt almost more cowardly than saying nothing at all.

But now I know that was stupid. I have to message her back. So I do, as neutrally as possible. I fill her in on how things are going with Callie, say it's probably best we don't message any more. I want to be gentle, but I can't be ambiguous.

I lay it all out, press send, feel ashamed. About the way I treated her, and about how things turned out between us. I hope that, one day, she'll be able to forgive me.

# 49

## Callie

In early June, Joel suggests celebrating my official moving-in day with stone-baked pizzas in town. They're so big we can barely finish them, but we still head down the road to a dessert bar afterwards.

'We deserve this after all those boxes,' I assure Joel, over mountainous portions of chocolate torte and cheesecake. 'Sorry I had so many. I could have sworn I didn't move in with that much stuff.'

'No worries. Reckon I'll be aching in some interesting places tomorrow, though.'

'Me too. I think my muscles have shrunk since the weather's been nice. I've only been topping in the tractor lately – I've barely broken a sweat.'

'Sounds all right for a day's work.'

'Well, yeah. It's not bad. Enjoy it while it lasts, I guess.'

Joel digs into his cheesecake. He looks handsome as ever tonight in a shirt of light denim, sleeves rolled up to his elbows. 'Exactly. Got to be better than winter, surely.'

I mull it over for a moment, shear off a corner of chocolate torte with my spoon. 'I don't know. Winter's just got something about it. Like . . . there's beauty in the bleakness.' I smile and shrug, because I can't really explain it. Most normal people detest winter, with its drab skies and sideways drizzle, the constant urge to shiver. 'Winter seems wilder, somehow. And I love that. Windswept landscapes, weather-beaten outposts – they're my bag.'

Joel grins. 'Nothing wrong with being niche.'

Smiling, I describe holidays from my childhood, how Dad and I were always exploring outside, going for hikes, collecting little artefacts en route. 'That's why I was drawn to Chile, I guess. It's that idea of the great outdoors – being really plugged in to the wilderness.' I go on to tell Joel about how great Latvia looks, enthusing afresh as I recount Liam's love for it.

'So how come you've never done it, Cal?' Joel's forehead crimps with a frown. 'I mean, you've got all those books and dreams about the stuff you want to see . . .'

Though I know it's not intended as a criticism, I shrink back in my seat a little. 'It's just never seemed like the right time. I'm cautious by nature, and my world's always been fairly . . . safe, even as a kid. And when I did try channelling Grace, doing things a bit differently, it all went horribly wrong.' I think back to my tattoo, to the horrible impulse-fringe disaster.

'No reason not to keep trying.'

'I know. And I would like to go to Chile and see that bird one day, if only to prove Dave and Liam wrong.'

'It's that rare?'

I draw the spoon from my mouth. 'It's a kind of . . . enigma.' In my mind, a shimmer of memory surfaces. 'My dad saw a rare bird once. Me and Mum were at the shops and Dad rang her in a flap, begging her to bring him a camera. So we had to jump in the car and race home to pick one up, then speed half an hour down the road to find him at the lake by the bypass . . . Mum was weaving in and out of traffic . . .' I laugh. 'I mean, I'm no birdwatcher, but I was only seven, and it was pretty exciting. I've never forgotten it. I felt like I was in some sort of TV police drama.'

Joel holds my eye. 'Well,' he says, 'maybe it's time for you to find a rarity.'

'Not now I've landed my dream job,' I say firmly. 'Travelling's going to have to wait.'

What I don't say is that it's not only about the job, of course. It's the idea of being parted from Joel – my own wonderful discovery, a longed-for rare find right here on home soil. It would feel so wrong to turn my back on him now. Even if only for a couple of weeks. Even if it was to chase a dream.

Back at the flat, I'm fumbling with the keys in the outside door when I feel Joel's hands around me, his smile on my neck. He mumbles something I don't catch, so I pull back, ask him what he said, and he tells me I can do anything I want to do, never to think I can't.

We fall into the hallway together then, and he presses me against the banister, our breath quickening through mouthfuls of kisses. We begin to tug at each other's clothes, not even bothering to shed our jackets, just unbuttoning and unzipping enough to make it happen. Somehow we find our way down onto the carpet, eyes locked and lustful, bodies trembling with longing. And as we start to move, I feel the full atomic weight of my love for him, as though my heart has just exploded into a thousand shooting stars.

# 50

## Joel

I've agreed to be Callie's plus-one at the wedding of Hugo, an old friend of the Cooper family.

It didn't take long to work out why Callie's parents had swerved it. It turns out moving to Switzerland after university and setting up in private equity hasn't done too much for Hugo, personality-wise. Twice after we arrived at his Jacobean manor-house reception he called Callie by the wrong name, before asking if I was with catering. (I assumed he was referring to my slightly too-sharp suit. But since he appears to lack even a knock-knock sense of humour, no one could really be sure.)

Hugo's new wife Samantha seems okay. (If a little clueless, since she's willingly marrying the douche-bag. Good luck to her, I guess.)

My dim view of Hugo dimmed even further when we were seated at a table alongside all of his most ancient relatives. Not one of them is compos mentis, so Callie and I have been left to amuse ourselves. Still, that's no bad thing. Sorting out our vegetarian food, for example, is proving to be an interesting intellectual challenge.

'There must have been a mix-up. It's meat.' Callie's talking through her teeth, staring at the miniature beef Wellington on her plate. Her smile looks like it's been programmed onto her face.

All day, I've not been able to stop looking at her. Wanting to kiss the contours of her collarbone, press my fingers against its smooth hollows. She's wound her hair into a soft bun, and her dress is a sweeping creation in vivid green. The earrings she's wearing are leaf-shaped and studded with emeralds, a gift from me once I'd seen her dress.

A couple of weeks ago I walked into the bedroom while she was trying on outfits. This particular one ended up on the floor, a silky shamrock pool, only moments later.

But I really can't think about that while surrounded by octogenarians. They're an unpredictable lot. One of them has just started swaying violently out of time to the string quartet, whose current number sounds alarmingly similar to Britney Spears's 'Toxic'.

Callie looks around for a waiter. 'I did tell them we were vegetarian, in the questionnaire.'

'Questionnaire?'

'Oh, yes. We had to fill one in, like a job application. And their gift list was positively autocratic.'

I swig my wine. 'How many stag dos did you say Hugo had?'

'Three.'

I lean closer. 'How many wedding days?'

'Two. This one, and one in Zürich.'

'How many honeymoons?'

'Two. One maxi, one mini.'

I raise my glass. 'Let neither of us ever become a Hugo.'

'Cheers to that.'

We chink and drink. 'Have I told you yet how incredible you look in that dress, by the way?'

'Six times. Seven, if you include that night it ended up on the floor.'

'I mean it, though. I'm not just brazenly trying to seduce you.'

She slides a hand to my knee. 'I don't mind. Have I told you yet how dapper you look in that suit?'

I smile, thinking back to stumbling suited-up with her into the department-store fitting room last week. As we fumbled with zips and buttons, I half wondered if we might get arrested. But then I very quickly realised I definitely didn't care.

A waiter appears. 'Can I help?'

Callie leans up, whispers to him that we're vegetarian.

He freezes as if bowled over by her beauty, which I can just about forgive him for. 'I'm afraid we received no requests for vegetarian food.'

*None? For a wedding reception of over a hundred and fifty guests?*

We wait for him to come up with something, but all he does is stare at us. He's clearly expecting Callie to say it's not a problem. That we'll just become carnivores for the day. Or maybe he's imagining they're making eye contact.

'Oh,' is all she says eventually.

He has the audacity to wink at her before walking away.

'Wow.' I smile. 'Something about awkward vegetarians really does it for him.'

Her forehead puckers. 'How do you mean?'

I lean forward. 'I think he liked you.'

'No, he was just confused.'

Oblivious, as ever, to how beautiful she is.

Callie bends closer to her plate, prods the beef Wellington with her fork. 'What do you think we should do?'

'I think we have only one option.'

'Go on.'

I raise my freshly filled wine glass. 'Liquid lunch.'

'I think you mean wedding breakfast.'

'Don't even get me started on why they call it breakfast.'

In the end we skip the food entirely and end up being first on the dance floor as soon as the lights go low. Callie's laughing, leading me by the hand. Her smile is like a bulb in the darkened room.

We dance, we sing, we laugh till we're dizzy. The perfect, perfect day.

At midnight we flee, wired and wild-haired. It's a clear night, the air potent with summer. Callie's shoes dangle from her fingers as we cross dampened lawns towards the wing where we're staying. Her dress swings as she strides over the dew-darkened grass, my palm locked in hers.

I look at the star-pocked sky above our heads, draw the moment to my chest. *I don't think I've ever been so happy as I am right now.*

Callie's talking about a book she's reading on wild swimming by a nature writer she loves. One man's quest, apparently, to swim his way through the British Isles. 'It just makes me want to jump into the nearest river. And it's the right time of year, isn't it? You can't get much closer to nature than actually swimming in it.'

We reach the top of another vast lawn. 'Well, now.' I pull her to a standstill. 'Look.'

'What?'

'Your ideal opportunity.'

At the bottom of a natural bowl in the lawn is an ornamental lake the colour of midnight, inviting as iced lemonade. The air is hot, and so are we: even to me, the idea seems delicious.

'Are you serious?'

Dropping her hand, I shrug off my jacket. Let it fall to the ground, then bend down to untie my shoes.

'Joel, we can't.' She glances around. 'They might escort us off the premises.'

I start unbuttoning my shirt. 'Then we'd better be quick.'

She breathes out a laugh. Looks over her shoulder, once. 'Okay.'

'Okay?'

'Okay,' she repeats, suddenly bold. She reaches over her shoulder, tugs down the zip to her dress. Pulling off the straps, she lets it drop like liquid onto the grass. She's beautiful in bottle-green underwear, her skin marked with maple-brown tan lines from long days spent outdoors. She snakes across to me, takes over unbuttoning my shirt. We're laughing, my undressing now a team effort.

I kick off my shoes while Callie unzips my trousers, flicks open my belt. And now we're running hand in hand in our underwear down the sharp slope towards the lake. Kinetic with momentum, neither of us stops before hurling ourselves into the water. It's deep-sea cold, a smack of liquid nitrogen. As we resurface we're hooting and gasping for breath, kicking wildly. We splash and thrash, like fish fighting capture. But though we're drenched and ridiculous and struggling to fill our lungs, our eyes collide and we start laughing again. We laugh so hard, we must be in danger of drowning. So we begin to kick instinctively for shore.

Eventually our hands meet mud. We haul ourselves onto the bank, membranes of pond weed attached to our calves. We're both winded, unable to speak.

Rolling onto our backs, we look up at the stars. We're panting like animals, brains and bloodstream recovering from the shock.

I'm first to speak. 'How was it for you?'

'Mind-blowing.'

I turn my head. Her hair's heavy with water, a glistening dark mass on the grass, like seaweed on sand. 'Really, that good?'

'We're going wild swimming,' she says, 'you and me. We'll join a club. Do they have wild-swimming clubs? We could do this every weekend, just us, together.'

I lean over and kiss her, run my hand down her body. Across that beautifully bizarre tattoo that makes me adore her all the more. 'You cold?'

She shivers as I unravel a weedy rope from her leg. 'Yeah.' Then, 'I want this to last for ever. This moment, right here, with you. I love you so much.'

My skin shudders and twitches.

She tips her face up to mine. 'Don't let me say anything else.'

I push a wad of wet hair away from her face. 'Why not?'

'Because I don't want to scare you.'

I want to tell her that nothing she says could scare me. But I'm not sure it's true.

The distant palpitation of the disco bassline drifts over from the Great Hall. A DJ from Italy, apparently, helicoptered in.

Callie slings one hand behind her head. Angles her face to the darkness, like she's searching the sky for the Milky Way. 'Because it is scary. How strongly I feel about you.' She announces this lucidly, voice crisp in the warm air.

'I know.' I bend down to kiss her again. 'It scares me too.'

# 51

## Callie

Next day, the morning sunlight is bleach-hot on my skin, a cutlass through the parted curtains. Joel's notebook is lying by his hip, so I guess he must have had a dream last night. He doesn't tell me unless he wants to, and I don't always ask.

'I've found you a club,' Joel whispers.

'Hmm?' My head feels like over-kneaded dough. I've just about managed to make us both a cup of sachet coffee with scant UHT before climbing back into bed.

'A wild-swimming club. Look.' He props his iPad up in front of me. 'They meet every Sunday morning throughout the summer.'

I shut my eyes. 'Oh, God. I remember.'

'Do you remember the lake?'

I groan.

'And what you did when we got back to the room?'

My eyes reopen, gunshot-fast.

'When you decided to hang your underwear out of our window to dry?' he prompts.

'Oh, no. Did it . . . ?'

'Oh, yes,' he says, like he's trying not to laugh. 'I went down there in my dressing-gown to try to salvage it.'

'Please, *please* tell me you succeeded.'

'I'm sorry, Cal,' he says, and he's really laughing now. 'I got the bottom half, but your bra's hanging off a gargoyle. There's no way of reaching it.'

'Oh, my God!' I sit up, a throb of planetary alignments taking place inside my skull. '*Please* tell me you're joking.'

He's beside himself. 'I wish I was.'

'Then we have to go. We have to check out right now!'

Joel climbs out of bed and moves over to the sash window, raises the lower frame and sticks his head through the gap. 'Yeah, I think you could be right. Sun's up. There's no hiding that beauty now. The green really stands out against the building. Still, on the bright side, it's drying well.'

I hurl a pillow at him, but despite my varying dimensions of suffering I'm laughing. 'We seriously have to leave.'

'Don't you think we could style out breakfast?'

'No!'

'How about a quick rendition of "Agadoo" from the shower? You sang it so beautifully last night.'

Abject horror floods my mind. 'We are going, right now.'

We pull in at a café on the way home, a dual-carriageway pit-stop where they serve only instant coffee in one size of mug, but fifteen variations on a fried egg.

Beyond the window, the road is a racetrack, the traffic motion-blur.

Joel looks tired, but in a good way – the kind of tired that reminds me of dawn kisses in bed, or late nights with music and candlelit conversation.

By contrast, I'm not too sure I want to know what I look like right now. I was so desperate to leave the hotel that I bypassed the hairdryer entirely. Ditto make-up – except for a touch of mascara and a reassuring squirt of perfume.

'You know you were the hit of the dance floor last night?' I say to Joel.

'In terms of most-mocked, you mean?'

'No, I'm serious! For a self-confessed hermit you had some good moves.'

'Hey, you're not so bad yourself.'

'Come on – I've got two left feet. Didn't you see me nearly crash into the band?'

He finishes his egg roll, wipes his fingers. 'They didn't seem to mind. I think they were flattered by your boundless enthusiasm.'

'Mildly alarmed might be a better description.'

'And you were very popular with the kids.'

That much was true. At one point I found myself surrounded by a gang of under-tens, teaching them how to do the Twist. After some gentle heckling Joel joined in, and for the next twenty minutes or so we were all dancing together – just us and a bunch of sugar-crazed kids – when a thought popped into my mind: *We'd be great parents. We'd have so much fun. How many children should we have – two? Five? Ten?* I was too happy and tired to restrain my imagination, so instead I just ran with it, enjoyed the fantasy – got drunk on it, almost.

I trace lazy patterns on Joel's forearm with my index finger. 'Where did you learn to dance?'

'My mum, actually. We'd have a little boogie together in the living room after school, while we were waiting for Dad to get home from work.'

A friction burn in my throat, then my eyes. 'That's so sweet.'

'Ah, you should tell my brother that.'

I look down at the table. The Formica is diseased with yellow stains that bring to mind the residue of a previous diner's curry.

Joel sets down his mug and rubs a hand through his hair, releasing a brief aquatic haze of hotel shampoo. 'You know, for such an idiot, Hugo actually managed to pull off a pretty great party.'

'Want to know what I think?'

Through coffee steam, he holds my gaze. 'Go on.'

'I think we *made* it great. I mean, I'm pretty sure you and me could have fun in a silage field.'

'Well, I've never actually tried. But we could find one on the way home if you like.'

Thinking of the lake, I shake my head. 'No more rampaging through open spaces.'

'Yeah, we're much safer in the car.'

I carry on sketching shapes against his skin. 'Be great to do this more often. It was okay, wasn't it? Being away again for the night?'

'Yeah,' he says, sounding almost surprised, like he'd not really thought about it until now. 'It was.'

'So . . . would you like to? Do this again?'

'Yeah,' he says, understated as ever. But as he flips his hand over to grip mine, his eyes are a silent movie, a love story without words.

# 52

## Joel

And then, just one month later, it happens. Exactly as I always feared it would.

The dream is harrowing, so real it sends a bolt through me.

Callie's whispering me awake, but I'm already there. I shake her off, roll away. Bury my face in the mattress.

*Please not Callie.*

*Not like this.*

*No. No. No.*

# PART THREE

# 53

## Callie

*I still think about us, Joel. Probably more than I should. The smallest of things brings you back to me.*

*I went swimming at the lido last night, and it took me back to that time you and I jumped into the lake together. A couple of weeks ago I baked some drømmekage, started crying halfway through. I've been invited to a hen do, and all I could think about was Cambridge, and the amazing night we spent there.*

*I've even started reading that sci-fi novel — remember? — and it's actually quite good! You should definitely give it a go. (Page seventy-nine made me laugh out loud, by the way. Try doing the voice in your head when you read it. You'll know what I mean when you get there.) Hopefully you'll still have your copy when you're reading this. If not, you can have mine.*

*It's been so long since we've laughed together. It keeps me going, sometimes, thinking about all the fun we had. The way you lit me up inside, every single day.*

# 54

## Joel

Outside, the sky is swollen with early-August storms. I'm standing at my bedroom window, waiting for the sound of the shower cutting off.

*This is worse than I ever thought possible.*

Above my head, floorboards creak. A new tenant, Danny, has replaced Callie upstairs. He works long hours, is barely around. Occasionally he surfaces to offer pleasantries in passing, before vanishing again like a ghost.

Already, Callie moving in a few weeks ago feels like a series of soon-to-be-forgotten memories. Her dad helping us lug boxes down the stairs, lecturing me about security as if I hadn't already lived here for a decade. Champagne on the sofa together that first night, a gift from her parents. Our favourite foods finally side by side in the fridge. Shared showers, pots of coffee. Watching Murphy chase balls from the back step. My fingers exploring the newness of her things. Her eclectic collection of trinkets and knick-knacks, to her an embarrassment but to me intriguing as treasure.

I blame myself entirely. I should never have let myself relax, put off calling Steve. Because maybe if I'd taken some kind of action, none of this would be happening.

# 55

## Callie

Eventually I make it out of the bathroom, stopping still by the chest of drawers that's spilling over now with my things. I like that, or at least I did – the not-quite-fitting, the idea we've already outgrown the space since I moved in, that we can't be contained by the world around us.

'I'm sorry,' Joel says, from where he's standing by the window like he could happily jump out of it.

Remembering what happened last night makes me want to cry all over again. It's too painful to think about the tears that seeped around the edges of his eyelids as he slept, how he gulped my name over and over like he was running out of air.

'Joel . . . this isn't a sorry thing.'

He hesitates – on the brink, it seems, of flooding the room with feeling. But at the last moment, he steps back. 'Can you cancel tonight?'

My mind chases its tail. *Tonight. Tonight . . . ?*

Eventually, I catch up – we've arranged dinner at Ben's, with Esther and Gavin. 'Of course.'

'I just don't think . . .' But his sentence goes unfinished, so I remain unenlightened as to what he doesn't think, let alone what he does.

'Joel, please don't do this.'

'Do what?'

'Shut me out.'

We just look at each other then, assaulted by sadness and powerless to stop it.

'I mean it when I say I love you,' I whisper.

'I know.'

'Not just you, but everything about you.'

He seems almost dazed with pain as, outside, the sky's stomach rumbles.

'It was about me, wasn't it?' I say. 'Your dream last night.'

His eyes are quite round now, dark as an owl's. He regards me wordlessly for maybe a minute, like I'm walking away from him and all he can do is watch me go.

His voice, when it comes, is gentle. 'You're going to be late,' is all he says.

## 56

# Joel

She's back just before six. I've spent most of the day outside, walking the dogs, then sitting in the garden with Murphy. As the clouds waltzed across the sky, I wondered what to do. What I can possibly say.

I found my gaze landing on Callie's flowerpots, filled now with bees and a frenzy of butterflies. Her window-box is erupting too with summer flowers, the blooms plump with nectar. They embody her so perfectly: splashes of colour against grey, life supplanting inertia.

Our robin chicks fledged ages ago, their nest box deserted now. But for a while the male was still prominent, warbling gutsily from next door's plum tree. Callie told me he was teaching his babies to sing. Who knows if that's true, but I liked the idea of it: a centuries-old song sheet, written on the air.

'Hi.' It's a tired *hi*, a breath exhaled. She drops her bag and puts her arms around my neck, kisses me. Sweat has formed a fine white tidemark on her face. She tastes of salt and sadness.

'How was your day?' I murmur into her hair.

'Awful,' she tells my T-shirt. I'm almost relieved, but only because I don't want to be pacified. Assured everything's okay when it's not. I'd rather she got angry, called this out for what it is.

A disaster, and one that's entirely down to me.

'I couldn't stop thinking about your dream.'

'We need . . .' I can barely get the words out. 'We need to talk about it.'

She pulls back from the hug. 'We do. Can we go somewhere?'

I'd prefer not to have this conversation in public. But since I'm about to take Callie's life apart, it seems only fair we do this on her terms.

We decide on the rooftop bar overlooking the river. It sounds nicer than it is. Pricey, and improbably positioned on the top floor of an office block, it's always been less popular than you might expect. The view's good, though the subject's nondescript: Eversford boasts neither distinctive architecture nor quirky charm. Instead it's a humdrum patchwork of offices and high-rises, church spires and roof tiles. Eras muddled together, character undefined. Still, we can see the river, silver in the sunlight like a seam of liquid mercury. And the morning's storms have passed now. The sky's wide and clear, a pale blue parachute above our heads.

There are more trees, too, than I ever realised. They erupt between the buildings like little green volcanoes.

We take a corner table against a tall glass panel, presumably there to stop us plunging to our deaths. I need to think clearly, so I order a coffee, but Callie opts for a glass of white wine. Can't say I blame her. The floral dress she's changed into is so incongruously cheerful it's almost painful to look at.

She's first to speak. 'You dreamt about me last night, didn't you?'

A nod, but no words. My mouth's become rubber.

'You were saying my name over and over. You were so upset. God, it made me . . . so sad to see you like that.'

My chest constricts: it's my turn now. But even after a full day of running everything over in my mind, I still have nowhere near the words I need to make sense of this.

'Cal, I'm scared that what I say—'

She cuts me off. 'Then don't. You don't have to say anything. I'll ask, and all you have to do is nod, or shake your head.'

I breathe in. Or maybe it's out. Her resolve has thrown me slightly.

Across the table, her eyes find mine. 'Sometimes words are the hardest part.'

'Tonight they are.'

It only takes three questions in the end. Three questions, and a matter of moments.

'Did I die?'

*Yes.*

'Do you know how?'

I force myself to picture her again lying lifeless on the ground. No injuries. No blood. No clues. *No.*

'Do you know when?'

*Yes.*

We're quiet then, eyes picking up where our mouths leave off. Hoots of laughter drift over from a nearby table as, down on the ground, Eversford's traffic moves. The world has refused to stop turning. Life rumbles heartlessly on.

I know I have to speak. Outline what scant plan I have. 'There may be something—'

'Wait.' She covers my hand with hers. It feels curiously cold. 'Don't say any more.'

'But if you—'

'I mean it, Joel. I don't want you to say any more. You need to listen to me.'

So I stop talking, train my eyes numbly on her flying-swallow necklace instead. It's the same one that so struck me all those months ago, when I first met her at the café.

'I don't want to know anything else. Nothing about what you dreamt. I don't want to know what you saw, or when it will be. Ever. I *never* want to know. Okay?'

I stare at her. The tears in her eyes have been swapped for steel. 'Cal, I don't think you—'

'I do.' Her voice cuts through the sweet air of the evening. She withdraws her hand from mine. 'I do understand. All I know, right now, is that I'm going to die. I don't know how it happens, or when it will be. I'm no different to anyone else here tonight.' She glances at our waiter, then a raucous group of drinkers a couple of tables away.

'But *I* know.'

'Yes. And if you told me, you'd be giving me a terminal illness. Right here, right now.'

'Cal,' I say, 'how can you not want to know this? There may be something we can—'

'But there isn't. You've already said you don't know how it happens. You're as helpless as me, Joel, and you know it.'

'Callie.' My voice buckles with emotion. 'Please let me just—'

'No, Joel. This is my decision. I can't deal with a death sentence.'

I think of my mum, denied the precious time she wanted to prepare. That all my fears about love since she passed away are playing out now with Callie is almost more than I can bear. 'Do you really mean that?'

She nods, just once.

I take her hand again. Grip it hard. Maybe I'm trying to squeeze it full of sense. 'I can't live with me knowing and you not.'

'You want to unburden yourself?'

'No, it's not that.' But then I wonder if it is.

'You know what this means, don't you?'

'It means too many things.'

'It means you love me.'

Trust Callie to see the upside. There's even the softest of smiles on her face. 'Callie—'

'You can say it, now. The worst has happened. You don't have to be afraid any more.' And then she leans across the table, kisses me.

But as I kiss her back, all I can see is her body on the ground.

There's not a single twinge of movement, and her skin is cold as milk.

## 57

## Callie

In the week following Joel's dream I struggle to maintain normality. Instead of joining Fiona and Liam in the yard at lunchtimes, I make my way down to the river and climb the old willow alone. Conversations with my colleagues have already assumed a different colour – it's hard to chip in to discussions about last night's TV, or the rise of the discount supermarkets, when Joel and I are spending our evenings blighted by discord over the date of my death.

On Friday night, flagging from hours of pushing an industrial mower through meadows, I climb the tree, then remove my boots and socks. Blending in with the branches as walkers pass beneath the bare soles of my feet, I feel the pleasing sensation of blood rushing through my calves to my toes. Dragonflies buzz by, tiny shiny helicopters, and from the marsh on the opposite bank comes the primal ache of calling cattle. All day the air has been warm and still, static with summer, save for the hot popping of exploding seed heads.

I can only think of Joel – warm-blooded and full-hearted, his self-contained demeanour masking a fever of agonies within. I try to imagine him telling me what he knows, the seismic repercussions as the ground-swell passes through him to me. I consider the ways in which our lives would change, and what we would become.

There's no knowing who I'd turn into, whether the information would be toxic, alter me entirely. It's no accident, surely, that we're biologically programmed to be ignorant of this stuff.

I envisage weighing out my days, how the chemistry of every experience would change. Perhaps I'd jettison everything dear to me, and all the while, the end would be drawing near, winding ever closer like the dark finger of a tornado.

I just don't know how Joel and I could hope to build a life for ourselves, with so much to fear.

But Joel carries all that with him already, and he has nowhere to stow it. If I truly loved him, maybe I'd be encouraging him to say what's in his heart, agreeing to share the load. Because love isn't only about the easy choices, the simple solutions – it's about the hard graft and the tough calls, the sacrifices you don't actually want to make. *Nothing worth having ever comes easy*, my dad always says.

I stare down at the furrow of my initial next to Grace's in the tree bark before scrabbling for my phone and dialling her, waiting for the beep.

'I'm just in our tree, thinking about you. Well, thinking about Joel, actually. I wish I could talk to you, Grace. I'm pretty sure you'd know what to do – or, at least, you'd know what to say. I think you'd tell me to stay blissfully ignorant and keep living for the moment. Am I right?

'You always said you wanted to die doing something you loved. Well, I'm sorry you didn't get to do that. But you died without knowing it was coming, which has to be the next best thing, at least.' I shut my eyes. 'Look, Grace, just give me a sign or something, will you? Just something – anything – so I know what I'm supposed to do . . . You'd have adored him – Joel. I know you would have loved to see how happy he makes me. It would have made you happy, too, I think.

'So, don't forget, all right? Just . . . give me a sign.'

Pressing call end, I lean back against the rigid spine of willow bark for a few more moments. Stupidly, I'm already looking out for it – the signal from my friend to let me know she's heard me. But the air remains quiet, and the river stays still.

## 58

## Joel

A fortnight since my dream. Two weeks of paralysis. I've been turning the pages of Callie and me over in my mind, like a book I was always afraid to open. I know I'm at risk of losing her, but I can't just wait for the tide to take her. I have to try everything.

Steve's out of breath when he answers the phone. 'Joel?'

I'm walking Bruno. It's only now I think to check my watch, and it's nearly nine p.m. 'Sorry, mate, were you—'

'Just some push-ups before bed.' He punches out excess breath like an army sergeant. 'You're alive, then.'

'Yeah, sorry, I've been—'

'Ignoring my messages.'

I feel momentarily like a client he's chastising for dropping out of boot camp. 'I think I'm ready to see Diana.'

'That was a long time coming.'

'Yeah, sorry.'

'And you're serious?'

'Very.'

'How's the – you know – dreaming been?'

'As bad as it could possibly be.'

He goes quiet for a few seconds. 'This to do with Callie?'

'I can't explain right now. Just . . . can you set it up for me?'

'Of course, mate. Of course.'

As I hang up I realise, perhaps too late, that friends like Steve are hard to come by.

## 59

## Callie

Sitting up, I let my eyes find the clock. It's two a.m., and I've been jolted into consciousness by the buzzing of my phone.

Joel is comatose next to me. I reach over with my free hand and gently slide the headphones from around his face. He must have fallen asleep with them on.

I stare at his shut notebook for a moment, imagining the words it must contain about me. I consider how easily I could change the course of my own future just by turning a page.

'I checked Grace's voicemail,' Ben says. 'What was all that about you and Joel?'

*Oh, no. He checks her messages.*

'Sorry,' I whisper, performing a tiny face-palm. 'You can just delete it.' A couple of weeks have passed since I left that message, and I'd forgotten about it.

I climb out of bed and pad through to the living room, Murphy at my heels. The night air is congested with humidity, like a swimming-pool changing room. I perch between the pots on the windowsill and tilt the blinds so I can see the night sky.

'I need to know you're okay,' Ben says.

'I'm okay.'

He waits a beat. 'You were right, you know.'

'About what?'

'What you said in your message. When people say they want to die doing something they love, what they really mean is they don't want to know it's coming.'

It was true that Grace had always said that, which is why I sometimes wonder if she should have died while she was climbing Table Mountain with Ben, or running that half-marathon in Lanzarote. I still don't know the answer – though I do know she shouldn't have died at the hands of someone else as she was rushing along that awful backstreet, late for Pilates. But I guess that's life's disquieting reality – you don't get to choose.

I curse my own insensitivity. 'I'm sorry, Ben. I didn't think.'

'Cal, tell me to mind my own business if you like, but . . . what's going on with you and Joel?'

His question, though well-intended, feels sharp as a dart. 'It's complicated,' is all I say, a feeble oversimplification.

'All right. But let me just say this. If you've found true love, Cal, don't let it go. You have no idea . . .' He skips a breath or two. 'None of us know what we've got till it's gone. Yes, it's a cliché, but that's because it's true.'

My mind a cyclone, I think of Joel. 'Ben, can I ask you something?'

'Sure.'

'Do you really believe . . . do you believe it was better Grace went quickly? Or do you wish you'd had more time, you know, to . . . prepare?'

'Prepare like . . . cancer?'

'Sorry,' I murmur. 'You don't have to answer, if you don't want.'

'No, it's all right. If I'm honest, Cal, where Grace was concerned, I'd have to say ignorance was bliss. Yes, it was a shock when she died. Brutal. It felt as if that bastard had ploughed into every one of us. But I don't think Grace could have handled a death sentence.'

'That's what I thought.'

'You're not ill, are you?' Ben's voice becomes a plucked string of fear.

'Not as far as I know.'

'I might be wrong,' he says then. 'Maybe Grace would have preferred a few months' notice. Maybe she'd have made even more of her life, if she'd known.'

I smile. 'I don't see how that's possible.'

'Yeah, me either.'

# 60

## Joel

Diana's invited me to meet her at the university where she's based. It's mid-September, just before the students return. I try to see that as a good omen. A fresh term, a new page. The chance to begin again.

'Take a seat.'

The office we're in is cramped and airless, with breeze blocks for walls and not enough light. The whole place feels distinctly correctional, so I angle my chair towards the door. Just in case.

She introduces herself, asks how she can help. Though not unfriendly, her tone's brisk and she speaks at a clip. She must be mid-fifties, yet she doesn't seem nearly eccentric enough to be a professor. She has an ergonomic chair, for one thing. And with those Buddy Holly glasses, black skinny jeans and canvas high-tops, she could easily have just clocked off from brainstorming straplines at an ad agency.

'Steve said he spoke to you. About my . . . condition.'

Unnerving: she's scribbling on a notepad already, not looking at me. 'You say you're psychic?'

'Well, I don't "say" I am. I am.'

She nods just once. Doesn't comment.

I shift awkwardly in my very un-ergonomic chair. 'Is this . . . anything you've come across before?'

'Not personally. Can you tell me a bit about what you experience?'

In my mind again, a cliff edge. That doctor at uni, a sneer on his flaky lips. But I'm here now. So I take a breath, remind myself Steve's already told Diana everything. And still she agreed to meet me.

I start with something simple. My dream last night. Tamsin, Neil and Amber on a half-term trip to the local safari park in six weeks' time. (Lions and tigers no credible threat, though monkeys cause minor damage to Tamsin's car. I guess I'll use YouTube to help forewarn them nearer the time.)

I keep talking, move on to Luke and my mother. To Poppy and the car accident, my sister's pregnancy. I tell her about the not-sleeping and the tortured nights. About my dad. And then I tell her about Callie, about what I know will happen a few short years from now. Unless Diana can help me. Unless she can do something.

'I only dream about the people I love,' I reiterate.

The scientist in her flinches.

'Steve mentioned something about . . .' I look down at my notebook. It's open in my lap, for prompts. '. . . my temporal and frontal lobes. And my right hemisphere?'

'Have you ever had a head injury, or a serious illness?'

'Never.'

'Does anything ever slip through the net? I mean, do significant things happen that you *haven't* dreamt about?'

'Yes. All the time. I can't see everything. There's so much I don't know.'

'Have you ever dreamt anything that hasn't . . . come true?'

'Only if I take some sort of action. Do something to stop it happening.'

She doesn't delve into what that might entail, asks instead about my medical history.

'Well.' Eventually she looks down at her notes and circles something (I'd kill to know what). 'I'll make some enquiries with my colleagues. We could potentially explore funding to carry out some research, subject to ethical approvals.'

'How long would all that take?'

She sidesteps the question slightly. 'We'd have to look at funding cycles, decide whether or not to make an interdisciplinary application. That's if you're happy for me to share your information with my colleagues, make some initial enquiries?'

'Yes,' I say dully. But though I came here to ask for it, I feel strangely wrong-footed by the idea of scrutiny. Like I've been trapped somewhere dark for so long, I need easing into the dazzle of daylight. I try to refocus. 'So . . . you think you might be able to help?'

After all these years, I'm still not sure I dare believe it.

Diana leans back in her chair as far as ergonomically possible. Bafflingly nonchalant, she glances again at her notes. Taps the tip of her pen against them. 'Well, that depends on what you mean by help. Evidently we can't change the future for you. But perhaps we could do something with the dreams themselves.'

'You mean, stop them happening?'

'At this stage, I really couldn't say.' She clearly won't promise some-thing so outlandish as restoring me to normal.

A thought toboggans through me. I've been so fixated on preventing the dreams, I've barely stopped to consider what that would actually achieve.

Because if Diana can't help Callie, is there even any point?

Ever since I dreamt about her death, it's Callie I've been worried about. Not my own jumble of lopsided brain cells.

'Something I haven't asked,' Diana's saying. 'Does anyone in your family share your . . . condition?'

Inside my mind, a key begins to turn. 'I . . . I'm not sure.'

'I'd like to run through your family history as a starting point.'

My breathing becomes rigid, mechanical. Why hasn't this occurred to me before now?

*I'm not even your father!*

'Actually,' I say suddenly, shutting my notebook and getting to my feet, 'don't share this with anyone just yet. I'd like some time. To think everything over.'

'Take all the time you need.' Her tone implies she's got a ton of other research on her desk that she'd frankly find far less of a ball-ache.

'Thank you for seeing me.'

'Give my regards to Steve,' she says. But I've already disappeared.

I walk back through the concrete maze of the university campus towards the car park. The place is eerily quiet, except for the whistle of an autumn breeze between the buildings.

Questions are strobe-lighting through my mind.

I've been focused on finding a cure for so long that I've never stopped to think about what would follow. Maybe cutting off my dreams would leave me worryingly adrift. Like the implausible anti-climax of a lottery win, the fingertip fear of a house offer accepted. Be careful what you wish for.

Because maybe what I'm actually wishing for is a way to stop the future happening. And no academic in the world can help me with that.

The only person who can do that is me.

# 61

## Callie

On the same day of Joel's appointment with Diana, I have a near-miss at work. A plastic felling wedge springs from a tree I'm helping to cut down just as I've lifted the visor on my helmet. Thick and squat, like a doorstop but sharper, it misses my face by millimetres. Any closer and I could have been blinded – or worse, if it had struck me in the neck. It's a stupid, careless error and it rattles me.

I wonder if I'll always be jumpy, now that Joel's dream has alerted me to my own mortality. Maybe this is what it's like for stroke or heart-attack survivors – forever afraid a tight chest or headache is the beginning of the end. Perhaps it will always be there now when I wake in the morning – that caged bird in my stomach, a small but insistent quiver of fear.

I must be young when the end comes, I've realised that. I can tell from the intensity of Joel's distress. A vision of me dying grey-haired and weary-boned, peacefully in my sleep, would hardly have tormented him to the degree he's now experiencing.

I run through all the ways it might happen – being crushed by a tree or falling from the shoulders of one I'm felling, drowning, suffocating, a clot or a tumour, a smashing of bones . . . I wonder if there is pain, and whether Joel is there, and where *there* is . . .

Closing my eyes briefly, I attempt to steady myself. *Stop. You're just in shock. This agitation will pass. The fear will fade.*

'Hey, Cal,' Liam calls, lowering his own visor again in preparation for the next cut. 'Don't overthink it. Seriously – happens to the best of us.'

Liam's being nice, but I'm shaken, and I wonder if perhaps it would be best to sit Joel down and ask him to tell me everything. But then I remind myself that a permanent ticking clock would be far, far worse than the occasional brush with mortality. It would be the most ominous of pendulums, counting down the sunsets, the summers, every kiss.

I can see why they say ignorance is bliss. Because if the end was revealed to be imminent, brutal, or both, I know I couldn't live with the dread.

Minutes later, Liam and I stand back to watch the tree finally fall. It's a diseased oak, dangerous and close to a public footpath, so it had to come down. We say nothing as it descends, felled like a king on an ancient battlefield. It first saw sunlight in the era of Queen Victoria, its acorn wriggling through soil to become a bright green sapling under the watch of Charles Dickens, George Eliot. And now, nearly two centuries on, the whisper of leaves crescendoes to a roar as it topples to the ground with a crack louder than thunder. I feel history exhale, a thousand kept secrets decimated, and I'm suddenly overcome.

'Awful, isn't it?' I say to Liam, as the fen falls silent once more and the storm of stirred-up undergrowth settles. Birds have scattered from the boughs of trees still standing, like seeds blown off the head of a dandelion. 'Watching something so old meet its end.'

'Yes and no.' Liam removes his helmet, rubs sawdust from his hair. 'Worse if a limb falls and kills someone.'

I say nothing.

As Liam and I begin sawing the felled oak into logs, I try to envisage how my life would look if I let Joel tell me what he knows. Though he truly is blameless, I wonder whether I'd start eventually to resent him for filling in the one gap we all take for granted, for snuffing out the warm glow of possibility. For giving me the full stop I never really wanted.

But we are where we are, and maybe I love him enough to surmount all that. Grace always used to say, *I'll either find a way or make one.*

I'm late home after staying to help quad-bike logs back to the yard. Though Murphy's in his usual spot by the hearth, the flat feels empty, still as a stopped clock.

I spot a note against the kettle on the kitchen worktop.

*Gone to Newquay for a couple of nights. Explain when I'm back xx*

I sit unsteadily on the sofa, stare at the scrap of paper I'm holding like it's a ransom note. Murphy nudges his nose onto my lap, looks up at me with eyes of liquid woe.

I know Newquay's the area code for the number in the book Joel found. All I can hope is that whoever lives there might be able to help us, before it's too late.

# 62

## Joel

He looks like me, just twenty years older. I recognise the dint of my own chin. The crow's feet and Cupid's bow. His eyes, dark as galaxies.

'Steady, steady . . . Hey, you okay?' He must think I'm about to pass out, because he's making that face people do when they're watching a natural disaster unfold on the news. He grabs me by the elbow, steers me inside.

His living room reminds me of Callie's when I first met her. It's packed out with stuff, bursting with colour. There are house plants, wall hangings, pictures of waves. Three surfboards propped up against a cabinet. A throw on his sofa that looks as if it's fresh out of a souk. An old-school stereo beside a pile of CDs. A bona fide lava lamp.

'Here, take a seat. Tea?'

Though I manage a nod, he hovers.

'This happen often?'

'Turning up on the doorstep of strange men? I try not to make it routine.'

'No, I meant the colour of your skin. You've gone a bit . . . chalky.'

'A shot of brandy in that tea might sort it.' I put my head right down between my knees, like I'm praying for something. Perhaps I am.

He claps me on the shoulder. Lets his hand linger there for a moment or two. 'Coming right up.'

\*    \*    \*

His name's Warren Goode, he told me on the phone. That's all I know. I dialled the number inside my mum's thriller as soon as I got back from my appointment. We had a short conversation, then I got into my car and drove to Newquay in one hit and fifth gear. Callie was on loop in my mind the whole way.

It all slotted into place during my meeting with Diana, and I just couldn't wait any longer. Time isn't on my side, after all.

He brings me a mug of tea laced with brandy, and a glass of the neat stuff for himself. Uncertainly, he sits in the armchair opposite me.

I sip the tea. Let the room fall silent, so my next sentence can get the airtime it needs. 'I think . . . I think you might be my father.'

A full moon of a stare, lambent with a lifetime's wondering. Then, eventually, 'You're right. I am.'

I feel my pulse quicken. My blood's rushing with sentiment.

He clears his throat. 'You said on the phone . . . you found my number last Christmas.'

There follows a pause, long enough for me to wonder if I've made a mistake in coming here. Clearly he's expecting me to say something. But what? *Is he annoyed I've left it so long? What does he think – that I should have jumped in my car and floored it all the way along the M4 on Boxing Day?*

'Yeah. So . . . why was it written in that book? The one Mum was reading in hospital.' (I'd mentioned it only briefly on the phone, figuring I'd prefer to hear the details face to face.)

Warren shakes his head, like he's trying to nudge his thoughts into order. 'I went to visit her, Joel. Just before she died.'

'Why?'

'I wanted to see her, one last time. She told me about you that day. I thought she might want to pass my number on.'

'You didn't already know about me?'

Another headshake.

'What were you – an affair?'

'No, we were together just before she met . . . well, Tom.'

*Tom.* So Warren knew my dad once, too. 'Did you love her?'

'Yes, I did. Very much.'

'So why—'

'Fancy getting some fresh air? Blowing the cobwebs away?'

'How did you know Mum was ill? You're not in touch with my . . . Tom, are you?'

'Nope. Heard through a friend-of-a-friend.'

There's a fresh onshore breeze tonight, straight in off the Atlantic. A few surfers are braving the lines of white water, but most people are sticking to solid ground. Walking dogs, strolling along the headland. The September sky is saturated pastel, purple and pink like sentimental notepaper.

'So what were you doing when you met Mum?'

'I was about to go off round the world in my camper-van,' Warren says. 'I'm a surfer, you see. Or was.'

A globetrotter. So we're different in that way at least. 'What do you do now?'

He makes the same face I do when people ask me about work. 'Teach kids to surf, earn pocket change from photos here and there. I was trying to bring out my own line of boards, but . . .' He looks away from me, out to sea. 'Money dried up.'

We emerge from the beach and pick up the incline towards the headland, past the Victorian hotel on the clifftop. It's grand and palatial, epically romantic.

Romance. The idea seems almost obscure to me now. Like a beloved patch of landscape viewed through a misty window.

'So why'd you break up?'

'The surf was calling. I thought I was going to be the next world champion.' His laugh is wistful. 'I left your mum behind, Joel. I always was a selfish bugger. And soon afterwards she met Tom. Your dad.'

His honesty, at least, impresses me. 'That's it?'

'Pretty much,' he says, but like he wishes it wasn't.

'Would you have stayed if you'd known she was pregnant?'

He skirts the question. 'I always told Olivia I didn't want kids. I told her that life wasn't for me. Maybe that's why she decided not to tell me.'

*Olivia. Olivia.* A name I never hear. The sound of it travels back to me like music.

'You know, being with Tom really was the best outcome for your mum – and for you. What life could I have given you, living out of a camper-van, obsessed with chasing the perfect wave? I had no money, no possessions, no job . . . not a thing to my name.'

I think of my dad, those regimented office hours. His lifelong dedication to order and hard graft. Like a soldier reporting for duty, every day of his life.

'Was Mum pregnant with me when she met my dad?'

'Yes. She got a job at his firm, as I remember it. But they didn't start dating straight away.'

I stare up towards the headland. At the acrobatic herring gulls taking on the breeze. Dad's lifelong hostility towards me is explained now, at least. I wasn't an accounting anomaly, a miscalculation he could quickly fix. It was more like Warren had graffitied his name all over our house, forcing Dad to look at it every day of his life.

'Your mum was the easiest woman in the world to love,' Warren says now. 'Everybody did. Not that she had any idea, of course.'

I think of Callie, and my heart fills.

'So, Doug and Tamsin . . . they're only my half-siblings?' I ask.

'Yes.'

Heat spreads through my chest as I picture Tamsin, what her face would do if she knew. We've always been so close.

'And Dad's parents . . . aren't my grandparents at all.' All those half-term trips to Lincolnshire, where the welcome was always so warm. Did they know? Did a small part of them never suspect, when this dark-haired urchin turned up on their doorstep?

'I'm sorry,' Warren says quietly. 'My parents – your biological grand-parents – died years ago.'

We walk on, strides matching exactly. The Atlantic has become a furnace, the setting sun its red-hot core.

'What did Mum say to you when you turned up at the hospital?'

'She was happy to see me. We talked, and she asked for my number. It was sort of a funny moment, in the end.'

'I guess she forgot to give it to me,' I say, recalling how the palliative chemo had attacked her memory.

'I guess so,' he says, voice gruff.

I look at him. Feel the first fronds of anger take hold. 'So why didn't you ever try to get in touch? Mum died *twenty-three* years ago.'

He frowns, works his jaw. For a moment I think he's trying to come up with an excuse. 'Oh, wow. This is hard.'

My anger intensifies. 'You're telling me.'

'I did, Joel. I did try. More than once.'

My heart derails. 'What?'

'The first time was a couple of years later. As soon as I'd got everything straight in my head, I contacted Tom. You were only fifteen, then.'

Gusts of wind gallop by.

'He told me you were too young. Said to try again when you turned eighteen. So I did, but he insisted you were busy with exams, and after that, university. He always claimed it wasn't the right time. Once you'd graduated I tried again, but he told me the two of you had sat down and talked. That you'd said you weren't interested. That you never wanted to see me.'

I gape. 'And you took his word for it?'

'He made me afraid I'd ruin your life, Joel. He told me you were sensitive, that I'd unsettle you, cause big problems. I'm sorry – I guess he was just trying to protect you.' Warren swallows. 'But, look, a few years later, I . . . had a dream. About today.'

'What sort of dream?'

We stop still and face each other. Warren says nothing, just eyeballs me until I know for sure.

I feel a strange, animalistic urge to howl. With what – relief? Joy? Frustration? 'You have it too. You have it *too*.'

He takes my arm. 'It's okay.'

'You've been waiting for me? You knew I was coming today?'

His skin flares amber in the sunset. 'Yes.'

*It's hereditary.*

I turn away from him, hold my face against the wind. The salt invades my nostrils, stiffens my hair as I try to take everything in.

It's a few moments before I feel steady enough to walk on. 'How long?' I'm unable to digest yet what he's told me about Dad.

'Since I was a kid.'

'And you haven't found a cure.'

Warren hesitates before relating his own dispiriting journey. Drugs and heavy drinking in his youth, then a slightly more orthodox approach than mine – multiple GPs and counsellors. Hypnotherapy, acupuncture, medication. But we both came up against the same brick wall in the end.

He has his own sodding notebook too. Black and hard-backed, just like mine.

'Do you sleep?' I ask.

'Rarely.'

'Have you got a girlfriend? A wife?'

'Too complicated.' He bolts me a look. 'And you?'

I laugh, loosely. 'Why do you think I'm here?'

'Don't tell me you're a lifelong bachelor too.'

I think of Callie and my dream. And then my heart cleaves in two all over again. 'I tried to be. I wasn't strong enough. I caved.'

Because he has only half the story, he treats this as good news. 'You have no idea how happy that makes me.'

Later, he offers me a bed for the night. But it feels too soon. I need space to shelter from the blizzard of thoughts in my mind, so he rings round for vacancies at local B-and-Bs.

While he's on the phone, I notice a framed photograph hanging in his hallway. A surfer, wet-haired in a rash vest with a Hawaiian *lei* around his neck. He's being lifted above the heads of a crowd. At first I think it's Warren, then peer a little closer. It's been signed in gold pen. I can just make out the name. *Joel Jeffries.*

So maybe Mum named me after Warren's favourite surfer. A way to remember him, perhaps.

I'm pretty tired the next morning after less than four hours' sleep. And I don't envisage the net-curtained confines of the B-and-B's dining room doing much to pick me up. So instead I go back to Warren's, with strong coffee and egg rolls from a local café.

We eat outside, in Warren's garden (which is really just a patch of yellowed, wasteland-style grass and a headstrong Cornish palm tree angled against a fence). The air's briny from the beach, a cardigan of cloud across the early-autumn sky.

Warren unwraps his food. 'This has been a long time coming.'

'Hungry?'

He laughs. 'No, I meant this moment. I dreamt about it. Well, this and when you turned up last night.'

I stare at him. 'You dreamt about . . . what we're doing right now?'

Weird. I've never stopped to think about how it would feel to be the subject of a dream.

'Dreamt you got the coffee black, too.'

I raise an eyebrow.

Warren peels back the lid of his cup. 'Chip off the old block.' He smiles. 'Can only drink it neat.'

Between sips of black coffee and bites of egg roll, I tell Warren about Diana. But I deliberately steer clear of my dream about Callie. Maybe because I can already see he has high hopes for my love life.

'Diana's right, you know,' he says, when I'm done.

I look at him, take in the folds of his skin. The creases at the corners of his eyes. He has the kind of weather-worn complexion that always carries a tan. Even in the middle of winter, when the sun hasn't shone for about six weeks. 'About what?'

'Well, maybe she could stop the dreams. Maybe. After a few years of you as her lab rat. But she can't change the future.'

'What are you saying?'

'We have this affliction, Joel. But we also have each other now. Ever since I dreamt about this weekend, I've been trying to get myself sorted. Make the house a bit nicer, go surfing more often. Stop being quite so much of a hermit.' He pats his belly. 'Lose a few pounds.'

It's a heart-warping thought, strangely sweet: Warren beavering away all this time, preparing for my arrival.

'I want to help, if I can. Don't make the same mistakes I did – mess up your relationships and career and—'

'Ship's already sailed on that front.' I tell him the story of how I became the world's worst vet. Then Warren reciprocates with the tale of his own promising surfing career. How he screwed the whole thing up with booze, recreational drugs.

'But we can get *you* back on track,' he says. 'It's not too late.'

My thoughts drift to Dad, to everything he denied me by turning

Warren away. Warren could have been my confidant all this time, seen me through some of the toughest periods of my life. 'I'm not sure I can ever forgive my dad,' I tell Warren now.

'Don't be too hard on him. He was probably afraid of losing you, after Olivia died. I guess he saw it differently from me – he'd done all the hard work, then I turned up uninvited expecting to muscle in.'

I frown, sip my coffee.

'So what now?' Warren asks.

'All I've ever wanted is for the dreams to stop,' I say eventually. 'I've been fixated on that for so long, but . . .'

'Now it comes down to it, you don't think you can handle not knowing what's to come?'

I exhale. Consider it. 'Maybe. How messed-up is that?'

'Well, you've lived with this for so long, it's understandable you might struggle to live without it. Like those old folks who spend their whole life waiting for retirement, then haven't got a clue what to do when they get there.'

'So what's the answer?'

'Forget science, forget cures. Just go out and live – you and Callie. Make the best of your lives.'

'I have no idea how to do that,' I say. Because the dark cloud of my dream overshadows us now, the threat of devastation just a heartbeat away.

# 63

## Callie

I'm with Dad in his garden, picking vegetables for Sunday lunch, a throwback to days gone by. Mum's left us to it, as she tends to do – I like to think, as she's watching us from the window, she's remembering all those days I'd totter about after him in my little splash suit, clutching a plastic bucket and trowel, bullied and buffeted by the wind and rain.

Maybe it's the sentiment that stems from childhood memories, but I suddenly wonder if I'm being selfish by electing oblivion. Whether I should prepare my parents, forewarn all the people who love me. Perhaps I could even consider one of those living funerals, where everyone gathers and says nice— Oh, no. How morbid. No one should have to experience their own funeral. No one.

'So where's he gone, then?' Dad's quizzing me about Joel's impromptu trip.

'Cornwall.'

'And that's all right with you, is it?'

'Of course, Dad. We're not—'

'Joined at the hip? Oh, I know. You kids do things differently these days.'

I smile. I guess, in my dad's eyes, I'll always be his little girl.

Joel and I FaceTimed yesterday, then again this morning. He confirmed what he'd already suspected – that Tom's not his real dad – and said he was staying until Tuesday night to try to figure everything out. Overwhelmed on his behalf, I told him I love him, to stay as long as he needs to get his head straight.

'Dad, can I ask you something?'

'Of course.'

'Do you think your patients . . .' I swallow '. . . do you think they were grateful for having time to prepare before they died?'

'Sometimes,' he says simply, uprooting a carrot. 'Sometimes they were glad to have that time. Sometimes they weren't.'

'What were their reasons for not wanting it?'

'Well, they varied. People are different. A drawn-out death isn't everyone's ideal way to go. People often think they'd rather have time to prepare, but of course they end up spending their last months and weeks paralysed by sadness, and fear. It's not always how it seems in the magazine articles.'

'You mean, it's not all bungee-jumping and touring the States in a Winnebago.'

Dad smiles sadly. 'Hardly, sweetheart. Not everyone feels emotionally able to tackle last-chance to-do lists, even if they're physically capable. I'm sure I wouldn't.'

We carry on picking for a few moments. The faint churn of farm machinery floats over from nearby fields, as at the garden's far boundary a quiver of swifts skims the hedge. It's always so peaceful here – free from shunting traffic and fired horns, the stereophonic rumble of urban living.

'So, what would you prefer?' I ask him. 'To go quickly, or . . .'

He looks over at me, a smear of mud on his left cheek that Mum's bound to tut about later. 'Callie, this conversation's starting to worry me . . .'

'No need,' I say quickly. 'I'm just curious.'

'You'd tell me if—'

'Dad, it's nothing, honestly. Actually, forget I said anything.' I straighten up, suck in fresh air. 'What's next?'

'Parsley, please,' he says, but like he's not entirely reassured.

Later, as I'm getting ready to leave, I say, without really intending to, 'Dad, how much do you think you should sacrifice for someone you love?'

'That depends on what you're sacrificing,' Dad says.

'Well, if it was something that would make the other person happy, but your life a lot worse, should you do it?'

Dad frowns. 'I can't really answer that, Callie, without knowing the circumstances.'

*Well, they're the worst*, I think. *As bad as you could possibly imagine.*

'Found it!' Mum calls from upstairs, where she's been hunting down a newspaper clipping she's saved for me.

I reach up to kiss him. 'That's fair enough. Love you, Dad.'

'In the end, I suppose, it all depends on whether Joel loves you back.'

Busted. I look down at the carpet.

*He does love me, Dad. He just can't bring himself to say it.*

# 64

## Joel

Warren and I are sitting on the deck of a bar overlooking Fistral Beach, a pint apiece and a portion of nachos between us. The sky and sea are shimmering, the surf pumping.

Even though it's just after lunch on a Monday, there seem to be plenty of people around. They're chatting on the sand, pausing by our table in shorts and flip-flops to shake Warren's hand and comment on the waves. I'm starting to feel distinctly suburban, sitting here in my trainers and jeans. Though I fit right in in terms of having nowhere else to be, I guess.

This is how we've spent the last couple of days. Mostly outdoors, in front of a series of spectacular vistas. Tentatively getting to know each other. Trying to make sense of the missing years.

He doesn't introduce me to anyone as his son. He just says, *This is Joel.* And people shake my hand too, ask how it's going.

'Do they know?' I ask him now.

Warren dips a nacho methodically between sour cream, guacamole and salsa. 'Do who know what?'

'Friends, acquaintances. About you. The dreams.'

He shrugs as he chews. 'Some do. Some don't.'

I stare at him, incredulous. 'And what do they think?'

'You'd have to ask them.'

'I don't want to. I'm asking you.'

'I reckon some think I'm bonkers. Some believe me. Most don't care.' He plucks another nacho from the pile, pulling a string of cheese with it until it twangs. 'One thing you learn as you get older, Joel, is that people care far less about your private business than you might think.'

'But . . . why? Why did you tell them?'

He smiles. 'Because I finally decided it's easier than carrying the thing like a dead weight around my neck.'

I sip my lager, stare out at the waves. Then I recount the story of my university doctor. Explain how judgemental my dad and brother can be.

Warren looks out to sea as he listens. 'People are a bit more open-minded, these days,' he says, when I've finished. 'Look at Callie. And your friend . . . Steve, is it?'

I frown, say nothing.

'Or maybe it's just the people I knock about with. The things some of them do . . . Once you've ridden a forty-foot wave, you start to see life a little differently. It's a kind of narcotic, and most of the people I know are on it. They wouldn't give more than a passing thought to me and my crazy dreams.'

'You've surfed forty-foot waves?' I say, after a moment.

He snorts. 'Not me. Big waves and old men don't mix. You, on the other hand . . .'

'You're out of your mind.'

'Exactly, Joel.' He leans forward. 'If there's one thing I've realised over the past few years, it's that getting out of your own head for a bit works wonders. Doing something different. Trusting the world around you.'

'You're not going to start talking about surfing being the source, are you?'

He laughs. 'Ha. I might.'

'But are you really happy?' I press him. 'You're not—'

'With anyone?' He leans back in his chair. 'There's more than one way to be happy in this life, Joel.'

I smile too. I have to. Because, despite everything, it feels so good just to talk with someone who really understands. To actually know, for the first time in my life, that I'm not alone in this. 'Do you know what, Warren? I think you might be a bit of a hippie.'

'Is that a compliment?'

I raise my eyebrows, swipe the last nacho for myself. 'I haven't decided yet.'

After four nights in Cornwall I drive home. In the early hours I stop at a service station, drink coffee in their weird little amphitheatre-café. Try to rest my eyes before making the final push back to Eversford.

At a nearby table, a woman's comforting a baby. Her partner's next to her, scarfing a doughnut as he blinks into UV-grade lighting. But it's the woman I'm most interested in. Her eyes are shut and, though she's trying to rock her baby to sleep in a service station at two a.m., she looks pretty happy. Calm and content, like she's listening to a harpist or getting a massage.

She reminds me of Callie. Same heart-shaped face, same long dark hair. Same profile when she turns her head. The similarity's so striking, I can't stop staring (until her partner starts to look as though he might get up and make me, which is both reasonable and my cue to leave).

I swing onto the M4 again, begin the last leg back to Eversford. But Callie's double with the child in her arms keeps tweaking the sleeve of my consciousness. And before long a thought corkscrews through me: if this condition is hereditary, then, for me, kids can never be an option. Despite that beautiful fleeting moment a few months ago, when I pictured Callie pregnant . . . I couldn't inflict the way I live on an innocent soul.

But where does that leave Callie? Though she's never said as much,

I'm pretty sure she wants children. Or, at least, she's never given me reason to think she doesn't. Her parents have dropped a few hints about it. Plus she has that rare and natural gift with kids that makes them cling to her legs, cry when she leaves. I picture her playing with my nieces and nephew. Teaching a floorful of under-tens to twist at Hugo's wedding. She was thinking about working in childcare, for God's sake. And if a family is something she wants, I can't be the one who stands in her way.

Adoption? For some reason I can picture my sister suggesting it, worried as always I'm denying myself life's joys. But adoption doesn't feel like something I'd want to explore. Because I'd still be the same: fixating on my dreams, worrying about Callie. And even without having passed on my condition, I'd mess the kid up somehow, I'm sure. Hand down my neuroses, infect them with anxiety.

I imagine the years rolling by, Callie and I stagnating as I count grimly down to her death. In those early days of agony with Mum, when I knew about the cancer before she did, all I could think about was how things would be four years down the line. Life lost its colour, turned gradually greyer. How can I go through that again, and still make Callie happy? It's not possible. It's just not.

I remember what she said to me, as we drove home on Boxing Day last year. About seeing my dreams as a gift. And I feel a fresh onrush of sorrow, because I know now that to me they will always be a curse.

It's nearly four when I get in. I can't bring myself to wake her, so I stay in the living room with Murphy.

Sitting down on the sofa, I google Joel Jeffries. He's British, same age as Warren. But, unlike Warren, Joel's a champion surfer with the lifestyle to match. House on the beach, wife, kids, crew. My instinct is to feel sad on Warren's behalf, before I think back to what he said at the beach bar yesterday.

*There's more than one way to be happy in this life.*

# 65

## Callie

I wake at about half six, just as light is starting to leak through the blinds. Something tells me Joel is home, so I pull on the tractor T-shirt he gave me at Christmas and pad through to the living room.

I find him on the sofa. He's slung his head back against the cushions and is staring at the ceiling, completely still.

'Hello,' I whisper, sitting down next to him and taking his hand. 'What are you doing in here?'

The look on his face is enough to break me. 'Sorry. Didn't want to wake you.'

'How was Cornwall?' I reach down to ruffle the dog's ears. 'We missed you.'

'I missed you too.'

Our eyes meet as, close to the open window, a bird performs a solo.

'Name that bird,' Joel murmurs.

'Robin. He's been singing all night.'

'All night?'

I nod. 'It's the street lamps. He thinks it's daytime.'

'Seems unfair, somehow. That he doesn't get any sleep.'

'Neither do you, night owl.'

A moment passes.

'They only live for two years, you know,' I say.

'Who do?'

'Robins.'

He leans forward and kisses me then, and it's a kiss for all the feelings words can't cover. He tastes of exhaustion and coffee. As he moves
down to my neck, his mouth hot and damp, I am seized by an almost
frenzied hunger for him, to show him just how much he means to me,
how much I hate to be away from him. And he must be feeling the
same way, because our kissing swiftly becomes urgent, our movements
frenetic. As our T-shirts come off I tremble at the touch of his hands
on my bare skin, and he too seems almost to shake with desire as he
eases his hand between us to tug down my underwear. All at once he's
inside me, lowering his eyes to mine, and I take in nothing but this
moment, his face, the sound of him gasping my name.

Afterwards, as we collapse flushed and unclothed against each other,
the whole world draws to a pause. Light is suspended against our skin,
and the morning holds its breath.


Over coffee, Joel explains more about Warren and his parents, their
heart-breaking history. He reveals Warren has the same condition, that
he's gone through all the same things Joel has. Tamsin and Doug are
only his half-siblings, he tells me, Tom having succeeded at keeping the
three of them in the dark until now.

I picture visiting Warren in Cornwall in happier circumstances.
Perhaps he'd have taught me and Joel to surf. I envisage sea spray and
sunshine, salted water rushing rocks, and feel regret ratchet through me.

'That's so much to take in,' I say, when he's finished talking, reaching
for his hand.

'I can find a way to deal with all that, Callie . . .'

*It's the other stuff you can't.* 'Did you tell Warren what you dreamt about
me?'

'No. I couldn't. I think . . .'

I wait.

'. . . it might have broken him.'

'I can understand that. It would break me, too.'

He stares down into his lap. 'The thing is . . . after seeing Warren, I can't stop thinking about my mum. The way she looked at me, when she told us she had cancer.'

'How? How did she look at you?'

'Like she wished I'd told her sooner. It's the biggest regret of my life, Cal, that I kept it to myself. That I didn't give her more time to prepare.'

Though my stomach spins with sympathy, my mind is resolute. 'You don't know how it happens with me, though. There's nothing either of us can do.'

'But I know *when*—'

'No.' I've never felt so certain of anything. Looking over at Joel, I let my eyes traverse the sweet shades of his face. 'No suggestions, no clues. I told you I didn't want to know, and I don't. I couldn't live my life if—'

'Callie, please, just—'

'*No.* Once the words are out there, you can't take them back. Everything changes for ever.'

He nods slowly. 'I'm just not sure that I can go through life,' he says, 'and not once give you a clue, or something you take to be one.'

I wonder if he's right, if I will start seeing signs in everything now – a low mood, a shed tear, a prolonged pause. Is our life together destined to become one long series of second guesses?

The room becomes quiet as a canyon.

'You don't have to stay,' he says eventually.

Tears swarm my eyes. 'With you?'

He nods.

'That isn't what I—'

'I know. But I need you to know that . . . you don't have to.'

'I want to stay, Joel. Because I love you.'

We share a look a mile long.

And then, 'I love you, too,' he whispers.

I stare at him. After all these months, he's finally said it back.

Though his eyes are glazed with tears, he doesn't look away. 'You're right,' he says. 'What's the worst that can happen now? I was stupid not to say it before. I love you, Callie. I love you so much. I always have.' He encircles me with his arms, presses his face against my neck and murmurs it over and over, against my flushing skin.

That night in bed my hands find him, desperate to stop us spiralling off onto opposite flight paths. His mouth is on mine straight away, fierce and tender all at once. But it's a sad sort of tenderness, the kind you see in black-and-white films. Like we're kissing through the open window of a steam train, just before the whistle blows.

# 66

## Joel

It's early October, a fortnight since my return from Cornwall. For the past few hours, Callie's been at dinner with Esther, Gavin and Ben.

I backed out at the last minute, claiming a headache she didn't buy for a nanosecond. But I'd been struggling all day. On top of everything else, I was still feeling unsettled by a dream I'd had about Buddy a few nights previously, falling off his pushbike.

'We're still a couple, aren't we?' she asked me, thirty minutes before leaving the flat. She was half dressed in front of the mirror, her hair in rollers. I was sitting on the bed behind her. I'd have forgiven her for wondering, as she looked at me looking at her, if what we had was nothing more than an illusion. Something she could see but felt cold to the touch.

'Of course we are,' I murmured. Still, where was the evidence? Every day I wait and hope for something to change, a solution to present itself. But nothing ever does.

'Then I'll stay at home with you.'

'No, I want you to go.' Because I did. I wanted her to have fun, forget everything that's going on. I didn't want to drag her down with me.

I guess she must be having a good time. It's midnight, and there's still no sign of her. No messages to say she'll be home soon.

I'm shivering in the garden on the phone to Warren, looking back at the flat. Our flat, where we'd started making memories. There's a single light on in the kitchen, throbbing orange like a dying flame. Above ours, Danny's windows are dark and still.

'I dreamt about Callie.'

'I'm sorry,' Warren says.

'It's not good.'

Warren clears his throat. 'You know when she's going to . . . ?'

'Eight years,' I manage, before my composure landslides.

He just lets me cry for a while, supportively silent as a helpline volunteer.

Once I've recovered he asks for details. There are scant few, of course.

'I don't know how it happens,' I finish by saying. 'I got no clues in the dream. And not knowing that . . .'

'. . . is the worst part,' Warren surmises.

I agree, describe Callie's fierce resistance to any intervention.

'What about her dad?'

'What about him?'

'Didn't you say he was a doctor?'

'Ex. He's retired now. But I can't ask him for help.'

'Why not?'

'You're suggesting I tell him? Everything?'

'Not everything. Just sound him out. You could see if there's any family medical history that might be relevant. There are ways to frame things.'

'I'm not sure.' Callie's dad is pretty smart. He does the cryptic crossword every day, for one thing. He'd decipher me in seconds.

'You need to try everything, mate.'

It's that innocuous *mate* that does it, that feels so unexpectedly incendiary. *I wish I'd had you*, I want to rage. *I wish I'd had you to help me through this, all these years.*

But I don't. I just sling my head back and stare at the sky, pinned up above me by a million stars.

'I dreamt Mum died,' I tell him, after a few moments. 'I knew she was going to die from cancer, and I never said anything. It's the biggest regret of my life.'

'You were just a kid, Joel,' he says softly.

'But the way she looked at me, when she found out . . .'

'Telling Callie when she's going to die won't bring your mum back, Joel.'

'What are you saying?' But I think I know.

'Well, if Callie's adamant she doesn't want to find out then ultimately, you have to respect that.'

'No. I can't live with knowing. I can't carry this with me, every day, and still make her happy. It's not possible.'

A long silence.

'Well, then, maybe you're no longer the guy to make her happy.'

It feels like a punch, telescopic, all the way from Cornwall. Confirmation of my very worst fears. 'That's not what I wanted to hear.'

He sighs. 'I know. But if lip service is what you're looking for, you dialled the wrong number.'

Furious, I cut off the call.

*No, Warren,* I think, despite myself. *I'm not giving up.*

Hours later, I'm dreaming again. It's just over three years from now, and I'm watching Callie walking along a beach, hand in hand with . . . oh.

Though dark, it looks hot and stormy. There are palm trees, and white sand, its appearance familiar somehow . . . Is it Miami? (Not that I've been. Netflix is the closest I'll ever get to transatlantic travel.)

Callie seems happy. They're laughing about something. Heads inclined, torturously in tune.

And then I see the ring on her finger, and everything inside me goes dark.

# 67

## Callie

Days dissolve into weeks, and soon it's late October. The air becomes crisper and the days contract, like the world is steeling itself for winter. Joel and I are at stalemate, unable to move forward.

Esther knows something's up, has asked if everything's okay more than once. Maybe she sensed something that night Joel ducked out of dinner. Or perhaps she's spoken to Ben, and he's filled her in on my voicemail to Grace. But, of course, I can't tell her, so whenever she asks I end up mumbling something about just being tired from work.

Joel and I are almost beyond discussion now – talking about it is like inching through gridlock, only to arrive at the wrong destination every time. But I have noticed that Joel has assumed a calm determination, an air of resolve that makes me quietly curious.

It feels to me like he's planning something, but what it is, I couldn't say.

It helps that I love him so completely. I have no idea what our future will bring, but if I shut my eyes and think only of now, we're somehow slowly getting through it. We're still a couple – we can't simply give up, turn our backs on the best thing in both our lives – which means we still go out, still have sex, still laugh our stomachs sore. But it's a bit like holding up a roof with your bare hands: all it takes is one change in the wind, and you're no longer strong enough.

\* \* \*

We've spent the day at Tamsin's, celebrating her birthday. Doug and Lou brought an elaborate cake shaped like a unicorn that was really more for the kids than Tamsin, but there were also mocktails and old-school party games, which were definitely more for us than the kids. It's been a joy-filled, hilarious day – a day that reminded me of everything Joel and I could be.

I dithered over helping myself to cake earlier, just for a moment. I've been agonising on and off about cleaning up my diet, cutting out wine entirely, filtering my water, investigating yoga. It's what people do, I suppose, when they're reminded of their mortality – they give their bodies the best possible shot at making it. Maybe I should have a subtle word with Dad, ask him for some health tips.

But all of a sudden Amber was tugging at my sleeve, a slice of cake on a paper plate in her hand. 'I saved you the unicorn horn, Auntie Callie,' she whispered. 'If you eat it, you'll live for ever.'

I could feel Joel's eyes on me across the table, but I couldn't look up. If I had, I might have cried.

'You know,' I muse now, as we walk home through the woodsmoke-scented air of late afternoon, 'it's been nearly a year since Bonfire Night.'

He squeezes my mittened hand. 'So it has.'

'I knew I liked you that night. I had a bit of a crush on you.'

'Just a bit?'

'Okay. A fairly major crush.'

'Understandable. I *was* something of a catch.'

'Total catch.' My insides bunch up as I say it. *Please believe it. Please believe how much I still love you.*

We take a few more steps, our feet scuffing fallen leaves, strides in perfect sync. Last night the clocks went back, and the light's already slipping from the sky.

'So, did you?'

'Did I what?'

'Have a crush on me too.'

'A gentleman never tells.'

'Yes, but you can tell *me*.'

His hand firms up around mine. 'It was more than a crush, Callie. I knew that from the start. There was never any point in me fighting it.'

We walk a bit further in silence. This is the area of town where Grace died, though I haven't been down the road where the accident was since that night. I doubt I ever will again. Briefly, I wonder if the same fate awaits me – but Joel said he doesn't know how it happens, which means he can't have seen a car, onlookers, tarmac . . .

But just as my thoughts are beginning to domino, Joel brings me back to the present. He's pulling at my hand, gesturing at something over to our right.

'Look, Callie,' he says urgently. 'Look.'

He's pointing to the low wall in front of an abandoned house, halfway along a terrace earmarked for demolition. The front door and windows are shuttered with graffitied chipboard, weeds winding like tentacles round the guttering and brickwork.

Behind the wall, a brown tail is protruding, utterly still.

Before I can blink, Joel's left my side.

I follow, almost afraid.

'He's been abandoned.' Joel's already on his knees, running his hands across the coat of a young-looking white-and-tan dog. I squat down next to him. The dog's not reacting to Joel's touch.

'What's wrong with him?' I ask, struggling to hold back tears.

Joel starts gently to examine him. 'Not sure. An infection of some sort. He's in a bad way. His gums are really pale – see, here? And he's cold. We need to get him help, urgently.' He scrambles to his feet and dials a number, murmuring a few words into his phone. I hear him give the address of where we are. 'Kieran's on his way,' he says, after he's hung up, before kneeling down again next to me on the ground. 'Let's just keep him warm for now.'

Together we ease the dog onto our laps. Joel takes off his jacket and I remove my coat, and we wrap him up, huddle over him for warmth. Still there's no response – he's passive and floppy, like he's already dying.

'Will he be okay?' I ask Joel.

He meets my eye. 'Sorry, Cal. It doesn't look good.'

I bite down on my lip, try not to cry.

Kieran drives us to Joel's old practice, me and Joel on the back seat, the dog across our knees. As Joel offers Kieran his assessment, I vaguely register mention of IV fluids, anaemia, internal bleeding. Then Kieran gets on the phone to someone at a local charity, who agrees to cover the treatment costs, after which he and Joel start debating the best plan of action.

As we pull into the car park, I spot the dog's collar lying loose on the seat. There's no tag with a name or phone number, nothing at all to identify him. I pick up the collar, slip it wordlessly into my pocket.

'You go home,' Joel says to me, as we get out of the car. 'This could take a while.'

It's dark by the time he makes it back to the flat. He finds me in the bath and perches wearily on the edge of it, smelling faintly of disinfectant.

I sit up, sloshing a little water over the sides. 'How did it go?'

'Okay, I think. He had a pretty severe worm infestation. We gave him a blood transfusion, antibiotics. It's touch-and-go, but Kieran's taking him home tonight.'

'Thank God you spotted him.'

'In the nick of time. We've just got to wait and see.'

I take his hand. It feels limp in mine, and his eyes are blank, unseeing. 'Are you okay?'

He draws his other hand down over his face. He's pale, like he's aged somehow. 'Just a bit drained.'

'You were incredible. Really calm . . . Do you miss it?'

He looks up at the window, where the lights from other houses are like bulbs in the blackness. 'I miss helping animals.'

'So maybe you could—'

'I'm not up to the job.'

'You *are* up to it, Joel. You proved that tonight.'

'This was one night, Cal. That's nothing compared to doing it again full-time.'

I know I shouldn't push it – I know that. But I want Joel to see what I see: his huge talent and tender heart, the warm, kind core of him.

'Joel, what you did tonight—'

'Any vet would have done what I did tonight.'

I look down, scuffing strawberry-scented foam with my hand. 'Why do you do that?'

'Do what?'

'Downplay everything, say you're not a proper vet.'

'Because I'm not one. I haven't practised for nearly four years.'

'But you're so great with animals.'

'You have to be more than that, Cal.'

'Why did you really leave?'

There's a pause filled only with the popping of bubbles, like abandoned champagne at the end of a pretty crap party.

'Joel?'

'I made a huge mistake, Callie, and I didn't think I deserved to be a vet any more. Okay?'

'No, it's not okay,' I say softly. 'You've never told me.'

'I'm sorry. But I find it hard to talk about.'

'Please tell me.'

He eases his hand from mine, works invisible putty with his fingers. 'What do you want to know?'

'I want to know what happened.'

The darkness of his eyes seems to deepen somehow. 'I made a mistake, and the consequences were . . . as bad as you can imagine.'

'What was the mistake?'

Eventually he tells me he was distracted at work. He was on part-time hours back then, a way to try to claw back some sanity as he was going through a rough patch following several unsettling dreams. He was constantly hung-over and sleep-deprived, neglecting to exercise or take care of himself, arriving at work exhausted.

'I had one client, Greg. He suffered from depression, and his dog was his life. He used to talk to me when he came in. I just listened. I think it helped him a bit. He told me he'd been on the brink of suicide more than once, but the thought of what would happen to the dog had stopped him. Sometimes that dog was literally Greg's sole reason for living.'

Saying nothing, I just listen.

'Anyway, Greg brought the dog in one day – he had diarrhoea, some lethargy. I was sure it was nothing to worry about, but I should have done more. I should have followed up, run some blood tests, but I just sent him away, told Greg to keep an eye on him and bring him back if he got worse.'

'That sounds . . .' *Reasonable*, I want to say. *Entirely reasonable.* But, really, what do I know?

'Looking back, I know I made him feel he was wasting my time. I remember being short with him. Not intentionally, but . . . I was no better than the GP I saw at uni. I did the same to Greg as that doctor did to me.'

'What happened?' My voice is featherweight.

'Well, he brought the dog back a week later, by which point there was nothing I could do. His liver was already failing, and it was my fault. I'd missed the crucial symptoms.'

'I'm sure you did your best. You can't blame yourself—'

'Callie, I *am* to blame. I didn't even carry out a simple blood test. I was unfocused, not paying attention. And that dog suffered because of me.'

'Joel,' I say, reaching out to take his hand again, 'please don't beat yourself up. Mistakes can happen to anyone.'

He stares at me. His eyes are round as portholes. 'You don't understand.'

'I don't have to be a vet to know that if you—'

'Greg committed suicide a couple of weeks later,' he says abruptly. 'The dog was his lifeline, and I took it away from him, out of sheer bloody incompetence.'

The shock shuts me up. For a few moments I go mute, the bathwater cooling around me.

'I'm so sorry.'

'I'm responsible for Greg's death,' he says, his voice reedy and unrecognisable. 'It's that simple.'

I'm beginning to shiver. 'No. It's not that simple.'

'You wanted to know why I say I'm not a proper vet. That's why – because I don't deserve to call myself one.' He lowers his gaze to meet mine. 'And if you want to know why I have to tell you what I dreamt, it's because I can't live the rest of my life knowing I could have done more. Not with you, Callie. *I can't do that when it comes to you.*'

'Please don't,' I say, feeling my throat thicken. 'That's not fair.'

'I'm not sure I care about what's fair any more. I care about what's right.'

He gets to his feet then, turns his back on me and leaves.

I stay in the bath for maybe a half-hour more, tears hot against my skin as the water goes cold.

# 68

## Joel

On Halloween morning I call Warren while I'm out with the dogs.

It's hard to believe it's been a whole year since sparks were flying between me and Callie at the corner shop. We've gained so much in that year. But have we lost everything, too?

I hope every morning when I open my eyes for a way forward, an epiphany. That zero visibility will somehow have become sunlight. But it never has.

'So I did what you said,' I tell him.

'What did I say?'

'I . . . Where are you? Why can I hear screaming?'

'The beach. I don't know – something about sand and water makes kids scream.'

'What? It's October.'

'Last weekend of half-term.' I picture him shrugging. Big shrugger, I reckon, my biological dad.

'Are you supposed to be there in a supervisory capacity, or . . . ?'

'I'm teaching in ten minutes. What's up?'

'I went to see Callie's dad. To find out if there's any family history I should be worried about.'

'Good on you. Anything?'

It wasn't as awkward as it might have been. I doorstepped him while Callie was at work, and we sat together in the kitchen. I mumbled something vague about having had a bad dream, not wanting to worry

Callie. Then, just like that, he gave me the information I needed. (Not that it helped. Squeaky-clean bill of health, the whole Cooper family.)

He assured me our conversation would go no further, which was pretty generous of him. I knew if Callie found out, she might think I'd betrayed her, given her parents the heads-up. And there'd be a good chance then she'd never trust me again.

Anyway. 'Nothing.'

'Ah.'

'Yeah, so that didn't work out.'

A pause, cut through with the coarse cry of seagulls. I wonder if I should tell Warren about my dream of Callie on the beach in Florida. I've not been able to shake it from my mind.

But the thought of sharing it with Warren riles me for some reason. Maybe because I don't want to prove right his theory about me no longer being the guy to make Callie happy.

I walk a few more paces, picture Callie at home. Still warm from the shower, drawing a comb through her hair, skin damp and glistening. I feel a throb of longing for the nape of her neck, the low lamp of her voice.

And yet. 'You think I should give up, don't you? Let Callie go and live her life, find someone who can make her happy. That's what they say, isn't it? If you love someone, let them go.'

The seconds lengthen. 'That is what they say.'

'So that's it, then.'

'Not yet. Not necessarily. Don't do anything hasty.'

'Time isn't on my side, remember?'

'Yes. But, look, if it does come to that, you'll know when the moment's right.'

'Well, cheers for your help.'

'I'm so sorry I can't fix this for you, Joel.'

'You had a chance to fix this thirty-seven years ago.'

'What are you—'

I can't help what I'm about to say. It's pure frustration. 'You could have fixed it before it started, by not having a meaningless fling with my mum.'

'It wasn't meaningless.'

'You swapped her for a surfboard. How much more meaningless could it get?'

That night I dream about Callie again, just under a year from now. She's wrapped up against the cold somewhere, I'm not exactly sure where. But it's remote and expansive, exactly the kind of epic landscape she loves. She looks fervent and alive in a way I've not seen for a long time. Has binoculars around her neck, and a camera in her hand. I can hear the wind whistling, see a soaring-blue sky. And from the horizon a volcano rises, imposing as a cathedral.

I'm shaking when I wake. I climb out of bed and grab my notebook, turn in the doorway to look back at her as I always do. She's curled up on the mattress like a comma, face pressed against my pillow.

A comma. Somewhere to pause for breath. A chance to make sense of things.

'You deserve more,' I whisper from the doorway. 'I don't want you to miss out on a single thing.'

I think back again to what Warren said. *Maybe you're no longer the guy to make her happy.*

Back at the start I should have gone with my head, not my heart. I know it now as I knew it then. It was on me to hit the brakes, as soon as I sensed my head was losing the battle. I could have been smart. I *should* have been. Saved us both the agony of this. Because now I've had a preview of the good things destiny has in store for her, I'm not sure I can bring myself to deprive her of them.

Callie's got time to move on. Make a life for herself, do all the stuff she's always wanted to. She can be the person, I realise, she can only ever half be with me.

# 69

## Callie

'Seen this?' Liam skims a postcard over to me while we're cleaning chainsaws in the workshop.

I wipe my hands and pick it up. It's from Dave, a bird's-eye view of the Amazon rainforest on the front, a précis of his latest adventures on the reverse. My heart pumps a little faster as I picture his life now, close to the Equator – the boiling landscape and exotic discoveries, the shimmering wilderness of the rainforest.

'Weird, isn't it?' Liam says.

'What is?'

He shrugs, like it should be obvious. 'That a year ago Dave was hanging around here, eating crisps and mucking about on the quad-bike, and now he's on the other side of the world. Bet he never comes home.'

I flip the postcard over. 'Yeah. Weird. Sounds like he's having a blast, though.'

Liam removes the engine casing from his saw, sets it on the bench. 'Not my cup of tea. But yeah.'

I laugh. 'I know. Six months in a rainforest would be your idea of hell.'

He shudders as though we're talking an actual means of torture. 'Surprised you've never done it, though.'

Smiling, I turn the postcard over again. 'Done what?'

'Travelled,' he says, characteristically blunt. 'You're always on about it. You should go to Chile, find that bird.'

Blinking back an image of Grace expressing similar sentiments, I slide a smile Liam's way. 'I thought you said I'd have a better chance of seeing a snow leopard.'

He almost-but-not-quite smiles back. 'Well, I'm sure you'd have fun looking for it. What's stopping you?'

I shrug and turn away, mumble something about timing. Liam's monosyllable disorder must be catching.

'Timing's perfect, isn't it?' he counters. 'Your contract must be nearly up.'

It's true – it's up in a few weeks, and there's no news yet on the money they'd need to renew it. Fiona's assured me they want me, but it's just a case of when and how. At the very least, she says, they could offer me scrub-clearance work in the interim, which would be better than nothing. 'In a month,' I tell Liam.

'They said what's happening yet?'

'Nope. They're keeping me in suspense.'

Liam frowns. 'Didn't they just get a load of new funding in from the grants award scheme? Sure I saw an email about it last night. You could go off travelling, and then—'

And it's at this point, with impeccable timing, that the workshop door opens and Fiona sticks her head through the gap. 'Callie, can I have a word?'

# 70

## Joel

Taking a seat at Dad's kitchen table, I try to remember how long it's been since the two of us talked properly. Perhaps it was when I'd just quit my job. He was sounding off at me in the back garden, aided by Mrs Morris next door (who'd eavesdropped on the whole thing and just so happened to agree I was most irresponsible).

Good times, good times.

Pink-skinned and still in shorts from his Monday-morning badminton session, Dad hands me a coffee. I notice he's got one of those straps on his glasses, to hold them to his head while he's doing something sporty.

For a moment I wonder if it's cruel to spring this on him without warning. But the clues are starting to mount up fast. I was here only last week when my phone rang from the living room and Amber yelled Warren's name. I darted back in there, stomach sawn in two, but thankfully Dad had popped upstairs for something. Still, it can only be so long before he clocks what's going on.

'Well, this is a nice surprise,' Dad's saying, which really is the most woeful of misjudgements.

I take a moment to survey the kitchen, as if for the last time. Overripe bananas, Bella's nursery tea towel, marigolds spread-eagling the tap. I look at it all like nothing will be the same once the words are out of my mouth. I suppose in many ways, it won't be.

'I know I'm not your son, Dad. I know about Warren.'

The colour slides from his skin. He doesn't say anything, or even move his mouth.

'Dad.' I lean across the table. 'It's okay. I know everything.'

The kitchen clock grinds on through the silence. Dad's become a waxwork, too still to be real.

Eventually, he speaks. 'How?'

'Does it matter?'

He exhales heavily, which I take to mean no. 'He didn't treat your mother well, Joel.'

'I know.'

Dad's eyes golf-ball. 'Have you seen him?'

'Once. He lives in Cornwall.'

A tut. Like Warren's some kind of philandering tax-dodger and Cornwall is code for Bermuda.

'You should have told me, Dad. That he'd tried to get in touch.'

Dad frowns. 'I panicked. I didn't want him back in our lives. He had . . . no right to you. No right at all.'

*Other than being my biological dad, you mean.* 'But you had no right to keep it from me, either.'

He sighs. Pinches his temples. I can see this conversation's going to test his commitment to non-communication. 'I suppose I thought you'd find out one day. I was probably just trying to delay the inevitable.'

I let the clock tick on. What can I say, really? I can't forgive him this yet, but still I want to hear his side.

'Your mother did try to tell him she was pregnant, back then. But Warren said he was off travelling before she could get the words out.'

'So you stepped in.'

He exhales. 'Not at first. She wouldn't even agree to a date with me until your first birthday.' A thin smile. 'That's why you were always so close, I think. You had that time together, just the two of you, in that funny little bedsit of hers.'

I trace the outline of a heart onto the table with my index finger. I did always have a special bond with Mum. She'd dance me in her arms around the living room, whisper me stories when my siblings had gone to bed. Confide in me like an old friend. I always assumed it was because I was her firstborn. But news of that year spent together, just the two of us, already feels like treasure to me. Something precious unearthed from freshly turned soil.

I sip my coffee. 'So you went on a date and . . . ?'

Still hesitant, he clears his throat. 'She moved in soon afterwards, fell pregnant with your brother. We got married, then Tamsin came along.'

'Why didn't you ever tell me? Before, I mean. When I was younger.'

'We always planned to. But after she died, I didn't feel it was my place. I suppose that's partly why I was so angry when Warren turned up. You have to understand, Joel – we'd built an entire life together by the time she passed. We'd never heard from Warren. I didn't *want* to talk about any of that again.' He frowns. Fiddles with his glasses. 'Maybe some of my choices weren't perfect. But in the end, your mother and I were married for twelve years. We had three kids, a house, money, friends. And I believe – I truly believe – she was happy.'

Honestly? I believe it too.

'Look, maybe she didn't love me in the . . . wild, crazy way she loved Warren. But when she had you kids – well, that was a different kind of wild, crazy love. A better kind. And Warren never wanted a family – that was one of the first things he told her when they met. He knew that much about himself, at least.'

I agree with Warren's stance. But, luckily for me, I guess, he failed pretty spectacularly to stick to it.

'He knew what he'd lost, though.'

I nod. 'Must be why he tried so hard to make contact.'

'No, long before that. After your mum got ill for the last time, I saw him leaving her ward at the hospital. He'd obviously had a few regrets.'

'You saw him?'

'Yes. I'd have known him anywhere. Funny, though.'

'What was?'

'Well, she'd only been admitted that morning. I hadn't told a soul. I suppose your mother must have got in touch with him. I mean, the man's a lot of things, but he's not psychic.'

Somewhere inside, a rush of realisation.

Dad shrugs like it's irrelevant in the end, that his wife's ex-lover rocked up at her deathbed. 'So how do you see things working out, between you and him?'

'I . . . I don't know. Do you mind – me keeping in touch with him?'

'No,' is the extent of the encouragement he's prepared to give me. 'But be careful. That's all I'd say.'

A surge of affection, warm as bathwater. 'You'll always be my dad.'

His frown deepens. 'Likewise. You'll always be . . .'

He doesn't finish the sentence. But that he even made a stab at it is good enough for me.

'Friend-of-a-friend, my arse.'

'Joel?'

I'm in my new favourite bolthole, the garden, staring at frost-fringed roofs. The air's icy tonight, but I haven't bothered with a coat.

'You didn't hear Mum was dying from a friend-of-a-friend. You dreamt about her, right at the start. You dreamt she'd die of cancer, and you finished it because you wanted her to go and live her life, before it was too late.'

A sigh. 'I suppose you were going to figure it out one day. You're far cleverer than me, thankfully.'

'Yeah, yeah. Tell me the *truth*.'

'I dreamt . . . I saw her in hospital. Then two nights later, I dreamt about her funeral.'

'So you knew she'd have kids, go on to have a full life. You weren't a selfish bugger at all – you were the opposite. You ended it because you wanted her to be happy.'

A yawning jaw of silence.

'Yes, all right?' he says eventually. 'Yes. She had fourteen years left, and I knew with all my issues and lack of money and drinking, I wasn't going to make her happy, in the short term at least.'

I breathe my pain into the rimy air, watch it balloon into tiny, angry storm clouds. 'So that's why you've been telling me to let Callie go.'

Warren exhales. The line crackles. 'When I went to see your mum in hospital, I knew I'd done the right thing. That she'd lived a good life. That she was dying happy. I chose not to mess up what time she had left, and for what it's worth, I think I made the right decision.'

Unexpectedly, I feel the boulder of guilt on my back lighten a little. Not much, but enough for me to notice. *Warren knew too, Mum.*

Maybe subconsciously I didn't want to mess up the time Mum had left, either.

'Just so you know, Joel, with me and your mum it was true love. As a person I was fairly useless, but I loved your mum. When we held hands and looked at each other that last time, everything had been worth it, to know she was happy.'

I think of Callie cocooned in our bed. Of her present and her future and the end. I think about all those things. And then I know what I have to do.

# 71

## Callie

The night after Guy Fawkes, I call Joel while I'm knee-deep in water in the middle of a marsh to ask if he fancies dinner at the new tapas place in town.

For the past few days I've been mulling something over, and now I'm buoyant with excitement about it. All afternoon as I'm trudging around in waders and wellies while the rain pours, I imagine revealing my plan, a beatific smile on my face. I picture myself assuring him that this – *this* – is why it was the right call not to tell me. Because I'm able to plot a future now that I simply wouldn't be bothering with otherwise.

In the end, I don't bring it up until dessert.

Joel seems subdued tonight, distracted. His mind is elsewhere, and I start to worry that perhaps my timing's all off. I know he's barely slept lately – he's been as exhausted this week as I've ever known him.

But the evening's escaping, and I can't wait any longer.

'I had a meeting with Fiona on Monday.'

Joel turns his dark eyes to me, and my nerves are quelled. Despite the low mood, his expression remains loyally loving. 'About your contract?'

'They've offered me a permanent role.'

'Cal, that's . . . that's amazing. Monday? Why didn't you say?'

'Well, I've been . . . The thing is, she's tipped me off about this cottage that's coming up for rent on the far side of Waterfen. An old reed-cutter's place. She took me to see it yesterday. It's gorgeous, Joel. We could live there, you and me, and we'd be right on the reserve, surrounded by the trees and the birds and the reeds . . .'

His eyes meet mine now, but I can't quite interpret the look on his face. Is he emotional with pride or something sadder?

'Fiona said she could give me a few weeks' break between contracts, too.' I smile, look down at my half-eaten dessert. 'They never need much persuasion to save a bit of cash.'

His expression asks me to fill in the blanks.

*Here goes.* 'You remember Dave, the guy who left soon after I started, to move to Brazil? Well, he sent us a postcard.' I slide it across the table to him. 'And it got me thinking . . .'

Joel picks up the postcard, scans it quickly. 'You want to do this? Go to Brazil?'

'No. I thought I'd go to Chile, to Lauca National Park. Try to find that bird.'

Joel smiles at me – for possibly the first time tonight – and swigs from his glass. 'I think that's a brilliant idea.'

I spoon up a little more *crema catalana*. I'm pleased I decided to have three courses – I mean, there are ninety-year-olds all over the place who've eaten cheese and drunk whisky and smoked like chimneys their whole lives. 'And I was thinking . . . once I'm back we can move into the Waterfen cottage, and I'll work at the reserve.'

He nods – but so slowly it feels almost redundant. 'Well, maybe you shouldn't come back, Cal.'

I do a sort of mental double-take. 'What?'

Another swig of wine. 'I think . . . you should go to Chile for as long as you want.'

'Yes, a few weeks, like I—'

'And after that, you should go wherever the wind takes you.'

'Well,' I say nervously, 'the wind would bring me back here. To you.'

'No.' Though definite, the word sounds wrong, strangely out of context. Like the call of a migrant bird blown off-course.

'No what?'

'You need to live your life, Cal.'

'But I would be—'

'No, I mean, really *live*. Forget about me. Do all the things you want to do, and more.'

I laugh. 'What are you talking about? I don't want to forget about you.'

'It's for the best.'

'Joel, no . . . What?'

'This . . . isn't going to work, Cal.'

Though the restaurant's warm and full, pleasantly buzzing, our table feels suddenly cold.

'Joel,' I breathe. 'We have to try. If we don't, then we may as well give up.'

The look on his face burrows deep into my gut and stays there.

'You are,' I realise slowly, my eyes jumping with tears. 'You're giving up. You're giving up?'

'I'm . . . accepting reality. That what we have . . . we can't make it work.'

Across the table, I take his hand. 'No, this is . . . *No*. We belong together, Joel. No one . . . no one can make me laugh like you do. It makes me happy just to wake up next to you every day. No one's ever made me feel as if the world's out there for the taking the way you have. Without you, I'd probably still be working in the café, watching my life go by. You've made me excited for the future again. We can get through this . . . I *know* we can.'

He shakes his head. 'I'm only going to hold you back, Callie. I don't want you to miss out on the . . . amazing life you deserve.'

'No. *No*. An amazing life – that's the one I have with you.'

Somewhere behind his eyes, a door swings shut. I notice his fingers tighten around the stem of his wine glass. He's hardly touched his dessert. 'Not if I can't do what you need me to do.'

'What do I need you to do?' But I know, I know.

'You need me to carry on as if nothing's happened, to live with what I dreamt every day, pretending I didn't. I can't do it, Cal. I just . . . can't.' The words heave from his chest like a dying breath. 'You should forget me now. Get out there and live.'

What I want to say is, *How?* But instead I say, 'You're wrong.'

'Someone . . . someone else could give you so much more than I can.'

I take a sharp breath, startle back from even the thought of it.

Joel's voice splinters. 'I can't deny you a future, Callie. Possibilities. Nothing would make me happier than to see you happy. And while we're living with what I dreamt every day, that's never going to happen. You know that, don't you?'

Piece by piece, this conversation is taking me apart. My fingers have gone numb, my toes are detached from my feet – but still I'm going to fight for us. 'No. I love you, Joel, and I know you love me. This is too good to give up. There's got to be a way we can . . . Why don't you go back to Diana?' I say, in desperation. 'She said she might be able to help.'

'But she can't change the future, Callie,' he whispers, his eyes full of sadness. And as he speaks, the weight of everything he's saying takes me down, because I know he's ending it here, tonight, now.

'This is all for nothing,' I say, one last attempt to get through to him. 'Because even if you told me what you know, our lives wouldn't be better. They'd be worse. Telling me isn't the answer.'

'Then there's no more we can . . .' But he trips over his words and can't finish.

I keep staring, and we keep saying nothing, and soon my tears are too heavy to hold back. Because maybe if what he's saying is true – if he really can't live with it – then there isn't a way forward.

Maybe there just isn't.

'Something has to change, Cal,' he says eventually, softly. 'One of us just needed to say it.'

I'm shaking my head now. Not because I still think I can change his mind, but because I'm winded, in shock. 'I can't . . . believe this.'

His expression says he can't believe it either. So sudden and brutal, like a heart attack or a car crash.

As my eyes start leaking tears, the flame from the tea-light seems to flicker sympathy. 'I've had the best year of my life,' I say, because I need him to know.

'I think for you,' he whispers, 'the best is yet to come.'

'I wish you hadn't had that dream.' My words are a riptide of regret. 'I wish that more than anything.'

Our gazes fuse. 'I tried so hard not to love you, Callie. But that was impossible, because . . . well. You're you.'

Feeling the stares of nearby diners swivelling one by one towards me, I reach for my napkin and start wiping my eyes. By now my mascara is probably all over my face.

Perhaps reflexively, Joel leans across the table to help, which makes me cry harder, grab his hand. 'How can it end like this?' I say, as his fingers grip mine, perhaps for the last time. 'We're not finished yet.'

'I know.' His eyes cling to me. 'That's what makes this so hard.'

But he's right. I can see that now. We've finally run out of road, with no way of turning back.

Releasing a breath, I attempt to steady myself for the toughest part, the part I'm not sure I can force my body to do. I manage to get to my feet, though I'm swaying a little.

I can't look at him, because if I do, I won't be able to go through with it.

'I'll stay at Esther's tonight—'

'No, don't. I'll go to Tamsin's.'

I pause then, because I can't leave for ever without saying it. 'Just . . . trust people to love you, Joel. Because they do, so much.'

And now I'm through the front door, negotiating the road somehow, not caring about the cold. As I reach the opposite pavement, I manage to turn around and blink back at the restaurant, as if to check it's still there, half hoping this is all just my mind's illusion, a mirage created by strangely angled light.

At our table with his back to the window, Joel has lowered his head. The traffic goes silent around me, and the street melts away. It's just me now, staring at Joel through a pane of glass, like he's already an artefact, something to be loved but never touched again.

Then comes the hiss of bus brakes, a whistle of wind. People push past, and sound swells around me. The world is moving me along, and a current's clipping at my feet.

I breathe in and then out, step forward, let it take me.

It's only when I crash-land on Esther's doorstep twenty minutes later that I discover I'm still clutching my dessert spoon.

# 72

## Joel

Once Callie's left the restaurant, I stay where I am for maybe thirty minutes, an hour. Eventually the candle at our table burns out. But none of the waiters come close. They must have seen what happened. A relationship smashed into pieces, right here in their restaurant.

I can't stop staring at her empty plate.

In the end, the waiter lets me take it home with me. I arrived with the only girl I've ever truly loved, and leave just two hours later with a single plate and a broken heart.

We haven't even made it to a year. Let alone a lifetime.

# PART FOUR

# 73

## Callie

*Life is so different, these days. Whenever I stop to think about it, it's hard to believe how much has changed since the last time I saw you.*

But when was the last time you saw me, Joel? Do you ever see me in your dreams? Sometimes I wonder how much you know about the way I live now — the things you've been privy to, the details and the colours. I've thought a lot about what you said — I think for you the best is yet to come — *and I've wondered for so long about how much weight to give that. If my sadness is misplaced. If I should feel only optimism.*

*I know all you ever wanted was for me to be happy. But I also know, for that to happen, I'm going to have to learn to let you go.*

*I'm trying, Joel. To pick my heart off the floor, love what we were, and finally let you go.*

*Just know, every day, that I'm trying.*

# 74

## Joel – six months after

I've got a dodgy back and permanently jarred neck from all my disjointed nights on the sofa. I've been sleeping there since Callie left. It's a small price to pay for not having to lie next to the empty space where, in another life, she should have been.

A week after she moved out, Esther and Gavin came over to pick up her many things. I couldn't face being there, so I took the dogs (minus Murphy, of course) for a ten-mile hike. When I got back, the flat was empty again. Lifeless, just an echo. Exactly as it was before she moved in.

At first I thought it might help not to be surrounded by her stuff. I hoped the blankness might snuff out the memories. But there were traces of her all over the place. Still are. Hairbands under sofa cushions, in drawers, hooked on doorknobs. Odd socks hidden among my things. The flowerpots on the patio, redundant and weed-filled now. Her favourite work fleece (Esther forgot to take it) still hanging by the front door, filling my hallway with the faint smell of bonfires. Strands of cut reed from her boots against the kitchen kickboards, because I can't yet bear to sweep them up. Last week, I trod on a stud earring, one half of a pair I'd bought her.

I didn't even care when it drew blood.

I miss her like she's been stolen from me. Like I've been robbed in the dark of something irreplaceable. Since that night in the restaurant I've been unable to walk past the coffee shop, or go anywhere near Waterfen. I can't even pass the end of the road where the Sicilian pastry shop is. I failed to celebrate Christmas, watched back-to-back action films on Valentine's night. I live from cereal box to cereal box, dog walk to dog walk. Occasionally I surface to check on Tamsin, Amber and five-month-old Harry, then head back to the flat to carry on staring at four walls.

It's a good job I have only a hypothetical neighbour to consider. With Danny hardly about, I'm not obliged to care what he might think of me right now. I don't have to make small-talk or pretend to be okay. And, best of all, I don't have to come up with crap like *It is what it is* and *I actually think it's for the best* (which was as much as I could say to my family during those first few weeks).

Dad and Doug, though they liked Callie a lot, seemed unsurprised by our break-up. But Tamsin was devastated. And I'll never forget the way Amber's face crumpled when I told her she might not see Auntie Callie again. It felt like the most careless kind of cruelty.

When I got home that night, I sobbed.

One afternoon in early May, I tune in to the sound of my intercom buzzing. For a good ten minutes now I've been staring at the patch of floor by the hearth where Murphy used to lie. Conjuring up the warmth of his body against my thigh, the sunlight of Callie's smile by my side.

It's the little things that take me down. Like turning my head to speak to her, before remembering she's gone. Wondering what she might fancy for dinner. Coming across a mug she's left behind as I boil the kettle for tea. Reliving our best kisses. Those times when just to touch her sent me spinning off into the stratosphere.

And Murphy. How he'd patter around after me, always hopeful of dropped cheese or a handful of words he could understand. Appended to me like a shadow. Gentle as a lamb, unquestioningly loyal.

After twenty seconds or so the buzzing stops, only to be replaced by the aggravation of my phone ringing. Glancing at the screen, I'm alarmed to see Warren's name flash up.

I stretch to peer through a crack in the blinds at the bay window. He's standing on my goddamn doorstep. Spots me straight away.

'You can't stay,' is all I say when I open the door. He's got a suitcase and everything.

'I'm worried about you.'

'I can't do this right now.'

'You don't have to do anything. Just let me in, so at least you're not alone.'

Without warning, that gets me. I break down beneath a torrent of tears, the kind that make your body convulse. So he just holds me and holds me until I can't cry any more.

Later he goes out to buy pineapple fritters and chips. It's the first hot food I've had in maybe a fortnight because, honestly, what's the point when you can ingest cereal by the fistful? We eat off our knees, side by side like old men at the beach. Fingers shiny with fat, lips stinging with vinegar.

'You've lost weight,' he remarks. 'You look pale, too.'

Why do people keep telling me this? As if I didn't already know, or no longer have access to a functioning mirror.

'When I split up with your mum I postponed my trip for a bit,' Warren says. 'Just sat in my bedsit and forgot to eat for a month. Lost touch with friends, got miserable.'

*Yeah, and meanwhile she was pregnant with me,* I think. *Have you ever wondered how she was feeling?*

'And then I realised,' he continues. 'You know what solves everything? Salt water on your face.'

I stare at him blankly, half wondering what he's here to try to sell me.

'You need to duck-dive a few waves, mate. Come surfing with me. It'll help, I promise. You'll feel like a new person. If I ever have a problem, the sea sorts it out.'

Right now, I don't want Warren to be my mate, or to feel like a new person. I want to travel back to the night of my dream and consume caffeine at quantities that would cut short a coma.

'Come to Cornwall, stay for a bit. I'll teach you to surf, help you move on.'

'I'm not ready to move on.'

Warren brushes salt from his fingers. 'This is no good. Look at you – you're making yourself ill. You need to get out more, see people . . .'

'There's a decent hotel by the river. It's not too expensive. I'll give them a ring.'

Warren sighs heavily. 'Okay. I'll check myself in tomorrow, if you insist.'

'I do.'

'But tonight I can kip here.' He pats the sofa cushion. 'I'll be no bother.'

Perhaps the rumpled duvet should have given him a clue. 'Actually, that's kind of my bed at the moment.'

He looks at me pityingly. 'Come on, Joel.'

'Look, no offence, Warren, but you don't get to tell me how to live.'

'You did the right thing, you know. Letting her go.'

I think about my mum. The decision Warren made that enabled her to live her life.

Still. 'Right doesn't make it easy.'

'I know. But I'm sure Callie wouldn't want you to—'

That does it. 'Maybe you should just go.'

He eyeballs me helplessly. 'That's really what you want?'

*Just . . . trust people to love you, Joel.*

'I can't do this right now,' is all I say.

After he leaves I sit on the sofa, the air congealing with chip-shop fat. I try to imagine what Callie's doing now, wonder if I'll ever stop feeling this way. I think about her until my heart is alight and my mind ablaze, and then I finally fan the flames with a double shot of Scotland's finest.

## 75

## Callie – six months after

The months have leapfrogged into May, yet I've never felt more damp, more grey, more lonely.

Friday nights are the worst. That once-golden time of the week, a sensation of supreme release – like slipping into a warm bath, letting out a held breath. But now just the act of arriving home at the end of the week is enough to trigger a landslide of memories from those glorious months before Joel's dream, when life – and our love – truly felt infinite.

Back then, Friday nights meant Joel, a crackling fire, the enticing sight of chilled white wine. A weekend waiting for us like a cork to be popped, long lazy kisses that ushered in evenings lost to love-making, our skin pink and slick, heartbeats thundering. Slow showers together before nights out in town, candlelit dinners, drinks with friends.

My mind filters out the messier stuff, like when Joel couldn't sleep, or got snagged on the meaning of a dream. Because none of the hiccups mattered, not really. I loved him fully, for the whole person he was.

Six months on, I still do.

Life has barely been life since I left the restaurant that night. I couldn't bear for Mum and Dad to go through my pain second-hand, so I crash-landed straight away at Esther and Gavin's. It was the only place to go, really. Because, inside, I felt almost as I did when Grace died.

Esther wasn't quite sure what to do with me at first. We'd experienced the aftermath of Grace's death together – drinking too much, staring numbly at each other and occasionally voicing reminders to eat and wash. Now she was watching me go through it all again alone, and the ugliness of grief is no spectator sport. Shut out in the cold, she kept begging me to let her in.

There's still so much she doesn't know. Like exactly why Joel and I broke up (I only ever tell her, 'It just couldn't work,' before I'm forced to turn away). Or why I started spending so much time in her little basement kitchen, staring at the spot where Joel and I stood that night at her party, to share a kiss I'd remember for ever.

After a few weeks, Esther's bewilderment at the state of me grew gradually into incentive. So I finally moved out and into the cottage at the edge of Waterfen, because there's only so long you can skulk around your friend's house like a ghost. Poor Gavin must have wanted to hang out the bunting when I eventually left.

I'd accepted the full-time job from Fiona by then too, asking for no break between contracts, because I couldn't bear the thought of stepping on a plane to Chile.

But now, in my darkest moments, the idea of escape is beckoning me once again, winking at me through the blackness. I've been pulling the travel guides off my shelf more regularly, flicking through them over breakfast or after I've climbed into bed.

Maybe one day soon I'll use some leave to fly away, attempt to rebuild my mind.

The cottage is no-frills, but it's exactly what I need. Perfectly isolated on the edge of the reserve, it's surrounded by reeds and tall trees, overlooked only by kestrels and owls. There's no one to hear me crying here, no one to urge me to eat or to inform me I look like death – although I know I do, but I just can't seem to care. And because access to the cottage is via a long, potholed track requiring permission to cross train tracks, I rarely have to worry about unannounced visitors. Much of my social contact moves onto my phone, and that suits me fine.

Sometimes, after dark, I'll take long hikes across the reserve, just me and Murphy and the moon. And sometimes I'll howl out loud, release my agony into the night sky, and wonder in the moments that follow if I'm actually going mad.

It's the little things that spark the worst kind of loneliness – smiling as I start to think about the weekend, or opening WhatsApp to ask how his day's going, before the thunderclap of recollection comes. And I can't even deny reality, the way I did with Grace, by leaving messages he won't ever receive. Because he *is* still here, he *is* only down the road – but he's just not mine any more.

When Esther fetched my things from the flat, she brought back some of Joel's T-shirts by mistake. I've spent whole evenings curled up on the sofa, holding them to me as though I'm holding him. I well up if I hear a robin through the kitchen window, insist on meeting Dot far away from the coffee shop whenever we get together, bake *drømmekage* in batches that I then fail to eat. I scroll endlessly through the pictures on my phone, unable to look away from his lovely face, fighting the urge to call.

Always, always fighting the urge to call. I've heard nothing from him since the day I walked out of the restaurant, and can only take that to mean he wants no further contact.

Though Joel is my greatest weakness, I have been strong enough to prevent my mind from wandering too far ahead – to how, and where, and how long I have. When that thought does flicker to life, I've become adept at snuffing it quickly out. I don't want to give it oxygen, or all this pain will have been for nothing.

I've added the dessert spoon from the restaurant to my small collection of memories, the things that will for ever remind me of us. The hotel shampoo from Hugo's wedding. The collar from the abandoned dog Joel saved, that bravely pulled through in the end. The tractor T-shirt's in there too, because I can no longer bear to wear it, and the note Joel wrote urging me to apply for the job at Waterfen. Jewellery he's given me, the glasses and carafe from Christmas the year before last. A bittersweet medley of our time together, short as it was. A story only half told.

## 76

## Joel – eleven months after

'You're a natural.'

'You think?'

'Look at the way he's gazing at you,' Tamsin says. 'Sure you don't fancy moving in, letting us sleep for six months? We'll pay.'

I smile, bounce Harry up and down on my knee. Miraculously, he's stopped yelling, though we definitely can't relax yet. He's not *exactly* gazing. I'd say he's scrutinising my face while considering his next move. Master tacticians, babies.

'Actually, Joel, I do need your help with something. Non-childcare-related.'

'Go for it.'

'It's to do with the other day. When you called and told me not to get on the tube.'

I saw the tube station in a dream, only a few hours ahead of time. A massive stampede, blind panic, screaming. I couldn't make out the station, but I did know Tamsin was due to visit an old uni friend in London that day with Amber and Harry. (I had no idea at that point why the stampede started, or how. Had nothing at all I could bother TfL with.)

'Oh, that.' I bounce Harry up and down again, talk directly at him. Pull a series of astonished expressions, like people do when they're playing for time.

'Yeah, that. You see, I'm a bit confused.'

'About what?'

'About how you could possibly have known. You rang me hours before it happened.' The thing was covered widely on the news, took over social media for most of the day.

A trapped-wing flutter inside my chest. 'I told you. It was just a feeling.'

'Come on, Joel.'

I remember what Callie said to me on Boxing Day nearly two years ago. About my visions being a gift. And her words as she was leaving the restaurant.

*Just . . . trust people to love you, Joel.*

I glance at my sister. She looks pretty no-nonsense today (hair pulled back, khaki dress, kick-ass boots) but old habits die hard. Years of keeping the words in, burying my secrets.

'I'm going to tell you something now,' she says.

I swallow, uneasy. *Isn't that my line?* 'Okay.'

'Remember when I was here last year, and I told you I was pregnant? Just before I left, I went to use the loo.'

I raise my eyebrows at Harry again. Say nothing.

'Well, when I came out you guys were in the hallway, and I heard Callie saying to you, *A brother for Amber. And Harry's just perfect.*'

I stare at the blue-eyed culprit in front of me. *Come on, Harry. Now's your moment. Scream, fill your nappy. Projectile vomit if you have to. Anything.*

'Anyway, I was really confused. I'd always known if I had a boy I'd want to call him Harry, but I'd never told you that.' Her gaze glides over me. 'So I started to think, and add things up – your supposed paranoia, your anxiety all these years. You knowing Harry's name and gender before I did. The tube. Your skittishness, how you were after Mum died.'

'Okay,' I say, rubbing Harry's chubby arms with my hands. He almost looks as if he's smiling now, the cheeky little beggar. Clearly he has zero intention of helping his favourite uncle out. 'Okay.'

'I know I always tease you for being a bit . . .'

'I know.'

'. . . but you can trust me, Joel. You can tell me anything.'

I meet her eye for just a second. A few months ago, Dad and I told Tamsin and Doug about Warren. It ran a razor blade through my soul, to watch my sister cry the way she did that day. This has been one of the hardest and weirdest times of my life, filled with arguments, accusations, questions. And now here I am, about to put her love to the test all over again.

But, ultimately, I know Tamsin's world is one of optimism. Of straight, sunlit paths, long, sweeping bends. She refuses to believe in cliff edges and dead ends, darkened corners. She thinks anything is surmountable, and for her so far it has been. If ever I needed proof of that, it was telling her we were only half related. Because in the end she accepted the whole thing fully and generously, let absolutely nothing between us change.

So I take a breath and then a leap. Hold my nephew close. Keep talking. 'I see . . . what's going to happen, Tam. To the people I love. In my dreams. I see the future play out, hours, days, weeks in advance.'

Harry gurgles sceptically, which is fair enough. But Tamsin's sitting very still. She puts a hand to her mouth, eyes bright with tears.

'Please believe me,' I whisper. I didn't realise until now how much I need her to.

'I knew it,' she says slowly. 'All this time . . . I mean, I *knew* it, Joel.'

'How?' My voice barely grazes the air.

Her mouth gapes. She shrugs wildly, like I've asked her to explain why we need oxygen. 'You're never surprised. By anything. You've always got a subtle warning here, a casual suggestion there. You always seem to know . . . when we've had an argument or something's happened. And last week, when Dad . . .'

'Yes,' I say quietly. Having dreamt about his particularly violent stomach bug (lucky me), I asked him, without thinking, over Sunday lunch how he was. Forgot he'd not actually told any of us. I brushed it off quickly, insisted he had. But I felt Tamsin watching me.

'It's all been adding up, over the years, and then with Harry, and the tube . . .'

Harry makes a starfish with his hand, reaches for my nose. I dip my head, let his fingers touch my face.

'Is it medical?'

'Inherited,' I confess. 'I got it from Warren.'

Tamsin swears on the exhale. 'Why the hell didn't you tell me, Joel? It's *me*, for God's sake. You could have trusted me.' I have a sense that if I wasn't holding her son, she might choose this moment to chuck something at my head.

'It's hardly standard information, Tam. And I didn't want to risk my relationship with you. I couldn't have dealt with that, especially after Mum. Me and you . . . we were always so close.'

'Which is exactly why you should have told me.' Tamsin rummages in her handbag, withdraws a pack of tissues. 'Joel, is this why Callie left?'

In my arms, Harry does a great impression of an earthworm angling for air. 'Sort of,' I tell her, because of course I can't give her the full story. 'But it wasn't her fault.'

We carry on talking well into the evening, until Harry makes it clear that he really would like us to wrap things up.

Tamsin hugs me hard when she leaves, assures me she's here for me. Insists she'll always love me. She tries to say, too, that she's sure I can work things out with Callie.

It's the only point in almost three hours at which I nearly lose it.

But I don't. I wait until she leaves before I let myself break down.

It's been nearly a year, now. I knew that night in the restaurant had to be the last time we saw each other. But, somehow, I still can't believe it actually was. That I can't now roll over and touch her arm in bed. Kiss her on the sofa when she says something lovely. Feel a high-five in my stomach when she doubles up with laughter over a joke I've made.

I still give all our haunts a wide berth. I can't risk running into her, jeopardising my resolve. Warren's suggested that if I'm craving a way to feel close to her, I should book myself into the wellness retreat she gave me a voucher for two years ago. It's expired now, of course. But perhaps he's right. Maybe if I went there, it would be a comfort, somehow. A quiet connection to her again, like hands linking up in the dark.

But I know I'm not ready. Maybe one day I will be. But not yet.

Still, wellness comes in many forms. A couple of months back, Steve asked me to try training with him. He suggested I start with one of his odious riverside boot-camp sessions (using telling phrases like *All levels* and *Your own pace* and *No judgement*). After some pestering, I agreed. Because I had to do something to stop myself thinking about her.

It was the boxing drills I got the most from. Punching out my anger, swinging my fists with frustration. I'd think about the impossible waste of it all while I was punching. *Why, why, why, why, why?* Then, when I was done, I'd have to crouch to the floor, so the person holding the pads wouldn't see I was close to tears.

Spotting my slightly dysfunctional preference for using my fists, Steve invited me to the gym proper. So three times a week now I'm one-on-one with my old friend, punching the whole thing out. Steve just stands there, pads raised, sturdy as steel.

It helps, a bit. Not just to unleash my anguish, but to feel I'm not alone.

## 77

## Callie – eleven months after

Late in the afternoon on my first full day in Lauca National Park, I'm crouched covertly low to the ground, my guide Ricardo at my side. I bumped into him last night in the lobby of my hostel, binoculars around his neck, explaining to a couple of other travellers what was so special about the park. To my dismay they quickly glazed over, but I was enthralled.

So I caught him as he was leaving, asked about the bird I was desperate to find. I could hire him as a guide the next day, he said, instantly animated. I might have to work in with a few other sightseers but, yes, he could take me to see that bird, and whatever else piqued my interest along the way. He high-fived me before he left, which would have utterly convinced me if I wasn't already sold.

The temperature's sliding now, and even wrapped up in my coat and hat, I'm on the verge of a shiver. Though that could just be excitement, the thrill of anticipation.

We're gazing over the boundless rocky moonscape of the *altiplano*, across rambling hummocks of vegetation and a theatrical skyline, the air growing earthy as it cools.

'There,' Ricardo says, lowering his binoculars so he can point. 'You see?'

A gust of wind jerks my hands as I raise the binoculars Ricardo's lent me, train my sight on the diademed sandpiper-plover perched atop a clod of earth in the cushion bog.

Finally, it departs the branches of my imagination. I'd know it anywhere – that white belly with the faint black barring. The fawn wings and black head, patched red at the back, like a blotch of rust.

*After all these years.*

My heart is soaring, helium-high. I am spellbound, breathing gasps of joy, my eyes laced with tears. To be looking at something so scarce, so precious – to have such a rare experience – is unmatched by anything I've encountered in the natural world before.

'You see it, Callie?' Ricardo says again.

'I see it,' I whisper, my voice shaking with delight. 'I see it.'

'Shall I take a picture?'

I think of Dave and smile. *If you ever get a picture, make sure you send it to me.* 'No,' I tell Ricardo, fumbling for my camera. 'No, I'll do it.'

We sit together for nearly twenty minutes, taking pictures and exchanging observations as the bird begins to move, lowering its beak to forage for bugs and grubs in the bog. My mind is buffeted by the sight of it, dwarfed beneath this towering panorama – the formidable volcanoes with their snow-dipped peaks, a crayon-blue sky where condors soar. A landscape that feels almost cosmic, extra-terrestrial. I am surrounded by the vastness of nature, and I take two or three rich breaths, trying to reel in the moment like a prize.

'You okay?' Ricardo looks concerned. He's been hyper-vigilant about altitude sickness, carries oxygen in the back of the 4x4.

I nod.

'Headache?'

'No, I'm fine, just . . . trying to take it all in. So I don't forget.'

'You won't.' Ricardo smiles, with a shrug that says, *Because that would be impossible.*

He's right, of course. It's like the hot black road we took to get here was a highway to another planet – one that exists far beyond the gravity of Joel and me, and everything we've lost. To be here is to forget my pain, fulfil a dream.

Liam would love it, I think, this edge-of-the-world terrain with its shrill chorus of winds.

'Shall we go and get the others?' Ricardo says eventually, gesturing back at the 4x4. He means the three other travellers from my hostel, who were interested in finding the thermal springs up the road, but not my little bird.

I don't want to leave – I could stay out here all night, shelter beneath the swathes of stars – but the thermal springs will be closing soon. 'Thank you,' I tell Ricardo, 'for showing me. I've wanted to see it for so many years.'

'If we're quick,' he says, 'we might still catch some flamingos.'

My trips out with Ricardo in the 4x4 over the next few days bring about a series of wondrous encounters – vicunas and llamas, alpacas and deer, rich scatterings of birds. Together we explore, picnicking on the toes of volcanoes, hiking up to marvel at lagoons. I am treated to yawning canyons and bright rivers, to immense picturesque plateaus, and I soak up every scrap of Ricardo's expertise. I'll always be grateful for the incredible things he's shown me.

My first time beyond Europe, and my eyes are now wide open to the world.

'So where's your next stop?'

It's my last night here before I journey west to Arica for three days, then south to the Atacama Desert via more national parks. After that, on to Santiago for three nights before flying home, concluding my three-week trip. I'm in a bar in Putre with Aaron, another traveller from the hostel, who invited me out for a drink. I said yes, because I've seen him around and he seems friendly enough. Plus I fancied the company.

We've chatted casually over the last few days. Originally from Cape Town, Aaron works in Rio but is touring South America for a few weeks by himself. Charismatic and quick, he seems interested in me, and makes me belly-laugh, but . . . he's just a little *too* perfect. He's tall and athletic, energetic and charming, all winks and cheekbones, flawless in the way that Piers seemed to be when I first met him. I prefer to see a person's kinks, I think. You don't get such a shock, that way, when the dazzle of the early days first begins to dim.

I outline my itinerary, then ask Aaron what his plans are. He's heading off in the opposite direction to me, across the border into Bolivia. He says I can come if I want to. And maybe if things were different – if I didn't still feel so raw about Joel – I might consider it, do something a bit crazy.

But I know the way to get over Joel isn't to supplant him with someone else. So I lean across and peck Aaron on the cheek, thank him for the excellent wine, wish him safe travels.


En route to Heathrow a week ago, the tsunami of memories was constant. All I could think about was leaping from the train and rushing home, telling Joel how much I still loved him. Even at the airport, I kept glancing over my shoulder, wondering if I might see him scrambling through the crowds to reach me, the way they do in films.

And once I was on the plane, for almost the whole flight to Chile, I kept asking myself what I would have done if he *had* turned up at the airport. Would I have succumbed to the madness of temptation, kissed him right there where I stood in the departures hall?

But finally I realised I was missing the point. Joel wouldn't have turned up at the airport because he *wants* us to move on. I thought back again to that last night at the restaurant, when he gripped my hand and urged me to see a better future for myself. *I think for you the best is yet to come.* And while I can't yet picture a time when being without him will feel okay, I know all he ever wanted was for me to be happy. So I made a pact with myself before we touched down that in Chile, I would try to ease slowly forward. The next few weeks should be about my life and what it could look like, because as yet I honestly had no idea.

The dessert spoon from the restaurant was nestled in the bottom of my rucksack. I brought it with me as a reminder. That life – if I could yet believe it – was here to be savoured and enjoyed. Sampled and tasted, as many flavours as possible.

When I get back to the hostel, I email my bird photo to Liam, Fiona and Dave –

**Saw a unicorn today!**

Then I sit on my bed and take a pen and postcard from my bag.

My hand is shaking slightly as I write the first word. *Joel.*

Despite my resolve to move on, I've been hit today by the strongest compulsion to tell him how I'm feeling. It came to me earlier while I was in a thermal pool, basking like a turtle in the water. I had both eyes on the raptors circling the sky when, without warning, a film reel of flashbacks began to spool through my mind. The lake at Hugo's wedding. Joel ribbing me about wild swimming the morning after. What we snuck off and did next, on our way home.

Because we did find a field to have fun in, that day. We parked in a lay-by, rushed hand in hand along a margin of ripening wheat before tumbling together between its sun-baked tunnels, the crop like hot rope against our skin. Afterwards we lay flat on our backs and stared up at the sky, where raptors wheeled above our heads.

And it's got me thinking. How everything we did together was like a bittersweet prologue to all that I'm doing now. And it feels wrong, somehow, not to be sharing it with him. So I do. I keep hold of the pen, and I write Joel a postcard.

Though I'll probably never send it, it's a kiss blown across oceans, from my heart to his.

## 78

## Joel – eighteen months after

Dawn patrol. I'm a pretty decent surfer now, since I started making regular trips to Cornwall and Warren shoved me into lines of white-water, told me to paddle and try not to kill anyone.

I look across. Give him the thumbs-up, a salty grin. It's only May, so the sea's not had a chance to warm up yet. Even through five milli-metres of neoprene, the breaking waves steal my breath.

But the swells are prolific and the summer crowds haven't peaked.

I sit up on my shortboard, watch the sets roll in. Picking my wave, I paddle, take off, charge left. Vaguely aware of Warren to my right, for a few exultant moments I no longer have to think. The water becomes thunder, deafening as a military fly-past.

I let it drown out everything. The past, the future and everything in-between.

Later, we head to the pub. I get lost in the crowd, start talking to someone. End up back at her place, a nondescript semi miles away from Newquay. I have no idea if she lives here or if she's transient like me, but the sex is good. Nothing close to the magic of being with Callie, but good enough. Just like the waves, it helps me forget.

The next morning I find her in the living room. Petite and dark-haired, she's sipping coffee in her dressing-gown. She lives here, I realise. There are framed photos everywhere, fresh flowers on the coffee table, pairs of shoes in the porch.

An excruciating silence. I haven't done this in so long.

She smiles shyly. 'Coffee?'

'Actually, I'd better . . .' I jerk my thumb clumsily over my shoulder, like a hitchhiker.

Something breaks over her face that might be relief. 'Yeah, I wanted to say. I'm not really looking for anything—'

'Me either,' I say quickly. 'Sorry.'

'No! Don't be. I'm sort of . . . getting over someone, so . . .'

'Oh, good.' My mind hiccups then stalls. 'I mean, not *good* . . .'

She laughs nervously. I can actually see her toes curling. (Is this honestly the effect I have on women, these days?) 'It's okay. I know what you meant.'

I glance at the photos on her mantelpiece. She used to have long hair. The crop must be a recent thing. 'Is that your . . . ?'

'Little boy. Yeah. He's five now.' She wraps her hands even more tightly around her mug of coffee. Takes a protracted sip, like she's playing for time. 'It's sort of on-off, on-off with his dad at the moment.'

'Oh. I hope I haven't—'

'Not at all. I mean, technically it's off, but I just can't quite seem to . . . get over him, you know?'

Something contracts in my chest. 'I do, actually.'

'You got kids, John?'

I half laugh, about to correct her before thinking better of it. 'No.'

A silence follows. Through the party wall drifts the sound of a baby crying. The muffled syncopation of an argument.

'Sorry,' she says, after a few moments. 'That was all a bit insensitive of me. I did have fun last night.'

I take her in, wonder briefly if this is how it will always be. A series of half-connections, nights devoid of true emotion. Never quite feeling the way I did with Callie.

'That's okay,' I say, reaching for my jacket where I left it on the armchair last night. 'I think we were both on the same page.'

She leans forward. 'You're such a nice guy, John. Honestly, there aren't enough like you.'

I pull on my jacket and smile again. Well, the sentiment's there, at least.

'Don't,' I say to Warren, when eventually I make it back to his place. (Long walk, bus, cab.)

He smiles. 'Didn't think you were in the market.'

'I'm not. What market? I'm not.'

Warren holds up his hands like I've whipped out a gun. 'Forget I said anything. Listen, we still on for next week?'

Warren's coming back to Eversford with me next Saturday for the barbecue Dad's finally agreed to host. For the first time we're all going to gather in one place and get to know one another. The whole family.

'Reminded Dad before I left.'

'It'll be weird to meet him properly. In a good way, I hope.'

I don't tell Warren that Doug is in fact my main concern, given his general inclination to behave like an arsehole.

Six months ago, with Tamsin and Warren's encouragement, I eventually went to see a GP. I knew by then that I could never be anyone's project, so had turned down Diana's offer of help for good. But I had noticed a subtle uplift in my wellbeing simply from throwing punches at Steve several times a week. And there were people I'd told now supporting me. The timing felt right.

Far more understanding than my university medic, this GP listened properly. Referred me straight to a counsellor. And now, gradually, by way of twice-weekly sessions, I've started working through the mess in my mind. Begun contemplating the idea of a future.

It's been more challenging than even I thought possible. But in a way it needed to be, to stop me thinking about Callie. The idea of her death is like an insect in my mind, a moth that stirs at the merest hint of light. I can't allow myself to dwell on what she's doing now. Because if I do, I'll be devastated by the thought of losing her all over again.

So instead I'm focusing on fitness, my mental health, and a rainbow of attendant benefits. Like improving things with my dad, and with Doug. Being a good uncle. The possibility of becoming a vet again. I've been gradually increasing the time I spend asleep each night, the end goal being not to fear it. I'm learning how to cook, cutting down on caffeine.

Callie would be pleased for me, I think. And that's the desperate waste of it all. Yes, I can try to live a life Callie would be proud of. But it will always break my heart that my dream became a chasm so wide between us that we had no hope of crossing it.

Because although she decided against saving herself in the end, I'd never have been able to stop trying.

I miss her still. All the little things. Like anticipating her smile as I cracked a joke. The way she'd press her face into Murphy's neck when she got home from work. How her head would nod and jerk as she fell asleep in front of the TV. Those first sky-high moments of kissing her. Stirring to hear her singing in the shower.

The last song she ever murdered in there was 'I Will Always Love You' on our final morning together. Two days later, after Esther's message to say Callie wasn't coming home, I went into the bathroom and just stood there. Tried to conjure up the sound of her voice. Her towel had slipped off the rail, become a crisp crumple on the floor tiles. A bottle of her favourite coconut shampoo was still balanced on the rack behind my shower gel, cap flipped open.

I picked it up and held it for a moment. Took a giddying breath in, before pressing the lid back down.

I did that for months afterwards. Inhaled it every morning, so I could start each day with only thoughts of her.

## 79

## Callie – eighteen months after

I see him on the boardwalk every morning. We're staying at the same site on the north-western tip of Latvia, in rustic beachside cabins where pine forests end and the Baltic Sea begins. The place is tiny – there's only around twelve of us checked-in. I realised he was British when I overheard him chatting to a birdwatcher one morning, as I was returning from a stroll along the sand at dawn.

There are lots of birdwatchers here. I'm not among them, *per se*, but migrating birds often touch down at the wildest extremities of earth. I can see why Liam loves it here so much – it's mesmeric in its desolation, a place of arresting remoteness, of sweeping sands and sprawling forests, where sea segues into sky.

I've been in Europe for a fortnight – my first trip abroad since returning from Chile last autumn. I wanted to surround myself with solitude once again – the vast beaches I'd seen between the pages of books, the pine woods I'd pictured in daydreams. Ricardo, my guide from Chile, recommended an atlas's worth of other destinations to me too, before I left South America, but they'll have to wait until I've topped up my bank account. Esther and Gavin's first baby is due in a couple of months, and they've asked me to be godmother, so I'm fitting in some time away now – because once the baby's born, I won't want to miss a thing.

We're both early risers, Finn and I. When he introduced himself to the man in the gift shop yesterday I was behind him in the queue, and made a mental note of his name. Two cabins along from me, he attempts to greet me in Latvian each time I pass him, the phonetic jumble that results about as amusing as mine. He's here by himself – at least, I've not seen anyone with him.

On my penultimate night, I'm sitting on the wooden bench outside my cabin with a beer and some bread and cheese, breathing in the view. The sky is strewn with candy-floss clouds, the sun like an orange being squeezed into the sea.

I've just finished writing Joel another postcard. There are several now in an envelope at Esther's house – a time capsule of all my thoughts, my adventures. I've been passing them to her for safekeeping, in case anything should happen to me. Because if it does, I need to be sure Joel has a way back to my heart.

Postcard written, I capture the sunset on my phone and message it to Liam. *Wish you were here?* I add an emoji on purpose, because he always gets so grumpy about them.

Then, flip-flops on the boardwalk.

I turn to see Finn heading to his cabin. He raises a hand in greeting.

I smile and set down my beer. 'Hi.'

Cautiously, he returns the smile. 'You're English?'

'Yep.'

'Ah. Sorry about my pidgin Latvian, then.'

I laugh. 'Mine too.'

He exhales, looks up at the sky. 'Nice night for it.'

'Beautiful.'

Just as I'm expecting him to move on, he lingers. 'You staying long?'

'I leave the day after tomorrow.' I hesitate. 'Would you like a beer?'

The smile reaches his eyes, and he walks over. 'Love one. If I'm not disturbing you?'

'Not at all. Unless you had plans to . . .'

'I was pretty much going to do what you're doing.' He laughs. 'I'm a sucker for a sunset.'

I uncap a beer and hold it out to him.

He thanks me and sits down. Six-foot-plus, he's blond and open-faced, with blue eyes that grip tight. He looks laid-back and beachy in shorts and flip-flops, a baseball cap.

I glance down at my beer and feel a twitch of anticipation, deep in my solar plexus.

'So . . .'

'. . . Callie.'

'Callie. I'm Finn.' We shake hands, his dwarfing mine. 'Did you come here for the birds, or the solitude?'

'A little of both. I'm not really a birdwatcher. More of a bird . . . appreciator.'

He laughs. 'Nicely put. So you're here on holiday?'

'Yep. You?'

'Same.' Eyes sparking, he nods. 'Nice T-shirt, by the way.'

The tractor T-shirt Joel gave me for Christmas, nearly three years ago now. Finally I've been able to wear it again, remember his smile with one of my own. I feel braver, somehow, when I think about him, these days.

My thoughts still drift to him a lot – to what he's doing now, who he spends time with, the things he dreams about. To whether he's got a job, or a love interest, or a different outlook on life since we split. But slowly, incrementally, the sharp edges of my memories are beginning to blunt. They wound me less, feel more like scratches now than stabs.

'Thanks,' I say to Finn. And then, so I don't have to explain, 'How long have you been here?'

'Nearly a week now. You?'

'Here, only three nights. I went to Estonia and Lithuania en route.'

Finn looks impressed. 'Both on my bucket list.'

I smile and tell him more, about spotting storks in the forest and eagles over lakes, about losing my way in an Estonian bog as night was closing in.

Finn leans in as I talk, listening intently, eyes spilling good humour. 'God, I need to do more travelling,' he says, when I've finished, sipping his beer.

'Anything stopping you?' The question people have been asking me my whole life. It feels weird to be the one saying it, for a change.

He grimaces. 'Money. Annual leave. Being organised enough. Argh. I hate real life.' He swigs his beer. 'You sound like you're pretty sorted, Callie. I'm jealous. What's your secret?'

'This is all new to me, actually. You know the story – too terrified to make the most of my youth, then start panicking as I hurtle towards forty.'

Finn fixes his smile. 'Ah. Here you were enjoying a peaceful sunset, and I come along and land you with an existential crisis. Okay. Let's rewind – tell me all about you, and don't let me speak for the next half an hour at least.'

'Half an hour?'

'I'll time you,' he says, looking down at his watch. 'Start by telling me why your other car's a tractor.'


'Is my time up yet?'

'I have no idea.' Finn's eyes are shining, like ship lights far out at sea. He's leaning forward, elbows resting on his thighs. He's been laughing at all my jokes, digging into my stories, asking questions. He's funny and self-deprecating, arrestingly handsome with a winning laugh.

He asks about my job, offers up smart questions on tree-felling, carr woodland and habitat management. I realise as we chat that I'm not comparing him to Joel as I thought I might. I'm not comparing him to anyone. Maybe that means I'm giving him a fair shot, or maybe it means I still think Joel's beyond compare.

'So what about you?' I ask Finn, conscious I've been running on for a while now. 'What do you do for a living?'

He looks into his lap, just for a moment, then back up at me. 'I'm an ecologist. That's kind of why I'm here. To catch the migration. Brush up on my ID skills.'

I stare at him. 'That's . . . You should have said.'

'I wanted to hear about you.'

So many questions spring to mind. 'So you actually . . . What kind of ecology?'

'Well, I'm with a consultancy. Lots of time out in the field. Surveys, assessments, reports, all that jazz.'

'Do you love it?'

'Yeah,' he says. 'I love it. It's what I was born to do.'

*I know that feeling,* I think, as we stare out at the sea together, now swathed in darkness.

He tells me he's a Brightonian born and bred, with a big family, lots of friends. He's a fan of dogs and romantic comedy, a lover of good food. Hopeless with technology, he's shocking at DIY, is someone who tries not to sweat the small stuff.

'So if you don't mind me asking,' he says, glancing down at the carpet of pine needles beneath our feet, 'is there anyone waiting for you, back at home?'

My mind journeys to Joel. I picture him in his garden, hands stuffed into his pockets, staring up at the stars.

I wonder, just for a second, if we're looking at the same spot of sky.

Then I return my gaze to Finn. 'Not any more.'

Later Finn and I kiss, lips cold and then hot against the backdrop of the Baltic Sea. It's a kiss that feels foreign and evocative all at once, a kiss that taps back into a long-forgotten thrill. There's not been anyone since Joel – and I'm trying to forget him now, the way his touch coursed through me in currents. Because I fancy Finn, and I already know that this could be something good.

It's time to move on. Joel said that was what he wanted for me, and kissing Finn beneath the stars tonight seems like a pretty great place to start.

And then, because I want to, because it feels right, I ask Finn into my cabin.

There was a time when I couldn't imagine wanting to be with anyone other than Joel. And that almost terrified me more than the idea of moving on. I feared being dogged for eternity by subconscious comparisons I'd never be able to override – because how could anyone ever kiss me the way Joel did?

But being with Finn reminds me that there are a million kinds of mind-blowing. He's confident, I soon discover, as our kisses intensify. He's really *good* at this stuff – bold and undaunted, emphatic, vocal. And in the end it is this self-assurance that saves us, because Finn's hot in a way I can't ignore, in a way that blazes straight through any thoughts I might have had of Joel. We don't once stop for breath, and it's the most thrilling surprise, that Finn has roused something in me I was worried I'd lost for ever.

The next morning we're up at first light, sitting on the rocks atop a spear of sand. We're the only ones out here, watching the air turn apricot as the sun begins to rise. Like we're shipwrecked on our own private island.

Up in the sky, a river of migrating birds is rushing over our heads, a surging torrent of beating wings. Finn points all the different species out to me as they pass. I can hardly keep up, but not just because of the birds – I feel dazed and quietly jubilant that this man is by my side, charismatic and attentive, a warm hand around mine and a cloud-nine smile. He woke me this morning with kisses at dawn – kisses that took only seconds to become more.

We spend the morning on the beach, walking hand in hand like we've been together for years. Snatching glances at each other, stealing kisses against trees. At midday we drive to a local café, where Finn makes a valiant attempt to order lunch at the counter in Latvian.

'What did you ask for?' I whisper, when he joins me at the table I've bagged.

He laughs. 'I have absolutely no idea.'

In the end the food is excellent – two mountainous salads, drinks, and cakes stuffed with cream. We follow it up – unwisely, perhaps – with an afternoon dip in a river nearby. And when the light begins to dim, we drive deep into the pine forest on the trail of capercaillie, windows wound down low. And though we don't find the bird we're looking for, and we nearly get the car stuck doing a twenty-point-turn, we can't seem to stop laughing and I can't help thinking, *I could really fall for you.*

Still, I'm trying hard not to expect anything, because there's a tiny part of my heart that will always belong to Joel.

Twenty-four hours later, at the airport in Riga, I feel elated to glance down at my phone and see a message from Finn:

Hey Callie. Haven't done this in a while (!) so not quite sure what the rules are here . . . BUT can I just say it was amazing to meet you and I would love, love to see you again. If that appeals.

Then another message pings through:

To me this felt . . . well, pretty epic.

And another:

(Should add that if it didn't to you – no hard feelings at all! But here's hoping.) x

Then one more:

Okay, shut up Finn. Gonna let you catch your plane now. Safe flight, travels, everything. Speak soon, I hope x

I think about switching off my phone, waiting until I'm home and a few days have passed before responding. But after five minutes or so of smiling to myself and rereading his messages, I realise I don't want to.

So, as they're calling my gate, I tap out a reply:

Amazing to meet you too. A meet-up sounds good. Your place or mine?! x

# 80

## Joel – two years after

Kieran stops by a garden wall, either for a breather or to throw up. I guess I'm about to find out.

'What the hell's happened to you?' he wheezes.

I take advantage of the break. Lean down on my knees, let my lungs fill. They're burning a bit, but it's a good kind of burn. Like the kind you get with happy tears, or laughing till it hurts.

Tonight's the first of what I'm hoping will be regular Wednesday-night runs together. Kieran's brought Lucky with him, the dog we saved that Kieran eventually adopted. (Sadly, my other canine charges are all too old to join us now.)

I glance at Kieran. 'Could ask you the same question.'

'Oh, cheers. Kick me while I'm down.' His face is red as rhubarb, skin slippery with sweat. 'I'm dying here, mate.'

I channel Steve. 'Pain is just weakness leaving the body, you know.'

'I tell you what I do know,' he gasps. 'You're a smug—'

I laugh. 'Sorry. Couldn't help myself.'

We resume the jog. I could go a lot faster: a better diet, training sessions with Steve and regular surfs with Warren have done wonders for my cardiovascular system. But I'm enjoying tonight's easy pace because it's a chance to talk to Kieran.

Steve, Tamsin, Warren and my counsellor all reckon the time is right.

'I've been thinking about what you said to me, a long time ago.'

'Was it when I agreed to come running with you?' Kieran growls. 'Because I take it back.'

We come to the end of the road. It runs into a car park with a view, and it's late, so the place is empty. There's a bench nearby, looking out across Eversford. You can see the river from up here, and the church spires. Across the sea of rooftops there's a smattering of attic windows, lit up like tiny life rafts.

Though it's November and the air is alive with ice, we're both warm enough to take five minutes out. So I sit down next to Kieran, who's already sprawled against the back of the bench like he's been shot.

Lucky settles on the ground next to us. He's barely panting, the athletic bastard.

'I've been thinking about coming back to the surgery,' I say carefully. 'If you'll have me, that is.'

Kieran hauls himself into a sitting position. 'Amazing. Of course. That's brilliant news.'

'I'd need to look into training.'

'Already done it, mate, aeons ago. I'll email you. What made you change your mind?'

I finally filled Kieran and Zoë in on my dreams this summer, over pints at the pub. I was twitchy and clammy-palmed, afraid of saying what I couldn't take back. But they seemed to accept it fairly readily (with any lingering doubts seen off pretty quickly via an introduction to Warren). The relief I felt was visceral.

I stare down at Eversford. It's a map of moving lights, and brightly lit smoke from industrial chimneys. 'Fitness. Sleeping better. Getting out of my head. Realising that hiding away doesn't help.'

Still, it feels like grief to me that Callie and I can't be sitting here together. Self-improve until you're flawless, but if the person you love is nowhere to be seen, something will always be missing.

Not that it was ever really about me. If Callie's happy now, with eyes firmly trained away from her fate, that's all that matters.

Kieran smiles slyly. 'So you've not . . . I mean, this isn't to do with a girl?'

'Nah.'

'How long's it been now – two years?'

'Yeah.'

'You ever hear from her? Callie.'

I shake my head.

'Stalk her?'

'Er—'

'Online, online,' Kieran says quickly.

'Oh. No.'

'Yeah, you're probably right.' He stares down at Eversford. 'You'd only end up torturing yourself. That's the problem, these days. You can never really escape your past because it's all there online every day, staring you in the face. You looking, then?'

'For what?'

'Someone else. I can hook you up, if you like. Zoë knows loads of people.'

'Thanks,' I say, feeling a bit blank inside. 'But you're all right.'

'Joel,' he says. 'How long are you going to wait?'

*Six years, Kieran,* I could tell him. *Callie's got six years left. I can't even think about dating properly again yet. Maybe I never will.*

But how do you explain that flings and chance encounters are all you're really capable of, without sounding like a snake?

By my side, Kieran's still breathing hard. 'Can't believe I can finally stop worrying about when I'm going to get my best vet back.'

'Get your breath back, did you say?'

Kieran snorts. 'Ha. The job does come with terms, you know.'

'Such as?'

'Such as no sarcastic comments about your boss running slower than your average ninety-year-old.'

'We can fix that,' I tell him. 'I know a guy.'

That night, I dream about Callie again. And it's a dream that floods me with joy, brings me slowly round with a smile on my face.

Three years from now, early in the morning. Callie's on a bench halfway along a promenade, eyes glimmering from beneath the brim of a knitted hat. Her gaze has drifted out to sea, and she's swigging intermittently from a travel mug.

It looks like a seaside town. There's a hotel in the background, light bulbs strung between lampposts. She must live there, I guess, unless she's visiting. But there's no luggage with her, and she's alone.

Alone except for Murphy by her side and the double buggy by her feet.

She's rocking it gently back and forth, with a smile that tells me her heart is full.

And to know that, so is mine.

## 81

## Callie – two years after

'I hate leaving you,' I say with a sigh, as I'm getting ready to catch the train back to Eversford on a sodden Sunday night in late November.

'Then don't.' Finn's topless on the bed, fresh from the shower and smelling of citrus soap. Propped on one elbow, he's pretending to watch me pack, though the look in his eyes is a full invitation. I'm half tempted to give in and kneel beside him for a kiss before remembering that I really do have to go. Kissing Finn on a bed without it turning into something more is, as yet, unheard of.

He sits up. 'I'm serious. Move in with me, Cal. You and Murph. Come on, this is crazy, all this back and forth. Move to Brighton. I love you, why not?'

*Why not?* would be Finn's epitaph, I think. That's just the way he's been brought up. *What's the worst that can happen? Worry about it later. It's better to beg forgiveness than ask permission.* He says yes to everything, turns very little down. So different from Joel, and his quiet, understated reserve.

And so different from me, too – Finn's my opposite in many ways, though being with him has made me more adventurous by default, I think. We're always out, these days, and we probably overspend on adventures, like skydiving and gig tickets and invites to overseas weddings. He drove up to see me on a mid-week morning once, threw me a surprise birthday party when we'd been together just a few weeks. Finn has the whole world on speed dial, can make friends in an empty room.

People keep telling me it's good to be with someone who balances you out. You can't be all yin and no yang, they say. And I'm sure they're right.

Sometimes I find myself wondering what would happen if Joel and Finn met – whether they'd be wary of each other or hit it off straight away.

But, like Joel, Finn is thoughtful too, always *interested*. He listens to what I say, rubs my feet while I talk, remembers the small details – that I prefer coffee on top of milk, love raspberries and Ryan Gosling, never remember my umbrella, can't stomach tequila.

All the ways he reminds me of Joel are comforting, and all the ways he doesn't are charming. Like his unexpected passion for acid-house music, the library of nature books even bigger than mine that takes up almost his entire living room, that he can tolerate Scotch bonnets without so much as blinking. He has a gift for naming birds in flight – seriously, *any* bird – plus a secret and much underrated talent for baking. He's passionate about local and regional politics, too, in a manner that makes me think of Grace.

This isn't the first time Finn's asked me to move in. His argument is that he owns his flat, so it makes more sense for me to live here. It's set back from the seafront, on the top floor of a large Regency apartment block. The proportions are minuscule, but we're only minutes from the sea. We can see it, just, from two of the rooms.

And I do love it here. I adore throwing open the windows, listening to the seagulls, breathing in the salty air. My memories of the first few weekends I spent here are deliciously primal – we barely left the bedroom, resurfacing only to eat or drink, pee or shower. We consumed everything in the flat – why waste time shopping or eating out? – took semi-ironic bubble baths, worked our way through everything on Finn's iTunes, laid our heads in each other's laps and talked about the future.

It's been only six months so, yes, we're moving fast. But fast can be exciting – like when a plane's about to take off, or a rollercoaster plummets. Scary, but exhilarating. Finn told me he loved me after only a fortnight, so when he brought up the idea of moving in together just a few weeks later, I shouldn't have been surprised.

I still think of Joel, sometimes, especially when I'm back in Eversford. I've even ventured into the café a few times, sat in his old window seat and ordered a thick slab of *drømmekage*. I've thought about how he is – whether he's happy, what he's doing now, if there's been any change to his dreaming. Dot's assured me he's not been in since we broke up, so I don't need to panic about running into him. Which is good, because I have no idea what I'd do, or what I'd say, if I did.

Occasionally I find myself questioning if I did enough – if perhaps I should have fought harder – for us. Maybe he needed more from me, and I let him down, failed him when it mattered most.

But then I run through all the reasons we let each other go, and I try to feel at peace again. Let it settle back down, the sadness that sleeps quietly inside me.

Slowly, I come to realise, Joel is strolling away. And in his place stands Finn, a lighthouse of a man, committed to loving me one hundred per cent.

'Champagne?' Finn calls from the kitchen.

The bottle in the fridge is an expensive one, Finn's birthday gift from a jet-setting uni friend who always does her shopping in duty-free.

Because I'm moving to Brighton. I said yes. In the end, I couldn't think of any reason to keep saying no. Six months is long enough, I reminded myself, and Finn says he's got plenty of contacts who can help find me a job (which I don't doubt). I'll miss Mum and Dad, of course, and Esther and Gav and their gorgeous new baby, Delilah Grace. But they all adore Finn, so I'm sure they'll be thrilled. And, in the end, Finn's right – all the back and forth was starting to seem slightly crazy.

Because I want to be with him. I do. How strongly I feel about him . . . it's nothing short of chemical.

So I said yes, and the joy on his face could have lit up a continent.

He reappears in the bedroom now, a T-shirt on like he thinks the occasion deserves that level of formality, at least. He's brought the bottle with him and two glasses, pops the cork. The champagne erupts all over the carpet, and I laugh as he swears, chuck him a towel from the pile on the bed. Murphy, who comes with me whenever I'm here to stay, sniffs the wet patch suspiciously.

'Well,' Finn says, as he passes me a full glass, 'let's just say, I'm really glad I stumbled across you on a beach in Latvia, Callie Cooper.' We toast and I take a sip. It's fresh from the fridge, sumptuously cold.

I look into his pool-blue eyes. 'Me too. You were an excellent find, Finn Petersen.'

'These past six months have been the best of my life,' he says, his smile filling the room.

I smile back at him. 'I'll drink to that.'

In the small hours of Monday morning, something shakes me awake. I had to catch the late train back to Eversford last night because until I can make the move to Brighton, normal life must resume.

I pull on a hoodie, head out into my cottage garden with Murphy at my heels, and blink into the dense blackness of the sky. I can't see any stars tonight, maybe because of light pollution, or maybe it's cloud.

There's a cloud inside my mind, too. It's not guilt, exactly – more a sense of quiet unease.

I've never betrayed Joel by telling Finn about his dream, and I don't intend to. But if we're committing to a life together, I can't help wondering if Finn has a right to know.

Trying to picture how he would react, I find myself imagining he'd simply laugh it off. It's not that he'd trivialise it – more that he wouldn't dwell on something he couldn't change. His view of life is *laissez-faire*, philosophical. He doesn't worry too much about money, or being punctual, or what other people think of him. I already know he'd see no need to get to the bottom of the thing, shine a torch into all its dark recesses. He'd accept from the start that no answer exists – or, if it does, that it's as ephemeral as air.

I could have one year left, or ten, or fifty. Finn and I are creating our own future now, and the idea of that dwarfs everything. Joel's dream has already started to dissipate, slip slowly into the shadows of my memory.

No. I won't trouble Finn with something that seems less and less palpable with each new day that dawns.

When we first met, Finn asked why Joel and I had broken up. I told him, quite truthfully, that we'd wanted different things. Finn smiled in recognition, said the same thing had happened with his ex. And then we carried on walking, and we never discussed it again.

## 82

## Joel – three years after

'Give me two more!'

'No, I hate you.'

'Two more! Come on!'

I can tell Steve won't be releasing my ankles until I've squeezed out two more sit-ups. Torso burning, I oblige. Then I collapse in a pool of sweat and resentment, start groaning loudly about cancelling my membership.

'Yeah, yeah.' Steve shoves a water bottle in my face. 'You want easy? Stay in bed.'

'Wish I had,' I growl. Rejecting the water, I roll over. Do my best not to throw up.

Steve agrees to suspend the sadism for five minutes while I catch my breath.

'How was it, then?' he asks me.

'How was what?'

'The spa, you idiot.'

I got back this morning from the wellness retreat, the one Callie bought me the now long-expired voucher for. The place is still going strong, squeezing juices for people with bad habits, massaging their vital organs. There was yoga and meditation. Acupuncture, some chanting. A couple of ceremonies involving bare feet, and a bit of half-hearted clanging.

I felt I owed it to her, somehow. Even after so long, at least to honour the thought of it. Her kindness to me that Christmas, the hope she'd had on my behalf that I sometimes dare to feel myself these days. Despite knowing what's to come.

'A bit bonkers,' I tell Steve. 'But I feel good. Weirdly enough.'

'They get you sleeping like a baby?'

'I've never understood that. Babies are famously bad sleepers. Speaking of which, how's Elliot?'

Steve and Hayley had their second, a little boy, two months ago.

'Still a tyrant. Literally a monster in a Babygro. I don't think he's shut his eyes for more than five minutes since he was born. Love the socks off him, though,' he adds, with a smile. And then, 'You've not . . . ?'

'No, of course not.'

We have an agreement, Steve and I, that if ever I dream about my godchildren again, he'll be the first to know. *Whatever it is, good or bad, you tell me straight away.* I have the same understanding with Tamsin, Warren. Most people, it seems, would want to know.

I wonder briefly, as I sometimes do, how things would have panned out if Callie had wanted to know the truth. Would we be married with kids now, a family of our own? Might I even have had a chance to change the course of—

'Right,' Steve says, springing to his feet. 'Burpees. Come on.'

'What? That wasn't five minutes.'

'Joel, what am I always telling you? You snooze, you *lose*.' He says this very emphatically. Makes an L with his thumb and forefinger, brings it up to his forehead.

Just in case I haven't got the message from the last ten times he's done it.

They didn't get me sleeping like a baby at the retreat, actually, despite the acupuncture and reflexology, and the nauseating quantity of essential oils. I've been much better on that front recently, but I still get nervous when I'm away from home at night.

The disquiet gave me a strong urge to get absolutely wasted, but I didn't want to go there. It reminded me too much of my past, of darker times. Somehow, I had to stop myself dashing to the nearest twenty-four-hour supermarket. So I took to roaming the grounds after dark, wrapped up in a thick coat, scarf and hat.

On my last night, cravings thankfully all but gone, I bumped into someone doing much the same as me.

'Sorry! God, sorry.'

She swore, tugged her headphones down around her neck. 'You made me jump.'

It was past midnight, sub-zero. She was wearing only a T-shirt and tracksuit bottoms, the flimsiest of cardigans.

'Sorry, I wasn't expecting to . . . see anyone.'

I'd come across her a couple of times before at breakfast (quietly begging for coffee, wondering out loud where the croissants were). Once at meditation. Twice in yoga, where she caught my eye as we were semi-inverted and we both struggled not to laugh.

'So what are you in for?' I asked.

She leant against the brick wall we'd collided at the end of. 'A multitude of sins.'

I smiled. 'Sounds serious.'

'So I'm told.' She checked them off on her fingers. 'Not getting my five-a-day. A fairly serious caffeine habit. Reaching my thirties with absolutely zero knowledge of yoga, which I'm led to believe is a crime, these days. You?'

I took her in. Blonde hair that skimmed her shoulders, powder-blue eyes. Lips patched indigo by the cold. 'Ah, I kind of . . . promised someone I'd come here. So.'

She smiled, didn't press me. 'I'm Rose, by the way.'

'Joel.'

Firm handshake, full eye contact.

'So, Joel. Are you . . . just getting some fresh air?'

'Actually, I've been fighting the urge to go on a massive bender. You?'

She laughed again, gestured to her headphones. 'Can't sleep, so . . . affirmations.'

I smiled, thought back to the early days of trying to free myself from dreaming. Decided not to share with her my repeated lack of success.

Turned out, she didn't need me to.

'It's all slightly odd, though, isn't it?' she said. 'Declaring how much I love myself *ad infinitum*. It actually has the opposite effect, if I listen to it for long enough.'

I laughed. 'Yeah, it goes against the grain a bit.'

She brushed the air with her hand. 'Ah, they probably won't make you do it. Compared to most people here you look the picture of health.'

I was caught off-guard by the compliment.

'Just to say – fully aware I look the exact *opposite* of health right now. Death. I look like death. And not even warmed up because I've literally never been this cold.' She raised her eyes to the sky, teeth chattering softly. 'Misjudged it.'

I smiled. 'Funny, I was about to ask.' I took off my coat then, put it around her shoulders. 'Here. Don't want to see those mantras going to waste.'

She stared at me. Let out a little shiver as I pulled the lapels together for her. They drew her hair in with the collar, made a ribbon down her face.

'Night, Rose. It was really nice meeting you.'

I walked away from her through the garden, soaked up the stillness of the night. Hoped that some of it might filter in, settle inside my mind.

## 83

## Callie – three years after

We've been in Florida – another of Ricardo's recommendations – for a fortnight, exploring the wetlands and nature reserves, swimming off white-sand beaches, hanging out with people we've met along the way. I've lost track of how many conversations Finn's struck up while we've been here, this man for whom charisma is instinct. He still makes actual new friends when he goes on holiday, something I pretty much lost the knack for as soon as I hit puberty.

After an al-fresco dinner at our new favourite Cuban place, Finn suggests a stroll, one last chance to enjoy a sultry evening before journeying back to colder weather tomorrow. So now we're wandering hand in hand through Miami Beach, in the direction of . . . well, the beach.

'It's flown, hasn't it, Cal?' Finn's saying.

For a moment I think he means a bird – force of habit from the last two weeks – then realise he's talking about the holiday. 'Can't believe it's work on Monday.' Not that I mind, not really. After a couple of months of looking, a friend-of-a-friend of Finn's gave us the heads-up on a job going at a nature reserve around thirty minutes from Brighton. I love it there now, almost as much as I did Waterfen.

A small part of me was relieved to be leaving Eversford and my perpetual fear of running into Joel. I was always so afraid I'd not know what to say – that, if faced with him, I'd feel something I didn't want to feel. Sometimes I thought if he saw me while I was sitting in his old seat at the café, or when I happened to be wearing a pair of earrings he'd given me, he might think I'd never fully got over him. And then I started wondering if perhaps he would have been right.

Finn has as much stuff as I do – more, if possible – so I didn't feel as self-conscious about my clutter when I was moving in, the way I did with Joel. Not that Joel ever cared about my boxes blocking his doorways, or the things that were strewn around his flat. Still, it mattered to me less, somehow, moving in with Finn. We shoved as many of my belongings as we could into drawers and cupboards before the housewarming Finn had arranged for that first night – even though it wasn't technically a housewarming. By early evening half of Brighton, it seemed, was crammed into the flat, drinking and smoking and dancing like we'd all become students again. Midway through the party, as Finn enthralled a ten-strong throng of people with the story of how we met, I looked at him and thought, *I can't believe you did all this for me.*

The highlight of Florida has been getting to spend quality time with Finn. Though he's in his quiet period at work – survey season ramps up during spring and summer, his hours becoming long and unsociable – we never seem to stop, in our free time. Finn's a people-person, and there are people – always – turning up at our flat, or calling us to join them for drinks at a nearby bar. Weekends are fully booked with family gatherings because Finn has two brothers and a sister, and an endless number of cousins. We spend midweek nights with friends, in pubs and restaurants and live-music venues, barely pausing between commitments. But we've been that way from the start – racing forwards, rarely stopping, the occasional glance to check the other is still there before forging on.

I don't mind – a man with such a full life can hardly be a bad thing – but sometimes I wish it was just us, enjoying each other the way we did during those precious first thirty-six hours in Latvia. Because Finn is a person *so* worth savouring. He's generous and hilarious and opinionated and wise, and sometimes I simply don't feel like sharing him. But I know this to be selfish in a way that Finn rarely is and, anyway, that's not the way life works.

'Cal,' Finn whispers now, as we reach the beach. Instinctively, we bend to take off our flip-flops, let our brown feet sink into the sand. 'There's something I wanted to ask you.'

As I turn to look at him, he drops to one knee, removes a box from his pocket. My hand flies to my mouth as, from somewhere nearby, I register a whoop and then cheers from a group of passers-by.

'I have no idea how to do this,' he breathes. 'So I just figured the old way's probably the best. Callie, I love you to the ends of this crazy earth. Will you marry me?'

'Yes.' I want time to slow down and speed up all at once. 'Yes, yes, yes.'

And there, in front of the high-rises and the palm trees, beneath the stormiest, most spectacular of skies, Finn and I agree to make it for ever.

## 84

## Joel – four years after

I'm at a service station off the M25 of all places when my past catches up with me.

'Joel?'

I turn, feel an unexpected rush of pleasure to see Melissa. 'Hello.'

She takes me in for a moment, then introduces me to the Adonis at her side. 'Leon, this is Joel.'

Warily, I offer him a hand, wondering if he might opt to punch me instead of shake it. But he doesn't. He just greets me with a half-smile, which is a whole half more than I probably deserve.

Melissa laughs. She's wearing the kind of hot pink lipstick that demands impeccable teeth. 'It's all right. I've only ever spoken extremely highly of you, of course.'

I shoot Leon a look that's supposed to mean, *You can punch me some other time, I promise.*

'Might go and grab some coffees,' he says. 'Back in a minute.'

In the middle of the thoroughfare we face each other. A torrent of travellers rushes noisily past.

'Are you . . . How've you been?'

'Good.' She smiles. 'We're just off to Heathrow, actually.'

'Lucky you. Anywhere nice?'

'Barbados.' She extends her hand so I can see her ring. 'Honeymoon.'

'Wow, that's . . . Congratulations.'

Her long hair's cropped short, and I can see the floral jumpsuit beneath her coat and scarf. Barbados-ready, classic Melissa. It's good to see her loved-up and luminous in a way she never was with me.

She looks as though she wants to say something but can't quite find the words. So, ever the gentleman, I jump in first. 'Leon's all right, is he?'

'Well,' she says, 'he's nicer than you.'

'Good. That's a start.'

'Just joking. He's great. Really great.' She looks longingly in the direction of the coffee concession he's wandered off to. 'So, where are you heading?'

'Oh – Cornwall. Not quite as exotic as Barbados.'

'Holiday's a holiday.'

'Er, no – I'm actually moving down there. Fresh start.'

'Wow. I'd have had you living in that flat until you died. No offence.'

Her trademark lack of tact almost stirs up a kind of nostalgia in me. 'None taken.'

'What prompted that, then?'

'Family stuff. Long story.'

She tilts her head. 'So you're not still with the girl who lived upstairs?'

*The girl who lived upstairs.*

'No. She's . . . with someone else, now. Married, I think.' (Actually, I know. Doug told me – turns out he has an acquaintance in common with Gavin.)

Melissa nods. And, for possibly the first time in the history of our relationship, fails to make a quip. 'Have you got a job down there, then? In Cornwall.'

'I have, actually.'

'You're going back to vetting?'

'Yep.'

She nods again, more slowly this time. Meets my eye and holds it. 'Well. Congratulations.'

I feel unexpectedly moved. 'Thank you.'

Some seconds pass, then she reaches up to hug me goodbye. It's strange to feel her arms around me again. Like rediscovering a favourite piece of clothing, breathing in a familiar scent. 'What are all those batty old ladies going to do without you?'

I swallow. It's not been a great year on my street, mortality-wise. 'Just the one now, unfortunately.' (Iris hanging in there, tenacious as ever.)

Melissa pulls back from me. 'And you're not seeing anyone?' Like she doesn't quite believe I'd have any other reason for moving to Cornwall.

I sigh. 'I'd love to, Melissa, but you're on your honeymoon.'

She laughs throatily in a way I've kind of missed. 'You know, it was a shame you and I could never be friends.'

'I think we're friends.'

She lingers for a moment, and I realise she's finding it hard to say goodbye. 'Well, take care of yourself. Try to meet a nice girl.'

'I did. It didn't work out.'

One last, mischievous wink. 'Joel, what can I say? I'm married now.'

I've rented a place ten minutes from Warren's in Newquay, with a small garden and a spare bedroom for visitors. I stopped off at a garden centre just after crossing Devon, bought a basketful of house plants for my new living room. And I threw in a window-box too. Because even though I've moved here for a fresh start, I still can't live without reminders of Callie.

By early afternoon I'm more or less straight, so I head round to Warren's.

'Tough goodbyes?' he asks me.

'Tamsin was a wreck. She wants to come down next weekend, bring the kids.'

'Be good to see her,' Warren says. 'How are you feeling, about being here?'

'Nervous. But good-nervous.'

'That's the best kind. Haven't had enough good-nervous in my life.' He smiles. 'All set for Monday?'

'Think so.' I've been working part-time with Kieran for just over a year now. I plan to split the next six months between my new practice in Cornwall and refresher courses in Bristol.

'Not sure if I said it before, but I'm proud of you, mate. You've really turned things around.'

'Cheers.'

'And for you to be down here, with me . . . well, that means the world. It really does.'

I nod. 'Waves any good?'

Warren checks his watch. 'Right now?'

'Yep.'

'They are.'

'Fancy a quick one?'

'Always, mate. Always.'


That night I dream about Callie.

I wake just as I'm telling her I love her again.

My face is wet with tears, my shoulders shaking with sadness.

## 85

## Callie – four years after

Finn and I got married in the summer, having agreed a long engagement wasn't really our thing. The sheer number of people wanting to wish us well necessitated a reception far bigger than our budget could cater for, so in the end Finn's sister Bethany, who lives on a farm, hosted it for us. She strung bunting between barn beams, scattered wild flowers over haystacks, baked us a cake strewn with edible blooms. There were animals everywhere, the air was warm, and as darkness fell, two hundred people danced and laughed beneath lucid lines of festoon lights, strung between the pantiles.

Over dinner, Finn's speech about meeting me in Latvia and everything that had happened in the two years since was like a love letter read out loud. A natural orator, he moved everyone alternately to tears and then laughter with his words – to see the whole barn ripple with emotion like that was something I'll never forget. Between that, my parents' jubilation, Esther's beautiful speech about Grace, and Dot's drunken snog with the best man, the day was happiness in its purest, most perfect form.

But still I want time to slow down occasionally. So I can stop to savour the present, instead of always moving on to the next thing. I want to spend more time hand in hand on the beach, or kissing on the sofa, or even just walking companionably through town. That was the way it was with Joel, and I feel sad, sometimes, that I seem never to have that with Finn.

We're in Australia for our belated honeymoon – Finn has relatives in Perth, so we've spent our last week here with them. Drunk on sunshine, we've swum in the sea, lapped up the open spaces and breathtaking beaches. It's winter at home, and though there's an enduring appeal to that season I'll always cherish, I can't deny the switch to shorts and flip-flops has been immensely cheering – especially as my last few days at work were spent battling the elements in waders and wellies.

I woke early this morning. Finn was still sleeping and I didn't want to disturb him. He looked so handsome and peaceful, brown and barechested next to me on the mattress.

So I crept into the bathroom alone where, five minutes later, I wept quiet tears of happiness.

We're working off breakfast with a walk along the Swan River. Everything this morning is an exultant shade of blue – the sky, the water, the glass faces of the high-rises. Finn's talking about taking his family out for dinner somewhere, a thank-you for their hospitality, before we fly home. I'm listening but also drifting, tuning in and then out, struggling to focus.

'Finn,' I say, as we reach the water's edge. He's wearing a baseball cap and shades, is mulling over our options for restaurants later.

He turns to me. 'Yeah, you're right. I guess that might be a bit heavy on the seafood. We could try that Greek place instead?'

'Finn, I need to tell you something.'

Perhaps instinctively, he takes my hand. I like to feel the ring around his wedding finger – it still seems like a novelty to me, to be Mrs Callie Petersen, to have a ring around my own finger too.

'Cal, what's wrong?'

'Nothing's wrong,' I say quietly. 'I'm pregnant.'

The softest of gasps, then the warmest of kisses, cheeks wet with tears, shoulders shaking in disbelief. He wraps me in his arms and we stay like that for several minutes while around us our life quietly trans-forms, becomes rich with new colour, lustrous with light.

He pulls gently away and levels his face to mine, removing his sunglasses so I can look right into his eyes. 'When . . . when did you . . . ?'

'This morning. I've been feeling a bit queasy.' I lined my suitcase with pregnancy tests when we left the UK, just in case.

It's something we've talked about from the start. Finn's from a big, loving family, and he's made no secret about wanting children of his own. That was something I wanted too, but I was nervous about things he didn't see an issue with – like how he would cope with stepping back from our social life, how we'd fit a baby into our tiny flat, whether Murphy would deal with the upheaval okay. Not to mention whether I'd even *get* pregnant, being in my late thirties – I'd read so many horror stories about the dreaded biological clock. We've been trying for five months, so the relief and gratitude I feel now is immense. It's all come together. I just have to hope we can adjust to the change we've got coming, the different lifestyle that lies ahead.

'Callie . . . I love you so much. This is the best news.'

'I love you too. I'm so excited.'

'Are you feeling all right? Sure you want to walk? It's pretty hot. We could just go and—'

'I'm fine.' I laugh. 'Actually, the fresh air's helping.'

'Can't believe I didn't notice.'

'It's only been the last couple of days. I didn't want to get your hopes up, in case it was nothing.'

He grins. 'Well, we should make plans. Although . . . what should they be? I haven't got a clue what we do next.'

'Me either. That's part of the fun, I guess.'

'Should we Skype everyone? Tell them?'

*I want to tell Joel.* The thought is urgent and alarming, until suddenly I realise.

Joel already knows. He has done for years.

*I think for you the best is yet to come.*

'Callie?'

I ease Joel from my mind, squeeze Finn's hand. 'Let's wait until we get home. I quite like the idea of this being our secret, just for a while.'

He smiles, puts an arm around my shoulders. 'Well, we should celebrate, at least. What can you have – cake?'

I smile. 'I'm still full from breakfast. And slightly nauseous, if I'm honest.'

'Is it weird?' Finn asks me, after a moment. 'I mean, apart from the nausea . . . how do you *feel*?'

I don't even need to think about it. 'I feel euphoric.'

And that's it – the best and only way to describe it.

## 86

## Joel – five years after

'And finally, I'd like to thank my three children. You make me proud every day. All of you.'

The room murmurs approval. Glasses are raised in our direction.

It's Dad's seventieth, so we're celebrating with him at the dingy old rugby club down the road. There's everything you'd expect from a party at a dingy old rugby club: a jaded-looking DJ working through Doug's Beatles-centric playlist, a limp buffet consisting of tuna and chicken (with the odd chipolata thrown in for good measure), lots of people standing statically in groups, trying to make their drinks last. I know simply from looking at it that the white wine's warm, and that eighty per cent of the conversation here is heavily accountancy-based. Still, it's Dad's party, organised by Doug. It was hardly going to feature award-winning cocktails and Idris Elba on the decks.

Or maybe it all feels predictable because I've already dreamt about it. Two weeks ago, in a dream that seemed to last a lifetime.

After the speeches I find Tamsin at a table near the back with Harry and Amber. Harry, who's almost five, is absorbed in a book. Amber, now twelve, has her headphones firmly on.

Wise girl.

I catch her eye, mouth, 'All right?'

She looks up from her iPad, shrugs. 'Boring.'

'Blame your other uncle,' I mouth pointedly, gesturing at Doug. She grins.

I lean back in my chair, grab a handful of dry-roasted peanuts. 'How's it going, sis?'

Tamsin bites her lip, adjusts her sea-green dress at the shoulder. 'It's a success, right? He's having a good time, isn't he?'

I glance over at Dad. He's telling a story to a group of his badminton buddies that they all appear enraptured by. God knows what it could be. That time he nearly lost the shuttlecock? 'Absolutely. Look at him. Haven't seen him this animated since the 2010 Budget.'

Tamsin smiles, sips her wine. Winces. 'God, this stuff is *tepid*.'

'How are you, Harry?' I ask my nephew.

'Good,' he says meekly. (He's not wrong, actually: Harry is the most angelic child I've ever had the pleasure to encounter. No wonder we're only half related.) 'Nearly done it.' He lifts up his activity book for me to see. It's all about outer space, looks frighteningly scientific.

'Good stuff,' I tell him encouragingly, then pull a face at my sister. 'Christ, Tam, that's virtually homework.'

She holds her hands up. 'Don't blame me. He wanted to bring it. Won't put the damn thing down.'

'You've given birth to a genius,' I whisper. 'Can't we just exploit him on YouTube for a bit and then retire?'

She shoves me softly on the arm. 'Nice that Kieran and Zoë could make it.'

I look at my friend and his wife, charming the socks off a couple twice their age. Even Steve and Hayley are here somewhere (though I have a sneaky feeling Steve's touting for business. I caught him brow-beating two octogenarians earlier into touching their toes).

'Hello, you two.' Warren sits down next to me, claps me on the knee.

I'm pleased Dad invited Warren. I'd thought he might not want to, but in the end he just shrugged and said okay. Like we were merely discussing an acquaintance from times gone by. Neither he nor Warren seems to have the energy for jousting over Mum, or me. It's so exhausting, one-upmanship: to be honest, I don't think either of them can be arsed.

I told Dad and Doug, eventually. About the dreams. They were the last to know (not that they realised or would have particularly cared). The conversation was short and stilted, and we've not discussed it since. Who knows if they even believe me? But I've been honest with both of them, at least – perhaps for the first time in my life. Surviving my break-up with Callie's made me fearless in many ways, perhaps a touch reckless. Lots of things are now a breeze, I've found, after getting through that.

*Just . . . trust people to love you, Joel.*

As Warren starts talking to Harry about the solar system, Amber leans absent-mindedly against me. I put an arm around her, kiss the top of her head. And for once she doesn't pretend to vomit, or tell me to get off.

I smile at Tamsin, and she smiles back. *It all worked out*, we're saying. *We're doing okay.*

After the party, Warren goes back to Cornwall. But I'm staying a few more nights. The next day, I drive for about an hour into the country, where I've arranged to meet someone.

I spot her white-blonde hair from across the pub. She's bagged the best spot in the place, close to the open fire.

She smiles when I approach, and I bend down to hug her. It feels easy and right, not awkward as I'd worried it might.

'Sorry. Am I late?'

Her eyes are Arctic-blue, but her laugh is full and warm. She looks casual in a T-shirt with a slogan I wouldn't be able to read without staring, a loose toffee-coloured cardigan. 'Not at all. I was early.'

Rose contacted me via the surgery a few months ago, asked if I remembered her. I did, of course. Suggested meeting up when I was next in her neck of the woods.

'Cheers.' We chink glasses, her white wine against my lime and soda.

'So how did the retreat work out in the end?' I ask. The morning after we met, I left before it got light. I'd started thinking about Callie again, and I wanted to go home.

'Well, I've carried on with the yoga. And I'm down to a coffee a day.'

'That's pretty impressive. Fruit and veg?'

She runs one hand through her hair. The air turns briefly sweet with her perfume. 'Still pitiful. How about you?'

'Oh, my problems were more . . .' I trail off. I can see myself opening up to Rose in a way I don't feel fully ready for. What do I say?

'In your head?'

I nod, sip my drink.

A pause. Her eyes are captivating. 'Well, I guess we were all there with issues of one kind or another.'

'True.'

'Or, in the words of my ex-husband, when I got home: *You go somewhere like that to be fixed, not for a holiday.*'

I smile. 'Ouch.'

She winces, then laughs. 'That was . . . my clumsy way of saying I'm divorced.'

'Oh, I'm sorry.'

'No, don't be.' She sips her wine. 'Funnily enough, it was going on the retreat that made me see the light.'

I raise an eyebrow. 'The power of affirmations?'

'Yes! Cheers to that.'

We chink glasses again.

'And you're a vet,' I say.

'Sure am. Did you like my ruse?'

In her email to the surgery, she pretended we'd met at some conference I'd never heard of. A quick search of Google confirmed she'd invented it, of course. But it also revealed that Rose Jackson was a vet.

We chat for a while about our jobs. My time out and route back in, her practice and mine. The pros and cons of outsourcing out-of-hours work (her surgery does, mine doesn't). Compassion fatigue. Treating wild animals. Being on-call at Christmas. I like her straightforwardness, her quick sense of humour. The way she touches my forearm occasionally when I've made her laugh. The warmth of her smile.

'So you know I'm divorced,' she says, when our conversation eventually lulls. 'What about you?'

'Single, but . . .'

She's nudging a beer mat around the table with her fingertips. 'Not looking.'

I frown. 'I'm sorry. It's complicated.'

'Someone else in the picture?'

I think of Callie. 'No,' I say honestly. 'But I'm just not sure if I'm ready to get to know someone again . . . in that way, quite yet.'

She smiles. 'Fair enough. Thanks for being straight with me.'

We drink up after that. Rose tells me she's got tickets for a comedy night later she was half thinking she might invite me to. And perhaps I would have gone, if she hadn't asked me so directly about my situation. But I realise I'm glad we're ending it here.

Because I like her. I'm attracted to her in a way I haven't been to anyone since Callie. And I don't want to mess that up, turn it into something throwaway through carelessness.

If that means missing the boat with her, that's just a chance I'll have to take.

'I'd like to keep in touch,' I say, as we're getting ready to leave.

Rose smiles. 'Like pen pals?'

I wince. 'Sorry. Just heard that back in my head. That was lame.'

'The lamest,' she agrees. 'Lucky for you you're so charming, isn't it?'

I'm not sure *charming* is how I'd describe myself right now. But as her compliment's overly generous, I accept it without further argument.

'Oh, I nearly forgot,' she says, standing up. 'This is yours.'

She hands me the coat I put around her shoulders at the retreat two years previously. She's had it rolled up on the chair next to her this whole time. I didn't even notice.

'Keep it,' I say.

She blinks once or twice, then puts out a hand. A formal goodbye. 'Okay. Just . . . call me, then. If you ever want it back, I mean.'

'Deal.' I take her hand, shake it. Meet her eye and smile.

## 87

## Callie – five years after

After the twins' first feed of the day, once Finn's left for work, I head out with the buggy and Murphy for a walk along the seafront.

It took us a long while to pull off the miracle of both babies feeding and napping at roughly the same time, but we're finally starting to emerge from the mayhem of the first few months. We feel bruised with exhaustion and more than a little dazed – I mean, we've still barely recovered from the shock of having *twins* – but somehow, we've made it through intact.

Euan and Robyn are five months old today. I still can't quite believe it. I'm not yet over reaching out to touch them, wondering if they're really ours.

When they were first born, Finn's enormous social network came into its own. Friends and family supported us in shifts, cooking and sterilising and washing and dog-walking. And now we're through those tough first months, I'm feeling increasingly lavish with love, ambrosial with fortune. When I hold my babies close to my chest, the rise and fall of their bath-warm weight feels like my heartbeat outside my own body.

The one-way street where we live is narrow and cluttered with cars, and there's plenty of weekday traffic, but once I'm on the promenade, I have only to look out to sea to feel washed over with calm.

Thankfully, my usual bench isn't too damp. It's the same one Grace and Ben sat on together the morning after they met on a night out in Brighton, with hot tea and bacon sandwiches, and giddy beating hearts. I know because she took a selfie, posted it on Facebook a few months later (*The day after we met!*), and I remember the hotel in the background.

I settle down with the decaf Finn made me this morning before leaving for work. He does that every day now, because it's easily more trouble than it's worth for me to try to manoeuvre the double buggy into the café at the end of our road. I've brought along a slice of *drømmekage* too, because if you can't have cake for breakfast when you're a new mum, when can you? We eat it a lot, these days – ever since Finn found my recipe and baked it for me as a surprise while I was out one afternoon. I didn't have the heart to give him the history.

I rock the buggy with my foot, make faces at the babies, adjust their hats and socks. I swig from my travel mug and tuck into my cake, break off a chunk for Murphy.

And then a sense. That he's close by, somehow. The feeling's so strong that I start and swivel around, scan the people on the pavement for his face.

I turn back to the twins, glance down at them. *You're crazy. Joel's not here. Why on earth would he be?* I haven't thought about him – not properly – in weeks. Maybe it's the lack of sleep, the black magic it performs inside my mind.

During my pregnancy I experienced terrible insomnia, the nights like vast lakes of unspent minutes through which I had to wade. To stop myself staring at the ceiling, I would get out of bed and do laps of the flat in my pyjamas while Finn slept, Murphy trotting after me like he knew I could do with the moral support.

Sometimes we'd sit by the living-room window together, where I'd talk to Grace in my head. And sometimes – only sometimes – I'd imagine Joel was awake too, that we were looking out of different windows at the same dizzying tessellation of hot blue stars.

But for the sake of the babies cocooned in my womb, and for Finn curled up in our bed, I couldn't let my thoughts wander too far into the future. If the past few years have taught me anything, it's that being in the present is what counts.

Finn and I had a drink last night – our first proper one together since the twins were born. Finn wanted to make an occasion of it, so he decanted a nice bottle of red unknowingly into the carafe Joel bought me for Christmas six years ago. We drank from the matching glasses, too – and just for a moment I let myself imagine Joel's smile, the way he said, *So you can always be at a pavement café, somewhere in the Med.*

Finn must have sensed my thoughts were wandering, because he nudged me with his foot, asked if I was feeling okay. And I smiled and said yes because, actually, I was. We had made it. We'd got through the soupy slog of those first days of parenthood, and we were coming out the other side. This felt like a toast to that. And it seemed only right to remember Joel in that moment, too, to raise a glass to him in my mind and thank him for all he'd given me.

# 88

## Joel – six years after

'Had a dream about Warren last night,' I say to Kieran and Zoë over breakfast. They've come to Cornwall for the weekend, their boys (now teenagers) safely ensconced at Kieran's parents'.

'Tell us everything,' Zoë orders. She tears into a croissant, attacks the butter. Freshly showered and fully made-up, she's one of those annoying people with a complete immunity to hangovers.

Kieran, on the other hand, looks positively malarial. 'Wait,' he says. 'Was it good or bad?'

'Good.' I lower my voice. 'He meets someone.'

'*Meets* meets?' Zoë says.

'Yeah.' I smile. 'She seemed nice. We were on the beach. She was laughing at his jokes. And they were holding—'

'Morning.' A grey-skinned Warren appears. He stayed over last night, opting to pass out on my sofa rather than attempt the short walk home.

'Joel has news,' Zoë says. She and Warren are like kindred spirits, honestly. They finish each other's sentences, share an identical sense of humour. Though Zoë's tolerance for late nights far outstrips his.

'Yeah?' Warren says. 'You got any—'

'In the pot.' I gesture at the stove. (I'm on the green tea myself. Still trying to get a handle on my caffeine habit.)

'Go on,' he mutters grimly. He fills a mug with coffee, keeps it neat. Flops down beside me, sticks his head into his hands.

'You suffering, mate?' Kieran asks him, with a smile.

'*This* is why I don't drink any more.' Warren's words come out all stuck together.

'Yeah, those Jägerbombs should really come with an upper age limit,' I say. 'Or at least a ban on buying in bulk.'

Warren waves a hand at me, presumably to bat away the memory of his demise last night. 'What's your news?'

'It's more your news, actually. I dreamt you met a girl.'

He looks up. 'What.'

'Well, a woman. You've got six months to sort yourself out.'

Despite himself, a smile. 'Jesus. What's she like?'

'She seemed nice. Willing to laugh at your jokes, for one.'

'From round here?'

'Hard to say. But we were on the beach.'

He groans. 'It's been a while. Probably won't last.'

I clear my throat. Lower my voice. 'I beg to differ. You were . . . holding hands.'

Zoë whoops. Warren winces. 'Sure it was me?'

'Yep.' I finish my croissant and tea, feel delightedly smug in the face of the room's communal hangover. I slept longer last night than I have in years. 'So that's something to look forward to, isn't it? Right. Anyone joining me for a run?'

They literally heckle me out of the room.

I take my fitness addiction to the coast path. Feel the burn of elevation in my calves and lungs. The wind is a swinging blade through the air, mud spinning beneath my feet.

My mind drifts to Callie. I picture her eating breakfast, the children in their high chairs. She's laughing with her husband about something, wiping flecks of food from the twins' chins. Her face is radiant, warmed by the sun from a nearby window.

My stomach briefly seizes with jealousy that it can't be me. But then I remember all the reasons why it can't. At least this way she's happy, and for now I've found a form of balance.

Ultimately, I know, we couldn't have done that together.

I fill my lungs with frigid Atlantic air, run on.

## 89

## Callie – six years after

I stare at the invitation in my hand. 'I still can't believe Ben's getting married.'

'Will it be weird for you?'

I smile, let a twinge of sadness subside. 'Grace will have been gone nine years by the wedding. I think that's possibly weirder, if that makes sense.'

'It does. Mia's great, though.'

'I love Mia. And Grace would have loved her, too.'

Nearly eighteen months old now, Euan and Robyn are propped up between us against the sofa cushions, bewitched by CBeebies. I reach down, absent-mindedly stroke Euan's hair.

'And the wedding looks pretty cool,' Finn says.

It's a railway-arch venue in Shoreditch, open bar. Mia works in advertising and moves in terrifyingly hip circles.

'I might use the opportunity to see Mum and Dad for a few days while we're up that way. Give them some quality time with Euan and Robyn.' Mum's always nagging me to visit more, and they come to Brighton as often as they can.

Finn smiles, scooping Robyn onto his knee and bending to kiss her head. 'Great. Your mum will love that.'

I glance down at the invite again. 'I'm a bit surprised they're letting kids in, actually. They do know children are legally obliged to disrupt the vows?'

'I reckon Esther had a firm word in Ben's ear.'

I laugh and reach down to stroke Murphy. He's up against my knee, chin resting on my thigh. 'Probably.'

'Never mind the kids, though, I'm not even sure they should be letting *us* into this wedding. Are we cool enough?'

There's nothing quite like having children for making you feel like a bona fide grown-up. Our breakneck social life, our holidays – those hallmarks of a child-free life – seem almost to have belonged to someone else, now.

Not long after the twins were born, I'd sometimes find myself looking back through our photos, just to remind myself it had all really happened. After confessing this to Finn, I returned to the flat one night to find he'd blown up our best shots in black-and-white, framed them and hung them on the walls. Our very first selfie, shot against the sunrise, the morning I left Latvia. The two of us on the boardwalk of a nature reserve in Florida, brown-skinned and beaming, thumbs up to the camera. Our last breakfast in Miami – omelettes and strong coffee – the morning after we'd got engaged. Abseiling somewhere near Tunbridge Wells. Laughing with a group of friends, high up on the Downs. But in pride of place, Finn had positioned a photo that came before all of that: my diademed sandpiper-plover, nestled in the foothills of a Chilean volcano.

'I mean, how do you even dress for a wedding like this?' Finn's saying. 'Should I wear a suit, or will everyone be in pyjamas or something?'

I hope he'll wear a suit – he has one he brings out especially for weddings, gunmetal-grey. He usually pairs it with a floral shirt, sometimes shades, and he looks . . . Well, if there was such a thing as upstaging the groom, I'm pretty sure Finn would do it every time.

'Well, that's kind of the beauty with events this cool. We could probably turn up in our wellies and look like we're setting a trend.'

'Can't believe we're already calling Ben's wedding an "event",' Finn says.

'There'll be people with earpieces.'

'Security checks.'

'A social-media blackout.'

'I love you,' Finn says then, across the top of the twins' heads.

I smile. 'I love you too.'

'I don't know . . .' He trails off, looks down.

'What?' I say, happily surprised by this sudden onrush of affection. There's been so little time for it of late. We tend to talk in snatched half-sentences now (*Have you done the—, I just need to—, Should we quickly—*) and though our sex life has made a tentative return, it's an open secret between us that, given the choice, we'll opt to shut our eyes rather than pounce on each other when we finally hit the mattress at night.

'. . . I don't know what I'd do if I hadn't met you, Cal. You're the best thing that ever happened to me – you and the twins.'

I lean over, kiss him on the lips. It sparks something inside me, and I think perhaps tonight I might pounce on him after all.

Later we undress and finish the kiss, urgent beneath the covers, our hands hot and damp in the cool of the room. Perhaps because it's been a few weeks, or because we're obliged to do everything at full-tilt these days, it feels vital and frantic in the very best of ways. The heat and the vigour take me back to that very first night in Latvia.

Afterwards I roll back towards him, about to whisper that we should really make the effort to do that more often, when the shrillness of a child crying rises from the room next door.

Finn starts laughing. 'Ah, for once, kid,' he murmurs, still breathless, his skin damp with sweat, 'your timing's perfect.'

## 90

## Joel – six and a half years after

I'm heading to Nottingham with Doug to catch up with our cousin Luke and some of our other relatives.

I got back in touch with Luke just over two years ago. Building bridges felt good, and I wanted to do more of it. Surprisingly, for someone so inherently grumpy, my brother felt the same way.

Luke never did return to school after the dog attack. His family moved to the Midlands a year or so after it happened, so he could stand half a chance of escaping the flashbacks. These days, he's a celebrated chef, having steered two restaurants to Michelin-star status. We've eaten twice at his current place, had boys' nights out together.

I haven't yet told him about my dreams. Or, rather, one dream in particular. I've been getting to know him again first. Building a relationship before I bare my soul.

But I dreamt about tonight a month or so ago. (Highlights: Luke takes us to a blues bar where we're treated like VIPs; Doug gets absolutely hammered.)

As we're waiting for our train, my brother starts to get twitchy. He's wearing his weekend uniform of jeans I suspect to have been ironed, and a slightly too-tight T-shirt. 'Dying for a fag.'

'Tell me you're not still smoking.'

He shrugs. 'Only socially.'

'And yet you're *dying* for a fag.'

Doug huffs. 'Oh, I meant to say. Dad's worried about you.'

I smile, wonder if Doug will for ever respond to criticism by batting it straight back where it came from. 'How come?'

'Says you're looking too thin.' A disdainful glance in my direction. 'I happen to agree.'

'Ah, it's nothing.'

But the truth is I've not been myself recently. Time is accelerating, the years slipping by like landscape past a train window. I've been thinking about Callie, plagued with agonising doubts. Have I done the right thing? Should I get back in touch, make one final attempt to save her?

I've been having a recurrent dream lately, my first ever. It's the one about Callie dying, and it's grown progressively lifelike. I wake up soaked in sweat each time, shouting her name.

Doug looks away from me. 'Good to know. I was only saying to Lou the other day, you're finally starting to act normal for the first time in your life.'

I smile faintly at the turned face of my half-brother. He's so different from me. And yet, weirdly, I wouldn't change him for the world. That I can rely on his rudeness is strangely comforting somehow. When I think of all the turmoil that's to come.

## 91

## Callie – six and a half years after

He's standing on the opposite platform with his brother, chin sunk into the collar of his jacket as it so often was, hands stuffed into his pockets.

He looks thin, I think. Slightly haunted, not himself.

Or, at least, the himself I used to know. It's been nearly seven years, now. But already the intervening time has melted away, and I can only see him as I last did, facing me across the table in the restaurant. *Forget about me. Do all the things you want to do, and more.*

My heart on a string, I can only pray he'll look up and see me.

I've taken a few days' annual leave for Ben's wedding, but Finn's been working in Ipswich this week, so I'm travelling from Mum and Dad's to London alone with the twins. Finn's meeting us off the train at Blackfriars, and already I can't wait – to be reunited after three nights apart, and for the second pair of hands. It's the first time I've travelled with the twins by myself, so I have Euan on my hip, Robyn in a single buggy by my feet.

I don't want to alarm my children – and the rest of the platform – by calling out. Joel's deep in conversation, and just as I start to think he might never look up, he does, and I am once again stilled by his satellite gaze.

*I never forgot about you, Joel.*

The world falls away. Sounds become echoes, my surroundings fog. I can see just Joel, feel only the spin of my stomach as we take each other in.

But within moments comes the hydraulic rush of my approaching train, the flash of lights.

*No, no, no. On time – for once – today?*

I mouth, 'Joel,' but then the train divides us and the crowd around me starts to move. And I need to move too – trains to London are only every thirty minutes, time's already tight, and delay will mean keeping Finn waiting, rushing to find a cab, panicking about missing the wedding, the potential humiliation of being turned away by a band of doormen masquerading as Tom Ford models.

I have no choice. We have to board the train.

The temperature in the carriage feels stifling, like the AC's on the blink. Mercifully our seats are at a table for four, where the only other occupant is a friendly-looking pensioner, who seems as though she might not tut too firmly if my two-year-olds decide to kick off. After checking with her, I stand up and open the top window before settling Euan on the seat next to me, pulling Robyn onto my lap.

But the whole time I'm straining, desperate to see if I can spot Joel outside. At first my eyes land only on strangers, until eventually they locate Doug, who I see with a jolt is now standing alone.

And then there's a tap on the window behind me.

I turn, and it's him. Lovely, luminous him. He must have sprinted across the overpass.

My eyes spring with tears as I mouth a hello.

*You okay?* he mouths back.

I nod fiercely. *You?*

He nods too, then hesitates. *You happy?*

I swallow the tears away, hold my breath for just a second. And then I nod again.

Because how can I paint for him the whole picture, the winding roots of the truth, through a window as the whistle sounds for my train to depart? What can I say in the space of five seconds to express all that I feel, in front of my children and a curious stranger?

On the other side of the window, Joel puts a palm flat against the glass. I reach out and do the same, and suddenly we're together but divided, just as we always seemed to be.

Then comes the distress flare of a whistle before slowly, agonisingly, our hands begin to peel apart. Joel breaks into a jog, trying to keep up, but of course he can't. My heart is tethered to him, a thread seconds from snapping. Then at the last moment he reaches up and drops something through the open window above our heads. It helicopters into my lap like a falling sycamore seed.

I grasp it, then look urgently up, but the station has already become the grimy façade of the railway depot. He's vanished, perhaps for the last time.

I stare down at Robyn on my lap. Her face is raised to mine, like she's trying to decide if she should burst into tears, and it occurs to me that it must have been a bit frightening for her, the unfamiliar figure at the window with the urgent eyes and muffled voice. So I draw her closer into me, cover her tiny hand with mine, give it a reassuring squeeze.

'I love you,' I whisper into her shining spirals of dark hair.

'Are you okay?' the old lady asks me quietly, her eyes wrinkled in sympathy.

I nod, but can't speak. I'm afraid that if I do, I'll lose it.

'The one that got away?' is all she says, her voice gossamer-soft.

I glance down at Euan by my side. He's staring up at the opposite window, absorbed in the sight of life rushing by.

*Oh, how it rushes.*

I blink just once, release a couple of hot tears. And she nods gently, because we both know there is nothing more to say.

Moments before we pull into Blackfriars, I unfold the paper napkin.

On it, scrawled in biro, are just five words.

*I'LL ALWAYS LOVE YOU, CALLIE x*

## 92

## Joel – eight years after

I wait for her at the bend of the river, by the crooked old willow I saw in my dream. Though the air today is tonic-fresh, the light feels prophetically gentle. Soft-hued with sympathy, as if it knows what's to come.

I look up at the sprawling tree, magnificent as a monument. Recall the loop of Callie's *C* scraped into the muscle of its wood. I picture the letter in time-lapse over all the years ahead. Warmed through with sunlight, powdered with frost, until eventually it's lost beneath layers of lichen.

I've told none of Callie's loved ones about today. The only thing she asked of me was to keep what I dreamt from her, and I couldn't risk the secret spilling out. So though it's crushed me to do it, I'll honour her wish to the last. If I don't, the past eight years will have been for nothing.

I guess she must be visiting her mum and dad, the children with their grandparents. I'm sure whenever she's in Eversford she returns to Waterfen, drawn back towards it like a bird migrating.

Since I saw her on the train eighteen months ago, she's been at every turn of my thoughts. A whisper on the breeze of my memory.

The weather grows sombre while I wait, the countryside excreting moisture like tears. Cold is pinching my skin as the sky slowly marbles with cloud. On the opposite riverbank, bare-boned trees bow their heads.

For so many years I've been praying my dream got it wrong. That Callie won't show. That I'll stand here alone until darkness, growing more and more euphoric with every fading gradient of light.

Because even though we're apart, I simply can't imagine waking up tomorrow without the comfort of knowing she's out there. Without knowing that somewhere she's happy, living a life of a million colours. When I saw her on the train that day, I wanted to break down the window, climb inside the carriage. Tell her I'll never stop loving her, that it's impossible to picture a world without her in it.

I'm counting down the minutes on my watch. I want to stop the earth turning, hit the brakes on time.

*Please let me be wrong. Please.*

But now there comes a shift in the air, the dampened strike of footsteps. And my heart hollows out, because she is here.

She's humming as she makes one last meander along the riverbank. Lost in the landscape, she's burrowed beneath a coat and scarf, like she's just another winter walker. Like this is any other November day.

But it's not, of course. Because I can already hear the air ambulance from across the fen, helicopter blades whirring like dragonfly wings. I made the call a few minutes ago, so she wouldn't lose a second. I needed to be sure I'd done everything I could.

Even as she pauses now, delighting in the dart of a kingfisher, I'm trembling with hope. That she'll simply turn around, exhale, and walk on.

*Turn around, Callie. There's still time. But you need to do it now.*

'Joel?' She has seen me.

My heart breaks open as we face each other. And for a moment that seems like an hour, I hang on to the sight of her and don't let go.

But already her eyes are asking the question. So, as gently as I can, I nod. *I'm sorry, Callie.*

The softest of smiles, a whispered 'Oh.'

Then she puts out a hand.

Seconds still as, for the final time, I close my fingers around hers, feel the warmth of her skin through the wool of her glove. I place my other arm across her back, draw her calmly to my chest. Without saying anything she rests her cheek against my shoulder, perhaps for comfort. And then I kiss the top of her head, tell her one last time I'll always love her.

After that no words are left. But in another life, we are turning to walk off down the footpath together, hand in hand towards a sunset that sees us home.

And now, here it comes – the buckle in my arms, the faint gasp for air that feels more like a cough. As gently as I can, I lower her to the ground, brush the hair from her face. I loosen the scarf from around her neck, my tears falling into its folds.

After all this time, I'm still not ready to say goodbye.

*Ten.*

My heart is punching out the seconds.

*Nine.*

'Callie,' I whisper, 'I'm still here. I'm not going anywhere, okay? Stay with me.'

*Eight. Seven.*

In desperation I take off her glove, rub her hand with mine like I think it might stop her slipping away.

*Six.*

Maybe it will. 'Come on, Callie. Don't let go. I'm still here, stay with me.'

*Five.*

And then. Perhaps I'm imagining it, but I swear I can feel her try to grip my hand. Like she's fighting so hard to hang on.

*Four.*

My heart upturns and the tears get fiercer. But still I keep whispering, squeezing her hand. 'Stay with me, Callie. The ambulance is coming. Don't let go, okay?'

*Three. Two. One.*

But at last I know. She cannot answer me because she is gone. So I try with everything I've got to restart her heart as, somewhere nearby, an ambulance lands.

Minutes later, the helicopter becomes a bird soaring skyward above the trees, carrying her away.

I did everything I could. All that's left now is to wait. Hoping so hard it hurts, praying she'll pull through.

# EPILOGUE

# 93

## Joel

Callie passed away that day from cardiac arrest. They couldn't find any evidence of an underlying heart condition in the post-mortem, so the cause of death was given as sudden arrhythmic death syndrome.

I didn't leave a trace with my 999 call and failed to give the paramedics my name. So no one knew I was with Callie in her final moments. But it was noted in several news reports that she'd been found by a passer-by. A few days later, Kieran sent me a link to an article in the local paper. Finn was imploring whoever had called the ambulance to come forward, so he could thank them personally for their efforts to help.

I stayed anonymous, of course. I didn't want to give Finn any reason to suspect Callie and I had been in contact while they'd been together. She'd been faithful to the last, of course she had. She loved him.

I'm not sure if anyone notices me slip into the church. Taking a last-minute seat in the rear pew, I end up sitting next to Ben and his wife Mia. They've got a baby of their own now, run an advertising agency together in London. Ben and I end up man-hugging halfway through the first hymn, which is 'All Things Bright and Beautiful'.

I do my best to avert my eyes from Finn. I couldn't have imagined a nicer guy for the love of my life to end up with. He's in bits, of course. Has been sat down the whole time, head in his hands. Callie's parents are next to him, equally shattered.

Finn's brought Murphy with him on a lead. He's so old now, and slightly arthritic. His movements are stiff and he struggles to lie down, but his whiskered eyes are faithful as ever.

I have to look away from the dog, or I'll break.

Eventually, Finn comes to the front of the church to make his speech. It takes him a good minute or two to compose himself, once he gets up there. He chokes on his words, unable to speak at first. But when he finally does, he floods the church with light. He tells us the story of how he and Callie met. About the fun they had, their incredible life together. Their two amazing children. 'They say there's one person for everyone,' he concludes, his voice wobbling. 'And for me, that person was Callie.'

I leave the church before the last hymn, in no doubt as to just how fully Callie lived her last eight years. How hugely she was loved.

While everyone filters off to the crematorium, I do a lap of the block. I want to avoid running into Callie's parents, Dot, or any of her other friends. Then I head back between the yew trees, where Esther's asked me to meet her.

She approaches alone. Her face is eclipsed by an enormous pair of bug-eye sunglasses. We hug.

'I'm really sorry,' is the first thing I say. And then, 'It was a lovely service.'

'Thanks. I think Cal would have liked it.'

I picture the flowers trailing the nave. They were woven into the wicker of her coffin, strewn across the top of it. The air was suffused with fragrance, sweetened by love.

'Not going to the crematorium?' I ask Esther.

'No. Cal would have understood. I'm a bit of a wreck with stuff like that.' A stiff ejection of breath. 'First Grace, and now . . .'

'I know,' I say softly. 'I'm sorry.'

I detect a brave smile beneath the scoop of her sunglasses.

'Actually, I've got something I need to give you.' She withdraws a thick envelope from her handbag, passes it to me. 'Callie wrote you postcards, Joel. After you broke up. She . . . passed them to me, for safekeeping. Anyway, she asked me to give them to you. If she died.'

My mouth makes soundless shapes. The envelope feels heavy as a house brick in my hands.

'She wanted you to know . . . how happy she was.'

I finger the envelope. There must be . . . what – twenty postcards in here? Thirty?

'I'd do it all again,' I say then. 'Even if nothing could change. I'd love her again in a heartbeat.' And then my voice breaks, and I can't say any more.

A long silence, punctuated only by birdsong.

'So, that mystery passer-by never came forward,' Esther says eventually.

I gather myself. 'No.'

She pushes her sunglasses up on top of her head. 'It's nice to know someone was there with her, though. You know – in her final moments.'

I meet her dewy eyes, nod once. And that's it.

'You coming to the wake?'

I shake my head. 'I think this is where it ends, for me.'

'All right.' She pauses. 'Thank you, Joel.'

'For what?'

She shrugs lightly, like she'd hoped I'd know. 'For what you did.'

I remain in the graveyard for a few minutes after Esther walks away. The sky is in mourning, overcast. But just as I'm about to leave, a slant of sunlight breaks cover.

As the earth brightens at my feet, a robin lands on the gravestone next to me, tilts its head.

'I'll always love you, Cal,' I whisper. Then I tuck the envelope into my jacket, turn and make for home.

# 94

## Callie

*I was thinking this morning about the day I met you. Do you remember? That time you forgot to pay and I gave you a piece of cake, gabbled, went all weak at the knees.*

*Anyway. We have* drømmekage *all the time now, me and Finn and the twins – silly, I know, but I just like finding little ways to remember you.*

*You should know that Finn . . . he's a wonderful person, Joel. It feels strange to tell you that. But please know I don't say it to hurt you. I just want you to know I'm happy – that I'm sure we made the right decision eight years ago, heart-breaking though it was, and as wrong as it felt at the time.*

*Anyway, I've been in Eversford this weekend, and I'm just heading down to Waterfen now. I'll be thinking of you, as I walk along the river.*

*Because I still love you, Joel. There's a part of my heart that will always be yours. Even when I'm gone, whenever that may be.*

# Acknowledgements

I'd like to thank my brilliant agent, Rebecca Ritchie at AM Heath, for everything you've done on my behalf. Any writer would be lucky to have you in their corner. Thank you.

I'm hugely grateful to everyone at Hodder & Stoughton, for making me feel so welcome and for championing this book so passionately. In particular Kimberley Atkins, for your enthusiasm, for your wise editing, and for caring about my characters as much as I do. Sorry for the sobs! A big thank you also to Madeleine Woodfield, as well as Natalie Chen, Alice Morley, Maddy Marshall and Becca Mundy. And the incredible rights team, particularly Rebecca Folland, Melis Dagoglu, Grace McCrum and Hannah Geranio – I've truly been blown away by all you've done to introduce *The Sight of You* to readers around the world. Also Carolyn Mays, Jamie Hodder-Williams, Lucy Hale, Catherine Worsley, Richard Peters, Sarah Clay, Rachel Southey, Ellie Wood, Ellen Tyrell and Ellie Wheeldon. And Hazel Orme, for the eagle-eyed copyediting.

At Putnam, I'd like to thank Tara Singh Carlson and Helen Richard, for your meticulous and insightful edits – it's been a complete pleasure to work with you both. Much appreciation too to Sally Kim, Ivan Held, Christine Ball, Alexis Welby, Ashley McClay, Brennin Cummings, Meredith Dros, Maija Baldauf, Anthony Ramondo, Monica Cordova, Amy Schneider and Janice Kurzius.

I also owe an enormous thank you to Michelle Kroes at CAA.

I'm very grateful as well to Emma Rous, for the speedy reading and expert advice on all things veterinary-related. Any mistakes are of course my own.

Finally, thanks to my friends and family, and especially to Mark.

# A Conversation with Holly Miller

**What is your novel, *The Sight of You*, about?**

*The Sight of You* tells the story of Joel and Callie. Joel has prophetic dreams about what the future holds for the people he loves, the good and the bad – dreams that disturb him so much he has vowed never to fall in love again. And Callie, who is grieving her best friend, knows she must try to live a fuller life, but can't seem to find a way to get there. Despite their private struggles, when the two meet, it feels meant to be – a love that could last a lifetime. But then Joel has the dream about Callie he has always dreaded, and the two face a heartbreaking decision that will alter the course of both their lives forever.

**Tell us a little bit about Joel and Callie. What do they each see in the other that makes them such a perfect couple?**

Callie is attracted straight away to quiet, understated Joel's huge heart. A former vet, he is full of compassion, modest and a little mysterious. And Joel can see how smart Callie is, how quick-witted and capable, how she can light up any room. He feels drawn to her in a way he never has to anyone before.

**Typically, the main question in a love story is whether the two main characters fall in love. But you begin your book by revealing that Callie and Joel are no longer together. Why foreshadow their relationship in this way?**

When I started writing *The Sight of You*, Joel and Callie being perfect for each other felt like a given – and I wanted this to be the case for the reader, too. Because in many ways, for both characters, the real story begins after they fall in love, not before.

**The chapters alternate between Callie's and Joel's voices. Why did you choose to format the novel this way?**

On the face of it, *The Sight of You* would appear to be the story of Joel – his prophetic dreams and their effect on his life and relationships. But it is equally Callie's story – who she is at the start of the novel, and who she has become by the end. I wanted to give equal weight to both characters' experiences, and alternating chapters felt like the most natural way to do this.

**Callie's passion for the natural world defines the arc of her life. Why isn't she able to embark on her ecology career earlier, before meeting Joel?**

Callie is by nature risk-averse – a trait inherited from her parents – and has always lived a relatively safe life in the shadow of her more outgoing friends. Before meeting Joel, she felt as though living cautiously protected her from disappointment or failure, but Joel encourages her to see that taking risks can lead to beautiful things.

**Joel feels responsible for others because of his dreams, yet this responsibility stands in the way of his relationships. How is he able to break free from the burden of his secret?**

Joel is so strongly drawn to Callie that he is able to persuade himself to tune out thoughts of what might happen if he dreams the worst about her, putting the weight of responsibility to the back of his mind.

But later, having been inspired by her courage and fortified by her love for him, he knows the way to honour what they had is to live the very best life he can and face up to his fears, or the choice they made will have been for nothing.

**When two people choose to become partners for life, they assume the burden of, perhaps, being the one to watch the other die. How is it that most of us are able to move through that knowledge and build lives unencumbered by that fear?**

Most of us are fortunate enough not to know when our loved ones will die, so we can live freely and boldly without a ticking clock in the background and the perpetual, daily fear of knowing what will come. I think this explains why so many people I have spoken to would choose not to know how long they had left . . .

**If given the opportunity, would you want to know exactly how long you have left?**

I would absolutely not want to know! Though I can fully appreciate the benefits of knowing – being able to plan, say my goodbyes, and achieve everything I wanted to – for me, every experience would be coloured by the knowledge of when the end was coming (and if it was imminent, I know that information would paralyse me rather than liberate me!).

**If you could do one thing before you die, what would it be?**

I'm lucky enough to have met the love of my life and achieved my lifelong dream of becoming an author. So my bucket list is all about travel. I'd love to visit Russia, South Africa, Iceland, Finland, Prague . . . the list is endless and probably far from achievable, sadly! Still, it's good to dream . . .

# Reading Group Questions

1.  *The Sight of You* is a book about love, loyalty, and how to handle a heartbreaking decision. How do you feel the author portrayed these themes throughout the novel?

2.  Callie and Joel's attraction in the novel is "solar-plexus level", as Joel puts it. Was there a time in your life where you felt like this? How do you feel about that person now?

3.  In the wake of her best friend, Grace's, death, Callie decides to keep Grace's dream alive by working at the café she loved. Do you think Callie made the right decision? What would you have done if you were in her shoes?

4.  *The Sight of You* has a colourful cast of characters that all play an important role in Joel and Callie's relationship. Which characters did you relate to the most, and why?

5.  Which scene between Callie and Joel was your favourite?

6.  How do you feel about how Joel handled his past relationship-building, or lack thereof?

7.  What is one piece of advice you would give to either Joel or Callie about love, heartbreak or grief?

8. Would you choose the ability to see into the future, like Joel, if given the option? If so, how would you use it?

9. What do you think about the novel's ending?

10. Do you think fate played a part in Joel and Callie's love story? Do you think it plays a part in yours?

11. Would *you* choose love, if you knew how it would end?